HEAT SEEKER

HEAT SEEKER

Lora Leigh

St. Martin's Griffin
New York

HEAT SEEKER. Copyright © 2009 by Lora Leigh. All rights reserved. Printed in the United States of America. For information, address St. Martin's Press, 175 Fifth Avenue, New York, N.Y. 10010.

www.stmartins.com

ISBN 978-1-250-03664-3 (trade paperback)
ISBN 978-1-4299-2965-3 (e-book)

St. Martin's Griffin books may be purchased for educational, business, or promotional use. For information on bulk purchases, please contact Macmillan Corporate and Premium Sales Department at 1-800-221-7945 extension 5442 or write specialmarkets@macmillan.com.

First St. Martin's Griffin Edition: March 2013

10 9 8 7 6 5 4 3 2 1

Sharon, you've made life fun. You've taught me how to be strong and you've become more important to me than I could have ever imagined. You are my very bestest friend.
This book is for you.

HEAT SEEKER

PROLOGUE

Brisbane,
Australia

LIGHT CRASHED AND THUNDER boomed. Rain poured down in sheets as Brisbane experienced one of its hardest thunderstorms in years. Inches of water fell, saturated the ground, and ran in streams along sidewalks and roads. The wind howled and raged, and inside the tiny bungalow just outside town, the woman who had always hated the thunder, detested the lightning, and scowled at the rain paid little heed to the storm.

Through slitted lids she watched as Trent Daylen, the tough, sun-darkened, laughing Australian Secret Intelligence agent she had been paired with on the mission they'd just finished, kissed the arch of her foot with greedy arousal.

Bailey wanted to moan at the sight. She'd never, at any time, had her foot kissed by anyone. It was almost like being a virgin all over again, because the sensations this man inspired inside her assured her that she had much more to learn.

"Like silk," he whispered, the low, slow drawl of his accent sending shivers up her spine as his lips slid to her ankle.

Bailey fought to simply breathe. She hadn't expected this. She'd wanted it, ached for him, dreamed of him, but she had never expected to actually find herself in his arms when the mission was over.

"Come on, love, let's get those jeans off. Let me see those gorgeous legs."

Legs he'd watched through the months, making her so wet she'd nearly had to change her panties several times. She'd worn short skirts and skimpy tops to play a waitress in a low-end dive in Brisbane as they searched for an Australian naval officer selling secrets of a top-secret military base both their countries were conducting operations out of.

They'd caught the officer. They'd celebrated with drinks. And now they were celebrating with each other.

Bailey watched as his fingers, long and strong, moved to the clasp and zipper of her jeans. They came loose easily, the rasp of the closure audible even over the storm that raged outside.

Her stomach clenched, her sex heated as the material parted and he gripped the hem, drawing the pants over her thighs and down her legs.

He was still dressed. She wanted him naked. But his lips at her hip bone stilled her hands as they moved for the buttons of his bush shirt. Her nails raked against the hard muscles of his shoulders, and the involuntary arching of her hips surprised her.

She could feel the dampness building between her thighs, soaking the sensitive folds there, sheening moisture along her thighs. She had never been so wet in her life, so ready for a man's touch, his kiss.

"Trent." She moaned his name. She couldn't help it. She needed more, so much more that she wondered if her need would ever be sated.

"Patience, love," he soothed her gently as he moved back up her body, one hand easing the fabric of her shirt up her stomach, to her breasts. "Let's get these clothes off that gorgeous body of yours. I swear I've dreamed of kissing every inch of that perfect, silky flesh."

There was nothing perfect about her body and she knew it. But he sounded as though he believed it. As though he saw perfection somewhere in her.

Heat sizzled under her skin when his palm raked over a tight, hard nipple as he drew her shirt farther up. Then he was gripping the hem, pulling it over her head. Before it cleared her head, his lips were back on hers and she was sinking into a morass of rich, sensual sensations, into a pleasure that rocked her, drew her tight against him.

Her arms wrapped around his neck as his lips took hers. His tongue pushed past, brushed against her own, then retreated. He sipped at her lips, caressed them, then came back with a hungry demand that had her crying out into the kiss.

Desperate fingers fisted into the material of his shirt as she tried to drag it up his body, fighting to touch his flesh. Hard, hot flesh that invited her hands, muscles that flexed above her.

Bailey writhed beneath him, her hands reaching beneath the shirt to clench on his back, her nails scraping against his flesh as she gripped her thighs tightly closed and fought for enough sensation against her clit to ease the ache building in it.

"Don't stop," she cried out as he drew back.

"Stop? Not on your life, sweetheart." He tore his shirt over his head, his normally serene gray eyes stormy now as he revealed the dark blond scattering of hair that covered his hard chest and arrowed down the darkly tanned stomach and tight abs.

His own jeans hung low on his hips, teasing her with the bulge beneath them. It looked huge.

Shaking, Bailey reached out her palm, flattening it against the center of his chest and smoothing down the silky hairs that covered it. She felt him flexing beneath her touch, the hard muscle and tough skin reacting to the caress as his expression tightened with hunger. His gaze was murky, swirling with shades of gray and sexual power as her fingers caressed to the snap of his jeans.

Bailey couldn't resist. She ached. She needed. She'd been working with him for months and all she'd been able to think about was the lean, muscular body and sensual swagger. How he would kiss, taste, touch. What it would be like to kiss, taste, and touch in turn. So far, it was like fireworks erupting through her system.

She fought to breathe. She fought to hold back, to enjoy every sensation, every heated touch.

She pulled at the snap as he rose on his knees above her, his gaze narrowed as he stared down at her. The zipper loosened easily, and Bailey felt her mouth go dry a second before it began to water in hunger.

Long, thick, the heavily aroused shaft throbbed, the darkened crest flared out and sheened with moisture.

"You make a man lose his mind." His voice was rough, thick with arousal.

The sound of it sent a clench of desperate sensation straight to her womb. He sounded hungry, desperate for her. The thought that this man, so incredibly bold, so hard and rugged, ached for her sent the blood crashing through her veins and arcs of heated desire striking through the erogenous zones of her body.

"I've already lost mine," she panted as his fingers curled around the mound of one breast.

Her nipple peaked hard, desperately tight and hot. When his thumb raked over it, Bailey felt her heart trying to come out of her chest.

Lifting herself until she was sitting in front of him, she gripped the edges of his jeans and dragged them down his thighs as her lips pressed to those tight abs. Parting them, she licked the tough flesh, nipped at it, and was rewarded by the harsh, male groan that tore from his chest.

That was what she wanted to hear. Those rough sexy male sounds that assured her it was good, that she was giving him pleasure. That he wanted her. That maybe he ached for her as desperately as she ached for him.

She curled her fingers around the silk-and-iron length of his erection, pumped it slow and easy, and watched as more moisture beaded the tip.

The flared head was just beneath her lips, enticing her, drawing her hunger.

"Little tease," he moaned above her as his fingers threaded through her hair, tugging at the long strands, causing the ends to caress her bare back and send another sensual sensation arcing through her system.

"Tease?" she whispered. "I'm not teasing, Trent. I'm very damned serious."

Her tongue licked over the moisture beading the tip of his cock, causing a husky grumble to leave his chest.

He liked that. His hips arched closer to her, his muscled thighs clenched violently, and the throb of his flesh beneath her fingers intensified.

He drew her as no other man ever had. He made her wish things, want things she had never wanted before. Need for him drowned out the loneliness and the sound of the storm beyond the windows.

Bailey parted her lips, needing more of him, aching for it as she had never ached for anything else. She covered the hot crest of his cock with her mouth, sucked him inside, and, through the strangled groan he gave, laved the sensitive head with her tongue.

He tasted hot and completely male. Like the storm outside, wild and untamed.

Trent Daylen was like a surfer boy mixed with a killer. A delicate balance of rakish charm and irresistible danger. And for tonight he was all hers.

"God, Bailey, your mouth." His voice wrapped around her, urged her on.

With the fingers of her free hand she reached between his thighs, let the tips of her nails scour against the tight sac drawn close to the base of his cock.

His hands tightened in her hair. Bailey sucked him deeper, let her tongue lick over the engorged flesh, and felt her own pleasure rising.

Each suck of her mouth, each touch of her fingers brought a reaction for her. His hands tightening in her hair, his rough voice groaning her name, a sigh of pleasure passing his lips.

"Damn, you're enough to make a man crazed," he accused her, though he didn't sound in the least resentful. He sounded sexy and dark, dangerous and playful. "Suck it, sweetheart. Steal my mind."

What was left of it anyway. He was rakish, playful, an adrenaline junkie with a cause and she loved every facet of his personality.

She loved him.

Bailey almost paused. She almost hesitated in the pleasure she was giving him at the revelation that she could possibly love him.

She loved him. Over the months of working with him she had somehow managed to lose her heart to him.

"Damn, Bailey. Baby." His hips pumping, he fucked her mouth with the hard, straining length of his cock as his fingers moved to her nipples, plucking at the tight points and sending pleasure rocking straight between her thighs.

She moaned around his cock as she sucked and licked the throbbing head. She tasted him and grew hungry for more as her hands stroked over his thighs now.

"Hell yes." She could feel his gaze on her, watching her. Lifting her eyes, Bailey was caught by the storm swirling in the depths of his gaze.

"Let me watch you lick it, Bailey," he commanded, his voice harder now, more dominant. "Use your tongue on me, baby."

She drew back, her tongue extending, licking, stroking. God he felt so good, tasted so male. She'd been desperate to touch him, and now that she had him she was shaking with the wonder of it.

"Fuck me, yes," he muttered. "That's what I'm going to do to you, sweetheart. Lick your sweet pussy till you scream. Till you're begging for more."

She was ready to beg now. The very thought of his tongue stroking between her thighs sent her juices spilling from her sex to dampen the folds further.

"Suck me now." The hands in her hair pressed her closer until her lips were parting, taking him inside the wet warmth of her mouth as his cock flexed and throbbed and spilled a precious drop of pre-cum.

Bailey licked at it eagerly, hungrily. She was lost in the moment, the pleasure, and the man. Nothing mattered outside the walls of the bungalow, nothing mattered except this. Touching him. Feeling his touch.

She filled her mouth with the engorged flesh of his cock, taking a small amount of it, suckling at the head, licking at it, and finding her reward in the hard, guttural groans coming from his chest.

She glanced up at him, saw the hard savage pleasure that twisted his expression, and the blood thundered through her veins in excitement. She was an admitted adrenaline junkie herself, but no high she had experienced could compare to this.

Taking Trent into her mouth, caressing him, seeing his pleasure in her. It made her feel beautiful. She felt desired.

"Hell. No more." He was dragging her head back.

Bailey moaned in protest. She wanted more. She wanted to feel him exploding in her mouth, taking her, marking her.

"Enough," he ordered, the rich velvet of his voice roughening as she found herself on her back once again.

He held her wrists in one hand, stretching them above her head as he stared down at her, the thick sandy blond lashes shielding his dark gray eyes as he watched her.

His lips were fuller now. A dark flush mantled his cheeks as the long strands of dark blond hair fell over his brow.

"I'm going to eat you up like candy," he promised, licking his lips as Bailey fought back a sensual cry.

"I think you're just going to talk me to death," she accused him roughly.

His chuckle was dark and deep. It was filled with purpose and washed over her senses like a soft summer rain as his head lowered, his lips going to one plump nipple.

Bailey arched beneath him as the heat of his mouth surrounded the sensitive tip. Her fingers curled until her nails bit into her palms and she strained against his head.

"Oh God, Trent." She wanted to scream his name but didn't have the breath to do more than push out a whispered cry.

Her fingers fisted into his hair as he sucked at the hard point of her nipple. His tongue lashed at it, his teeth raked it. He tormented it, tortured it until she arched against him, strangled cries leaving her throat as she fought to hold him to her.

Perspiration sheened her flesh, desire dampened her thighs. She could feel the pulse and throb of blood inside her sex and the aching tightness of her clit.

She was on fire. Flames were racing across her flesh, tingling between her thighs. When he slid his leg between hers, the heavy muscle of his upper leg pressing into the aching folds between her thighs, she nearly came from the contact.

Arching into the pressure, her hips writhed as she rubbed the swollen knot of her clit into his hot flesh. She could feel sensation winding tighter in her womb, the need for orgasm becoming painful as his lips moved from one peaked nipple to the next.

When he moved back, his lips roaming down her body, Bailey was helpless against the desire tearing through her. Her legs parted for his shoulders, and when his tongue licked through the heavy juices built along the folds of her sex, she nearly came off the bed, the pleasure was so great.

It was like having a flame, sensual, wicked, laid to her flesh. His tongue licked slow and easy through the narrow slit; then his lips caught at the flesh, gave it a suckling kiss before moving to the sensitive folds on the other side.

His teeth rasped against the swollen mound, his tongue licking around her clit. And all the while his fingers played a rapturous, torturous little game as they circled and probed at the entrance.

"You're the tease," she cried out as her fingers clenched in his hair and she fought to hold him in place while he gave an exquisite little suckling kiss to her clit. "You're killing me, Trent."

"Loving you," he muttered against her sex. "God, Bailey, you taste like peaches and cream."

"Soap," she moaned.

His chuckle sent pleasure tearing through her.

"That's not soap." He kissed her again, a deep tongue-licking kiss right into the center of her pussy. "That's my baby. So sweet and hot I could melt right into her."

Oh God. She almost dissolved herself then and there. When his tongue thrust inside her again she swore she was going to do more than melt. She was going to explode. She was going disintegrate right there in his arms.

"You're killing me." He rose between her thighs. He reach out to the bed table, retrieved a condom he had opened earlier, and rolled it quickly over his cock. "Come here, Bailey. Come on, love. Have me now."

Have him now? She wanted to have him always.

Lifting her hips, she watched as the swollen head of his cock eased between the lips of her sex and nudged against the entrance of her vagina. She watched, wide-eyed, the breath stilling in her lungs as he began to ease inside her.

If she had felt on fire before, she felt more so now. With each shift of his hips, she could feel the burning stretch as her muscles fought to accommodate the width of his flesh. The folds of her pussy gleamed with her juices as the dark, heavy shaft parted them.

It was arousing, the sight of him taking her intensifying the pleasure until Bailey didn't think she could take much more. She was burning in the center of a storm; lightning erupted inside her, thunder crashed through her veins. She was lost in a turmoil of sensation and had no idea how to hold on.

"Hold on to me, baby." As though he knew what the pleasure was doing to her.

He took her hands and led them to his wrists, first one then the other. Her fingers wrapped around the strong breadth of them as her hips arched, a cry tearing from her as she took more of him.

"So sweet," he murmured. "There you go, love. Watch me take you. I've never seen anything so damned hot in my life as the sight of you taking my dick."

His hips bunched and moved, his cock stroked deeper inside her, sending her nerve endings into a maelstrom of sensation that whipped through her mind.

Nothing existed but the feel of him moving inside her, taking her, stretching her until she was crying out his name, begging for more. Deeper. Harder. The short delving strokes weren't enough. She wanted all of him. She wanted to feel him taking her, stretching her, burning her alive with his possession.

"Damn, Bailey. Wait a minute." His hands gripped her hips as he tried to hold her still.

Bailey's head thrashed against the pillows. "No. Please, Trent. Don't wait. Please don't wait." Her muscles clenched around him, spasming with the need she couldn't control as he threw his head back and thrust his hips forward.

Time dissolved. Bailey felt it sliding away, receding with reality as the deep pleasure-pain of his possession wiped everything else from her mind.

In one hard stroke he buried himself inside her. His cock throbbed inside the clasp of her clenching pussy. Flexing and pounding in rhythm to their shattered breaths, she nearly came at the feel of it. Nearly. Not quite. She was desperate to come. She could feel her orgasm hovering just out of reach as her nails bit into his wrists and her hips writhed beneath him.

"Hell, we've had it now," he panted. "Son of a bitch, Bailey."

Her lashes lifted until she could stare into his eyes. The deep gray was nearly black. His face was flushed, his lips swollen and damp. He looked like a sex god rising between her thighs, determined to possess her soul.

She watched as he shook his head, obviously fighting for control as she fought to help him lose it. She tightened her muscles around his cock. Her hips shifted and rolled as her lashes fluttered with the pleasure.

"Fuck me," she whispered.

His eyes widened as a sexy grin curled over his lips.

"Say it again," he ordered.

"Fuck me, Trent. Fuck me until I'm screaming for you."

It wouldn't take him long to make her scream. She was already on the verge of it. Already needing it. Her nails dug into his wrists as he began to thrust, to move. Bailey's legs lifted, curled around his thrusting hips. She tried to lift closer, to catch that last sensation, that last moment of intense, incredible pleasure that would send her over the edge.

Each thrust tore another cry from her, sent her flying higher. Heat tightened in her pussy, in her clit. It whipped through her, raced over her flesh, and finally detonated in her womb in an explosion so intense, so soul shattering that she could only cry his name.

Her orgasm filled every cell in her body and sent ecstasy tearing through her nervous system. It stole her breath, stole her mind, and left her a creature of sensation alone as she felt him thrust hard and deep before his body tightened and his release tore through him as well.

A moment out of time. That was what it felt like. Like a moment that would never return, and she was desperate to hold on to it. To hold on to him.

She was still fighting to catch her breath when he rolled beside her and pulled her into his arms. For a moment she froze, so unused to being held by another that for the slightest second it was completely alien to her.

She lay against his chest, listened to his harsh breathing, the thunder of his heart, and gave a desperate little prayer that she could hold on to it just a little longer.

"I knew you'd blow my mind," he finally said with a sigh.

"You would have to have a mind first," she quipped, suddenly uncertain of herself.

What did a woman do with a man like this? Did she try to hold him? Let him go? What? God, she had no idea how to play the most important game in her life, even though she had excelled at the other games she'd attempted in her career.

"I have a mind." He rolled her to her back, rising over her as he gave her one of those rakish devil-may-care grins. "And I used to have a heart. I think you stole that, too." He was suddenly somber.

Bailey stared up at him, her lips parting in surprised wonder.

"Your heart?" she whispered.

"It's very probable." He winked down at her before bounding from the bed and striding across the room. "Showering with me?" He glanced back at her as she watched his cute, tight ass.

"Later." She shook her head. She needed to get her bearings, needed to figure out where she was supposed to go from here.

"Later then." He nodded. "I'll step out and get us dinner after I shower. I have to check on a few things with a contact then I'll be back."

She nodded then watched wistfully as he disappeared into the bathroom. The sound of the shower seconds later had her blowing out a hard breath before she flipped the sheet over her body. A quick nap might get her equilibrium back. Besides, she was worn out, more tired than she could remember being in years.

A grin pulled at her lips at that thought. He had worn her out. Sated her. Made her feel treasured. She definitely wanted to keep him.

Long minutes later she felt the kiss on her cheek and his quiet "Be back soon, love." The door closed behind him.

She was sliding back into sleep when hell broke loose outside. The explosion blew out the windows, shattering glass over the bed and lighting up the stormy night as Bailey screamed in horror.

Jumping from the bed, she jerked the sheet around her and raced to the front door. Flames were licking up the side of the bungalow where he'd parked his Jeep. The vehicle was a mess of twisted metal. Flames greedily consumed it and destroyed the fragile dreams she had been building.

Neighbors from surrounding bungalows were running for the driveway. Someone was yelling for help. Someone else noted in hysteria that there was a body in the vehicle. And all Bailey could do was stand there, her fists clenched in the sheet, her soul shattered.

This was what she got for wishing, for hoping. This was what Bailey Serborne got for dreaming.

JOHN VINCENT STEPPED out of the bungalow, whistling quietly, a part of his soul lighter than it had been in years. The Australian night wrapped around his senses, a cool breeze riffling through his hair as a smile tilted his lips for a second.

As he moved off from the door, the smile eased away. A shadow stepped from the tree line and rushed across the short expanse of grass toward him.

The contact he was supposed to meet in town reached Trent's Land Rover in the driveway, agitated and obviously frightened.

"Thank God you finally came out!" Timmons Lowen was shaking from head to toe. His limp brown hair was saturated and plastered to his skull, his normally dull hazel eyes wide and glittering with fear. "Mate, Warbucks is on to us. They're looking for us."

Trent grimaced as he jerked the man beneath the awning of the house and gave him a quick little shake.

"What the hell are you talking about?"

Warbucks was a shadowy individual—or several individuals—acquiring and selling classified American information and hardware to terrorists. Part of that information was a list of Australian Secret Intelligence agents working with the CIA abroad. Agents who were turning up dead.

Trent's investigation into the Australian connection to Warbucks was turning up some surprising results, and information that Trent knew was more than dangerous.

"Somehow Warbucks found out what I've been doing," Timmons wheezed. "They sent a guy after me. He almost caught me in town. Listen to me, Trent, we're screwed."

"What the hell did they find out?" Trent felt like shaking the little man. Timmons was obviously losing his last grip on the fear consuming him. Hell, he should have known better than to use this man at the hotel where Warbucks was suspected to be meeting this month with a broker who would sell the new information Warbucks had. But Timmons was already in place, and the best pair of eyes he had.

"They found out about it," Timmons cried. "That I was watching for you. Who you are. All of it, Trent. Warbucks knows everything."

Trent paused. "How did they find out?"

Timmons shook his head desperately. "I don't know, mate. All I know is that it was from the agency. While he was in the bar looking for me I trashed his car and found an agency ID and pictures and info on us. We're tagged."

He had to get Bailey out of there. Glancing around, he watched the sky light up with lightning, felt the power of the storm, and knew he had to get Bailey as far from this mess as possible.

"Take the Rover." Trent dug his keys out of his pocket. "I'll met you at the safe house in Paddington in three days. Stay there, Timmons. Don't poke your nose out the door. Hide the Rover in the garage and play dead." He shoved the keys in his hands and pushed him to the Land Rover.

"The safe house. God, Trent, I knew I could depend on you."

Trent jerked the driver's door opened and pushed Timmons in the seat.

"Don't call me, don't call anyone," he ordered him. "Just lay low and don't open the door for anyone but me."

There was only one person who knew the details of the information Trent had been working on, as well as Timmons's part in it. His partner, Guy Warner. Even Bailey hadn't known who Trent's contact was or that he was tracking the connections in Australia to Warbucks.

Timmons jammed the key into the ignition as Trent backed away. The ignition started as Trent turned away to run back to the bungalow. Then the night exploded around him. Trent felt himself being catapulted through the air, his body landing hard enough to drive the air from his lungs as he bounced into the mud and muck of the swampy canal that ran past the bungalow.

The night was ablaze as another explosion rocked the night, sending more fragments of the vehicle hurtling through the air.

He fought to breathe through the pain, to make sense of the blinding light and pyrotechnic colors that danced in front of his eyes.

He could hear screams. A woman's screams, Bailey's. The sound of her cries tore through the night as he dragged his eyes open and fought to roll to his side.

He struggled to turn, blinking against the mud that covered his eyes and rain that poured over his face. As his vision finally cleared, he focused on the hell that had been the driveway, and saw his partner, Guy Warner.

He was racing from his car to the Land Rover. The agent had a curiously smug expression on his face. And there was Bailey, wrapped in a sheet, screaming for Trent.

It was too late, Guy had already found him. He fought past the constriction in his chest, tried to think, to find the closest route to Bailey when he saw Guy move to her. She threw herself in his arms.

Trent blinked as his vision began to blur. He fought to refocus, then watched as another agency vehicle pulled up and one of the American SEALs who had worked this last op with himself and Bailey moved into view.

Jordan Malone.

His gaze blurred again even as he fought it.

The night began to close around him, to smother him in darkness.

"Easy there, Trent." He was caught before he hit the ground and struggled to get free.

"Hold up," a dark male voice hissed. "We've got this one covered, buddy."

Trent tried to shake his head, to make sense of what was going on. He recognized the voice, he just couldn't place it.

"Bailey," he groaned.

"Bailey's covered. Let's move out."

He couldn't see. His vision swam with colors that didn't

make sense. His skin burned like fire, like acid. He felt singed from the inside out.

"Bailey." He groaned her name again as he fought the hands that forced him to move.

Bailey. He'd left her there. He'd promised to return. The first woman he'd ever promised to return to.

"Bailey's safe." Reno. That was his name. Reno Chavez. Navy SEAL. Part of the SEAL team working within the joint American–Australian operation they had conducted.

Dizziness washed over him again. Darkness covered him like a layer of ice. He couldn't fight it this time. He couldn't halt the tide of nothingness that washed over him and dragged him under.

He could feel death moving over him despite his battle against it. The breath stilled in his chest, fury rocking through him. Warbucks. The bastard had managed to defeat him before the battle had ever begun.

Atlanta, Georgia
Five Years Later

Bailey Serborne fought until she was gasping for breath, until breathing actually seemed exhausting, uncertain. She jerked against her bonds, screaming through the gag and she refused to cry.

She'd been captured tracking the international terrorist known as Orion, but she hadn't been captured by Orion. Oh no, even Orion wasn't this damned efficient. She had been captured by the team of unknown men guarding Orion's target, Risa Clay. The young woman had been marked to die by the bastard who had raped her eight years before. She was remembering who her rapist was: He had aided her father, Jansen Clay, in his white slavery operation and the kidnapping of a senator's daughter.

Bailey had tracked Orion to Atlanta, tracked him to a small group of the wealthiest men in America and had been working tirelessly to connect the dots among Orion, his employer and the deaths of her own family members.

She had gotten so close, so very close, only to be captured by the unknown suspected agents currently protecting Risa. Agents who refused to share information or to allow her in on an operation that she could benefit.

The men were known in underground circles simply as ghosts. The research she'd managed to do, the answers she had come up with concerning them didn't make sense. Among those men there was a former Navy SEAL, a former drug lord, an arms dealer, and a suspected terrorist. Of the five men she'd managed to identify, none was known as a good guy, but they were all surrounding Risa Clay. Which made her wonder at their covers.

Instead of getting answers, though, she was tied, gagged, and blindfolded as she was transported from the apartment building she had been in to an unknown location where she would be "interrogated."

Her own agency, her boss, a man who had been a friend to her parents, had betrayed her. He had given them the secret to breaking her, to stealing the information she was refusing to give them.

As though she wouldn't know that the men she was investigating were the same ones holding her. She'd been close enough to hear each of their voices. She was good at voices, good at identifying agents despite covers or alterations.

Bailey worked her hands against the ropes holding them, feeling the damp warmth of her own blood as her skin abraded. The thought of being drugged, of being forced, terrorized her. She was almost shaking with that fear. Being drugged by men she couldn't trust was even worse. Men whose names were synonymous with blood and death.

She could hear them talking. It was a hollow sound, a sound that indicated a cavernous area, perhaps a warehouse. She was lying on a cot. The drug would be given through an IV. She remembered that. It had been part of her training when she had worked with the Mossad years ago. It was the drug known to break her the fastest.

Bastards! She bit back the tears, the fury. If she let it take her over now, then she was going to break before they ever inserted the IV.

"The drug will be here within the hour," one of the men spoke up.

"I don't like this," said another, the one she'd heard called John. His tone was irate, and had been growing more so since they had arrived at the location.

"Chill," another voice advised him softly. "There's no pain involved. It's humane and efficient."

Why would killers worry about humane and efficient?

"Fuck your humanity and efficiency," John growled, his voice still low. "Let her the fuck go."

"Her people are on their way," he was told. "We'll wait for them outside, lead them in, then begin the interrogation. You keep an eye on her."

Her would-be knight had also been the same interrogator who had called her "cheap meat" hours before. Threatening to sell her to the local dog food company. But she'd heard the amusement in his tone, heard the playfulness.

Nostalgia had almost washed over her at the sound. If he'd had an Australian accent. If he had light gray eyes rather than dark, if his hair was a lighter blond. If he were another man and another time, then she would have known she was safe. If he were the lover she had lost, Trent Daylen, rather than John Vincent, a suspected arms dealer and killer, then she wouldn't fear the outcome here.

But Trent was dead. She had to force herself to remember that, to let that pain wash through her again. Trent had been killed in Australia.

Trent was gone.

She heard the men leave, but she was aware there was one still watching her. John. The arms dealer.

He was an agent, she knew he was. They all were. It was the only thing that made any sense. If they drugged her, she'd forget all this. She would forget their names, their identities, and the operation being conducted here. It would all be gone.

She felt movement around her, a brush of air against her

cheek a second before the gag was dragged down over her chin.

She stayed silent. At the moment, she decided silence was the better part of valor. It could be her smartest move.

"Picked yourself a hell of a fight here, didn't you?" His voice was low, filled with anger.

"What do you care?" She kept her own voice equally low.

He breathed out roughly. She felt a low sizzle of electricity as he gripped the back of her neck.

How odd. That reaction was rare. It was a reaction she had only known with Trent. She closed her eyes again and forced herself to breathe through the knowledge that she was truly alone. She had no partner, she had no agency backing. Hell, her own agency was turning against her for these men.

What the hell was going on here?

"I shouldn't care," he assured her. "You've asked for this. You could have given us what we needed and gone your way."

"Bullshit." She gave a hard mocking laugh. "Going my way wouldn't have taken me very far. Orion is mine," she hissed. "His death belongs to me."

"That isn't going to happen, baby," he assured her. "The bastard nearly killed you in Russia. Let it go now."

She couldn't let it go.

"You're lucky." Orion's voice washed through her memories. *"The right people want you alive, for the moment. Don't make the same mistakes your family has made, little girl. Go home. I cross you again, and I'll drink your blood for breakfast."*

The right people wanted her alive. People she hadn't cared to associate with since she was eighteen years old. The right people, those with too much money and too much power. People who hired this man's services and gave him his orders.

"I can't let it go."

She should have lied about it. She could have promised him the moon; what the hell difference would it make in the long run? She should give him what they wanted and bargain for her release and just fucking run.

She'd been running for more years than she could count. A few more surely wouldn't make a difference.

"What does the drug do to you?" he asked as she felt his fingertips running down her arm.

She wanted to smile. Trent used to do that when he wanted information from her, that or her attention, or just to touch her. The backs of his fingers over her arm.

These weren't Trent's fingers, even though the sensation was the same. There was a fine webbing against his flesh, as though his fingers were scarred or had suffered some trauma. He touched her as Trent once had, though, causing her chest to tighten with pain.

Her handsome, courageous Trent.

The blindfold eased slowly from her eyes and she found herself staring into the storm-ridden grays of John Vincent's. They were eyes that swirled with turbulence, with anger and desire, with lust.

He was rugged, rough. His face was sun-bronzed with creases at his eyes as though he had once laughed a lot but rarely did so now. His upper lip was a bit thin, his lower lip a bit full. They were kissable lips. Lips that would know their way around a woman's body. Lips that knew how to kiss, how to caress.

"Are you going to let me go?" Bailey could feel her heart racing in her chest as he hunched in front of her, staring into her eyes as though he were trying to figure her out.

"I shouldn't," he whispered. "I should never have walked into this little trap." She could sense the *but* in that sentence and would've loved to have known what he was thinking.

"What trap?" she asked, wondering at the swirl of emotions in his eyes.

"The Bailey Serborne trap." He sighed. "Big ocean-green eyes and the face of an angel. A face that traps a man's soul and never lets it free."

He sounded serious. Bailey wanted to sneer, but she

couldn't work up the mockery, the sarcasm needed. It wouldn't slip past the pain that pulled at her heart and left it aching.

"I know who you are," she whispered. "You're no more an arms broker than I am."

He laid his fingers against her lips. "You never want to say that again. Don't even think it. Don't become a risk, Bailey, or I'll never be able to protect you."

She tilted her head to the side. "Since when did I become your responsibility?"

Familiarity flickered in his gaze, confusing her. He watched her as though he knew her, as though he had touched her, and for a moment she could actually feel that touch.

His lips thinned, holding back whatever he wanted to say as he rose to his feet and dug his hand into the snug pocket of his jeans. He pulled free a small penknife, opened it, then moved around her.

A second later he was curling her fingers around it.

"I can give you five minutes," he told her. "There's a car parked at the back door, the keys are in the ignition. Drive out slow and easy and keep driving, baby. If you're taken again, I won't be able to save you. I won't be able to keep this from happening to you."

She stared back at him as he moved around her, her fingers gripping the knife as she made a decision she couldn't have imagined making.

"The information you wanted," she whispered.

His eyes narrowed.

She gave him the brief details he needed, most importantly the location of Orion's handler, information it had taken her years to track down. She would have known his voice in a heartbeat, but she wouldn't hear it again. She described the handler's voice as well as Orion's quickly while she worked the knife through the ropes. She ran through the list of details she had, reciting the last one as the ropes fell away from her wrists.

She dropped the knife and moved. Jackknifing from the

cot, she swiped his legs out from under him and sent him rolling before sprinting to the back door.

She was almost there. Her hands were reaching for the latch when she was suddenly grabbed from behind and jerked around. She bounced against the cement wall. The only thing that protected her head was the hard male hand that covered it. The only thing that dimmed the shock of the impact was his lips suddenly covering hers.

The fingers of his free hand gripped her jaw, keeping her from biting the tongue that swept across hers. Not that she would have bitten. Not that she could have bitten. She was shocked, held amazed, lost in a riot of sensations that she had felt only once in her life, and only with one other man. A dead man.

"Try that again." He jerked back from her, releasing her. "You can play dirty all you want to, baby, but remember, I've got your number, and I know damned well how to use it."

She flashed him a daring smile. "I expect to hear from you soon then."

Sliding the door handle down, she slipped out the crack she made in the double doors and escaped into the night. The car was waiting, the keys in the ignition. Within seconds she was pulling sedately down the alley and checking her rearview mirror.

He was watching her. Standing there beneath the moonlight, illuminated in an eerie glow cast by the nightly orb and the lights that struggled to ease the dimness in the alley.

And for a second, just the briefest second, it wasn't the arms broker/unknown agent John Vincent she saw. For just a breath of time, it was Trent. For a single heartbeat she saw him, felt him.

"Trent." She whispered his name as he turned and stepped back into the warehouse, dispelling the fantasy forever.

Trent was gone. He was dead. She couldn't ever let herself forget that.

Or was he?

Her eyes narrowed as she pulled the vehicle into Atlanta's

traffic. She had her suspicions where her cousin David Abijah was concerned, because God's truth, Micah Sloane could be no one but the Israeli cousin that she had believed was gone forever. She knew his voice, his movements, and the man who had interrogated her earlier could be no one else.

Micah Sloane was no more a former Navy SEAL than she was. He was a man without a true past. A man who moved like her cousin, a man who carried himself like the only family she could have called her own.

Bailey knew voices, she knew faces, she knew characteristics and movements. It was her strength as an agent. And she knew her cousin David, just as she had known her lover Trent. And now two men, one supposedly a dangerous criminal, both with the same characteristics, the same "feel," and they were working together?

She didn't believe in coincidence and she sure as hell didn't believe in an overactive imagination. She wasn't overly imaginative. She was fact-based. She knew herself. She knew the people she loved.

She was betrayed. It was a betrayal that struck into her soul and left her shaking in anger. A betrayal she wondered if she could ever forgive. John Vincent couldn't be Trent Daylen, but she knew for a fact that Micah Sloane and David Abijah were the same.

It was a betrayal she drove away from, just as her cousin had walked away from her. Just as Trent had been taken away from her.

As the night wore on and the car ate up the miles to DC, Bailey knew where she was going from here. She had spent too many years fighting other people's battles. It was time she fought her own.

CHAPTER 1

One years Later

IT WAS A WORLD BAILEY HADN'T expected to ever enter again. She had left home fifteen years before, vowing she would never return. After her parents' deaths seven years ago, there had never been a reason to return.

She stood beneath expensive crystal chandeliers, outfitted in a brilliant emerald designer dress and high heels, with emeralds and diamonds at her throat and ears. Diamond pins held her hair in place and a single emerald ring graced her hand as she lifted a champagne flute to her lips to sip.

Not cheap champagne here. This was some of the best she had sipped in her life. Perhaps better than her own coming-out ball when she had turned sixteen and her father had definitely splurged on that.

She stared around the ballroom, let the orchestra's music drift around her and pretended it was just another assignment. That she was still with the CIA, that the op she was on was blessed by its director, and that backup would be waiting if the shit hit the fan.

She knew better. In this world there was no backup. There was just Bailey Serborne, the Serborne heiress. The prodigal daughter without a family to welcome her back into the fold. Only the enemies surrounded her here.

"Bailey, how good to see you again." She lifted her cheek and allowed yet another vapid smile to cross her lips as a kiss was brushed against her cheek.

Janice Waterstone. She was in her sixties and still looked forty. Plastic surgery and cosmetics could accomplish miracles.

Janice was one in a long line of welcoming elite in attendance at the Serborne mansion, which Bailey had reopened a year ago.

She'd returned home, supposedly with her tail tucked between her legs, her pride smarting from her dismissal from the agency. And the dismissal was nothing more than the truth; she could still hear her director screaming at her in his office. Milburn Rushmore's face had been neon red, flushed and perspiring, he'd been so pissed at her.

"It's good to see you again, Janice." The smile was as patently false as the other woman's.

Janice was no more happy to see her here than Bailey was to be here. It was the social lie that mattered, though, the persona, the facade presented to the world.

The Serborne fortune was one of the twelve largest in the world. In more than three hundred years it had never dwindled, only grown. And her family had always remained in the top tier of the social elite. The cream of the crop so to speak. American royalty.

She stared around the ballroom, remembering her mother's balls here. The exquisite parties, the months of planning that had gone into them. Angelina Serborne had been an exacting hostess. Her parties were always enjoyed, and invitations were always envied.

"You have quite a crowd here." Janice looked around with a smug smile. "I believe I even saw Sheik AbdulRhamadin and his bodyguard. Not to mention several of this year's hottest actors."

"Every invitation was accepted." Bailey shrugged her bare shoulders.

"Of course they were." Janice blinked back at her. "A Serborne invitation hasn't been issued in seven years. No one was going to miss this party, even if it was such short notice."

In other words, it hadn't been planned a year in advance.

"I'm home. I wanted to remember the good times," she stated simply. "Mother loved the parties."

Janice paused at the mention of Angelina, then finally nodded as though her thoughts were pleasant for a change.

"Angelina and I used to plan her parties together." Janice sighed. "I've missed her."

Bailey finished her champagne. It was instantly snagged by a waiter and replaced with another. Reminiscing about the past wasn't on her list of priorities tonight.

"Pardon me, Janice, I see someone I need to talk to." Bailey excused herself before making her way across to the room to her nemesis.

Some men were so power-hungry that they would do anything to achieve the position they sought. One of those men was Raymond Greer, a former CIA overseas operative.

Raymond had managed to slide into the elite by the way of marriage to one Mary Grace Altman, a widow he'd met on a European cruise while undercover. Bailey wondered if Mary was aware that at one time, she was the former agent's mark.

Raymond stood an easy six four, but he lacked the breadth and muscle that would have made his height attractive. His face was shaped rather like a weasel's, and she could honestly say she had never seen a real smile cross his lips.

"Hello, Raymond, I'm glad you could make it." She stepped up to the former agent and continued softly, "You've done very well for yourself."

"Not all of us are born into wealth." His smile was tight, almost angry, as he spoke back just as softly. "Some of us definitely have to work for our retirement."

Bailey's brows arched as she glanced several feet from where they stood from Raymond's delicate wife.

Mary was one of the sweetest people Bailey knew and one of the few who understood the word *sincerity*. She was a sister to one of the men Bailey hated most in the world and the aunt to the girl who had once been Bailey's dearest friend.

"Some things should never be considered work," she stated softly as she turned back to him.

He glared back at her.

"Really, Raymond, I'm your hostess, don't you know you're supposed to kiss my ass." She brought her glass to her lips to hide her own gloating smile. "You're letting your roots show, my friend. That's considered impolite."

"What do you want?" He ran a hand over his thinning brown hair, and his hazel eyes flickered back to her in suspicion.

Bailey shrugged at his question. "We should be friends. We've come from the same world in some ways. The same dangers. We could trade war stories."

Not in this lifetime and she knew it. Raymond despised her for her birth, just as she despised him for his arrogance. But that arrogance had been an inborn trait of his. He was finally where he had felt he had belonged all along. It didn't matter how he'd had to lie, cheat and perhaps even kill to get here.

Raymond's gaze narrowed on her at her suggestion. "Funny, you were never interested in discussing anything with me before."

She smiled at that. "We never had anything in common before. We're both a part of this society; we see each other often. We should make the best of it."

"You're not interested in returning to the agency then?" he asked her, a hint of calculation in his voice and in his gaze. "After a year I'd assume you've missed it."

It was a question she had been asked several times over the past months since returning home.

"You don't have to insult me," she informed him coldly. "I think we're both aware that's never going to happen."

Let him get his strikes in. She could handle them as she had never been able to before.

"Because you were fired." He smiled in gloating satisfaction.

Bailey gave a low, light laugh. "I quit. Rushmore just felt

he should fire me in retaliation. Haven't you heard? He
didn't like having someone on his team who didn't believe
he had a direct line to God."

Raymond's brow arched curiously at that. She was re-
peating his own insults concerning Rushmore.

"Figured that out, did you?" he asked smugly. "I did warn
you, Bailey. Rushmore believes he's above the rest of us.
One of these days someone should put him in his place."

"Six feet under," she muttered before directing another
tight smile in his direction. "If you'll excuse me now, Raymond, I need to mingle. We should talk again later, though."

She moved away from him but glanced back, giving
him the impression that she was considering more than a
bullet through his head. She was considering much more.

Bailey had worked a year to incorporate herself back into
the society she had run from so long ago. For twelve months
she had lied, schemed and worked herself to the point that
she knew Orion's employer, Warbucks, would contact her
soon. He would have to. Only Bailey could supply information he needed now. Information that would lead him to a
prize she knew he had all intentions of selling.

As she greeted her guests and sipped at her champagne,
the image of her parents flashed through her mind. Ben and
Angelina Serborne had been gracious, enduring. Her mother
had smiled with genuine amusement or fondness; her father
had had a deep belly laugh that never failed to make others
laugh in turn.

Her father had been a patriot. A man dedicated to his
country and its freedoms. It was a dedication she knew had
ended in his and her mother's deaths.

She should have returned sooner, she thought as she
stared around the ballroom, took in the bright colors of the
evening dresses, the dark tuxedos. This was Aspen's winter
finest, and mixed with them were six families who were part
of a very elite group of powerful men. The richest of the
rich. The most powerful. The most corrupt. She should have
returned years ago and learned the secrets she was only now

beginning to realize. Secrets that would avenge her parents' deaths.

There were reasons she had left home at eighteen, and turned her back on a fortune that would take four lifetimes to even put a dent in. She had walked away from her parents and everything she had ever known in her life because of the corruption and deceit she had seen here.

There were reasons why she was back now. One was to find the man responsible for the death of her parents. The man who had paid an international assassin known as Orion to kill them.

She couldn't ask Orion himself; he was dead. Taken out by an unknown group of soldiers or agents and killed in his bed. A shadowy force that didn't even have a name. The same group that had kidnapped her in Atlanta.

There were layers upon dark layers here, and she meant to uncover each of them. She would uncover them and learn Warbucks's identity. When she did, then she would have her revenge. As she hadn't had on Orion.

The thought sent a chill up her back as she forced it away from her. She'd walked away from Orion, knowing, even as she fought the knowledge, that she didn't have a chance of taking him on her own. She would never get the information she needed without returning here. She just hadn't expected exactly what she had found once she came home.

"John Vincent. What the hell are you doing in Aspen?"

Bailey swung around at the male exclamation. Ian Richards and his wife, Kira, were in Colorado for vacation. The ex–Navy SEAL had married one of the nation's most sought-after heiresses, Kira Porter, giving him entrée into some of the most exclusive parties.

And there, shaking hands with the burly ex-SEAL, was John Vincent. Every background check she had done on him had shown him as shady in his dealings as well as his business. He was a suspected hardware, information, and arms broker to terrorists and drug cartels. A middleman who ensured a smooth and honest transaction among thieves.

With that cover, it was only fitting that he would know Richards, whose father had been one of the most notorious drug cartel rulers alive until he was killed several years before.

Ian was accepted here because he was a SEAL, because drugs were as prevalent as the champagne that flowed like water, and because his wife was one very rich heiress.

"It's been too long, John." Kira was accepting a kiss on her cheek from lips that Bailey dreamed about much too often. "Where have you been hiding?"

Bailey watched as John's head lifted, glimpsed his laughing gray eyes, and ate every detail with her senses. The strong slope of his brow, the bridge of his nose, those kissable lips and broad cheekbones. Sun-bronzed flesh stretched over the broad planes and angles of his face as a dark overnight growth of beard shadowed his jaw.

He looked like a pirate. Like a man who took what he wanted and laughed at the opposition. He looked like exactly what he was supposed to be. Dangerously charming.

"Bailey, there you are." Ian turned his head to her, a smile lighting his handsome features as she moved toward them. "Come meet a friend of mine."

Meet a friend of his. Ian had been part of the Atlanta operation, though Bailey had glimpsed him only once or twice in the operation itself. Kira had been there as well, but Bailey had always suspected that the other woman was much more than she had ever presented herself as being. So many layers, and they were all converging here.

"Ian." She accepted his hand as she drew closer. "I'm so glad you and Kira could make it tonight."

"We wouldn't miss it." He grinned as he turned back to John. "I'd like you'd to meet a friend of mine." The introduction was done smoothly, casually, but Bailey could feel the hairs on the back of her neck rising in alarm.

She was being watched, closely. Someone was much too interested in this meeting.

"Mr. Vincent." Her gaze was held by his as he took her hand and brought it smoothly to his lips.

A chill raced up her spine to explode at the back of her neck as electricity seemed to charge her entire body. She could feel her breasts swelling as his lips touched the sensitive flesh over her knuckles and brushed against them. Her nipples were hard, sensitive, and between her thighs she was growing heated and wet. Her reaction to this man was immediate, blazing and confusing.

"Miss Serborne," he murmured as he lowered her hand. "It's definitely a pleasure to meet you."

She bet it was.

A smile curled her lips as she felt adrenaline pierce the haze of dark emotionlessness that had held her in its grip for too many months now. Suddenly she felt alive, she felt dangerous, she felt a thrill racing through her body that she couldn't control.

"The pleasure is all mine," she assured him, and it was. He was here for a reason, an operation. He was here, and she was laying money on the fact, to interfere in what she had begun just as he and his team had interfered in Atlanta. She was beginning to grow sick of all the noses continually poking into her business.

She was playing on her home ground now. No one was taking this from her, least of all a man who had already stolen the pleasure of Orion's death.

"Ian, you didn't tell me the scenery here was this exceptional," John murmured aside to his friend as he kept his gaze on hers. "I would have visited sooner."

"The scenery only acquired certain additions recently," Ian assured him.

Bailey kept her smile pleasant as she glanced at Ian and his wife. "Ian's being overly kind," she stated lightly. "So tell me, Mr. Vincent, are you here for business or pleasure?"

"Well, I'm a businessman." He grinned. "I like to combine the two whenever possible, but at the moment it's definitely pleasure."

It was definitely an operation. For a second, regret shimmered inside her before she pushed it back, ignoring it. She was nothing to him, and he was nothing to her, evidently.

She had to remember that; to remember anything else only threatened her control.

Her suspicions couldn't be proved, no matter the time and effort she had put into that investigation. It was wishful thinking, she continued to assure herself. She'd lost the man she loved and now she wanted nothing more than to find a way to bring him back when she needed him the most. There was no bringing back the dead.

"Would you like to dance?" Still retaining her hand, he stepped back from Ian and Kira.

Bailey allowed him to draw her onto the dance floor, holding her silence until she was in his arms, their bodies moving together to the slow, easy strains of the orchestra.

"What are you doing here?" She kept her lips against his shoulder to hide the words, her voice low enough that only he could hear her.

"We need to talk." He didn't answer her question, but she hadn't really expected him to.

"Too bad," she drawled. She luxuriated in the feel of his body against hers, even with the clothing that separated them. There was something about him that she couldn't ignore, couldn't forget. Something that drew her like a moth to a flame. It was a very dangerous position to be in.

"Come on, Bailey." His lips brushed against her ear. "Just a few minutes of your time. I promise, you won't regret it." His hand stroked from her hip up, along her back, then back again.

"I regret meeting you to begin with," she told him softly, noting the tension that tightened his body. "Why would tonight be any different?"

His hand tightened at her hip. "You never know, I could surprise you."

She almost laughed at that statement. There was no surprise in store for her. The best he could do was manage to amaze her with the delivery of whatever he wanted from her. She had no doubt why he was here.

"You're on my turf now," she warned him. "I doubt

there's anything that you could do here that would surprise me, John."

She surprised herself sometimes, though. Now was one of those times. She was amazed at her reaction to him, at the excitement that filled her. He had taken the prize from her hands last time, and he was no doubt determined to do the same thing this time. She should be outraged rather than aroused.

"It's important, Bailey," he told her. "We need to talk, after the party."

"After the party I'm going to be incredibly tired." The song drew to a close as she stepped back from his hold. "Maybe later. Leave your number with the doorman, I'm sure he'll make certain I get it."

He didn't let her go. Surprising her, he caught her arm, as he drew her from the dance floor and to the wide double doors leading out of the ballroom.

She had a feeling he wouldn't let this go so easily.

"I cannot leave my own party," she protested with feigned lightness, her temper beginning to burn.

"Just for a moment, Miss Serborne," he promised as they passed the wide doors and he headed unerringly to the back of the house.

Their progress was being noted. The tingling at the base of her spine was building, assuring her that whoever had been watching her for most of the night still had their eyes on her. She'd tried to pinpoint the sensation all evening and had yet to assign it to one particular guest, though she had her suspicions.

Whoever it was, they were good, better than she would have expected, considering the people she knew she was dealing with. Of course, they had been skating by for years now, they would have grown adept at hiding, she assured herself as John drew her straight to her own personal office.

The door had been locked earlier, but it wasn't locked now. Her brows arched as he opened it and drew her inside before closing and locking it.

"Thank you for making such a spectacle of me." She rounded him furiously. "You dragged me through my own party like a disobedient pet."

"And you were growling at me every step of the way," he glowered back at her. "What part of *We need to talk* didn't you want to understand?"

"The *needing to talk* part?" She opened her eyes wide in false amazement. "Did you somehow manage to misunderstand me?"

She crossed her arms over her breasts as she lifted her brow in curiosity. "You don't take no for an answer at all well, do you, Mr. Vincent?"

His lips twitched in amusement. Now, didn't it just make her day to know she amused him in some small part?

"I must admit, I have problems with that word," he finally replied. "Perhaps my mother said it too often when I was a child."

She gave a short little snort at that. She doubted any woman had ever told him no.

"So what was so important that you felt the need to make a spectacle of me at my own party?" she asked coldly. "I hope it's a matter of life or death, because really, there could be no other excuse for it."

His brow lifted. The dark blond color against his sun-bronzed flesh was incredibly alluring. He could have been a fallen angel, too ruggedly handsome for words, and too charming for his own good.

"You play the part of the society princess very well," he mused. "I wouldn't have expected it of you."

She gave a little shrug of her bare shoulders. "You could say it's in the blood," she retorted mockingly.

At least, that was what her mother had always assured her. That she had the blood of American royalty running through her veins and she should always remember it. There hadn't been a single member of her mother's or her father's families who hadn't married well, who hadn't married into true blood, if not blue blood.

"It's easy to forget when you're trussed up, blindfolded, and gagged," he murmured with a wealth of amusement now. "The society princess gets pushed behind by the gutter fighter then." He rubbed at his jaw where she had managed to head-butt him months before in Atlanta.

"Back any animal into a corner and it's going to come out biting," she promised him. "Now, are you going to tell me what the hell you want or do I have to start guessing? I really don't have time to guess, John."

His lips pursed thoughtfully. "You're still pissed over Atlanta, aren't you?"

"And why would I be pissed over Atlanta?" she asked him. "You just kidnapped me and nearly drugged me. You were directly responsible for my release from the agency and you refused to help me in any way while I was there. So what reason would I have to be pissed?"

John nodded. "As I assumed, you really have no reason not to help me then." His grin was confident and way too arrogant.

"And you live in a dream world that I can only envy, big boy. Someone should be kind and awaken you."

His eyes narrowed warningly. "We have a situation, Bailey, a very delicate one."

Now why didn't that surprise her?

"Sucks to be you." She wasn't about to admit that she was blazingly curious about his *situation*. No doubt, knowing him, the men he worked with, and Milburn Rushmore, she could count on the fact that they wanted nothing more than to use her. Forget working with her, or her working with them. It just didn't happen that way.

"You like pushing, don't you?" he asked softly, dangerously.

"I like wasting my time as well," she informed him haughtily. "Now why don't you get the hell out of my way and let me get back to my party? I was rather enjoying it before you decided to intrude."

She moved to grip the doorknob and slide the lock open

when he shifted, turned—and before she knew it she found herself with her back against the panel, his large body pressing against hers, heating it further.

A sharp breath exhaled from Bailey's lungs at the sensation of suddenly being flush against him, almost surrounded by him. It had obviously been too long since a man had touched her, too long since she had felt the warmth and hard thickness of an erection pressing against her, because her senses were rioting with it.

Bailey felt her knees weakening, her heart racing, her breath coming hard and fast.

God she wanted him. As though she knew him, as though suspicion were indeed fact rather than wishful thinking. Maybe she just needed an excuse. Maybe her brain just needed a reason to take what her body was demanding.

"Don't do this," she whispered, her hands pressing against his chest as his head lowered, his lips coming much too close to hers.

"Don't kiss you?" His lips quirked with sexy humor and dangerous intent and an oddly familiar playfulness. "Afraid you might change your mind, Bailey?"

"You like messing with my head," she accused him. "If you think you can use my body against me, John, then you'd better think again. It's not going to happen."

"Bet me."

The hard growl that left his lips was the only warning she had before his lips were covering hers and reality began to recede. Wicked, driving hunger rose to the forefront of her senses, a starving need for touch that she couldn't fight against, that her body had no desire to reject.

Need and knowledge warred inside her mind now. The need for this kiss that she couldn't seem to get enough of, and the knowledge that he was going to do exactly what she had sworn she wasn't going to allow him to do. He was going to use her body against her. He was going to make her hungrier, he was going to fill her senses with him and sap the strength to fight from her.

She'd known in that warehouse a year ago that he was

dangerous for her. She had known that her best course of action for her sanity and her heart was to stay as far away from him as possible.

She'd run as far as she could run and here he was, exactly where he shouldn't be.

Her arms twined around his neck as his hand gripped her hips, then slowly slid to her thighs while he pressed a knee between them. The hard muscle of his upper leg rode against the mound of her pussy, stroking the swollen bud of her clit as she fought for breath. Her hands speared into the overly long strands of dark blond hair, and she held on for dear life as her hips writhed against his leg.

The friction against that most sensitive part of her body was overwhelming. Lust clamored inside her brain; the need for release drove sharpened spikes of sensation racing over her nerve endings straight to her sex.

Her tongue rubbed against his, fought for dominance in the kiss, and finally conceded as he wrapped his fingers around the mound of a breast.

Bailey froze, her breath stilling in her throat as his thumb stroked over her nipple. She could feel the rioting pleasure rising inside her. She wanted to tear the material of her dress out of the way, she wanted bare flesh to meet bare flesh and she wanted to ride the wave of arousal surging through her.

In the arms of a stranger.

God, she had lost her mind. She had lost what little control she still had of herself, and finding it again seemed a lost cause.

He may be some super-secret agent. It could all be a game. He could be just what his background assured her he was: a killer, a terrorist, a monster. And here she was surrendering to him without a shred of certainty either way.

She was so desperate for the past that she was creating her own fantasy and she knew just how dangerous that was.

"No."

She tore herself from his arms, stumbling away from him as she covered her lips with the back of her hand and stared back at him in horror.

He even kissed like Trent. Just like Trent. With the same voracious hunger, the same lustful intent.

"Get out!" she panted desperately. "Get out of my home before I have you thrown out."

He looked as shell-shocked as she felt. Staring back at her, his gray eyes thunderous, his lips swollen from her kiss, he looked as though the pleasure had punched him just as hard as it had her.

"This isn't over," he warned her. "We will talk, Bailey."

"When hell freezes over," she snapped, furious with herself as well as him.

His lips thinned. "Invest in plenty of heat then," he warned her. "Because it's coming. And it's coming fast, baby."

He jerked the door open and stalked out. Every line of his body was tense and hard, furious lust practically sizzling off his body as he stalked down the hall and back to the front of the house.

Bailey followed behind him, her heels snapping against the marble floor as she silently cursed him, as well as herself.

She'd be damned if she was going to allow him to manipulate her or to destroy what she was working on here. She knew his kind and she knew him. He would take over, he would insist on dominance, and she had no intentions of allowing anyone to dominate her at this point.

He was too much like Trent. She had loved Trent, ached for him after his death, but she had always known that eventually they would clash. She could have handled it with Trent, but not with this man. She had loved Trent, she didnt love John Vincent.

Stepping into the foyer, she watched as he stalked past the doors the doormen pulled open for him. One hand pressed to her stomach, the other hanging at her side, she fought to find her equilibrium once again.

Breathing in deeply, Bailey licked her lips, then looked around, only to find her gaze caught and held by Raymond Greer's. Her head lifted as her lips tightened. Just what she needed, for the bastard to see a weakness in her.

He was watching her like a beady-eyed cobra waiting to strike. Calculating, manipulating. That pretty much described Raymond to a T.

She nodded toward him sharply before moving quickly back to the ballroom and the party she had organized so painstakingly. She was on a deadline. She didn't have time to be drawn into John Vincent's games. She didn't have time to allow her heart to be broken again. She had a past to put to rest, and trying to resurrect her lover in another man wasn't part of the plan.

CHAPTER 2

JOHN STARED OUT INTO the Colorado mountains from the cabin Jordan rented for the time the team would be in Aspen. A frown pulled at his brows as the rest of the men began to gather in the room behind him, their images wavering in the glass of the window.

Jordan had arrived earlier and set up a situation room of sorts. There was plenty of hot coffee, computers along one wall displaying a multitude of images, and several communication bases staffed by the redheaded spitfire Jordan had brought in just after the inception of the Elite Operations Unit.

Tehya Talamosi Fitzhugh was the daughter of a white slaver whom Ian Richards, and the SEALs he'd worked with at the time, had brought down. She'd spent her life running from the Fitzhughs and once that was over, she had been unwilling to step into any life other than the one she had learned how to live within. One of danger.

"I'm going to assume last night went about as well as you expected it to," Jordan announced as the rest of the team gathered around the large table set up in the room.

John turned away from the vista spread out beyond the cabin and faced a room filled with dead men. Noah Blake had once been known as Navy SEAL Nathan Malone. Then there was Travis Caine, a former MI-6 agent; Nik Steele, a former Russian intelligence officer; Micah Sloane, Bailey's cousin and former Israeli Mossad agent; and Jordan Malone, Noah's uncle and the commander who had fought to keep five dead men from living again. He had a hell of a job cut out for him, as two of them had already reclaimed parts of their lives.

"She's uncertain and angry." He shrugged addressing the question. "We expected that."

"Then find a way to work around it," Jordan ordered him. "We received word last night that Warbucks is getting ready to move on his next acquisition. We can't afford to let that sale go through."

"We're certain he's here?" Nik leaned forward, staring at Jordan intently. "There's no sense in drawing her into this and endangering her further if we're not certain."

Jordan stared back at the six-foot-five-inch Russian coolly.

"Would we be here if I weren't certain?" he asked.

Nik shrugged. "Knowing you, Commander, one can never be certain."

There were a few chuckles from the other men, especially Noah Blake. They all knew Jordan. He was sharp as hell and one of the best commanders John had ever worked with, but he was a bit prone to go with his gut rather than proof. Not that his gut had been wrong yet, but there was always a first time.

"You've read the same reports I have," Jordan finally grunted. "Code-named Warbucks, this individual or group of individuals is acquiring top-secret information and hardware and billions in sales on the black market. There's rumor that Warbucks has acquired this." Jordan turned to the large monitor on the wall.

The black screen flickered to show an image of a soldier holding a shoulder-mounted missile launcher. When he fired, they watched as the missile exploded from the barrel. Within seconds it took out a military drone flying above the accepted limit for commercial airliners.

"Code-named *CROSSFIRE,* the military's new toy has exceptional speed and reach," Jordan informed them. "But it has even more. It can be programmed to a specific aircraft either using a stealth transmitter that can be attached to the hull of the aircraft, or using the airplane's electronics themselves. *CROSSFIRE* can be programmed to the transmitter, fired in Colorado, and take out an aircraft in the air or on the ground in Washington, DC. It can't be tracked by conventional radar, and its stealth capabilities are exceptional. It's easily transported, hidden, and completely undetectable. Last week a launcher and six missiles were stolen from a military depot in DC. Two days later John Vincent's handler"—Jordan glanced to Tehya—"received a message that Mr. Vincent's services were being considered for a unique sale. We suspect that sale is *CROSSFIRE*."

"Several other messages went out to Libya, Syria, Iran, China, and Africa that *CROSSFIRE* had been acquired and bids would be taken," John informed them. "One of the messages was received by a suspected general with al-Qaeda and money began shifting through several different accounts associated with the organization.

"In three weeks the president is scheduled to arrive in Saudi Arabia to meet with several dignitaries, princes and Middle Eastern factions in secret talks aimed at drawing support for a new proposal for a truce in armed areas. This new plan has drawn support from some surprising factions. It could actually begin an initiative that could signal a turn in the tide of terrorism in the Middle East."

Micah Sloane, the former Mossad agent, got to his feet at that point. "This new peace plan has Jordanian, Israeli, and Iranian consideration so far. The talks are remaining highly secret until the meeting in Saudi, where all the area's leaders will gather. Several terrorist organizations have already learned of the meeting and have been planning ways to potentially sabotage it. This weapon is all they need."

"The planes will be checked for transmitters before liftoff," Travis Caine interjected. "How much success could they have?"

"The missiles can be programmed to individual aircraft signatures," Jordan answered him. "It can also be armed with a nuclear warhead large enough to take out the meeting area and anyone in it." He stared around the room as tension began to thicken. "We have three weeks to identify Warbucks and find the location of the missiles and launcher," he warned them. "John Vincent is being tapped to broker the sale." He looked to John. "Our hard work in all your covers and our previous operations is finally paying off. Vincent as the broker, Caine his bodyguard. Nik our Russian terrorist will be in place at the ski resort for bidding. Micah is our Palestinian terrorist Jerric Abbas. Noah will be here at the cabin with me to provide backup and logistical support."

John lifted his gaze back to the file footage playing on the wide screen and watched once again as the missile struck the drone plane. The warhead that could be attached to the missile wouldn't be large, but it was big enough. Big enough that it could take out the heads of more than half the Middle Eastern countries without a problem, and they had only three weeks to stop it.

"Bailey is an important part of this operation why?" Caine asked. "A disenchanted CIA agent?"

"Much more than that actually," Jordan answered. "Warbucks will choose his broker based on Bailey Serborne's approval of him. She's in whether we like it or not."

"How do we know this?" John could feel the almost violent sense of protectiveness rising within him. This was new information, and it was information he didn't like.

"This is via Warbucks's contact," Teyha informed him. "The call I received was quite specific. Miss Serbourne will choose the broker. Every broker contacted received the same message. This is now our best chance of identifying him."

Warbucks's connections and the information and hardware he was getting his hands on was beginning to concern not just the United States but also allied nations. The power behind Warbucks had already shown itself in previous sales. The theft of the items, their movements, and their subsequent sales over the years had led back to connections to six families. Families with enough power around the world to bring down any law enforcement agency that came after them. But even more, there was enough power that each investigation into Warbucks's activities had been betrayed and/or stopped in its tracks.

High-ranking political officials had died searching for answers, as had agents, investigators, and bureau directors of more than one law enforcement agency across the globe.

That kind of power could eventually result in complete global warfare or financial meltdown if it wasn't stopped.

"Bailey has connections into each of the six families," John continued. "And we know for a fact that she's running her own op into Warbucks. Her years at the CIA were peppered with various searches into each sale Warbucks made. We also have a file taken from Orion the night he was killed. That file included her picture and copies of e-mails sent to the assassin each time it was suspected he would cross her path. He was paid well to make certain he skirted around her rather than killing her. She had a no-kill order attached to her name that went out to not just Orion, but also several terrorist organizations. Warbucks is drawing her in. She knows it, and now we know it."

"She could be involved," Nik injected.

Jordan shook his head. "The families she's tied to are the connection. The Serborne fortune goes to charity, billions and billions of dollars if Bailey Serborne dies without an heir. That's the key to her good health and welfare to this point. She has no heir. That fortune is still up in the air, as well as the power that backs it. Until there's a way to claim it, Warbucks will not allow her to die. Instead, its been determined that he's going to partner with her, or develop a relationship with her instead."

The monitor changed from the missile firing to a dozen pictures of the reigning patriarchs of each family Bailey was connected to.

"You'll receive files on each family," Jordan informed them. "But of the twelve, we've narrowed down what's considered the four most likely, and we believe Bailey has narrowed that number down even farther. Read over your files, acquaint yourself with each family and their ties and connections into the Mideast deal coming up as well as their oppositions to it."

"And if you can't seduce Miss Serborne into helping you?" Travis Caine arched a blond brow as he stared back at John. "Just because she was enamored of Trent Daylen five years ago doesn't mean she's going to fall into John Vincent's arms now."

John scowled back at him. "She'll do her part. She wants this as bad as we do. One of the men on your list is Ford Grace, the man she suspects played a part in not just her parents' deaths but also a childhood friend's some years before. Bailey wants vengeance. She missed out on Orion, so she's now returning to the source."

She had let them have Orion, hoping that when she returned to her former life and her place in society, no one would give it a second look. That she could find her own justice, in her own way. She had been drawing Warbucks in, waiting for this chance.

The satisfaction for her would have been much more profound. However, there was no way Bailey could have possibly been aware of the extent of Warbucks's crimes or power. She was after the man who hired a killer, not an international terrorist.

"How much information are we giving her?" Noah asked, his blue eyes concerned as he watched John.

"Everything." John glared back at Jordan, very well aware that his commander was opposed to that. "She won't be aware of anyone involved but myself and Travis, but she'll be aware of the operation as well as the implications of failure."

The others nodded, though Jordan continued to stare back at him coldly. John wasn't always in agreement with his commander's tactics. Jordan liked to keep his secrets, and he liked to keep knowledge of the unit completely hidden.

He was still pissed that Noah's and Micah's wives were aware of not just the unit but also its operatives. He considered each one of them weaknesses. Which, in all likelihood, they were. But John often wondered if that wasn't what made both Noah and Micah as efficient as they were. They had a reason to return from a mission, a reason the rest of them didn't have or had lost.

"We have Ian and Kira as backup as well as Kell Krieger and Macey March," Jordan informed them. "Ian and Kira are playing within the upper crust of the rich and famous while Kell and Macey are working within the security details of two of the families. I'll make certain you get reports as information comes in."

"Travis and I have checked in to one of the hotels in Aspen," John told them. "We'll be moving into Bailey's mansion within the week."

"Confident bastard, isn't he?" Nik grunted, bringing a round of chuckles from the other men.

"Convinced," John informed them all coolly.

He knew Bailey, he knew the desire was still there, just as strong and just as hot as it had ever been. It hadn't gone away any more than his need for her had gone away.

It had begun five years before, only months before his "death." When he had met Bailey on a joint US–Australian operation. He'd commanded the small team searching for pirates, and Bailey had been the CIA's agent in charge. They'd struck sparks from the first second, and within days those sparks had grown to full-blown lust.

They'd had one night. One night that he had never forgotten, never gotten out of his mind. A night that haunted him until he wondered if it would eventually steal his sanity.

Seeing her in Atlanta had nearly destroyed him; letting her go had torn his heart out. He hadn't told her in Australia what she meant to him—that he'd seen the end of his bachelor days in her eyes. And then fate had taken the choice from him. Trent Daylen had died and John Vincent had been created from the ashes. And John Vincent had no right to Bailey Serborne.

Fuck.

He clenched his fists and moved from the table once more as the other men read over their files and discussed various aspects of the operation as it stood.

Everything hinged on Bailey and her decision to accept him as her lover. She wasn't an agent who would sleep with any man for a mission. She might pretend to, and she could be a damned good actress. But John didn't want an act, he wanted the woman. Just one more time. Just a few nights to store inside his soul and hold him over in the bleak, lonely days to come.

She was like a ray of sunshine that he hadn't known he'd missed until Atlanta. Until he had looked up and seen her haunted green eyes, her hollow expression as she watched Micah and Risa leave their apartment building.

He'd known why she was there. The assassin Orion had been hired to kill Risa, an assassin suspected to have been involved in her parents' deaths, and proven to have been involved in her cousin's death in Israel. She'd lost everyone in her life, and she had hungered for vengeance, for absolution. It had been a hunger he'd had to deny her.

Hell, he was fucked up here and he knew it. This mission had the potential to blow up in all their faces. The players involved weren't just the richest men in the world, they were the most powerful. They seated politicians and had the ears of presidents and kings. They weren't men whom any government agency dared to trifle with, which was why Jordan had taken the operation himself. It was one they had been working for years, gathering intel from various agencies, tracking movements, shipments, and weapons.

Warbucks somehow managed to steal the information or hardware. From there, he engaged the services of a broker to auction the items and transfer the goods. John had handled several smaller transactions with exacting detail. Whoever Warbucks was, John was a trusted entity to him, or them. John was also considered one of the most reliable brokers on the black market, where a man's word was about as good as the spit on the ground at his feet.

He was careful, he avoided assassins and betrayal and he had the connections needed to get the highest dollar for each deal. And this deal would demand a hell of a lot of dollars. It wouldn't be a simple transaction and transfer; even Warbucks would know that. The danger, the secrecy involved, and the weapon itself would require more trust than normal from all parties.

John had been contacted. The first move had been made.

"You going to be able to handle this, Heat Seeker?" Noah's voice was low at his side.

John turned his head and stared back at the man who had become a friend in the past five years.

"I'll handle her." He shifted his shoulders, preparing for the battle ahead.

Noah breathed out roughly at the answer. "I didn't ask if you could handle her. You going to be able to handle walking away again?"

John stared back at him for long moments, letting the question sink inside him before the anger that had once been carefully banked flared to the surface.

"Who the fuck says I have to walk away again? No one makes that decision this time but me."

"What the fuck do the lot of you think this unit is?" Jordan broke in furiously as he came in behind Noah. "A damned matchmaking opportunity? I don't send you on these missions to lose your damned hearts and create more risks than we need at this point. We have a job to do, Heat Seeker, try to remember that."

"Fuck you!" John snarled. "You don't own my fucking soul, you just bought it for a while."

"And you damned well better remember that your time isn't up yet." Jordan flattened his hands against the table as he glared back at John. "Seven more years, that's what you owe this unit and the men who gave you a fucking life back. Getting married and living happily-fucking-ever-after wasn't part of the deal."

"Putting up with your bullishness wasn't part of the deal, either," John sneered, the thought of walking away from Bailey a third time ripping at his soul as he shoved his finger in Jordan's direction. "You don't tell me what I'll walk away from, mate. Not you, not anyone. Remember that."

He turned and stalked from the room, then from the

cabin. He'd had enough. Orders, missions, decisions always based on the good of the unit or the good of the mission. This time, this mission, there was a hell of a lot more at stake. This time, it wasn't his life, it was his soul.

NOAH WATCHED AS HEAT Seeker stalked from the room and slammed the door behind him. Minutes later the Hummer he was driving started up and sped out of the driveway.

The Australian was pissed, and Noah couldn't blame him. Hell, Bailey had already been taken from him once. In every man's life there was one woman, one chance, and very few were given another shot if they fucked it up.

Noah had been given another chance with his wife, Sabella, and he'd almost fucked that one up. Now John was being given another chance with Bailey, and when it came to that Aussie, anything was possible.

"We're going to have problems with him," Jordan remarked as he neared Noah. "I'll have to have Travis keep a close eye on him."

Problems meant that Jordan was realizing the mistake it had been to bring John into this mission to begin with. Not that Jordan could have stopped Heat Seeker from being here, not with Bailey Serborne involved. But for some reason Jordan kept thinking he could control events. When it came to a man's soul, Noah thought that maybe his uncle was finally realizing that once a man lost his soul to a woman, it was gone forever. And life wasn't much worth living without her.

"Give him room, Jordan." Noah shook his head. "Crowd him and you'll regret it."

"My operatives keep acquiring wedding rings and I'm going to end up with a bunch of useless men as well as an ulcer," he grunted. "You guys get damned cranky when I pull you away from home and hearth."

Noah grinned at that. He did get damned cranky. He liked being close to home and hearth and living again. He'd been "dead" for far too long without his Sabella. Being with her again, being himself, a husband, a lover, and a father, was a miracle for him.

Pulling his wallet from his back pocket, he flipped it open to reveal the latest pictures of his wife and son. "This is what you're pulling me away from, man. It's worth getting cranky over."

For a moment Jordan's face softened as he stared down at the infant. Thick black hair and vibrant blue eyes combined with the dark Irish skin tone that his father and uncle both possessed.

Jordan was damned proud of his little nephew. He'd been there when the baby had been born, and Noah could have sworn Jordan might have been hiding a tear or two when the nurse laid the baby in Noah's arms.

"Gonna be damned hard to say that's not Nathan Malone's kid." Jordan sighed as he shook his head in concern. "You're taking a hell of a risk. We can't afford to have others realize that Nathan Malone might not be fully dead."

"He is Nathan Malone's kid." Noah grinned. "Sometimes we forget who I used to be, don't we?"

Noah never forgot. His name might have changed, to some extent he might have changed, but Nathan Malone lived on within him.

Jordan shook his head at that, his expression becoming almost haggard. "I never forgot, I never forget. And by God, I never stop regretting."

Before Noah could say anything, his uncle pivoted on his heel and stalked from the room.

Noah shook his head and replaced the wallet in his back pocket before breathing out heavily, his gaze connecting with Micah Sloane's. Over the past months he and the former Mossad agent had found common ground that they hadn't had before. Wives and children. Micah's wife had only recently presented him with their first child, and both men worried incessantly when they were away from their families.

Both men recognized something in Jordan that even Jordan refused to admit to. A man fighting a losing battle with the woman he couldn't stay away from, as well as a soldier's battle to fight a war he felt he was losing.

Jordan's responsibility for the operatives he commanded

and the missions they took often weighed on his shoulders. If they failed, he took the blame. If they succeeded, he gave them the glory. He took nothing for himself, took no solace, and neither man could figure out why.

Noah knew his uncle hadn't been like this before Noah had been sent on that near-fatal mission to uncover a spy who'd been attempting to aid a terrorist white slaver in using drug routes to smuggle terrorists onto American soil.

Jordan had changed during that time. Something had happened, had somehow scarred the soul of the man Jordan had once been, and Noah still hadn't figured out exactly what. Knowing his uncle, chances were Noah would never know.

He just prayed his uncle found a way to ease it, because at the rate Jordan was going, he wouldn't have a soul left when it was finished.

WARBUCKS.

John clenched his fingers around the steering wheel of the Hummer and felt his jaw tighten in rage at the thought of the elusive traitor stealing America's secrets and selling them for billions of dollars at a time.

Whoever or whatever Warbucks was, he was the number one threat to national security at the moment as well as to Bailey. The missile launcher and accompanying missiles Warbucks now possessed, and the buyers eagerly amassing their money to pay for them, could wreak havoc on the world's security. They could hold nations hostage.

How the hell that weapon had been stolen, they still hadn't managed to track down. Whoever Warbucks was, he had power and connections that no man or group should ever acquire.

And he had no conscience.

John wiped his hand over his face and fought to hold back the rage that threatened his control. Warbucks had been responsible for several Australian Intelligence officers' deaths before the strike that had ended Trent Daylen's life and begun John Vincent's. Several of those agents had been friends, just as Timmons had been.

Fucking bastards. John breathed out roughly at the fury pulsing through him. Warbucks had stolen John's life, he'd stolen the chance he had at love when he'd ended his life as Trent Daylen. Warbucks had stolen Bailey from him.

He glanced at his reflection in the mirror, remembering the post-surgery pictures he had been shown of his face after that explosion. It had been ravaged. Deep cuts, burns, and shattered bones had required a complete reconstruction. The months of agony had built a hatred inside John that he feared he'd never be rid of.

Now his search for vengeance had brought him full circle in a way, back into Bailey's life and whatever game she was playing here in Aspen. Whatever game Warbucks was playing with her.

John knew his lover. He knew Bailey in work mode, and she'd definitely been in work mode the night before. Somehow she had managed to convince the unidentified Warbucks that she could be an ally. The coincidence was too close, just as her release of the information in Atlanta had been too easy. She had tried to throw him off track. She had tried to help them acquire Orion, hoping she would throw them off the scent of past employers other than the rapist who had targeted Risa Clay.

Knowing Bailey and he did know Bailey, that was exactly what she had been trying to do.

Which meant she had more information now, information they needed even more desperately than they had needed the information on Orion.

She was a slick one, he had to give her that. Cool as a cucumber and just as dangerously calculating when it came to a job. Unfortunately for her, she was going to have to share this one. He had his own interest in Warbucks and he knew well just how far the traitor's power extended. It was why the Elite Ops had been given the operation: because Warbucks had too many connections into too many law enforcement communities as well as underground and black-market sources.

Rubbing the back of his neck, he blew out a hard, rough

breath. This wouldn't be an easy one and protecting his identity from Bailey would be even harder. She was damned intuitive and if he knew her, then she knew the man he had been. And the man he had been wasn't that far removed from the man he was now.

He was still the man who loved her, who ached for her in the darkest reaches of the night, his arms empty for the feel of her. He remembered her kiss, her touch, and relished each cry he knew he could draw from her lush lips. He was still the man who felt lost without her, and how the hell he had managed to let that happen, he still hadn't figured out.

How long, he wondered, before he betrayed his former identity to her?

Hell, she was going to be the death of him if he wasn't damned careful here. He had given her a part of himself that he had never given to another woman in his life, a part that still remained with her. His heart.

CHAPTER 3

BAILEY WAS AWAKE BEFORE sunrise the next morning. As the first spears of light began to spread into her bedroom, she was staring out the window, waiting, watching.

He was coming. She could feel him, almost as close as a caress against her flesh, she could feel John Vincent coming nearer.

Anticipation was sizzling just beneath her flesh. Her heart was beating faster, harder than normal as nervous excitement clawed at her nerve endings.

Her body was flushed, heated; damn, she was aroused. She could feel the damp warmth heating the flesh between her thighs, the spiked hardness of her nipples. She would have found it amusing if it weren't for the fact that she knew next to nothing about this man, and what she did know, she wasn't certain she liked.

Why, she wondered, was she letting him affect her like this? She'd met him once. Only once. In Atlanta, where he had helped steal the prize she had sought for so long. Orion's head.

Where he had kissed her. Where he had touched her as though he knew her and her body had responded with a familiarity that made very little sense.

Turning away from the window, she shook her head as she drew the thick, heavy robe from the chair next to her bed and drew it over the silk nightshirt she slept in.

She didn't have time to sit here waiting on a man who might or might not show up. A man she should pray never showed up. He could only be here for one reason, and that reason wasn't her. He was here to steal the prize again.

Grinning at the thought, she left her bedroom and descended the winding staircase of the huge cabin-style mansion her parents had had built more than thirty years ago.

She had returned here a year ago and begun the very subtle game of drawing Warbucks into her own little web. Her life had been secured time and again by Warbucks for only one possible reason. The Serborne fortune. Now that she had revealed her disenchantment with her country, once she had proven it by looking the other way when several military items had been compromised at a Serborne research facility, she knew she was close.

Stepping into the foyer, she shoved her hands into the pockets of her robe and gave a soft sigh before turning and heading to the kitchen at the back of the house.

Entering the kitchen, she inhaled the scent of fresh coffee before moving to the coffeepot and taking a cup from the cupboard. Filling it with the aromatic brew, Bailey went to the breakfast nook, sat down in one of the opulently cushioned chairs, and stared outside the wide picture windows that surrounded it.

She knew he would be here this morning. Glancing at the watch on her wrist, she lifted the cup to her lips and sipped as she cast her gaze outside once again.

A shadow moved.

Bailey pretended she didn't see it as she hid her smile behind the cup. It could be someone other than John Vincent, she told herself, but she doubted it. Only John sent this quicksilver punch of excitement rioting through her veins.

She watched the shadow shift again outside, this time closer to the house. Rising to her feet, she poured another cup of coffee and moved it to the table as those first fragile rays of sunlight lightened the snow-laden trees and evergreen shrubs that filled the property.

The mountain was beautiful in the winter. The snowy

blanket looked pristine and untouched as it piled around the
pine trees that surrounded the house.

There were bare spots beneath the trees, and if she wasn't
mistaken her shadowy visitor was using those bare spots to
slip up to the house without leaving evidence of his visit.

She would have done the same thing. She'd actually
helped her mother to plant some of the trees in the back when
she had been a teenager. At the time, Bailey had been fascinated by the subject of slipping around undetected. Several
of the trees had been planted with the idea of giving her an
easy, untraceable route.

She'd left before she could try it, and now she watched as
John used it instead, moving steadily to the patio and the
French doors that were unlocked and awaiting his arrival.

She watched as the doorknob turned slowly, the door
opened, and John stepped inside.

She was caught anew by the shock of primal awareness
that surged through her at the sight of him. The dark blond
hair that fell roguishly around his face. The high, almost flat
arch of his cheekbones, his expressive dark gray eyes. The
strong bridge of his nose.

"Coffee?" She arched a brow as he flashed her a quick,
devilish grin and pulled off his leather gloves and ultra-thin
protective jacket.

"It's a bit cold out there." He closed the door, locking it
carefully behind him as he stared around the breakfast room
and the kitchen.

"We're alone," she assured him as she indicated the coffee. "Have a seat, Mr. Vincent, and tell me why I shouldn't
shoot you for trespassing."

She slid her Glock from the pocket of her robe and laid
it casually on the glass-topped breakfast table beside her
coffee.

His brow arched in amusement as he glanced at the
weapon before moving to the table.

Bailey pushed out the opposite chair with her foot and
waved her hand toward it.

"At least you're going to allow me a cup of coffee before

actually shooting me," he said, chuckling. "How would you explain that to the authorities?"

"Explain what?" she asked with a shrug. "I'd simply hide the body. I wouldn't have to explain anything."

The dark, low laugh that vibrated in his throat sent a rush of sensation chasing up her spine. Damn him, she should shoot him for that alone.

"I knew you'd be trouble when I first saw you in Atlanta," he told her as he wrapped one hand around the coffee cup and brought it to his lips. "Pure fire wrapped in the sexiest package I've ever glimpsed."

She grunted at that as she leaned back in her chair and watched him cynically. He was definitely charming. Something about his smile, the movement of his body, invited a woman to trust him, to lean into him. She knew better than to trust or to lean into anyone.

"Compliments won't soften you?" he asked as he set the cup back on the table. "For shame, Bailey. Are you a bit conceited?"

"A bit disbelieving perhaps," she admitted, amused by him, turned on by him. "Now what the hell do you want? I have things to do today and I don't have time for your games."

"I don't play games." There was a glimmer of warning in his gaze.

"And I don't play at all," she told him. "So get to the point."

She wanted him out of here. She wanted him out of her sight and out of her life before it was too late. Before she lost more of herself than she already had to a too-charming man and her own hormones.

"An impatient woman as well." He shook his head as though he pitied her. "I had heard you were quite patient."

"I don't know where you heard such a thing." She widened her eyes in false surprise.

"Orion."

That shocked her for a brief second. Bailey could feel her training kicking in as she held her expression. Bland amusement, no surprise. She merely stared back at him with innocent curiosity, as though there was nothing Orion could possibly know about her.

She wondered if the bastard had actually kept files. How insane would that be for an assassin—to actually keep records? Of course, if he had, perhaps they held a clue to who or what Warbucks actually was.

"I rather doubt Orion had much to say about me," she finally said quietly. "What could he know other than how deep to slice my wrists to keep from killing me?"

She heard the anger that filled her tone, the edge of bitterness. And she was angry, just as she was bitter. Orion's death had been stolen from her. For so many years she had dreamed of being the one to pull the trigger and blow his fucking head off. She'd deserved the chance to do it. She had deserved the right to call his life her own.

"Orion wasn't that easy to find," he finally told her soberly, his gray eyes serious as he wrapped his hands around the coffee cup. "You couldn't have done it on your own. He wouldn't have allowed the payoffs to continue from whoever sent those deposits to assure that you weren't killed. You were becoming a risk to him, baby."

She had meant to become a risk. She had wanted him to come after her, to make that first move that she could have used to identify him and kill him herself. "What do you mean by that?" She feigned surprise at his statement.

John clucked his tongue as he shook his head at her. A smile tilted those beautiful male lips and for a second, all she could think about was kissing him, eating those lips until her need for him was sated.

"You knew he was being paid off to let you live, didn't you?"

What to tell him, what not to tell him?

She smiled back at him. "Where did you get your information?"

"Why didn't you tell me everything you knew in Atlanta?" he queried instead. "I helped you, Bailey, I got you out of there. You held back on me."

"Information wasn't part of the deal," she reminded him

coolly as she leaned forward and braced her arms on the table. "You released me without conditions, John, remember that. Now, how did you find out Orion was being paid off?"

He couldn't know who had been paying the assassin to not kill—otherwise, he wouldn't be here pumping her for information. He would be tracking another of Orion's employers instead.

"Orion was a very expensive assassin," he stated. "Only the richest of men, or women, could have afforded his services. He was careful. He was damned good at what he did and he wouldn't have allowed you to live if he wasn't being paid handsomely to do so."

Bailey tilted her head to the side and watched him curiously for long moments. She'd been right last night: He was here to poke his nose into her business again.

"I have no idea who was paying him," she finally admitted.

"But you knew he was being paid?"

Bailey tightened her lips for a second before nodding. "I knew. He told me in Russia, when he sliced my wrists. He warned me then to stay out of his way. That he wouldn't let me live the next time."

John's eyes narrowed dangerously. For a second, just a second, a flashing memory of Trent with that same look on his face, his body tightening protectively when she had been threatened, flashed across her mind.

"And you continued to search for him?" His voice lowered, became almost guttural with anger.

Bailey smiled at the sound. "Of course I did. If I backed down every time I was warned to do so, then I wouldn't have had a career for long, now would I?"

"You nearly didn't have one the way it was," he growled. "Orion was out of your league, Bailey. No lone agent could have taken him out, no matter how good they were. You didn't have a chance."

"So I let you have him." She rose from the chair and moved back to the coffeemaker, where she collected the pot and returned to refill their cups. "What's your bitch?"

She glimpsed the tightening of his jaw, the way his forehead tensed and had to force herself not to grit her teeth. Was it wishful thinking?

"My bitch is the fact that you haven't learned your lesson," he said dangerously. "You're still trying to bite off more than you can chew."

Now, this was just supposition, she thought in amusement. He couldn't be certain why she had returned home, no matter what he wanted to believe.

"I was fired from the agency, John, or did you forget that little piece of information?" She shoved the pot back into the coffeemaker before turning to face him once again. "I'm not on assignment here."

"You weren't on assignment in Atlanta, either," he grunted as he leaned back in his chair and crossed his arms over his chest. "Don't play games with me, Bailey. We both know why you returned here."

Bailey inhaled deeply, gritted her teeth and forced back the anger that rose inside her at his domineering attitude.

"This is my home, John. Where else was I supposed to go?"

"The same home you disowned fourteen years ago?" He rose from his chair now and faced her challengingly. "The same home you swore you'd never return to when your father refused to believe that his best friend had killed his wife and daughter? Is that the home you're talking about here?"

Control, control. She breathed in once, twice. She wasn't going to let him crack the shield she had promised herself she would keep in place.

"That was a long time ago . . ."

"Bullshit!" he snarled. "You came back one time, when your parents were killed. After that you began chasing Orion. You suspected he was involved in their deaths, didn't you?"

"Was he?" What else had John found when his group had assassinated the assassin? What other files had Orion kept?

Bailey shook her head slowly. "He was here in Aspen the night they were killed, that was all I ever knew. What did you find?"

If he'd kept the information that he'd been hired to let her live, then perhaps he had kept other information as well.

"We found his kill book," John revealed. "Your father's name was listed."

She swung away from him, her hand covering her lips to hold back the cry that would have slipped from them. She had known. She gripped the counter with her other hand to hold herself up, fighting the tremors that wanted to shake her body. She had known her parents had been murdered by Orion.

"Why?" She forced the word past her lips. "Why were they killed?"

She had to fight back the tears that filled her eyes, the pain that clawed at her chest as she felt him moving behind her.

"Bailey." His hands gripped her shoulders as he turned her slowly to face him.

She couldn't look up at him. Tears were a weakness. *Never let them see you cry,* her mother had always cautioned. *Never show anyone your weakness.*

"Why did he kill them?" She forced the question past her lips as she tried to pull away from him. "What did they know?"

"You know he wouldn't have had that information," he breathed out roughly. "No more than he knew why Warbucks wanted you to live."

She froze. This time, she couldn't hide her reaction, she couldn't stop the stiffening of her body or the way her gaze jerked to his.

"That's why you gave us the information on Orion," he stated calmly despite the anger that brewed in his eyes. "Isn't it, Bailey? You cut your losses in Atlanta. You gave us Orion so you could go after Warbucks."

When she pulled back from him, he let her go. Shaking her head, she pushed her hands into the pockets of her robe and breathed out heavily.

"I didn't know Warbucks was involved," she finally told him, hating herself because she really hadn't known. "I didn't know until after I came back last year. I decided to return to find out who hired Orion. I found Warbucks mentioned in one of Father's journals. No one knew he kept them, or where they were hidden. He mentioned in several of the journals that he suspected someone among his set of friends was a traitor. The last journal, he had the name Warbucks written and underlined with a question mark beside it."

She should have come home sooner, she thought again. It had been a steady refrain since her return. She had come home to find out who had hired Orion; she should have known it was Warbucks. She should have suspected.

She turned back to John, wishing she could make sense of the need, the demand inside her that she trust him. She didn't trust anyone; she had learned never to trust that anyone would still be with her tomorrow. They were taken, they were always taken away from her. Or they left.

"Warbucks is mine," she told him softly, determined. "You took Orion from me, you won't take this from me, John. I won't allow it."

"I don't want to take it from you, Bailey. I want to share it with you."

She almost laughed at the thought. "Share it with me? Like you shared with me in Atlanta?" she asked mockingly. "Really, John, what in the hell makes you think I believe you'd want to share anything with me? And even if you did, what about that snazzy little group you work with? I think I counted, what, four, five of you? How's the Israeli doing, by the way?"

The Israeli. Her cousin. The bastard. David Abijah had been one of her best friends as well as her cousin. Until his death. Until he'd died and been reborn and hadn't even had the courtesy to let the last of his family know he was still alive.

John's expression never changed. He was good, damned good. His pupils didn't even dilate.

"There's only me," he finally stated. "And John Vincent's bodyguard. I'm a broker. I negotiate sales of sensitive information and unique acquisitions. There is no group, and there is no Israeli."

"And there is no trust, and therefore, there is no sharing, period." She smiled sweetly as she turned and walked back to the table to collect her weapon. "You can see yourself out. Please make certain you lock the door on your way."

She moved to the doorway, intent on returning to her room and preparing for the day ahead. The life of an heiress wasn't bonbons and soap operas or even a round of boring parties and expensive dresses. She had to actually shop and socialize with the very people she had grown up despising. That was more nerve racking than chasing spies or avoiding assassins.

"I could make it worth your while."

She paused at the door at the suggestion. Turning her head, she stared at him, her eyes narrowing in consideration. "How so?"

"John Vincent was contacted several days ago to broker a sale, an acquisition Warbucks is eager to get rid of. I can let you in on this."

"And why would you do that?" she drawled mockingly. John Vincent would just let her in on this. There had to be a catch.

"You're bluffing." Wasn't he?

"Why else would I be here?" He crossed his arms over his chest, leaned back against the counter, and stared back at her knowingly. "I've been contacted, but the contract isn't assured. Several other brokers have been contacted as well and there are conditions."

"Then why do you need me?"

That one bothered her. If he'd already been contacted, if he was that close, then why bother even letting her know?

"Because the contract isn't assured," he told her again. "Warbucks will be careful about this transaction and who brokers it. Levels of trust that he has never been known to approach before will be required. And he made you a requirement. According to his offer to broker the deal. You'll choose the broker." Surprising. It wasn't shocking, but it was surprising. She had been working toward this, but she'd had no idea she was so close.

Warbucks was here in Aspen—she knew that, her father had known it. He was part of a select group of men, men powerful enough that they didn't have to worry about being caught. Rich enough that they could avoid the laws that governed others.

"You need an in," she finally said softly. "A level of trust that the others don't have. If you're my lover, then you're assured of the "in" you need."

He inclined his head in agreement. "I need a lover that he trusts. Someone he's certain wouldn't betray him. Someone he believes wants vengeance against a government that betrayed them one time too many. You're my ace, Bailey. But my question here is, why does Warbucks trust you now?"

Bailey licked her lips as she inhaled slowly, evenly. This was more than she could have hoped for. It was definitely more than she'd expected.

She had worked for this for a year. Days and nights of acquiring just the right information and placing it in the ears that she knew would lead to Warbucks.

She had no idea who he was, not yet. But she was getting closer. This was proof of that fact.

"Warbucks trusts no one," she finally answered him. "If he did, he would have been identified by now. He doesn't trust me. He's testing me."

"Why?" John leaned forward, his gaze intent, probing. "Why test you and no one else? Why has he focused on you?"

Pursing her lips, she leaned back in her chair before breathing in deeply.

"Because I have something he needs as well as something he wants. When you're going fishing, John, you have to have the right bait. Right now, I have the perfect bait."

Fate. Bailey believed in it as she believed in few things. Some things were just fated. From birth she had been destined to come face to face with Warbucks.

For years the traitor had paid to keep her alive. She wasn't always certain why, but she had suspicions. Her fortune was part of it. The Serborne fortune was lost forever if she died without an heir. A husband or a child. That meant that somehow Warbucks was tied to the six men who were a part of the Serborne holdings, the committee her father had set up to run the business holdings for her. One of those men was Ford Grace. But there had to be more to it as well. It wasn't just the money. It was the information and the protection she had provided over the past years. It was the game she had been playing with a traitor. A killer.

John shook his head slowly. "This is what you've been working toward for a year, isn't it, Bailey? You've planned this."

Bailey let a smile touch her lips. "Well, I have to admit, I was hoping for more than such an asinine test. Warbucks likes to play games, but this is going a bit far."

She had no doubt Warbucks didn't know exactly what he was doing, though.

John's lips tightened in irritation. She could see the anger brewing in his eyes, building inside him. He looked like he was ready to explode. For a moment Bailey felt the familiar excitement surge inside her. It was sexual, sensual, dangerous. She had just pushed past a boundary she had somehow instinctively known had a limit. She had made herself a target.

Inhaling slowly, deeply, she watched as he rose from his chair, his expression hardening.

"Tell me, Bailey, exactly how did you convince a man like Warbucks to test you? To believe he could trust you?" His hands flattened on the table as he glared back at her. "What have you done, Bailey?"

The sound of his voice sent a rush of sensation tearing up her spine. It was like a ghostly finger of pleasure. It radiated to the back of her neck where it seemed to explode in pleasure and excitement.

"What have I done?" The words were pushed between gritted teeth. She smiled again. A tight, furious smile. "I found his weakness, John. Information. Contacts. The type that can lead him to prizes far richer than he's had before. Prizes he can only obtain through me."

"Prizes like *CROSSFIRE*?" he snapped.

Bailey blinked back at him in surprise. "*CROSSFIRE*? The missiles?"

"The missiles," he snarled back. "Did you give those to him, Bailey?"

Bailey shook her head, realization dawning. "He has *CROSSFIRE*?"

"He does."

She nodded slowly. "He has the missiles, but guess what?"

John straightened. "What?"

"Warbucks needs me now, John. He has the missiles, but only I can provide authenticity to the sell, lover." Her smile was pure amusement. She had him now. Warbucks would be hers. "You see, he has the missiles, possibly the launcher. But what he doesn't have is what any buyer will demand."

"And that is?"

"The key to unlock the firing mechanism. And that is something that only I can get for him."

Bailey rose to her feet. She could taste the triumph now. After all these years, the blood Warbucks had spilled, the deaths he had ordered. He was finally going to pay.

"You see," she continued, "those missiles were developed originally as a toy for the CIA. I was there during its first test and I made sure I knew all there was to know about it. I have the code. And I'm the only one he can come to for it."

"So why not torture you to get it?" The anger was barely contained now. Bailey could almost taste it, it was pouring from him.

"It doesn't work that way," she laughed lightly. "Remember that Serborne fortune? He can't jeopardize that just yet. First he'll see if I'm as good as I'm pretending to be. He'll test me. He'll see if I'm ready to join him or betray him. He'll pull me in, implicate me, get me where he thinks he wants me. He thinks he has me where he wants me now. I guess he didn't bargain on you, huh?"

She loved it. She had worked for it. So many years playing both sides, protecting a traitor, fighting to learn his identity before he decided to kill her.

"Do you know what you've done?"

Before she could avoid him, John moved around the table, gripped her shoulders, and jerked her against him. "Do you realize the risk you've taken?"

She stared back at him. "I succeeded."

"Bullshit!"

Her eyes widened. "He needs me now. He had no choice but to let me in. He can't kill me. There's no way to get rid of me. You're just pissed because you can't have the upper hand. Admit it, John, you hate it because I did what you and your nifty little group of boys couldn't do. I got close enough to Warbucks to tempt him. He's mine."

"He'll kill you," John snapped.

"Then I guess you'll just have to protect me." She moved against him, let her lower stomach cushion his denim-covered cock as her hands smoothed up his chest. "Wanna be my bodyguard?"

She hadn't anticipated his reaction. Bailey had counted on his arousal, she knew it was there, but she had anticipated his anger rather than his lust taking control.

Before she could avoid his kiss, his lips were covering hers. Before she could pull back, his arms were surrounding her, lifting her to him as his tongue rubbed against hers.

Bailey felt the hand at the back of her head, holding her in place. His fingers rubbed at her scalp as his tongue licked at hers, his lips stroking against hers.

A second later his hand was at her hip, tightening, pulling her fully against him, his erection pressing fully against her now as she felt lust suddenly surging through her.

"You're insane," he growled, maneuvering her until her back was pressed against the wall and her senses were going haywire. "Damn you, Bailey, you'll be the death of both of us."

There was anger and lust surging between them, a fiery surge of intensity that poured through her system. Her fingers tunneled into his hair, gripped and held him closer. She fought to melt into his body, to consume his kiss as his hand gripped her hip and tried to drag her closer. They fought to get closer.

"John," she moaned his name as he nipped at her lips before moving to her jaw, her neck.

He dragged the sleeve of her robe over her shoulder as his lips followed. With his other hand, he pushed beneath the material covering her thighs.

Bailey drew in a harsh, ragged breath as his fingers found the moist, slick flesh between her thighs. She stilled, her lashes flying open to stare back at him as he parted the folds of flesh and found the hardened nub of her clit.

"There, baby," he crooned, his voice deep and dark. "Feel how fucking good it is. You want a bodyguard? Let me show you just how well I intend to guard it."

His fingers moved lower. She felt the width of two of them suddenly pressing against the clenched, hot entrance before he surged inside.

Fire erupted through her senses, sizzled over her flesh. Tremors shook through her. Bailey heard her own strangled cry, felt the violent clench of her body around his fingers, and the orgasm threatening to tear through her.

"Feel it?" he growled as he rubbed inside her, stroked her. "Feel it, Bailey."

She felt it. All of it. The hunger, the need, the racing sensations that threatened to tear her apart.

"John," she gasped his name again, then cried out as he pulled slowly away from her.

"No." Bailey tried to draw him back, fought to find the pleasure again as a chill of foreboding swept through her. "Why are you doing this?"

Why was he drawing away from her? He wanted her, she knew he did, wanted her with the same desperation she wanted him.

"You won't work me like you've worked Warbucks,"

he stated, his voice harsh now. "You made damned sure you're a part of this game, but you'll play by my rules, Bailey. And my rules include information. Now start talking."

"Your rules?"

"My rules," his voice hardened.

Bailey smiled. "Bodyguards don't give the orders, lover. This isn't your game this time. It's mine. You can share it with me or you can get the fuck out."

Evidently John's rules meant he walked. She watched in shock as he turned and left the house.

CHAPTER 4

IT INCLUDED HIM WALKING away from her and leaving her aching. That evening Bailey was still irritated, more with herself than with her early-morning visitor. John was determined to turn her life upside down and turn her operation against her. She could feel it. Almost as though even before he made the first move, she knew what he was going to do.

He'd left the house that morning after stepping away from her. He'd walked out, locked the door behind him, and disappeared the way he had come as she stared at his back in surprise.

He wanted her, yet he'd turned his back on her.

So much for that hard-on he'd tried to claim was so serious. He was probably perpetually hard.

Pulling her BMW into the front of the hotel he was staying at, Bailey turned her keys over to the valet before entering the lobby and moving quickly to the elevator.

She wanted answers. He hadn't returned to the house to provide those answers, so she was coming to him. It might not be one of her brightest moves. She was well aware of the fact that he had most likely maneuvered her into doing just what she was doing.

As the elevator slid to a smooth stop at his floor, she stepped out and came face-to-face with one of the men she had watched in Atlanta.

John had worked with five men on that mission against

Orion. One of them was Micah Sloane. Middle Eastern, perhaps Israeli, six two, his black hair short and framing an imposing, arrogant face. If what she suspected was right, this was a dead man walking.

"Excuse me." Aware of the other men standing behind him, Bailey pasted a polite smile on her face and moved to skirt around him.

"Ms. Serborne, yes?" He stopped her.

Bailey stepped back, staring up at him, her brow lifting as she detected a Palestinian accent.

"Yes?"

"Jerric Abbas." He extended his hand.

Jerric Abbas, her ass.

She extended her hand. "I remember you, Mr. Abdul." He did resemble Jerric, who had died in a messy little explosion several years before. If someone wanted to believe he was Jerric, it would work.

Come to think of it, there were a few slight differences in his appearance since she had seen him in Atlanta. It didn't change the fact that she knew exactly who he was.

"I would hope that you would have no problems with my presence in your fair town." His smile was shark-cold, rather like Azra's had been. Of course, Azra had been a shark. Without conscience and without mercy.

She lifted her hands up, palms flat in a gesture of casual disinterest. "Stay out of my way, I'll stay out of yours," she promised before moving around him and walking quickly to John's room.

She could feel the hairs at the back of her neck lifting in warning that "Jerric" and his friends were still watching her. She knew the other two men. They were a part of Samuel Waterstone's security detail.

Interesting that good ol' Sam, as patriotic as he purported to be, allowed his men to associate with suspected terrorists. Of course, Jerric Abbas had never been convicted. He was watched closely, until that explosion in which he was supposed to have been blown to bits.

Boy, there were a lot of men rising from the grave lately.

She stopped at John's hotel room door and gave a quick knock, her back still to the men who watched from farther down the hall.

She was gaining a lot of interest these days.

Within seconds the door opened slowly. John stood in front of her, shirtless, the fine hairs on his chest glistening damply. He looked sexy as hell, mouthwatering and dangerous.

"You're early," he announced as he stepped back and welcomed her into the room. "Come on in."

She stepped inside, feeling something shift inside her, some knowledge, a premonition that she had just entered something much more dangerous and deadly than simply a hotel room.

The door closed behind her, leaving her alone, defenseless, and suddenly feeling more determined and more confident than she ever had.

"So, lover." She turned to him slowly. "What happened to my bodyguard?"

JOHN STARED AT THE VISION that entered his hotel room and wanted to growl like an animal in rut.

Son of a bitch, she was the most gorgeous woman he had ever laid his eyes on. Dressed in a snug sapphire evening gown slit up to her thigh, matching heels, and emerald-green eyes. Her shoulder-length dark chestnut hair was swept up on her head with sapphires and diamonds among the curls.

Full, firm breasts peeked above the loose material of the gown that draped over the mounds and drew instant attention to the tempting curves. Long legs made a man think of firm thighs gripping his hips and the treasures to be found beyond.

He knew the treasures between those legs. The soft, silky curls that covered her pussy, the sweet syrup that could dampen her flesh. The thought of it had his cock hardening further, his heart racing.

Damn, he was so fucking hungry for a taste of her that he wondered if he would survive the wait. She was hesitant, reluctant. He'd be madder than hell if she jumped straight into bed with him, but on the other hand, he was going to die of need if she didn't.

He finally found enough of his senses to question her. "Weren't you supposed to come across with information first?"

Her brow lifted as she glanced around the room, then turned back to him as though in question.

It took him a moment, but he finally got the hint. "Room's clean," he said quietly as he turned away from her and headed for the bar on the other side of the large sitting room. "Want a drink?"

He sure as hell needed one. He could feel the sweat popping out on his brow, his internal temperature rising in direct relation to the way that damned gown shifted and moved against her body.

At the rate he was going his self-control was going to be shot where she was concerned.

"I'm not in the drinking mood, John," she informed him.

She followed him to the short bar across the room, though, and watched as he poured himself a drink. He could feel her behind him, the warmth of her body reaching out and stroking the bare flesh of his back.

Hell, he wanted to feel her touch so damned much that he could almost imagine what it had once been like.

"So are you ready to talk yet?" He turned to her as he leaned back against the bar nonchalantly.

Her brow arched. "I rather think you know what I want to talk about. In what way are you wanting to work together here and what assurances do I have that you and your team aren't going to move in and take this away from me?"

He shook his head. "There's no way to take this away from you, Bailey, and you know it. You're the key to the operation, as you said. You have access to the code, Warbucks needs you, as do we. But I won't work blind."

She tapped her fingers against the small silk purse she carried in one hand.

"When did he acquire *CROSSFIRE*?" she finally asked. "My sources haven't reported any attempts to steal it, now that it had been taken."

"This doesn't surprise me." He shrugged. "A cap was placed on the information going out until the they could be found," he stated. "That's how we managed to finally track the traitor back here. It's a very unique weapon. One War-bucks couldn't resist once a weakness was inserted in the security surrounding it. We were hoping to catch the thieves before they actually got away with it. Unfortunately, they slipped by us. But we manage to track the lines of informa-tion to four families: Waterstone, Grace, Claymore, and Menton-Squire."

They were names she knew, families she had grown up with and had suspected herself. "I've come up with the same names," she said. "But I've also placed Raymond Greer high within Warbucks ranks. And only he would know that I have that code."

"That leaves Waterstone, Grace, Claymore, and Menton-Squire." he pointed out.

Bailey nodded at that. "Raymond Greer worked for Ford Grace before marrying Grace's sister. I know he's been in-volved in the brokerage of the sales in several instances. Myron Falks is Samuel Waterstone's head of security. I've compiled quite a bit of circumstantial evidence against him as well. I know the two of them are involved, I just don't know who's giving the orders."

That was more than the unit had. Much more. She'd obvi-ously been working on this at a deeper level than they had imagined.

John tipped back his drink, finished it, and set the glass on the table.

"How did you manage to tie Greer and Falks into it?" He crossed his arms over his bare chest and watched her gaze caress the naked flesh.

"Tying Greer to it wasn't that hard." She shrugged, and the full slope of a breast flashed within the folds of material draping over it. "He's ex-CIA. He has the contacts to know about classified research-and-development projects. He still maintains friendships with very high-level individuals, and with his marriage to Mary Grace Altman, he has the power and financial backing to aid many of those individuals. Falks was easier, actually. His alias Mark Fulton was tagged several years ago during a sale of advanced electronics on the black market. We didn't have enough evidence for an arrest or conviction, but we know he was there."

"And each family has the power or resources for transportation and delivery," he stated.

Bailey nodded at that.

He blew out a heavy breath before wiping his hand over his face and staring back at her silently for long moments. He had actually expected her to know what was stolen. She had her own sources, her own contacts and assets. The fact that rumor hadn't made it back to her was in a way an indication that this operation was much more high-level that any of them had wanted to believe.

"When was *CROSSFIRE*?" she asked.

He nodded sharply. "It was stolen during transportation to a secret military base in DC several weeks ago. Word went out to terrorist organizations and nations days ago that *CROSSFIRE* was coming up on the auction block and that you would choose the broker. We have a major situation here with limited time to track the weapon, considering there's a highly classified multinational meeting in the Middle East in three weeks to discuss a new peace initiative that has garnered surprising support."

"So we have three weeks to ensure that Warbucks approves of my choice of John Vincent as the broker," she stated.

John nodded. "Considering the item, the price that will be attached to it, and the level of trust that will be required in this trade, any broker will demand a face-to-face with Warbucks as well rather than his middlemen, whom they've met with before. This is our chance to identify him and to take him out."

He watched her expression turn somber, her green eyes losing a bit of their brilliance as bleak bitterness filled them.

"Warbucks was one of Orion's employers," she said. "I suspect he was hired to kill Ford Grace's wife and daughter fourteen years ago and I know he hired out the deaths of my parents. I want him, John. I won't be pushed out of this one. Try to take me out of it, and you and your entire team will regret it."

He shook his head slowly. "This can't be just your operation any longer, Bailey. It has to be a shared venture between you and me."

"And your Jerric Abbas look-alike?" The tight, sarcastic smile she gave him was telling. "I met him outside the elevators tonight—with several of Waterstone's security team, by the way. He made a point of letting me know he was here, to have me verify his identity as Abbas."

John grinned. The identity of Jerric Abbas was the best cover they could have come by. Jerric had only been rumored to have been killed in that explosion; there was no proof. Several times after that explosion Micah had made forays into the criminal underground as the terrorist. The unit had decided that morning that Micah would make certain Bailey verified his identity. She'd come across Jerric several times in the field and she was the best verification he could have had.

"There have been some questions," he finally admitted. "He was fingerprinted, DNA'd. We managed to get our own results into each test easily enough, but we thought a verification by you would go farther."

She nodded at that. "The people you're dealing with aren't the most trustworthy. And arranging a meeting with Warbucks isn't going to be as easy as you think. I've been working for more than a year to prove my discontent with the agency and my country in general. He's only now beginning to test me."

Returning amid a scandal had done some damage to her social life, but not to the certainty that she would turn against the CIA if given the chance. John knew for a fact that rumors were already circulating that Bailey Serborne was now a disenchanted agent and possibly available to the highest bidder.

It was information that the CIA couldn't afford to act on, though, simply because of the power that backed her. They hadn't even placed a watch on her, which was a testament to the financial and political clout that existed within the world she had been born into.

So how did a society princess, an heiress unlike any other he'd heard of, end up risking her life and fortune in a career that could end any day with her death?

What sense of honor, injustice, or vengeance had led her here?

There were so many secrets, so much of her that he was only now realizing that he didn't know or understand. Parts of her that she hid, that she refused to share with anyone, man or woman. An intimacy she was determined to keep to herself.

"What proof do you have that Warbucks was involved in the death of your friend or your parents?" he asked her.

She shook her head. "I don't have time to sit and tell you my life story." She used a small flip of her hand to indicate the dress she was wearing. "We're going to be fashionably late as it is. Get in your best evening suit and we'll head out."

"To where?" he asked curiously. She was obviously attempting to assert herself and her dominance in this. For the moment, he was allowing it.

"Samuel Waterstone's get-together. He and his wife are celebrating their anniversary tonight. Forty-five years of marital bliss."

There was a regret disguised in the bitterness of her voice that made something in his chest ache. Made him regret choices himself. Could he and Bailey have been celebrating an anniversary this year? he wondered. If he hadn't "died." If Trent Daylen hadn't managed to get on the wrong side of Warbucks in Australia?

"The families we're watching will be in attendance at this party?" he asked her.

"Every one of them plus several dozen more. Add to that list a few box-office stars, a couple of very dull television personalities and even some of Aspen's finest political figures and you have a gallery of the rich and boring."

She had little respect for the world she had been born within. But John had realized in Australia that Bailey never simply gave her respect or trust. Male or female, people had to work to prove themselves to her.

As Trent Daylen, he'd done that somehow. Through the months that they had worked together, he'd found some way to earn that respect and trust. A respect and trust that John Vincent wasn't earning quite so easily.

"I'll make certain I don my finest threads, then." He quirked a smile in her direction and yet still received that strangely somber look in return.

He wondered if she knew what that look did to him. If she knew that he wanted to wrap her in his arms and protect her from the world when she looked so sad.

"That would definitely be a good idea." She nodded. "Tomorrow you'll come out to the cabin. I'll have my father's tailor there fit you with some new suits. You've done very well as a successful broker, but now you need to show your intent to rise higher in the world. You'll have one of a very few of the richest heiresses in the world that you're courting. You need to show your intent as well as your seriousness in the matter."

His brow arched. "Should I be looking for engagement rings then?"

She tilted her head and stared back at him coolly. "Call Cartier's in England, make an appointment with the manager to see his finest diamonds in, say, six weeks' time. That will prove your intent as well as give you ample opportunity to complete your job here before you have to actually buy the diamond."

He snorted at that. "I have my own diamond sources, my dear, I think I can take care of this on my own."

She shrugged. "However you wish to deal it, as long as word leaks out. Now, we'd better be leaving soon or we'll be more than fashionably late and end up insulting our host and hostess. That's something we really don't want to do at this point."

Insulting the Waterstones wasn't one of the things that was high on his own list of problems to avoid, but he would take her word for it.

"And once we arrive?" He moved from the bar, stepping over to her slowly, letting her feel the heat of his body as it mixed with hers. "Are we lovers, Bailey, or still tiptoeing around each other like a couple of teenagers?"

She inhaled deeply, her nostrils flaring with a hint of nervous excitement as a glitter of hunger lit her eyes. She wanted it just as damned bad as he did. The need that had erupted between them five years ago hadn't abated. If anything, it had only grown hotter.

As she stood still and silent, he let his hand caress her hip, feeling the heated flesh beneath the silk of her gown. Then looping his arm around her waist, he jerked her to his chest.

Soft, silken hands flattened against the bare muscle as her gaze widened and flew to his.

"This isn't necessary," she retorted breathlessly.

"Don't think you can dominate me, Bailey," he warned her carefully. "Don't think you can dress me, or tell me how to conduct my part of this little operation. I've been handling my own tailors as well as my own jewelers for years." His head lowered as he spoke until his lips were only a breath from hers.

Damn her. She was strong, resilient, but she hadn't yet learned that he was stronger and a hell of a sight more stubborn. She'd learned that lesson about Trent; now she had to learn it about John.

"This isn't a game we're playing between ourselves," he continued. "Don't pretend that it is."

"Isn't it?" A challenge flared in her eyes, like fire inside the purest emerald. "Don't lie to me, John. Don't pretend it's any more than it really is. It's a job. One we're both determined to complete, nothing more."

"Like hell."

He'd be damned if he would allow her to leave here, on his arm, believing that load of crap that she was trying to convince herself of.

She wanted to deny what was between them because she didn't understand it, because she didn't know who or what he was to her. He understood that. That didn't mean he would tolerate it.

Using one arm to hold her in place, he gripped the side of her face with his palm. As she parted her lips to blast him with that sharp tongue of hers, he took possession of it.

Kissing Bailey was like being engulfed in flames. The damp heat of her tongue, the satiny softness of her lips beneath his, were like a narcotic that he couldn't seem to rid himself of. The more he had of her, the more he wanted.

He felt her hands slide slowly up his chest, hesitant, trembling, her fingers stroking against his flesh until they clasped his neck.

She shuddered in his grip, as she had that first night in Australia. Tremors of need raced beneath her flesh as a soft, almost unwilling cry passed her lips.

John kept the kiss gentle. There was no need to take her roughly, to assert his dominance, his hunger. It was there in each lick of his tongue against hers, in the rub of their lips, the way her hands gripped his neck, the way he held her to him. Her body softened into his, as though it realized what her mind didn't. That she was his. That her heart, her body, belonged to him.

That slender, sweet body conformed to his now. Her hands held tight to his neck as she leaned into him, burning in his arms like a flame as he began to kiss her with hungry demand.

She asserted her own demand. She took what he gave and then pushed for more until lips and tongue were working together with heated moans and hands that couldn't stay still.

He wanted to slide the fabric of that dress up her thighs until he reached what he knew were the dew-shrouded folds of flesh between her thighs. She would be wet for him, hot. The remembered feel of her sweet pussy drove through his head and sent pulses of need clenching in his balls.

His cock was a wedge of pure steel, straining at his slacks as he lifted her closer, unwilling to release her for even a second, wanting more of her than he had ever imagined wanting of a woman.

She was his.

His hands tightened on her as he lifted her impossibly closer. His palms slid to her rear, tightened in the smooth, toned muscle as a groan tore from his chest.

His hips bunched, grinding his cock into the soft flesh between her thighs, feeling the heat of her pussy, flexing and throbbing for the remembered sensations of being buried deep inside her.

God, she had been so tight. She would be tight around him now. She hadn't had another lover in five years, but soon, very damned soon, she was going to have him again.

"Call it a game now, damn you." He tore his lips from hers as he stepped to the couch several feet behind him. Turning, he bore her to the cushions, pushing her dress up her smooth, silk-covered legs as he slid between them. "Tell me you're not as damned hot for this as I am."

He made the mistake of glancing away from her face. The draped material of her dress fell over one swollen breast, revealing the hard, velvet-covered tip. Tight and flushed, her nipple beckoned his lips, his tongue.

He felt starved for the taste of her, the feel of her.

"Look at you," he rasped. "You want me just as bad as I want you, Bailey, and you refuse to admit it."

"I don't deny it." Her breathing was rough, hard. "I never denied wanting you."

She denied herself the chance to take it, though. He wasn't denying himself.

Flattening his hands against her knees, he ran his hands up her thighs, feeling the silk stockings she wore until he reached the lace band.

She shook her head as he pressed her legs farther apart,

her fingers clenched into the cushions of the couch, but she didn't ask him to stop, she didn't deny the touch.

Pushing the material of the dress higher, he finally found what he was searching for. A sapphire-blue thong, the small triangle covering her pussy already damp, the folds of her flesh outlined beneath the material.

"Spread your legs farther," he ordered roughly. "Let me see, Bailey."

Had it ever been this hot before? John knew it hadn't been. Never had he seen her like this, watchful, waiting, uncertain in her femininity and her response to him.

Her legs parted, the silk tightening over her sex as he slid his fingers to the edge of the panties.

"This is mine." His palm covered the mound and the feel of the wet heat beneath it nearly had him coming in his pants. "Mine, Bailey."

She trembled beneath him as his fingers slid beneath the snug material and found the syrupy heat he'd dreamed of for five long years.

He couldn't stop the touch. He couldn't keep from dipping a finger inside the snug, clenched entrance or delving inside to caress the sensitive tissue inside. He couldn't stop the hunger that dragged a ragged groan from his chest or the demand that he take more, that he have more of her.

Another finger. Pulling the panties aside, he watched as his fingers took her, thrusting, working slowly inside her as her hips arched and a strangled cry passed her lips.

She was tight around his fingers, her muscles fluttering, vibrating around his flesh. He tore the panties from her, the scraps of material fluttering to the floor as he gripped her thigh with one hand and watched as he possessed her. Fucking her with his fingers, loving her cries, the way she arched to him, and finally the way her body tightened, jerked, and heat surrounded his fingers as her orgasm rushed over her.

The folds of her pussy became flushed. Her clit stood out like a tiny dark pink pearl that throbbed and glistened as her juices coated his fingers and the swollen curves.

It was the most beautiful sight he had ever seen. This,

watching the effects of her pleasure on her body, seeing her release, feeling it. Owning it.

"You're mine," he bit out roughly. "Mine, Bailey."

She shook her head even as she shuddered through the final pulses of release.

"All fucking mine."

CHAPTER 5

ALL FUCKING HIS.

John's words echoed through her mind that night and into the next morning as she fought her body's demand that she give in to the utter possessiveness that had filled his tone.

He had been very un-Trent-like. Trent hadn't been that dominant, that possessive. He had been more casual, more fun-loving. But hadn't she always sensed a darker core in him?

Driving along the mountainous road that led to Aspen the next afternoon, she fought to put aside the conflicting feelings that were making her crazy. She couldn't get her heart, or her body, to meet with her mind where he was concerned. Was he, like Micah, a dead man walking? A man much closer to her than he wanted her to know?

No, she didn't believe in coincidence, but she knew that she couldn't depend on her emotions right now, either.

That left the man and the mission. For the moment, those two things she could control.

As she reached the city limits her cell phone rang imperatively, drawing a grimace to her lips as she pulled it from the console of her Mercedes SUV. She checked the number quickly.

Her brows lifted. She'd expected John, not the man she had always considered her nemesis.

"Hello, Raymond," she answered as she slowed down to

weave into the mass of tourist traffic entering ahead of her. "What can I do for you this morning?"

"Good afternoon, Bailey. Mary was wondering if you'd like to meet us for lunch at Casamara's. That is, if you have nothing else planned."

Her brows lifted. "I'd love to. I always enjoy Mary's company."

He chuckled at that, another surprising reaction. "Perhaps we should allow the past to remain in the past," he said smoothly. "After all, there's no reason for us to remain at odds, as you said the other night. We've both learned our lessons the hard way where the agency is concerned."

"Trial by fire is more like it," she muttered into the link.

"Yes, the betrayal can often be a hard one," he said sympathetically. "Meet Mary and me, my dear. I think you'll find the afternoon a rewarding one."

She thought perhaps it was very possible.

"I've just entered town actually," she told him. "When would you like to meet?"

"Let's say an hour," he suggested. "That should give us plenty of time to arrive. I've already made reservations."

"I'm looking forward to it then." She added just the right touch of relief to her voice. "Thank you, Raymond." And that last touch nearly choked her.

She hated thanking Raymond Greer for anything.

"In an hour then," he reaffirmed. "It will be nice to merely visit rather than snipe at each other."

But sniping at him was so much fun, especially considering that she detested him.

The call ended, and as Bailey flipped the phone shut she drew in a hard, deep breath. She was certain she should call John and let him know about the upcoming meeting.

She grinned at the thought. Maybe five minutes before she actually met with Raymond would work. It wouldn't do to give him too much time to rush to the restaurant, not after last night.

Driving to the restaurant, Bailey left her car with the valet before entering and moving to the bar. Casamara's was one of the more elite restaurants in the city, with a cozy little bar for customers who stopped in for a drink rather than a meal.

There were several couples sitting inside the intimate atmosphere of the bar. Coffee, hot chocolate and lattes were in heavy demand with tourists and residents alike. Moving to the back of the room, Bailey slid into a booth that afforded her a clear view of the entrance and ordered coffee as she watched the maître d' greet guests and escort them into the dining room.

Casamara's had been one of her mother's favorite restaurants, she remembered. Shopping trips always began with coffee in the bar and then lunch in the dining room when she and her mother had been together.

As much as she hated shopping, Bailey had always loved shopping with her mother. Angelina had always made their trips fun, her witty asides about both friends and strangers, as well as her exceptional ability to convince Bailey to wear clothing creations she would have otherwise turned her nose up at, had never failed to amaze her.

She missed her parents. Ben Serborne had been loving and kind. He had seen the world clearly, but often ignored the parts of it that he didn't enjoy. The dirty, corrupted parts. He had ignored those traits in his friends as well, she thought. If he hadn't, perhaps he wouldn't have died.

Lifting her coffee cup to her lips, she considered the meeting Raymond had called. His wife Mary would be with him. Frail and kind, Mary couldn't possibly be a part of Warbucks's circle. The other woman was like a child sometimes. She'd been ill for most of Bailey's life, but she'd always been a gentle, guiding influence during Bailey's teenage years.

It never failed to amaze her how easily Raymond had stepped into her life, though. Bailey had always thought Mary had exceptional taste in friends, until she had met Raymond.

Bailey wondered if her friend had ever realized that her meeting with Raymond hadn't been an accident? Ten years before, Raymond's assignment had been to find a way to get close to Ford Grace and to learn if his European transportation company had been infiltrated by terrorists. There had been suspicion that Grace's interests there were being used to transport both people and weapons through Europe and into the United States.

It had been determined that the quickest way into Grace's inner circle was through the sister. One of the few people in his life that Grace didn't abuse.

Funny that, she thought. Ford Grace had terrorized his wife and his daughter, but he was known to spoil his sister outrageously and to worry constantly about her welfare.

Raymond had taken that assignment seriously. Within a year he had quietly resigned from the CIA and his engagement to Mary had been announced. An heiress in her own right, Mary had transformed Raymond from a stooped, studious appearance to a weasel in silk.

"Bailey. Bailey Serborne?"

Lifting her gaze from the coffee, Bailey felt a smile curl her lips as she lifted her head and met the frank, light green gaze of Wagner Grace.

"Wagner." Sliding from the booth, she came to her feet, her arms wrapping around his neck as he lifted her from her feet in a tight, carefree hug.

She hated Ford Grace, but Wagner had been her best friend's brother and the brother Bailey had never had.

"Damn, you're looking good." He laughed as he set her back on her feet and flipped the end of her nose gently. "Look at you, all grown up and pretty as a damned picture."

"And you're as handsome as sin." Standing back, she gazed up at him, seeing the face of the young man she had once treasured.

At thirty-nine Wagner was trim and lightly muscular. Dressed in a heavy sweater and jeans, he was the epitome of the successful mature male. His light green eyes gleamed with laughter, his sun-darkened face was creased in a smile.

"Bailey, you remember Grant." He moved back and only years of training kept Bailey's expression friendly.

Where Ford was the epitome of a successful mature man, Grant Waterstone was the epitome of a spoiled little rich boy.

At thirty-five Grant was handsome in a clinical sense. With his black hair, blue eyes and broad shoulders, he gave all appearances of success. Jeans, a light pullover sweater, and leather coat completed the look. But there was something in his gaze that set off warnings in her gut.

"Bailey and I saw each other at Rhamie's little party in Paris several months ago." Grant smiled, but it didn't reach his eyes. "She's looking as exquisite as always."

"Isn't she though," Wagner chuckled before turning back to Bailey. "May we join you for coffee? We were getting ready to hit the slopes later. You should join us."

Skiing was one of Wagner's favorite hobbies. It had been one Bailey had never quite been able to enjoy.

"Of course you may." Bailey smiled as she slid back into the booth, wishing the two would have continued on to the slopes rather than barging in on her thoughts.

"Father mentioned you were still here last night," Wagner stated as the waitress materialized with extra cups and another pot of coffee. "Actually, I believe I heard him screaming it over the phone." He winced slightly. "Still not getting along with him, dear?"

She shrugged easily as she sat back in her seat.

"Did Bailey ever get along with anyone well?" Grant asked then, his nasal accent grating on her senses. "Really, Wagner, I believe you're the only one of us that she really cared much for."

Wagner laughed as Bailey slid Grant a tight smile. "I guess Wagner just wasn't as abrasive as the rest of you," she stated coolly. "You should take lessons, Grant."

He sniffed in disdain. "I rather doubt it, sweetheart. Perhaps you've simply been associating with commoners for far too long. They've rubbed off on you."

She refrained from making a fist and ramming it into his face. The good thing about associating with real people was the fact that they were simply that, real. They might have an agenda, but it wasn't nearly as corrupt and diseased as those she had seen when she was younger in the people who believed they were so much better.

"I'll take that as a compliment, Grant." She tilted her head as she shot him a tight smile. "The good thing about common people is the fact that they don't pretend to be anything else, while I've noticed far more privileged people have a habit of being more common than those they look down their perfect noses on."

"Still a bitch, aren't you?" He glared back at her.

"Enough, Grant," Wagner's voice hardened with a snap at the insult. "If you want to be an ass, then you can head on to the resort and I'll meet up with you later."

Grant's lips thinned for a moment as he shot Bailey such a look of dislike that she was certain it should have seared her. Unfortunately, she really didn't care if Grant Waterstone liked her or not.

"I think I just might do that." He slid out of the booth as his lips curled into a sneer. "The company here is growing a bit stale."

He stalked away as Bailey refrained from calling out a "Good riddance."

"He spends too much time with Father," Wagner sighed as he lifted his cup and sipped from his coffee. "They've become rather close over the past few years." There was an edge of sadness in Wagner's voice, almost a regret.

"You never were much like Ford, Wagner," she stated. "Be thankful for that. Unfortunately, Grant is too much like him."

Wagner shook his head at that before staring back at her. "I've missed you, Bailey. It's almost like having Anna back when you're here."

The pain at the mention of his sister sliced across Bailey's heart.

"I miss her, too." It had been so many years since Anna and her mother had been killed, but the anger and the hatred hadn't dimmed.

Nodding slowly, Wagner finished his coffee before sliding

to the edge of the seat. Before leaving, he paused and glanced back at her.

"Father wants you out of Aspen." His voice was low, warning. "He'll make things hard on you."

"He's rather good at that." She smiled as though it didn't bother her. "I've been back for a year now, Wagner. I'm certain he knows by now that he can't run me off."

"But he's still trying," he told her. "Be careful, darling, I'd hate to see him succeed."

With that, Wagner left the table, stopping long enough to kiss her cheek before he left the bar. Bailey shook her head, wondering if Ford Grace had ever cared that his son was ten times the man Grant Waterstone could ever be.

He likely didn't, and if he did, Bailey doubted he cared. Wagner wasn't cold and power-driven as Ford was, or as Grant Waterstone was. It made sense that Ford was taking Grant under his wing and working with him. Not that Grant needed the help. His own father, Samuel Waterstone, thought his eldest son could do no wrong.

It was typical of those she had been raised with. It was typical of the society she had been raised within. The children were taught that they had no equals. They were superior, laws unto themselves. Those lessons had created adults with no compassion, no mercy, and even less honor.

Sipping at her coffee, Bailey bit back the anger that tore through her at the thought of the cruelty that existed here, thinly veiled and shadowed. She'd almost succeeded when she glimpsed Raymond entering the restaurant with his petite, smiling wife.

Mary was an attractive woman for her fifty years, much too attractive for the arrogant, cruel Raymond.

Rising to her feet, Bailey moved from the bar to the restaurant, keeping her stride slow and easy, taking her time. Glancing at her watch, she was pleased to see that she would be only be a few minutes early.

"Bailey." Raymond rose politely to his feet as the maître d' escorted her to the table several moments later. "Your timing, as always, is faultless."

And what a change. She allowed him to grip her hands with his own cool, baby-soft ones and place a kiss on her cheek with his too-damp lips.

She had to force back a shudder of revulsion before drawing away from him.

"Hello, Mary." Bailey turned to her friend and bent to kiss her pale face. "How are you doing?"

"Very well, my dear," Mary declared, a genuine smile gracing her lips. "I hear you've picked up a beau since coming home. A very exciting one."

Bailey glanced in Raymond's direction, knowing he would be more than aware of John's background and wondering how much he had told his wife.

"Mary enjoys listening to rumor, my dear." He smiled indulgently at his wife. "I believe one of the guests at a party last night mentioned that he might have a shady past."

"John, a shady past?" She grinned as though the thought amused her. "I'll have to ask him about that."

"There you go, spoiling all my adventurous tendencies," Mary pouted in amusement.

Bailey forced a believable laugh from her lips and kept her expression light. Rumors weren't circulating very well; thankfully, they remained for the most part contained. The families she grew up with gossiped among themselves, but it didn't go farther. Rather like honor among thieves. Or what used to be honor among thieves.

"Mary has always been fascinated by our pasts." Raymond's tone was surprisingly affectionate, as was the glance he shot his wife. "She believes agency work was all danger and romance."

"Boring background checks, stale coffee, and sweaty greasy-haired gunrunners and drug lords," Bailey murmured with amused mockery. "Don't we miss it so much?"

"Even after fourteen years?" Mary asked. "You must have enjoyed your work, dear?"

Bailey shook her head. *Joy* wasn't a word she would have used to describe how she felt about her career. "It was a job no one wanted me to have," she said, wondering if that wasn't the real reason she had chosen it. "I realized too late what I was turning my back on."

"Rebellion," Mary sighed. "Your parents worried."

"And Father screamed and yelled and totally disapproved," she revealed with a fond smile. "It took me a while to grow up."

She didn't glance back at Raymond, but she could feel him watching her as he took in her words, her tone, her expression. For all her hatred of him, she knew he had been damned good at what he did at the agency. She wasn't about to discount his instincts or training.

But she was damned good at what she did as well.

The conversation shifted to more general topics as drinks arrived. Bailey let herself settle into the routine of it as she forced back the revulsion she felt at sharing a meal with a traitor. She'd shared meals with worse, she assured herself.

"I hope you don't mind, Bailey, but I invited a few other guests to lunch," Raymond suddenly announced as the waiter appeared at the table. "It was rather last-minute."

Turning to him, Bailey arched a brow. "Of course not, Raymond. It was very kind of you to invite me as well."

His smile was more confident now and if she wasn't mistaken the thin curve of it was more arrogant. She would have thought it would be impossible for him to display more self-appoval.

He nodded to the waiter, who hurried off as though he were carrying top-secret information on a deadline.

A few minutes later she looked up and had to fight to control her expression. She could feel the rage rising inside her fast and hard, like a tidal wave beating against a flood wall, threatening to overpower it.

Where Bailey controlled the rage, held it back and hid it, Ford wasn't nearly as adept. He approached the table slowly, his weathered face tight, his dark gray eyes almost black with anger as he glanced between his sister and brother-in-law.

Slender, graceful male hands moved to the buttons of his silk jacket as he released them with an irritated jerk before he accepted his seat from the waiter with a brief "Thank you."

Bailey inhaled slowly, evenly. It would seem odd if she didn't show some reaction to his sudden appearance.

"You didn't tell me you had invited anyone else, Ray," he said stiffly to his brother-in-law.

"I'm sorry, Ford, Mary mentioned wanting to see Bailey. I felt the two of you should bury the hatchet, so to speak. This enmity isn't conducive to good business relationships. Besides, I know how you hate gossip," Raymond said evenly, smoothly. "People are beginning to gossip."

Ford tightened his lips as the waiter brought their menus. He ordered a stiff drink, his gaze turning on Bailey once again as the waiter moved off.

"You're not stalking off," he said, his voice low. "Or spitting curses at me." His gaze was calculating. Bailey imagined she could feel the searing presence of pure menace.

Bailey swallowed tightly. "Not yet at least."

She turned her gaze to the menu, aware of both Raymond and Mary watching them. Mary's gaze was concerned; Raymond's, more determined.

"Your father would have enjoyed a nice lunch with you before his death." Ford struck at the heart with the first parry and cut deep.

"So would I." She looked up from the menu, remembering the fierce arguments she and her father used to have concerning his friendship with Ford.

The man was a wife beater, a child beater, and yet her father had stood by him at their funeral, clasped him as the fake tears fell from his eyes, and mourned with him.

"You broke his heart," Ford muttered.

At least she hadn't taken his life, she wanted to retort. Instead, she held back the accusation and stared across the table at him bleakly.

"We saw each other more than you know, Ford. Father

knew I loved him, as I knew he loved me. He couldn't live my life for me."

His lips tightened.

"Ford, perhaps it's time to let the past go," Mary suggested gently. "Give her a chance to return home. You were her father's best and dearest friend. He would have wanted you to embrace her return, not guilt her over it."

Words of wisdom, even if Bailey's return home was all illusion. This wasn't her home, and these weren't her people. There was no one here who knew her, no one here who had ever understood the fight she had tried to undertake when she had left home.

Even her father hadn't understood. If he had, he would have never told his friends that she was working with the agency once he had learned what she was doing. He would have never interfered with her job and made certain she didn't receive the assignments that would have allowed her advancement within the agency.

Her director, Milburn Rushmore, had ensured she was never involved in anything too dangerous, just as he had always rushed to pull her out of it when she managed to involve herself.

"Ford and I will always have our differences, Mary," she told her friend as she glanced back at Ford. "I can live with them civilly, if he can."

His jaw tightened as he stared back at her with an odd expression of relief, as though he had expected something else, which he should have. But his expression indicated that the small concession she had given mattered to him. Of course it did. It would be hard to conduct illegal business with her otherwise.

"Good then," Raymond announced with a pleasant smile. "I'm still awaiting another guest if you'd like to take your time ordering. He mentioned he might be late."

Bailey nodded back at him with regal haughtiness as she maintained her own shield of arrogance. There were certain rules here, unwritten and unspoken, that she had never minded breaking before. It mattered now that she regain the acceptance she had always turned her back on before. It mattered because she finally had the chance to attain the justice she had always sought.

Raymond was no doubt involved in this. One man couldn't do it alone. Warbucks would be a group, a small one, with one man pulling the strings. She suspected the man pulling the strings would be Ford. But who else were they waiting for?

"Ah, and here he is now." There was a tone of satisfaction in Raymond's voice as he looked over Bailey's shoulder.

Turning, Bailey hid her smile as she watched John make his way to the table. Dressed in black jeans and a white long-sleeved dress shirt beneath a long black leather coat, he looked like the devil he was. Wicked, charming, dangerous. He was breaking the unwritten dress code, and she could tell he really didn't give a damn. Some rules were just made to be broken and he was damned good at doing so.

As the waiter pulled out his chair beside her, John leaned down to kiss Bailey's cheek. "I was wondering where you got off to," he commented just loud enough for the others to hear him.

"I wasn't too hard to find, now, was I?" she said demurely. "And you never mentioned wanting to do lunch today."

He took his seat slowly, his wicked lips quirking into a crooked grin. "It should have been understood."

Her brow lifted. "You should have been clearer."

"I'll make certain, in the future, that I'm very clear."

Bailey pursed her lips and held back a scathing retort. He was establishing possession and dominance and irking her independent streak almost past toleration.

"Bailey often disregards acceptable limits," Ford informed John tightly. "She's not quite tamable."

"Taming isn't what I'm after, Mr. Grace," he assured Ford quietly, firmly. "I don't want a servant, I prefer a partner." His hand covered hers warmly, possessively. "I think Bailey and I make wonderful partners."

She left her hand beneath his, cast him a sidelong glance and remained quiet. Silent assent. He had stated their position, he had made his own boundaries clear.

The game had begun.

CHAPTER 6

JOHN COULDN'T BELIEVE that Bailey had actually met with Raymond Greer and Ford Grace, the two suspects highest on her list, without informing him. If it hadn't been for the late-morning call he'd received from Grace himself, he would have never known where she was.

The woman was going to make him crazy, that was all there was to it. If he let her. The problem was, he damned sure didn't know how to stop her. She was independent, she wasn't subject to anyone's orders, least of all his and he doubted she would follow them if she was. She had her own agenda in mind and she hadn't yet deigned to inform him of what it was, exactly.

That wasn't going to be allowed to continue.

He had a pretty good idea of what she was doing, but it was time he heard it from her. It was time he got several things aired out with her.

If she was still the woman she had been five years ago, then ordering her wasn't going to work. But he knew what would work. He had learned that little lesson in Australia.

Pulling into the driveway of the Serborne mansion, he stared up at the imposing two-story cabin, if you could call a fifteen-room mansion a "cabin." Huge windows looked out on the driveway as weathered cedar siding gave the structure an aged, welcoming look.

It was a home she had turned her back on. She'd had a

family she'd walked away from, a fortune she had rarely dipped into. Because her father hadn't believed in her, because his friendship with another man had been more important than his daughter's belief that his friend had murdered his family.

A wife and a daughter who had been trying to escape him. She suspected Ford Grace had hired an assassin to create a convenient accident the night Mathilda and her daughter Anna had tried to run from the Grace mansion.

She was still searching for proof, still trying to prove to her father that the man he had believed in was a killer.

Tightening his lips in frustration, he moved from the SUV he had driven back, just as the butler opened the door for her.

With a quiet "Thank you," she moved away from the employee who'd helped raise her and entered the house. John followed closely behind.

"Upstairs," he told her, making certain his voice carried no farther than her ears. "We're going to talk."

Talk wasn't all he had in mind, but it would be a good start.

"Of course." Her tone was agreeable, but there was nothing agreeable in the tension that tightened her body.

It was hidden very well. To the casual observer, she was relaxed and smiling—but he knew her. He'd worked with her enough that he recognized the signs of stress ratcheting through her system. Stress that he didn't think was entirely attributed to their lunch.

Not that Raymond Greer and Ford Grace couldn't give the hardiest system heartburn. They could. Their self-importance could be sickening at times. But she had been raised here, she knew them, she understood that attitude and had developed her own, which she used with amazing grace.

Hell, there had been times he wished he had access to the financial freedom she had, but he was beginning to rethink that wish. It took a type of personality that he didn't possess, that he would never be able to acquire.

Moving into the bedroom behind her, John closed and locked the door before moving to her dresser where she had positioned a white-noise device. Turning on the small electronic bug neutralizer, he turned back to her and watched her silently for long moments.

She didn't appear the least nervous. Pulling off her leather jacket, she hung it in the large walk-in closet at the side of her room, then toed off her sneakers and placed them perfectly alongside designer shoes.

Returning to the bedroom, she moved to her dresser, removed her jewelry, and placed it in a small engraved silver box. She was quiet, her expression clear. But he could feel the tension emanating from inside her. Like a string wound too tight and humming.

"You should have let me know about the lunch," he stated as he leaned against the wall and simply watched her. "We're supposed to be working together here."

Her head lifted, and their gazes met in the mirror. "Like you invited me to the meeting you had with the rest of your team this morning?" she asked.

John hid his surprise. How the hell had she known he'd had a meeting with the team?

Bailey's lips quirked into a sardonic smile. "Don't expect concessions that I'm not given as well," she told him coolly. "I can be a hell of a team player if the team I'm on actually understands working together."

His jaw tightened at the statement. "You'll be a team player on this one regardless," he informed her. "You're going to have to accept that the team surrounding you will remain invisible, Bailey. It's the only way to do this. Don't make things harder than they have to be."

"Simply accept that I'm no more than an asset in this little game then?" she asked haughtily as she turned around, her movements slow and deliberate. "Do you really think it's going to be that easy, John?"

No, he didn't. He knew she was going to make it harder than hell for him to keep her away from the unit. That was the deal. She couldn't be a part of the team as a whole; if she was, then she became a liability when it was over.

"It's going to be that easy," he said calmly. "We both get what we want this way. That should be enough for you."

Her lips thinned in irritation as her arms crossed over her breasts and she glared at him from the other side of the room.

"So I'm to have no idea who's friend or foe," she stated tightly. "I'm to just follow your lead and be a good little girl when you need to take me out to convince the bad guys that you're just as bad as they are?"

He stared back at her, mocking. "That would be classed in 'only in my dreams,' right?"

"Pretty much," she retorted with false sweetness. "But even your fantasies couldn't be that good, John. I think you're smart enough that your sense of reality would intrude right into that little dream should it strike your mind."

The sarcasm in her tone sent his blood pressure spiking into pure unadulterated lust. Damn her, she knew the buttons to push every time. She could spike his dick harder, faster, than any woman he had ever met with a simple arch of her brow and the gleam of challenge in those emerald eyes of hers.

And she knew it. He watched as her gaze flickered down his body before jerking back to his. Staring back at her knowingly, he watched the flush that mounted her cheeks and knew she was well aware of exactly what she was doing to him.

"That is not an acceptable response to an argument," she informed him.

John grunted at that. "Since when does it have to be acceptable? And you're changing the subject. We need to come to an understanding here and now, sweetheart. No more meetings, lunches, dinners, or conversations if you don't invite me into your little loop."

"Like I'm invited into yours?" She rolled her eyes. "We're not a team until the rules go both ways, John. If you can disappear to one of your little meetings, then I guess you're just going to have to trust me when I disappear into one of mine."

Enough was enough. She was daring him deliberately,

challenging him in an area where she knew he couldn't back down and give her what she wanted. It wasn't possible. He wasn't working within an acceptable arena where the unit was concerned, and *need to know* meant people could die if they pushed and learned more than they needed to.

He was across the room before she could avoid him, pulling her to him, holding her to him. There were a lot of things a man could learn about a woman when he pulled her into his embrace. Especially a woman as willful as he knew Bailey could be. A woman as well trained.

She could have jerked away from him easily. She could have had him on the floor in a breath, groaning in pain. But the wide streak of femininity inside her, the arousal, the hunger he could see in her eyes pushed back the stubbornness. He could feel it in the subtle molding of her body against his, the way her hips melted against him, the way her lips softened beneath his.

The way she went wild.

John nipped at the lips that opened hungrily against his. His tongue licked against hers, twined against it. Lust, need, something dark, something too hot, too intense twisted inside him until he felt as though the sexual intensity were burning him alive from the inside out.

It had always been this way with her. From that first kiss in Australia to this moment, the arousal flared white-hot and intense, digging into his senses and tightening his balls until he wondered if he could stand the strain.

His hold loosened as he felt her clawing at the clothes he wore. She pulled at the shirt, jerking it up along his back until he pulled away, intending to unbutton it and shrug it from his shoulders.

She didn't give him time to unbutton. Running her hands to his chest, she gripped the edge of the material and jerked. Buttons scattered across the floor as his chest was revealed. The cool air of the room didn't have a chance against his heated flesh.

Dominance rose inside him, tightening his muscles and sending a surge of adrenaline tearing through his body. He jerked her back to him, because he had to feel her close to him. He needed more of her.

Gripping the hem of her shirt, he pulled back enough to rip it from her as she lifted her arms with sensuous grace, wrapping them around his neck and tugging him back to her for another of those heated, hungry kisses.

Damn her, she made him ready to howl with lust. It grew inside him with every stroke of his hands along her body, overtook him with each article of clothing that he nearly tore from her flesh.

Minutes later she was naked against him, her breasts branding into the naked flesh of his chest as he bore her to the bed. Nothing mattered but Bailey. Nothing mattered but touching her, tasting her.

Her arms wrapped around his neck, her lips opened to his. But it wasn't submission she gave him. It wasn't supplication. It was a woman demanding the man she needed, the man she loved. A woman who had lost too much far too long ago.

Standing on her tiptoes, for one precious second she commanded the kiss. Her lips parted, her tongue stroked over his, dueled for domination until with a harsh groan he took control. One hand threaded through her head, cupped the back of her skull, and held her still beneath his kiss. The other gripped her hip, held her in place, and guided the kiss.

For a moment.

Bailey wanted to laugh in joy as she felt his surprise when she nipped at his lips, stroked over them with her tongue, and refused to be dominated. Her fingers tugged at his hair as her nipples raked over his chest.

It was a passion unlike anything she had ever known, even with Trent that first night, so very long ago. It was a lust, an overwhelming hunger that she couldn't fight. With each taste of him, with each touch of his callused hands she needed more, she ached for more until she could barely breathe for the ferocity of it.

Shudders of pleasure were racing beneath her flesh as his free hand began to caress her, moving up her back, over her waist, and up her side to cup her breast, his thumb stroking over an engorged nipple.

Bailey wasn't to be outdone. Her hands lowered from his hair. She wasn't doing very well at holding him to her anyway. He was doing as he pleased, sipping and nibbling at her lips, destroying her control with each deep, tongue-thrusting kiss.

It was like being submerged in pure ecstasy. She let herself become lost in him, this time, in ways she hadn't allowed that first tentative night. The night she had thought she had lost him forever.

Tonight, she would take everything she could get from him. Tonight she would give him everything she had to give.

Her hands stroked from his shoulders, over his chest, to his hard abs. The feel of his hard muscles overlain with tough, sun-darkened flesh was like a narcotic to her senses. It infused the passion roiling through her and built the need for more higher, hotter inside her.

She could feel the heat of that need, that hunger as it spread from her sex, dampening the folds of flesh as it sensitized them.

Her clit ached. The swollen bundle of nerves felt too tight, too hot. The need for relief was like a biting inferno she couldn't seem to assuage.

"Sweet love," John groaned, that little bit of accent breathing against her ear and sending shivers racing down her back. "How I love your touch."

His lips raked down her neck, his teeth nipped at flesh so sensitive that each caress brought her to her tiptoes and had a hoarse cry tearing from her throat.

She needed him. Needed him until she wondered if she could survive it. Needed him until it was like a conflagration burning through her body.

One hand slid lower, her fingers searching for and finding the heated length of his cock as it pressed high against her belly. Thick and iron-hard, throbbing beneath her touch, the silken flesh was like a flame in her hands.

"Damn." He breathed hard against her ear as her fingers

stroked along the shaft. "Sweet mercy, love, you'll have me coming in your hand if you keep this up."

She nearly came in his arms at the rough statement whispered against the sensitive flesh of her neck.

"Then you'll just have to try to do it right the second time," she panted, a smile tugging at her lips as his chuckle echoed against her flesh.

"Think I'd get it right the second time?" His hand moved from her waist then, curled against her hip, then pushed between their bodies to find the flesh beyond.

"Oh God." Her head fell back, her hips arched against his touch as his fingers slid into the narrow slit and rubbed delicately against her clit. "I think we'd try the third time just to be sure."

"Practice makes perfect?"

She would have answered him. She would have come up with half a dozen smart-assed remarks if he hadn't chosen that moment to press his finger into the tight, clenched entrance of her pussy.

"John." His name was a cry of demand as her thighs parted farther and she felt her juices easing along his finger, lubricating her more, increasing the pleasure tearing through her.

It was wild, the way the sensation thundered through her, throbbed in every beat of her heart, and kept her on a ragged edge of desperate hunger.

She needed his touch now, soaked it in with a desperation born of the reality of loss and being found again. It was wrapped in joy, speared with pain, and through it all was a hunger she had never forgotten. A hunger she couldn't eradicate from her soul.

"Touch me," she whispered, the need pouring through her, ripping at her. "Oh God, John. Touch me."

Though how he could touch her more, deeper, or better than he was, she had no clue.

Then he did. His lips nudged against hers, rubbed against them, then opened them in a kiss so deep, so filled with wicked sensual hunger that it seemed to explode inside her.

She was on the verge of begging. The fingers of one hand stroked at the long, thick length of his cock as her hips writhed against the finger plunging inside her. First one, then a second, filling her, stroking inside her and caressing flesh rioting with such extreme sensation that she was shaking with near rapture.

The pad of his palm pressed against her clit, sending lightning bolts of fiery pleasure to tear through her nervous system.

She felt poised within the heart of a flame. Her vagina clenched around his fingers, fluttered against the rapid strokes that filled her, stretched her.

Five years was a hell of a long time to survive without touch, without affection. To exist within a void that was filled with nothing more than a memory.

She relished each touch now and reached for more. Her fingers stroked the hardened length of his cock, weighed the heavy sac beneath, and caressed him as she never had before.

"Baby, you're destroying me," he groaned.

She didn't care. He'd already destroyed her.

"Don't stop!" Her cry was a broken plea as his fingers slid from the aching center of her body.

"Just for a bit, darlin'," he swore, his voice rough.

A second later she was in his arms, a step later and they were in her bed.

Rising to her knees, she met him as he came to her. Her arms wrapped around his neck as her lips met his. Lips and tongues battled, dueled as he pushed her back to the mattress. Pulling her thighs apart, he slid effortlessly between them, tore his lips from hers, and let them roam her body.

"Not like this." She pushed against his shoulders, fought for supremacy.

His laughter was like a balm to the ragged edges of pain inside her. There was joy in the sound, playfulness. There was a willingness to tease, to tempt, not just to conquer.

Before she could process the sudden change in position he was on his back, his head moving between her spread thighs.

Bailey froze at the first stroke of his tongue through the swollen folds of her pussy. It flickered and probed, caressed and stroked, each lick light and easy, teasing and tempting as she braced her hands on his abs and fought to breathe.

Rising beneath her was the heavy length of his cock. The flushed, engorged crest throbbed, spilling a minute amount of pearly moisture that tempted her tongue.

She could barely think for the pleasure centered between her thighs. She could do nothing but feel, but ache for more.

Her head lowered, her hands wrapped around the base of the engorged shaft as instinct and hunger took over. Her tongue swiped over the head of the shaft, and Bailey began to give as good as she could get.

She filled her mouth with the heated width of the head of his cock, sucked it in, and laved it with her tongue.

John felt the first spear of sensation as her tongue swiped over his cock. Gripping her thighs and holding her to him, he speared his tongue inside the slick opening of her core, hoping to distract her. Hell, he should have remembered just how bold and adventurous Bailey could get.

But he'd never seen her adventurous in bed. That one night, a few fragile hours hadn't been near enough to know what she could deliver, even as she received.

And God help him now, but his Bailey was sure as hell delivering. It was all he could do to keep his head together, to keep his senses intact enough to pleasure her as she pleasured him.

He ran his tongue through the wet folds of her pussy, tasting the sweet syrup of desire, feeling the heat and need in every clench of tender tissue as he pushed his tongue inside her.

The taste of her intoxicated him, the touch of her, her touching him, him touching her—it was like a high no drug could deliver, no amount of alcohol could provide.

He flicked his tongue over her clit and fought to control his spinning senses as her mouth worked over the head of his cock. She was sucking at him with sensual delight, each caress of her mouth a testament to the pleasure he was giving her as well.

Her fingers were caressing the base, then his balls. She weighed the heavy sac, then moaned around the thick crest as he licked inside her once again.

Sweet Lord, she was making him insane. His hips arched involuntarily, giving her more, filling her mouth until she was forced to draw back just a bit.

John could feel the sweat gathering along his body. The heat building inside him as he fought to hold back his release. He wanted to explode deep inside her. He wanted to feel her sweet pussy clenching around him, drawing him in, holding him inside her delicate little body.

He hadn't realized how he'd missed her. Her touch, her kiss, all the sweet little tidbits that made up the woman. The way her hands stroked over his flesh, as though the touch of him was all that mattered to her.

As though touching her was all that mattered to him. His hands stroked over her thighs, her rear. He let his nails rasp against her flesh and felt the betraying little shiver of need it invoked as she moaned around the cock filling her mouth.

Each deep draw of her sweet lips, the suckling against the erect head was like shards of ecstasy raking through his cock. Blistering heat wrapped around him until John felt his body was close to exploding, disintegrating into fragments from the pleasure of her touch.

Cupping his hands over the curves of her rear, he brought her closer, licked around her swollen clit, sucked it into his mouth.

Distracting her from the deep, destructive suckling of his cock was becoming a priority. He was going to come in her mouth, and that he didn't want. Not yet. Not this time.

Drawing the swollen bud against his tongue, he licked against it, rubbed it, felt it pulse and throb against him as she began to stiffen, her body tensing with the sensations clamoring through her.

Moving one hand lower, his fingers found the delicate little opening to her pussy. Sliding in slow and easy, John worked two fingers into the clenched tissue, feeling it flutter against him as her orgasm began to build inside her.

But that wicked mouth didn't stop, didn't pause. Her tongue swirled around the head of his cock, her moans vibrated against it.

He pressed his fingers deeper inside her, moving them slow and easy in thrusts calculated to destroy her control as he sucked at the hardened bud of her clit and felt her flying higher.

And still she relished the flesh she had in her mouth. She sucked at him until he felt as though his soul were being drawn from his body. She licked, her fingers stroked.

Their breathing was rasps of desperation in the stillness of the room, their moans filled with tortured pleasure.

John felt his heels digging into the mattress as he fought back his release. The muscles of her thighs were tight, her body vibrating with tension.

"Enough." He moved quickly, lifting her from him and pushing her to her back. He jerked up the condom he had tossed to the upper corner of the bed and rolled it over his cock before he came over her.

"Like hell." She moved before he could push between her thighs.

John almost laughed in sheer delight as she pushed him against the bed on his back and moved over him.

His hands caught her hips. "You damned little wildcat."

"Remember it." She panted as she straddled him, moving until she was pressing the hot, wet folds of her pussy against the swollen head of his dick, nudging it against the tight opening.

Gripping her hips, he grinned up at her as he held her back, making it harder for her to impale herself upon the heavy length of his shaft.

"Oh, I'll remember it, love," he assured her, barely able to breathe for the silky heat cupping the tip of his cock. "I'll remember it very well."

He loosened the hold he had on her hips and nearly threw

his head back in ecstasy as she took him. Rapid bolts of fiery sensation tore through his cock, his balls. His thighs tightened, his hips arched, thrusting his shaft harder, deeper inside her as he fought back the release that nearly slipped his control.

God help him. Nothing in his life had ever been this good. Nothing had ever been this hot. Nothing had ever affected him as Bailey did.

"John." She whispered his name, and he could do nothing to hold back the groan at the need to hear more, his real name on her lips, the knowledge that she remembered the man he had been. That she knew the man inside her.

Reaching up, he drew her to him, her lips to his, a kiss that fueled the hunger raging inside them as their tongues fought and dueled, licked and stroked.

Hips clashed, writhed, perspiration built. There was nothing between them, nothing held back, and it was unlike anything John had ever known in his life.

It was like nothing Bailey had ever known, either. She had slipped past simple pleasure; now each touch of his flesh against hers was torturous ecstasy. It was blending of fire and ice, desperation and rapture. She felt as though she were being stroked with pure lightning, hot flames that whispered over her flesh with rapture.

Tearing her lips from his she rose above him, her hands braced against his stomach, her hips churning, writhing against him. Her clit rubbed into his flesh as he filled her to overflowing, stretched her beyond pleasure.

Her head fell back as that pleasure began to tighten in her womb. Pinpricks of sensation began to dig into her flesh as her nails raked against his stomach.

She could feel the whirling sensation as it attacked her senses. The feel of his cock inside her, throbbing, shuttling in and out in deep, rhythmic strokes. The steel-hard, iron-hot flesh stroked tender nerve endings revealed for the first time in five years. It rasped over them, throwing them into a conflagration of sensation that she couldn't control.

She had lost control long before this. She was riding a wave of such pure pleasure that control was impossible. It tossed her, churned around her, tore through her until she was crying out his name, begging for release, more than aware that he was controlling it, holding it back. Taking her into a maelstrom she had never known in her life until the explosion tore through her.

She was trying to scream his name, fighting to, but she couldn't find the breath to force it free. His hands held her hips fiercely as he thrust beneath her, plunging into her, throwing her higher with each stroke into an orgasm that threatened to destroy her.

Bailey arched her back, trembled and shuddered and fought to be free of the intensity of sensation racking her body. She was only barely aware of John beneath her now, thrusting hard and heavy inside her until, with a shattered groan, he gave in to his own release.

And she felt it. Despite the condom separating them, she could feel the hard, heated throb of his release. The fiery sensation of his seed spurting against thin latex, barely held back, but still heating inside her as another wave of sensation ripped through her.

She was flying. Color exploded behind her closed eyes, lightning struck through her veins, thundered through her body. She was lost inside a pleasure she couldn't control, lost in the man that no woman had a hope of controlling.

The ride was like being thrown into the heart of an exploding nova. Light and color, sensation and sound. Melding.

She felt melded to him. Inside his skin and sinking deeper by the second as she wilted against his chest.

His arms surrounded her, his hands stroked down her back as he whispered something at her ear. She couldn't process thought yet. Hell, she didn't want to process thought. She didn't want to hear, think, or rationalize at the moment. She simply wanted to feel. She just wanted to be a part of him as long as possible.

"Easy." She finally heard the soft word and realizing she was still shuddering, trembling in his embrace. "It's okay, baby, I have you."

John had her. She could feel him holding her, soothing her, wrapping around her from the inside out.

Her nails were still biting into his shoulders. Forcing herself to release that hold on him, she instead flattened her palms against his flesh, desperate to retain the feeling of being so much a part of him.

"You're like a flame against me," he whispered, brushing her hair aside and placing a kiss at the side of her neck. "So sweet and hot."

She had to fight back the tears even as she forced herself to restrain the words that rose to her lips. Was he Trent? She could feel it, that same touch, his kiss, a suspicion that was destroying her from the inside out.

If he was, then he had deserted her. He had taken the emotion that had existed between them and he'd walked away with a part of her that she had never been able to replace.

And she had existed in a void that had been empty, without direction.

Until John.

In that second Bailey realized the mistakes she had made in the past five years. How Trent's "death" had affected her. How it had nearly destroyed her own life.

She pushed herself from him and rolled to her side, eyes still closed even as she felt his hand stroke along her stomach.

Her skin was still so sensitive to the touch that a little shudder worked through her.

She had nearly destroyed herself because she had lost Trent. How weak was that? She, who had always thought herself so strong, so intent and determined. She had lost herself when she had lost Trent. Or John. Or whatever the hell he was calling himself on this operation.

"Bailey, stop drawing away from me." His voice hardened at her side. "I can feel you doing it."

She opened her eyes, turned her head, and stared back at him.

How ruggedly handsome he was. Dark blond hair, darker than it had been before, fell over his brow. The laugh lines at the sides of his eyes were always one of his sexiest features. His lips were swollen from their kisses, his dark gray eyes turbulent with emotion.

What emotion? she wondered. What was brewing inside this man she had given her heart to, and nearly given her life for?

Did he regret? Or did he justify his decisions?

And did it matter? If he was Trent, then the only reason he was here, with her, was to use her. Because he needed her to gain entrance into a society so elite, so powerful, that only a very few even knew of its existence.

She breathed in that truth.

No more lying to herself, she thought as she fought back the tears that would have fallen from her eyes. And no more weakness. She was a better woman, a better agent than she had been in the past five years.

Losing Trent had messed with her heart and her head to the point that surviving had been almost impossible. Moving on from his "death" had nearly destroyed her. She wasn't going to allow John Vincent to destroy her now.

"I'm right here," she finally answered. "It's been a long day, and a very trying week."

She forced herself from his side, sat up on the side of the bed, and willed her legs to hold her as she rose to her feet.

"Where are you going, Bailey?" Unashamedly naked, he watched as she snagged a robe from the chair against the wall and pulled it over her body.

The ultra-soft cotton enfolded her, but it wasn't as warm as it used to be. She still felt chilled, empty without his touch.

How long would it last this time? she wondered. That sense of loss when he left her for another mission. Perhaps even for another woman.

"I'm hungry." She forced a smile to her face as she moved for the door. "And I need coffee."

"It's late, and you didn't sleep much last night," he protested as he rose to his feet and snagged his pants from the floor. "You should be tired."

She was exhausted from the inside out.

"Food, then sleep." She shrugged as she headed for the door. "Care for a sandwich?"

She kept her back to him. He was too perceptive and he could read her much too easily. She had never been able to hide things from John and now she had a lot to hide.

The agent she'd once been had been so damaged when she thought he'd died, she'd barely recovered. She had forgotten her training in the past years and she'd forgotten how to use her instincts.

That wouldn't happen again. She had a life outside John, just as she should have had a life outside of Trent Daylen.

She wasn't losing this part of herself again. He owned her heart; he wasn't going to own her life.

"Bailey." He caught her arm as she opened the door. "Are you okay?"

She turned back to him and felt her stomach sink. What was that expression on his face? No, it couldn't be love. She had fooled herself into believing that once before. The heavy, intent look in his eyes might be caring—she had no doubt he cared—but it wasn't love. Love didn't walk away for revenge. It didn't desert the heart it had stolen and it didn't return for a job. It returned because it had no other choice. Because life was empty without that heart that beat life inside it. She was very much afraid her life would be even emptier when he left her. Again.

CHAPTER 7

THINGS CHANGE. EMOTIONS harbored so long inside a woman's heart can't always be denied. The need, the hunger, the feeling of a connection, a bond—there was no way to turn away from it. No way to ignore it.

Bailey awoke the next morning with that knowledge burning inside her, driving her from an empty bed to the shower, where she fought back the tears that would have poured from her eyes.

She awoke alone. After the most incredible night of her life, she was alone when her eyes opened. Just as she had always been alone.

Gathering clothes together, she forced herself into the shower, forced back the anger and the pain as she got ready for the day.

John hadn't made any promises and as much as she wanted to find ways to believe he was another man, as many traits as she could attribute to him, still more overshadowed them.

He was John Vincent, and John Vincent might not love her. He probably didn't love her. She was an asset, just as she had always been. She had been an asset to her father, she was an asset to those she had grown up with and she was now an asset to an agency that she didn't even understand.

Dressing seemed to take forever. It sapped the strength she knew she needed to face the man whose arms she had fallen asleep within just as it sapped the hope that had begun building within her. Not so much that he was Trent as that this emotion she felt inside would be returned.

Shaking it away wasn't easy. Forcing back the weakness was almost impossible. It wasn't permanent, she told herself. It was simply the afteraffects of a night in the arms of a very skilled lover and her own wayward emotions.

They had gotten her into trouble before; they had always led her onto the path of destruction. She was simply a magnet for heartbreak, it seemed.

A mocking smile tugged at her lips as she finished her makeup and flipped the brush through her hair one last time before surveying herself in the mirror.

She looked okay. She didn't look as though her heart was breaking and she didn't look as though another dream was slowly unraveling around her.

Vengeance.

She breathed in deeply, forcing that thought through her system, into her brain, into her heart. She might not have a chance at love, but she did have a chance at vengeance. For Anna and Mathilda, for her parents. Especially for her parents. She had a chance to make their murderer pay.

And for now, for a moment in time, she would have John. Not that it would ever be enough, but when it was over at least she wouldn't have the regret that she hadn't tried, that she hadn't fought for what her heart had tried to claim.

She'd let months go by before she had ever hinted to Trent that she desired him. It was time she had no intentions of wasting with John.

He was a secretive bastard. He was dominant, he edged at being controlling, but they were all traits she had as well. They would clash while they were together, but the memories . . . She smiled at the thought. She would have the memories when it was over.

If they survived the mission they were on. And that brought up another point she hadn't wanted to face. When all this was over, she was set to possess some very powerful enemies. The men in this little group liked to think that they policed themselves. That they kept themselves under control. They wouldn't appreciate her stepping in. And there was always the chance that more than one of them was involved. She wasn't overlooking that angle.

She hoped she wasn't overlooking anything. She'd been tracking Warbucks and Orion for years. After she'd eliminated those who couldn't possibly be involved, it had left her with four men who had the power, the resources, and the connections to accomplish the thefts and sales that had gone through.

Pushing her feet into a pair of well-worn hiking boots, she tied them quickly before heading downstairs for the coffee she knew the housekeeper would have prepared. Daylight filled the room, a cold dim light that sent a chill racing through her body despite the warmth of the house.

It would snow soon, she thought as she glanced out the huge front windows in the foyer. She could see the clouds lying over the mountains and bearing down on them. The forecast for the next week mentioned blizzard conditions nearing.

They had less than three weeks to accomplish the identification of Warbucks. The sale was coming soon. A broker would be chosen; within days negotiations would begin and a price would be set.

She had to ensure that John received the contract.

It amazed her how totally business-like these transactions now went.

Once upon a time things weren't nearly so civilized and in a lot of ways it had been much easier then to track and to apprehend the traitors involved in such sales. Now they were shielded by brokers, middlemen, and a professional atmosphere including background checks, moles in law enforcement agencies, and negotiations for pending sales.

It was becoming a pain in the ass, more so than normal, to apprehend the criminals hiding behind third-world nations and international connections.

Shaking her head at the thought, she turned and headed into the kitchen. The scent of smooth, rich coffee wafted through the air, tempting her. But something more drew her as well: the sound of hushed voices, male and female. John's and an unknown woman's.

She drew closer on silent feet, edging to the doorway but still unable to hear exactly what they were saying.

Lips thinning, she checked the holstered weapon she'd clipped at her back, beneath her light sweater, before straightening her shoulders and sliding into the room.

John turned to her immediately, his expression closed as the redhead standing close to him hid a quick smile.

Slender, toned, her red-gold hair flowing down her back, her sea-green eyes both amused and cynical, the other woman appeared both worldly and innocent, as well as familiar.

Dressed in jeans, boots, and a heavy sweater, the younger woman looked like a tourist out for a hike rather than someone who would be involved in what Bailey had decided was John's very dangerous life.

Tilting her head to the side, she stared back at the woman as she tried to ignore the stinging bite of jealousy. Though John seemed more irritated by the woman than aroused by her. Funny, but she could have sworn the curve of his lips, the way his nose flared, and the jut of his jaw were identical to Trent's when he had been irritated.

"Hello, Bailey. I hope you don't mind if I call you Bailey." The redhead didn't wait for an introduction. She moved across the room, her hand extended in greeting as a bright smile curved her lips. "I'm John's handler, Tehya."

"His handler?" Bailey arched her brow as she turned back to John, shooting him a curious look while shaking the woman's hand.

Distantly, she noticed the less-than-baby-soft smoothness of Tehya's palm, the firm grip, the warmth and lack of moisture. This wasn't a woman who would show nerves easily, or even feel them easily. She was confident, determined, and showed no signs of an agenda.

"My handler." He nodded. "Every good broker has one."

"It's what makes a broker good." Tehya grinned. "Every good assassin has one as well. That was Orion's weakness.

His handler was frightened of him rather than confident in his area of expertise. He knew Orion would have him killed when he retired."

"Seems like a good idea to me. When do I get to retire?" John snorted.

Tehya chuckled as she stepped back from Bailey.

"Last I heard, most handlers call rather than visit in person," Bailey pointed out as she moved to the coffeepot. "When did that rule change?"

"A good handler knows when to call and when to visit." Tehya shrugged her almost fragile shoulders. "Some information you don't want tracked over open phone lines, and even secure connections can be hacked."

That was no more than the truth.

"What was so important that you were forced to make the journey from England, then?"

Bailey timed the question perfectly. Turning, she caught Tehya's surprised look and the flare of suspicion in John's gaze.

Hiding her smile behind the coffee cup as she sipped at the fragrant brew, she let the knowledge that she had her own sources sink in.

"How did you find me?" Tehya seemed more curious than upset. "Better agents than you have searched for me."

"You were in Atlanta as well," Bailey stated. "Along with Jerric Abbas and Travis Caine. Once I tied you to all three men it wasn't hard to connect the dots and find you. You should be more careful."

"No doubt," Tehya murmured quietly.

No doubt. Bailey could sense the growing curiosity inside the other woman. It wouldn't be every day that she was tracked so easily. It was simply that Bailey had a driving reason to track the woman. The more she knew about the men she was tracking at the time, the better off she was. And sensing that Micah Sloane was her missing cousin had only given her added incentive.

She noticed the look Tehya and John exchanged then: Bailey shouldn't have been able to track her. Tehya was actually hidden very well, and pulling out background on the woman was like pulling teeth.

"So tell me, how did you track me to England?" Tehya asked bluntly. "You shouldn't have been able to."

"It wasn't that hard." Bailey moved to the breakfast table and the bagels and spreads her housekeeper had laid out for breakfast. "Residents of the village you call home recognize you. It's where you go when you leave there that I've had trouble following."

"Well, as least some secrets are still safe," Tehya quipped. "You're dangerously good, Ms. Serborne."

"She's dangerous, period, to herself," John grunted as he collected his own cup and moved back to the coffeepot. "What the hell were you doing tracking my handler?"

"At the time, I really had no idea she was your handler. She was tied to three men I was investigating; the connection points made her easier to trace." Bailey narrowed her eyes on the other woman again. The more she interacted with her now, the more familiar Tehya seemed. There was something about the way she held her head—her almost instinctive attempt to hide her face behind the veil of her hair, or by staying in profile—that piqued Bailey's memories. She just couldn't place it.

"We'll have to discuss that later, John," Tehya warned him.

John nodded sharply, and Bailey could almost see his concern. Whoever led the team he was a part of wouldn't be pleased with this information.

"So why is she here?" Bailey asked again.

Tehya slid into a chair at the table, crossed her jean-clad legs, and stared back at Bailey with a grin as John sat down in the chair between the two of them.

"It was business," Tehya sighed mockingly. "As a broker, John Vincent is in high demand. Fortunately, he's rather picky about the jobs he takes."

"Is he really?" Bailey glanced over at him.

He was leaning back in his chair watching both of them with a slightly worried expression. Now, why would he be worried? Unless he knew as well as she did that eventually Tehya's identity would come to her.

Bailey was drawing some amazing conclusions since Atlanta, since realizing her cousin was a part of the team John worked with.

If she wasn't mistaken, if her memory wasn't faulty, and it normally wasn't, then she was betting Tehya was just as "dead" as Micah. Perhaps just as "dead" as Trent.

"He is." Tehya nodded, obviously biting back a laugh even as she kept her voice low. "In this case, I felt it was in his best interests that I come to Aspen in case I was needed during the transaction."

John shook his head. "What Tehya is beating around the bush about here is the fact that Warbucks has made contact again. He seems rather interested in the fact that we're an item now. He contacted Tehya with a message that he's rather enjoying the fact that I've taken such initiative."

"He's also rather confident of the fact that you'll choose John over the others as well. He wanted to warn John that there would be no negotiation in terms of his payment, despite your relationship."

"I take a straight fifteen percent per sale." John shrugged. "I'm not willing to go lower. It's not worth my time otherwise."

Tehya shook her head. "Jerric Abbas is willing to go fourteen percent."

"Jerric doesn't have the connections I have, nor does he have the negotiating power." John grinned as Bailey barely kept from rolling her eyes at the mention of the other man's name.

"Jerric hasn't been in the brokerage game long enough to develop a name for himself outside his security abilities," Bailey stated. "He's a terrorist, and that's what he's known for, not his brokerage background."

"But his connections to the differing terrorist states could give him an advantage. Who do you think is going to be bidding the highest for the item?" Tehya asked.

"It doesn't matter." Bailey finished her coffee before rising and rinsing her cup. "Warbucks doesn't care who is going to be bidding for it. He's going to be concerned with the highest price and the most security. That's what John is known for, whereas Jerric hasn't had the time to prove he's capable of providing the highest quality of those two resources."

She glanced back at John in time to catch the surprise on his face.

She was revealing the time she had put into investigating him, as well as Warbucks. Jerric Abbas had never been known for his strength in negotiations before sixteen months prior, just after the explosion he'd supposedly escaped from.

Fortunately, Jerric hadn't really escaped; Micah had simply taken his identity. A little cosmetic work here and there, and he had slid perfectly into Jerric's life. So perfectly that there were moments even Bailey was amazed at her cousin's effectiveness.

Oh yes, there was no doubt in her mind that Jerric Abbas, Micah Sloane, and the deceased Israeli Mossad agent David Abijah were one and the same. She just wasn't so certain about John Vincent and Trent Daylen.

"You've put a lot of research into this," John said carefully.

"I've had a lot of free time in the past year," she pointed out mockingly. "And an overriding curiosity."

"Curiosity can be dangerous in this business," Tehya stated as she rose to her feet and carried her own cup to the sink. "I'd better be going now." She turned back to John. "Warbucks is supposed to be making contact in the next few days. I'll check in to a hotel in Aspen. I'll text you my location once I've settled in."

John gave a brief nod as she shrugged into the coat she had hung at the back door, then slipped out of the house. Bailey stared back at John silently for long moments, her eyes narrowed, her thoughts moving in several different directions. Overriding was the idea that John was still trying to keep secrets.

"Full disclosure," she finally said firmly. "I believe we may have discussed this already."

His lips quirked with irritating amusement. "I would have disclosed to you fully, sweetheart, if you hadn't shown up."

"But you weren't about to awaken me and allow me to be a part of the full conversation," she pointed out. "Possibly because more was discussed than simply Warbucks's message."

"Possibly." His lips twitched. "Some things are on a need-to-know basis, Bailey, you know that."

"Not in this game," she snapped angrily. "I'm either a part of it or not. There is no middle ground in this, John, I've warned you of that already. If you'd investigated my work background at all, then you'd know that."

His expression darkened. "I investigated enough to know that you drove the Australian agents crazy with your complete nosiness."

Ah yes, she was wondering how long it would take him to go down this path.

"All of them?" She arched her brow quizzically. "Oh, there might have been one who handled it fairly well."

She injected just enough sensual reflection in her tone to make her meaning clear.

"Trent Daylen." There was nothing in his tone to indicate that Trent was more than a name, a face, associated with her past. "You were lovers."

This was a hell of a game if he was truly Trent. God, she wished she knew one way or the other. She wished the suspicion would go away, leave her in peace. She wished the memories of her time with Trent would stop haunting her.

"We were lovers," she answered quietly. "Until he was killed."

He rose from his chair and paced back to the coffeepot, where he refilled his cup.

"Did you know Warbucks was behind Daylen's assassination?"

He surprised her. Bailey froze as a stabbing pain struck

at her soul, one that nearly took her breath and sent her stomach plunging.

She hadn't known that. Her investigation had shown that his partner had betrayed his identity as an agent to former enemies, not that Warbucks had played a part in it.

"You didn't know that?" He was watching her now, his gaze hooded, his thick dark blond lashes shielding his eyes. "He was investigating an Australian connection and the identities of several agents who had been sold on the black market by one of Warbucks's brokers when he was killed. He and one of his contacts were killed the same night."

Bailey stared back at him, fighting back the tears, the knowledge that Warbucks had taken more than she'd ever imagined from her life. She had placed herself in the perfect position, at first, to find the man who'd hired her friend's death. Bailey had feared that the investigation had resulted in her parents' deaths. And now to know he had been responsible for Trent's death as well sliced through her spirit like a hot, dull knife.

The pain was nearly overriding. It tightened her throat, made breathing hard, and locked a scream in her chest. She was alone, so fucking alone that sometimes she wondered why the hell she made herself get out of the bed in the morning. So alone that she couldn't forget the one night she spent with a man she had loved, even as another man filled her bed. Or was he the same man?

She couldn't make herself believe one way or the other, and she feared it was because she was too frightened of what she could lose either way.

"I didn't know." She finally forced the words past her throat as she turned her back on him, still fighting the tears. "My investigation didn't reveal that."

Where had she managed to miss that?

"It was something he was working on covertly, even outside the ranks of his agency," John stated.

"How did you know?" She turned back to him, the question snapping from her lips. "How could you have known if it was so secret?"

"His partner wasn't killed that night." John shrugged. "He was interrogated by an impartial group that had been investigating the tie themselves. Even the director of Australian Secret Intelligence had no idea what was going on. Trent hadn't had time to relay the information when the hit had gone out on him."

She hadn't known.

She was shaking, rage and bitter fury tearing at her insides as she forced herself to breathe through the pain. She felt as though her guts were being shredded. Burning hot and filled with acid, the pain lanced through her senses and left her fighting back the tremors that would have shaken her body.

"You loved him," John stated again.

Bailey shook her head as she turned back to him, wiping away the single tear that escaped her control.

"He was my life," she said simply. "Yes, John, I loved him."

"Do you still love him?" He paced closer, his expression closed, almost frigid.

"Do I still love him?" She wanted to laugh at the bitter irony of the question. "I love a memory, don't I? Trent is gone forever. Dead men don't rise from the grave, do they, John? They don't come back to the lovers who weep for them, and they don't hold the women who dream for them. They're just gone. Aren't they?"

She watched as he came closer, as his hand lifted out, his palm cupping her cheek as he wiped away another tear.

"They're just gone," he agreed quietly. "Except in memories. He'll always live, Bailey, because he'll always be a part of you."

And what the hell did he mean by that?

"That doesn't bother you?" She swallowed back the sobs that fought to be free. "It doesn't bother you that you're fucking a woman whose heart belongs to another man?"

"Don't call it that!"

Before she could evade him she was in his arms again, his hold tight, almost punishing.

"Don't call it fucking?" she cried hoarsely. "What is it, then? You aren't jealous that another man holds my heart? Don't you care that I want to call out his name when I'm coming around your cock?" Fury was enveloping her. She wanted to rage, fight. She wanted to smack the anger off his face, because he had no right to be angry. He had no right to stand and discuss himself as though he had truly died.

She was dying inside. She could feel it. The suspicion that he was Trent was eating her alive, and there was no way to stop it. It was destroying her. The knowledge that the man she had loved hadn't loved her enough to come back to her without a mission backing him was ripping her soul to pieces one small bit at a time.

"I don't have the right to be angry, do I, Bailey?" But he was. She could see the anger building in his gaze, flushing his dark skin. "I don't have the right to care."

It was stated so simply. It wasn't even an answer. It was an affirmation that he would leave when this was over, nothing more.

"No." She tried to push away from him. "You have no rights, period."

"I might not have the right, but I have the fucking woman." He jerked her back to him, holding her in place as he backed her against the kitchen island counter, keeping her tight against his body despite her struggles. "Deny that, Bailey. Deny the fact that you know exactly who's holding you in that bed. Don't you dare lie to me and pretend you're thinking of another man. You know exactly who's fucking you."

Did she? Did she know? If she knew, then why, God help her, why couldn't she stop suspecting he was another man?

"Is it enough for you?" she asked, her voice ragged. "Of course it is. You're not here for love, are you, John? The woman doesn't matter, just the mission."

He didn't have an answer for that. He didn't argue with her, he didn't deny it. Instead, his fingers gripped her hair, pulled her head back, and his lips covered hers with a desperate, painful passion.

She knew that passion, that desperation. She knew the pain that drove the senses to possess, to mark what belonged to her. It was the same intensity he used to mark her as his.

His tongue drove between her lips to tangle with hers. His free hand moved beneath her sweater, her top, pressing heatedly against the bare flesh of her back as his hips pressed into hers.

It was a kiss that seared the senses. A kiss that drove all thoughts of anything else, anyone else, from her mind. When she was in his arms, she didn't torture herself with questions, she didn't silently beg for answers. In his arms nothing mattered but this. The kiss, the feel of him, the driving need that shattered her control and overwhelmed her senses.

Nothing else mattered but this moment in time.

Her hands moved from his arms where her nails had bitten into his flesh. Hesitantly, almost warily they stroked up his arms, to the strong column of his neck.

Her lips opened beneath his as she began to mark him as well. Her tongue fought against his, licked and dueled until they were both moaning with the driving need tearing through them.

She wanted him again, here and now. She wanted to tear the clothes from his body and feel him hard and hot against her. She wanted the thick shaft of his cock pressing inside her, stretching her, burning her with the need that neither of them could deny.

She wanted so much and so much of what she wanted wasn't hers. It couldn't be hers. Because if he was Trent, the risk would be too great. And if he wasn't Trent, then the love, the instinctive need that Bailey knew she couldn't do without, wouldn't be there.

She loved Trent. Totally. Completely. Surely a woman couldn't love like this twice in one lifetime. It wasn't possible, was it?

"That's what fucking matters." He jerked back from her, his breathing as rough, as heavy as her own. "Figure it out from there, damn you. And be very careful, because saying another man's name in my fucking bed could get you a hell of a lot more than you want to deal with."

With that, he stalked from the room, leaving her panting, aching, and almost certain. John Vincent was Trent Daylen.

CHAPTER 8

HE SHOULD HAVE KEPT HIS damned mouth shut. John wiped his hands over his face the next day as he stared out Bailey's bedroom window. She was roaming the extensive back gardens while snow fell around her.

They'd spent the night further looking into the backgrounds of the suspects they'd both come up with. Ford Grace, Samuel Waterstone, Ronald Claymore, and Stephen Menton-Squire. Added to that list were Raymond Greer and Jerric Abbas.

She knew that was bullshit, she already had it out in the open. Micah's portrayal of Jerric was excellent, though, she'd give him that. Few agents would have known the difference. But she had.

She had, and something inside him that warned him that Bailey was slowly figuring him out as well, even as he watched her.

The temperature was still fairly moderate, just cold enough for a thick, heavy wet snow. The flakes caught in her dark hair and glistened among the strands as she trailed her fingers over a winter-dead climbing rosebush as it hung tenaciously to its trellis.

She was thinking, and he'd learned in Australia that this was never a good thing, unless it involved a mission.

In his case, John knew it was a very, very bad thing. She was already suspicious. He'd slipped into her laptop enough times to know she was already aware that Micah Sloane was her cousin, David. She was too fucking intuitive. She'd pieced that one together with such accuracy that it was frightening. And she was piecing together the truth about him with the same accuracy.

He hated hiding it. Every time she stared up at him with those inquisitive green eyes, every time he saw the questions in them, the pain and the loss she felt.

She was getting closer to piecing it together. Not through investigation or proof, but through her own intuitive strength. It was one of the reasons she had made such an excellent agent. Bailey could see beyond most disguises. She studied body movements, expressions, and characteristics. Things that were much harder to change. She looked beyond the skin and that made her incredibly dangerous to the Elite Ops.

If Jordan weren't being so fucking stubborn, she would have made just as strong an agent for the Elite Ops.

Shaking his head at the thought, he flipped open his cell phone and hit the secure line into headquarters.

"Morgan's Meats," Jordan answered on the first ring as John activated the added scrambler on his phone.

"Activate Black Jack," John stated. "We're moving."

He cut the line before it could be traced or descrambled. To this point, he hadn't needed backup, or hadn't considered it important. If Warbucks was getting ready to move, then he wanted Travis in place. As his bodyguard, Travis wouldn't be considered a threat or unknown. And if this was getting to move, then John would feel more comfortable with the knowledge that there was someone else watching Bailey's back as well.

She might not be certain that he was Trent yet, but she wasn't far from it. And the problem with that was, he knew he was slipping in front of her. Slipping in ways she couldn't miss. It was almost instinctive, as if a part of him needed her to know, even though realistically he knew she would only end up hurt in the end. God knew, he didn't want to see her hurt more.

Breathing out wearily at the problems he was facing, he turned and headed out to meet her. She looked like a fairy princess with the snow falling around her and hair lying about her shoulders like a cape.

He needed to be with her. Denying himself the pleasure of her warmth was more than he was capable of. He needed the memories when this was over. If he had to walk away from her or, God forbid, he didn't survive this mission, then he wanted her to know he'd given her every part of himself while he could.

Moving down the stairs, he snagged his long leather jacket from the foyer closet and headed to the back of the house. Wide French doors led to the gardens and the snowy wonderland that awaited there.

He loved the snow, even the cold sometimes. Shrugging on the heavy leather coat, he moved through the massing snow, following the dim prints of her footsteps, moving deeper into the gardens toward the gazebo where she had been heading. The shelter was as large as some rooms, surrounded by latticework.

Stepping up to the doorway, he watched as she sat on the cushioned bench and stared at the open fireplace that sat in the middle of the structure.

A blaze leapt hungrily at the logs she had laid fuel to, illuminating her thoughtful face as she curled into the corner of the wide seat.

She wore a long, heavy sweater over her jeans and cashmere top. Heat radiated from the fireplace, painting a golden hue over her as her head lifted and her gaze met his.

They hadn't discussed much other than the mission at hand since the morning before. She'd almost avoided him otherwise and she'd definitely avoided any references whatsoever to anything more personal than how to conduct themselves once they were back in the public eye.

"We have a party tomorrow night," she told him as he stepped into the shelter. "Stephen Menton-Squire had invitations issued this morning. I received one by text. It's formal—

most of them are. His Winter Ball. His wife, Josephine, was one of my mother's best friends. Her and Janice Waterstone."

"Your mother enjoyed throwing parties as well," he stated. "Your file is filled with references to her charities and the newsworthy balls she hosted."

A small smile tugged at her lips. "Mother always grasped the opportunity to squeeze out donations to her favorite charities. Her parties were mere excuses to draw the most moneyed of her acquaintances into one place and ply them with good liquor or champagne. Then, while their defenses were down, she would sweet-talk them like the southern belle she was."

He grinned at the thought. Her mother had been known as a kind, gracious lady who didn't mind getting her hands in the dirt if she had to. She had planted the gardens here herself, working with a few landscapers for the heavier projects, but her hands had helped shape it.

"Mother was an angel," she said softly. "Everyone loved her."

Especially her daughter.

"I often wonder if the man who hired Orion to kill them gave any thought to what they were doing to someone who had most likely cared for him," she said softly. "My mother knew the men we're looking at, she was friends with their wives, their children called her Auntie Angie. She would have had him at her dinner table. She would have kissed his cheek and smiled at him the night she was killed."

Benjamin and Angelina Serborne had died in a crash after leaving a party Ford Grace had hosted.

"You're convinced it's Ford, aren't you?" he asked as he moved to sit beside her.

She rubbed at her forehead wearily. "He had the most reason. I didn't know until after I returned home that Father even kept a journal. I was going through his things when I found several of them in a hidden safe that only myself and my parents knew about. The last week he was alive there were several references in his journal to business dealings he'd had with the four men we're investigating. There was something shady about them, he noted. The last entry was titled 'Who the Hell Is Warbucks?' "

He slid her a surprised look. "You haven't told anyone else about this?"

She shook her head as she stared down at her hands in her lap. "Father never believed that any of his friends could possibly be a killer. I've always suspected Ford had his wife and daughter killed. Father and I argued about it often and loudly. He never believed me."

"But you were certain," he said.

"His wife was leaving him, and Anna went with her. Ford used to hit them. The last time, he beat them severely. Mathilda was trying to protect her daughter, and they were murdered as they tried to escape. Who else would have reason to kill them?"

"There was no evidence they had been murdered," he pointed out. "The official report is that the car skidded on ice."

"There hadn't been snow for weeks." She sighed as she leaned back and stared up at him. "Orion's handler confirmed to me that he'd been hired for the hit."

"Did you ask him about your parents?" He watched her more closely now. He knew she'd made contact with the handler; he hadn't known how in-depth that contact had been.

She shook her head. "I haven't been able to find him. Someone hid him, and they hid him well."

John knew exactly where the handler was, and he made a mental note to get the answer to that question. If Ben Serborne had somehow suspected who Warbucks was, then Orion would have been called in. It made sense. Just as it was beginning to make sense why Orion had been given orders not to kill Bailey.

Until she became a personal risk, she was still a part of a very elite group. A group known for its loyalty to one another. Once it was proven that Bailey would strike against them, then she would be in danger as well. If they didn't identify and eliminate Warbucks during this mission, then she would never be safe again.

"Would he have confronted Warbucks without letting you know something was wrong?" John asked curiously.

"Of course he would have." Her smile was sad. "Father would have never told me, because he knew I would have done something about it. He hated my job and the danger involved in it. It was something else we fought about."

As John knew he would protect his own daughter if he ever had one.

"Your father was on to Warbucks, then. It would make sense. He was a closely knit part of the group. They could have been courting his membership if it's a group, or his help if its an individual."

"Or he could have been checking into something himself," she breathed out roughly. "Father was an armchair investigator. He loved solving puzzles and he was incredibly nosy. He could have become curious about the wrong thing, or the wrong person. Which makes more sense."

John could hear the grief in her voice, the need for answers, for vengeance.

"Warbucks has stolen so much from me," she went on. "My dearest friend. Anna and I were like sisters. My parents." She shook her head. "Trent." Her gaze deepened as she stared back at him. "I can't let this go, not until I find him. I won't let it go."

He reached out to touch her cheek, needing a connection to her, to comfort her. She had no idea how deeply she was entrenched in his heart.

"He won't take anything more from you," he promised, hearing the roughness in his own voice, the need. "I won't let him, Bailey."

It was a promise he meant to keep, even though realistically, he knew it could be beyond his own control.

She shook her head at the promise. "Tell me, John, what happens when this mission is over?"

"What do you mean?" He had a bad feeling he knew exactly what she meant.

She moved then, slowly, sinuously, like a lazy cat shifting in the sun until she was moving over him, straddling his lap as he leaned back, his hands cupping her ass until he could grind her against the hard length of his cock beneath his jeans.

"What happens when we've identified Warbucks and neutralized him?" She leaned forward and touched her lips to his. "You'll leave." It wasn't a question. "You'll ride off into the sunset and the next time I see you I probably won't even know who you are. I'll look for you in every man I meet. In every kiss I share with another. Because you can't stay, can you?"

He stared back at her, wishing he could deny it.

"Warbucks will have taken you away from me. Because of him, you came here, to me. And once he's gone, there will be no reason for you to be here any longer."

Because the mission would be over. Because he had sold his soul for vengeance against the shadowy traitor.

"Don't." She laid her fingers against his lips as he started to speak. "No promises, John. I don't want any. All I want is the truth. I don't want to ever believe in something I can't have again."

He moved her fingers from his lips, gripped the back of her head, and pulled her to him as he took in a kiss as gentle as the soft fall of snow outside the shelter that surrounded them.

It was like being surrounded by a dreamscape. A moment out of time that existed for them alone. Here, no one could touch them, nothing could threaten them. Right here, they were simply a man and a woman, aching, needing. There was no past, no future, only the present.

"You deserve better," he whispered as he brushed his lips over hers, then sipped at them delicately.

"I deserve what I want." She sighed, a hint of desperation filling her voice and cutting at his soul. "I want you, John. Here. Now."

With the firelight flickering over her, he could imagine her naked, stretched across the lush cushions of the bench, her naked body warm and inviting. The image was so strong his cock jerked in his pants, becoming so hard, so tight, it was agony.

Gripping her back he turned until she was lying back against the cushion. He lifted one leg, unlaced her boot, and removed it before taking off its mate.

Her feet were slender and delicate, the nails painted a rich, lush berry red to match her fingernails.

Lifting one, he kissed the tips of her toes, watched her eyes flare, then moved to the arch. Her feet were incredibly sensitive. He remembered that from the night they had spent in Australia. How her foot flexed, as it did now, and a low moan whispered from her lips.

That moan struck his senses like a match to gasoline, flaming through his body and erupting like a starburst in his balls. He was nearly coming in his jeans just from stroking her arch with his lips.

Lowering her leg, his fingers moved to the clasp of her jeans, released it, and slowly lowered the zipper. He wanted to undress her slowly, to bare each bit of flesh to his gaze like the most special present.

Leaving her jeans loosened but still in place, he moved to the sweater. Lifting her, he pulled her arms from the sleeves, left the cashmere beneath her, then pulled her shirt from her.

Her breasts were unbound, golden from the light tan she carried, her nipples hard and cherry red. John licked his lips with the need to taste her, to draw that delicate, tempting fruit into his mouth with greedy hunger.

As he drew back, he watched in amazement as her hands lifted. She cupped her breast, her fingers gripping the hard points of her nipples as her hips arched and her face flushed with arousal.

"You're so damned beautiful," he groaned as he practically tore the leather coat from his shoulders and tossed it aside.

He jerked at the buttons of his jeans, tearing the metal disks from their moorings before jerking his own shirt over his head without bothering to unbutton it.

He could feel the sweat beading on his forehead as she moaned with lush hunger and caressed the tight buds of her breasts.

"Feel good?" he asked her roughly.

"Not as good as your hands." She sighed in longing. "Do you like watching me?"

"God, I love watching you," he groaned. "I could watch you for hours."

A sensual smile twisted her lips as one hand lowered from her breast, her fingers trailed down her abdomen. John watched hungrily, with mounting excitement, as those delicate fingers pressed beneath the jean material, moving for the sweet, wet flesh beyond.

He gripped the waist of her jeans and pulled them over her hips. He nearly lost what was left of his mind as he watched her fingers circling the damp bud of her clit. The glistening little pearl peeked between the folds of her pussy, gleaming with arousal as she rubbed at it, stroked it.

He managed to get the denim off her legs, jerked a condom from his back pocket, thanking God that he'd pushed one in there earlier, just in case.

Oh yes, he remembered how sweet and hot Bailey could get. How many times in Australia had he missed out on that sweetness because he hadn't been prepared?

Rising to his feet, he toed his boots from his feet and stripped his jeans, barely aware of the chill in the air as the heat from the fireplace licked over his flesh and the heat of lust licked inside him.

As he lowered himself to one knee between her spread thighs, his gaze was glued to the journey her fingers were making from the tight bud of her clit to the slick entrance beyond.

He could barely breathe for the need striking inside him. His muscles were clenched from the effort to hold on to his control as he watched, his fingers massaging the muscles of her thighs as he watched her fingertips sink inside the delicate opening.

"Beautiful," he whispered, his voice guttural.

Pulling her fingers back, her juices glistening on the tips, he watched as she lifted them and stroked her lips.

Lust tore through him like a punch to his gut as he watched her juices glisten on her lips a second before her tongue swiped over the lush curves.

He could barely breathe now. He could feel the need for oxygen tearing at his chest as he panted, fighting to retain the mental capacity to hold on to his control.

His fingers were shaking as he tore open the condom and worked it over his cock. The flesh was so swollen it was painful, so hard it was like iron. The need to thrust inside her was a primitive, primal response that he could barely hold back.

Leaning over her he licked over her lips, moaning at the sweet taste as he let his fingers move between her thighs to tangle with hers. He stroked the silken flesh to feel the heat of her. He dipped his fingers into the tight entrance, stroked and caressed her as her hips arched to him and her moans filled his ears.

Her fingers gripped his wrist while her thighs fell farther apart, welcoming his fingers into her as a strangled cry tore from her chest.

She was burning alive beneath him. Sweet and hot, stealing his mind as he fought to hold back. Just a few more minutes. Dear God, just enough to imprint the memory of this into his mind forever.

BAILEY STARED UP AT JOHN, watched the firelight flicker over the dark, savage features of his face, and felt her heart expanding in her chest. There was nothing so sexy, so completely filled with driving lust and sensual excitement as this man.

As he kissed the arch of her foot, she saw Trent. As his lips grew heavy, his gaze flickered with need, and his expression tightened in the lines of a man intent on mating, she saw the lover she had thought was dead forever.

This was Trent, yet he wasn't Trent. He was different, harder, hungrier, but still the same man she had loved for five long, lonely years.

A part of her was crying out in joy, another part filling

with pain. He was alive. He hadn't died. He had deserted her instead.

No matter the pain, she couldn't pull away from him. This memory, this short time spent with him was all she was going to have. She couldn't bring herself to make him stop. She couldn't bring herself to deny him.

As his lips came to hers in a kiss filled with passion and torrential need and his fingers began to slide inside her, filling her, stretching her, she knew that a part of her would always belong to him. A part of her would never let go of the lover who had stolen her heart so long ago.

"You make me insane to have you," he groaned against her lips as she arched closer, driving his fingers deeper inside her.

"Not insane enough," she panted. "You're not taking me."

"Are you sure?" Two blunt male fingers thrust inside her, sliding through the slick juices that eased from her pussy and pushing past clenching, desperate tissue.

"Oh God. John." She was ready to scream out in need. It wasn't enough. She needed more of him. She needed all of him.

His fingers weren't enough, his kiss wasn't enough.

As his lips moved from hers to her jaw, her neck, and then lower to her breasts, she could feel her temperature rising, the need growing inside her to an inferno level. Her hips arched closer as his fingers began to fuck inside her with steady strokes and his lips closed over a too-sensitive nipple.

The suckling heat of his mouth, the lash of his tongue against her nipple, and the smooth, driving strokes of his fingers fucking inside her were too much. The pitch of excitement was rising, growing to a degree that she couldn't bear the sensations. Her stomach contracted, her muscles tightened and she could feel her orgasm growing, just out of reach.

Wrapping her arms around his neck she arched and writhed against him. His name was a ragged chant on her lips, drawn from the growing desperation building inside her.

Lightning-hot bolts of sensation tore across her nerve

endings, whipped through her body, and sent waves of clawing hunger washing through her.

She couldn't bear it. The need was tearing at her like a ravenous beast, filling her with a desperation she couldn't fight or control any longer.

"Please, John," she cried out, fighting to breathe through the hunger that tore at her senses. "Take me now. I can't bear it. Please."

"God, I can't let you go yet," he groaned against her breast as he licked at her nipple before turning to its mate. "Not yet, Bailey."

His fingers worked inside her, stroking and caressing tender tissue, stoking the fire burning inside her until she could feel the flames licking at her soul.

"No. No. Now." She arched, the muscles of her pussy tightening around his thrusting fingers. "Now, John. Please."

She couldn't bear much more. She needed so desperately to feel him inside her that she couldn't bear the sensations.

"God, you're killing me." His fingers slid free of her as he rose between her thighs. "Sweet sweet Bailey, you'll be the death of me."

She watched, licking her lips in anticipation as he stroked the sheathed flesh of his cock and moved closer to the aching center of her body.

She reached for him, gripped the hard shaft herself and lifted to him, drawing him to her and tucking the head of his erection into the clenching entrance of her pussy.

"Love me," she whispered. "Just this once."

His expression tightened, his gray eyes darkened to nearly black as he froze against her for one long moment. Their gazes locked, Bailey watched as something akin to grief swirled in the hungry depths of his eyes.

"Forever," he whispered, the word almost soundless, almost broken as his hips moved.

Bailey cried out, her hands flying to his hips while he thrust against her, pushing inside her, working his erection desperately into the tight depths of her sex as the world began to explode around her.

She saw stars. She saw a sunburst explode inside her mind as he thrust to the hilt, stretching the sensitive tissue as she clenched in reflex around him.

His groans mixed with her cries as he began to move. There was no time for slow loving now. They needed too much, had too many memories, too many sensations to store up inside their souls.

John felt as though his soul were pouring from his body into hers. He couldn't hold back the emotions any more than he could hold back the need that tore at him.

His balls were tight with the need for release, his cock flexing, clenching as he felt her pussy tightening around him and the hard arch of her body when her orgasm flooded through her.

His name was a steady chant on her lips. Love filled her voice, her hold, it wrapped around him until he could feel nothing, sense nothing but Bailey. Until nothing mattered but the woman, until he released inside her with a hard growl, his body arching, tensing until he felt as though he had been shattered from the inside out.

Until he knew, without Bailey, he was nothing. Pleasure would be a thing of a past. He would be like a ghost, haunting the world for the love of a woman.

God help him, how was he was supposed to walk away from her now?

CHAPTER 9

THE NEXT EVENING BAILEY stood amid the bright chandeliers, surrounded by the slow, sweet strains of orchestral music, and watched the eleven other couples in attendance at Ford Grace's dinner party.

These dinner parties were always excellently timed to coincide with other parties being held through the night. Tonight the couples in attendance would leave to attend a fete held in honor of one of Hollywood's leading men, who coincidentally was staring in a major production by a studio that Stephen Menton-Squire and his wife, Josephine, held major interest in.

Bailey had never enjoyed the rounds of dinner parties, despite her mother's attempts to instill a sense of excitement about them. They were boring, the food was too rich, and the guests were too self-involved. She had never understood why her parents had enjoyed them so much.

After-dinner drinks were served in the large family room of Ford's mansion. The chandeliers overhead were dimmed. Tastefully arranged lamps were set in place around a large seating area, which faced a crackling fire. Conversation flowed as freely as the alcohol.

"Interesting group," John murmured from where they stood next to French doors that led to an evergreen garden beyond.

It was an interesting group. Every suspect left on the

short list that had been compiled was in attendance. Was it possible that Warbucks wasn't one man, but a group of four?

"There's Raymond," Bailey said softly as John drew her onto the dance floor. "Whoever or whatever Warbucks is, he's here tonight. All the major families are in attendance."

"As well as a few well known criminal elements," John pointed out rather sarcastically. "Amazing the clout a few good drugs will get you."

It was amazing the amount of drugs that actually flowed in a party such as this one.

"No one has yet approached me," she kept her voice low, her lips close to his neck as she spoke. "Considering I'm the one that chose the broker for this deal, and the one with the code needed, you would have thought I would be approached by now."

"He's waiting to see what you'll do when confronted with the choice," he told her. "No doubt he's well aware of the fact that the brokers will let you in on the secret. Better you have one of them arrested than one of his men."

"True," she murmured. "Still, not exactly the wisest course of action where I'm concerned."

"There's no way he can know that one of us isn't who we seem," he told her. "My background is solid, darling, stop worrying. I'll be fine."

"Maybe it wasn't you I was worried about." She smiled before nipping his neck with her teeth. She was rewarded by the tightening of his hand at her hip and the hardening of his cock against her lower stomach.

That was how she liked him. Hard for her, hungry for her.

"I'll make you pay for that comment later," he assured her.

"Excuse me, Mr. Vincent, but perhaps you should give the rest of us a chance here." The deep, dark male voice at her side had Bailey lifting her head from John's shoulder to encounter the snake-mean gaze of an American broker known for his penchant for sexual torture and terrorist connections.

Ralph Stanford was the only son of a very successful Texas rancher. He had married an international model whose extremely good looks had withered away within years of her association with him.

"Ralph." John stepped back with smooth grace as the other man laid his hand on Bailey's hip. She almost felt her skin crawl.

"We could skip the dance." She smiled tightly as he began to lead her around the room. "Why not get a drink and have a seat?"

He chuckled at the suggestion. "And miss a chance to rub against you as Vincent was doing? For shame, Bailey, knocking the rest of us off the playing field so easily isn't exactly sportsmanlike."

"I never claimed to be a sportsman, Ralph," she drawled, well aware of the fact that John was watching the other man closely.

Tall, almost gangly, with rather long brown hair and fierce hazel eyes, Ralph Stanford could have been handsome if he didn't work so hard at being the bastard he was. The corrupt soul of the man seemed to darken his expression, his eyes, even his smile.

"I would have thought you'd at least be required to be impartial," he stated with no small amount of malice. "Fucking one of the competitors just seems a bit like foul play to me."

"I didn't see a rule book with the job," she murmured. "I'm well aware of all your reputations. I'll make certain the best man gets the job." She'd already made her choice as far as she was concerned. Warbucks was wasting his time with this little game.

"We were assured of impartiality," he stated, a glimmer of anger showing in his eyes.

"And I'm being very impartial," she promised. "If you don't like how I do things, then perhaps you should take it up with your potential client. I only make the suggestion, I'm sure he'll make the final choice."

Personally she would have preferred to have been asked to take the position, but beggars couldn't be choosers. The past year had been spent trying to convince Warbucks that she wanted her chance to get back at the government that had betrayed her. He was giving her the chance. Now, she had to play the hand she was dealt until the time came to cash in on her own vengeance.

Ralph's thin lips nearly disappeared into his face as he pressed them together in irritation. "I'll be certain to do that," he informed her coldly. "Until then, Ms. Serborne, I'd watch my back if I were you. You could acquire several very dangerous enemies with this job."

He walked away from her, leaving her in the middle of the dance floor as though he had cast her aside. Bailey let a rueful smile tip her lips at the curious glances from the other dancers.

"Were you deserted, darling?" John's arm wrapped around her as he pulled her against the strength and heat of his body once again. "For shame. Some men just have no manners."

Delight spread through her body at the feel of herself against him. She hadn't realized just how good his body felt against her own. Even clothed in the finely cut evening suit, the hard muscle hidden from view, she could sense the strength and the heat of him.

"I considered it a favor," she laughed lightly as he led her from the dance floor.

"I'm certain you did," John agreed. "But while you were away, I received a very interesting message."

He slipped the paper into her hand. Turning against his body to use it as a shield, she opened the folded note and read it quickly.

Ms. Serborne's choice is noted. Not that it had been approved, simply that it had been noted.

Refolding it, she tucked it into her purse, noting the narrowing of his gaze as she did so.

"Well, it seems we are indeed being watched," she murmured.

"Did you doubt it?" he asked her.

"I never doubt it, I simply hoped to figure out who it was

rather quickly," she sighed, though she knew she should have known better.

"Several other brokers are here as well as Stanford," he noted. "Abbas and his former mistress are here."

Former mistress, her ass. She knew exactly who Catalina Lamont truly was. The same redhead posing as John's handler. A few cosmetic alterations to her face, a lighter rinse on her hair, and perhaps some padding at her breasts, but it was definitely the woman she had met as "Tehya" the morning before.

Catalina Lamont had been caught in the explosion with the real Jerric Abbas. They had literally died in each other's arms. After the explosion, and the revelation that they had survived, the two had very publicly, and vocally, broken off the affair. They were now rumored to be mere business associates, nothing more.

It seemed Tehya was playing a variety of roles and ones she appeared to be well adept at playing.

"We also have a European arms broker in the mix, Terrance Dupuis," she pointed out. "And a Saudi sheik who often brokers deals with the various terrorist groups. A Russian mafia figure arrived in Aspen earlier today as well." She shot him a sidelong glance. "Ivan Olav. He's gaining a name for himself with his negotiations on stolen Russian military weapons to terrorists."

It all came down to terrorism. The various factions and cells in an age of terror and political and religious factions vying for supremacy however they could acquire it.

"We have quite a little mix," John murmured. "And we're about to add to it. Greer is coming up to us."

Bailey turned as Raymond stepped closer, his expression unreadable.

"Bailey, could I drag you away from Mr. Vincent for a bit? Mary was feeling poorly and wanted to visit with you before we leave."

"Of course." Bailey turned to John and saw the edge of worry in his gaze. No one would have realized it, or would have recognized it. But the familiarity to Trent slammed inside her. The same light in his gaze, the way the shade darkened even as she watched him, the slightest tightened curve to his lips.

"I'll be back soon," she promised. "I saw Ian and Kira arrive earlier, perhaps you could take the opportunity to invite them to lunch tomorrow as we discussed."

She hadn't discussed it, but she knew Ian was part of the group that John was working with, as was Kira. It was time to draw the players together and force the answers she needed.

"Don't be long, sweetheart." He lowered his head, kissing her cheek gently. "You know how I worry."

He had every right to worry, as they both knew. Turning back to Raymond, she gave him a slight smile before moving with him across the ballroom.

It wasn't an odd request. Mary often had bouts of weakness and retired to a bedroom or sitting room where she visited with her closest friends during the parties she attended. Crowds often made her jittery anyway.

"This way." Raymond stepped into the foyer and led the way to a short hallway that led from it. "Ford was kind enough to loan us his sitting room."

Kind enough. "Ford" and "kind" weren't words that she thought would be synonymous with the man. He was kind to his sister, he loved his son. His grandchildren treasured him. But he had terrorized his wife and daughter, and, she suspected, had ordered their deaths.

He was the same man who had cried at her parents' funeral and went to their graves on the anniversary of their deaths. The man whose servants had gossiped that he'd nearly destroyed the inside of his home the day his wife and daughter had been buried.

He played a damned good game, she had to give him credit for that.

Opening the door to the sitting room, Raymond showed her inside, but no one was there. Bailey turned quickly to find Raymond closing the door before clicking the lock slowly into place.

"Where's Mary?" She gripped her purse loosely, her finger lying on the trigger of the weapon within the silk folds of the small bag.

"Stand down, Bailey." He shot her a disgusted look as he moved for the bar, his stooped shoulders rigid with either tension or anger, it was never easy to tell with Raymond. "I'm not going to have you killed while your lover is waiting in the ballroom."

"It wouldn't be the first time you arranged it." She didn't move her finger, but she relaxed marginally as he fixed himself a drink.

"Whisky and Coke?" He turned back to her, his heavy brow lifting in question as he gestured to the drinks.

Bailey nodded carefully. "What's this about, Raymond?"

He finished fixing the drinks before moving back to her. "Have a seat, my dear." He nodded to the chairs that sat in a small grouping to the side of the bar. "We need to talk."

"Do we now?" She took her drink and accepted the chair closest to her as she watched him curiously. "And what do we have to talk about that would require such a private setting?"

Sitting down, Raymond leaned back in his chair, sipped at his own whisky, and let a smile touch his lips. "You're rather good," he stated after long moments. "I have to admit, even I had my doubts that you would turn your back on your own country until you covered our tracks in Iraq as you did just before your retirement."

"You fucked up," she snapped. "Damn, Raymond, I never thought you would have let yourself get burned so easily."

She hadn't been certain he had been involved until now. All she had known was where the trail had led, and the prints that had been lifted from the secured Army barracks that had held the confiscated plutonium found in a hidden, underground vault beneath Saddam Hussein's castle.

"Very nearly," he agreed. "We were working within a tighter schedule than we had assumed. Unfortunately, the prize wasn't nearly as rich as we had assumed. The plutonium was unusable, I'm afraid. Saddam, it seemed, wasn't nearly as bright as he led some of us to assume."

Bailey sat back in her chair, forcing herself to keep her expression enigmatic, not to give up the fact that she had never truly been certain that Raymond was involved.

"Warbucks appreciated your efforts," he murmured, watching her, his gaze narrow, thoughtful.

"That's always nice to know." Leaning back herself, she watched him for long moments, seeing a side to Greer that she had only suspected existed. She had always known he was cold, hard, superior, but what he was showing now was a casual confidence, a self assurance that attested to the fact that he now had the upper hand.

"I haven't figured out exactly what you'd hoped to gain in the past years though," he finally sighed. "We've watched you, of course, especially since I took over the day-to-day operations of the ventures he partakes of. You've gone to great lengths to protect him. Why?"

Bailey crossed her knees, rested her elbow on them, and sipped at her whisky as she considered the question.

"Whoever he is, he's someone I've grown up with." She finally shrugged. "Father didn't completely fail in raising me, Raymond. I understand my duties to the men who have always watched my back. I looked after Warbucks's interests, and he kept me alive. It was a beneficial arrangement."

Raymond's lips quirked in amusement. "How did you know he kept you alive?

"Orion had a big mouth," she sniffed. "He warned me several times that he was being paid not to kill me and that one day there wouldn't be enough to walk away from the temptation." She grinned ruefully.

"You were rather a thorn in his side," he sighed. "We paid quite a bit of money to ensure he didn't harm you. Perhaps you could have done us a greater favor and let him be," he suggested.

Bailey leaned forward. "He killed my family. My cousins suffered at his hands. There was no amount of money that could have made me turn back. And evidently it wasn't too large a price to pay or Warbucks would have made the request that I back off."

"And would you have?" Raymond asked.

"Probably not. It would have been according to how strenuously he had asked." She lifted her glass to her lips and took a fortifying sip as he grinned back at her in amusement.

"That's rather what we assumed." He finally nodded. "Your past endeavors to protect him have always surprised him. Because of this, he's decided that perhaps you would make a worthy partner."

A worthy partner? Oh now, this was much more than she had ever hoped.

"He's looking for partners, is he?" Bailey let her surprise show, to do otherwise wouldn't have been in her best interests.

"Not just any partner," he assured her. "You have contacts, Bailey, many that I can only guess at, you've proven that over the years. But even more, you're his equal in ways that no one else could hope to be or to become."

"Is he looking for a partner or a wife?" she sniffed.

Raymond laughed, a low dark chuckle that sent a chill racing up her spine. "He's not in the market for a wife, my dear, though you'd make an excellent one. What he is in the market for are your invaluable services in several endeavors he'd like to undertake in the future. Your help with this one in particular is greatly appreciated."

Bailey sipped at the whisky again before setting her glass on the table. "No broker that he's contacted is going to take *CROSSFIRE* without a meeting first," she finally assured him. "Warbucks has so far managed to keep his identity a closely guarded secret. The days of that are at an end if he's not extremely careful this time."

Raymond nodded. "We've discussed this at length, which is one of the reasons we've given the choice of brokers into your safekeeping. You know the risks he'll be facing as well as the brokers most likely to secure the job and to secure it correctly. We ask that though it seems you have chosen a worthy lover, that you give due consideration to the other parties as well."

Bailey stared back at him, knowing how she appeared to him. Her gaze was flat and cool, assessing.

"It would have helped if I had known that I would be choosing from the parties concerned before they arrived," she stated.

Raymond tilted his head in agreement. "But in doing so we would have lost the element of surprise as well as our own strength in assessing your true intentions."

"In other words, you had everything in place to see if I went screaming back to the agency." She gave a light, amused little laugh. "Tell me, Raymond, did you ever regret your choice to work with Warbucks?"

"Never." His response was instant.

"Then I suspect, neither will I." She lifted her glass, finished her drink, then stared back at him questioningly. "Do we have any other business to conduct?"

Raymond arched his brows, his lips tugged into a reluctant smile.

"Very well, then, we'll discuss fees," she suggested. "The brokers you've chosen all charge a fifteen percent rate of the total sale. Though I'm certain a few will go a few points lower, Vincent won't. I wouldn't suggest using anyone willing to take a cut on their pay at this point."

"And your fee?" he asked.

"Partners don't charge a fee." She rose to her feet and stared down at him with the assured self confidence and feminine arrogance she had learned before leaving this world. "I expect to see Warbucks at the point of sale. I don't partner with men, or with women, that I don't know or can't put a face to."

A gleam of amused respect seemed to lighten his gaze. "I'll be certain to pass that along."

"Do that." She nodded. "Because it's non-negotiable. And I'll need his answer before the process goes much further. By the way, I'd drop Stanford if I were you."

"And why would I do that?" he asked, his gaze narrowing.

"Because he's an informant to several individuals within

certain law enforcement agencies, namely the FBI, when the price is right. And I would assume they would pay quite a hefty price for information on this sale. Discretion is called for at this time, I believe. I'd mark him off your list and send him home."

"We could kill him," he suggested.

"We could." She lifted her shoulder in complete uncon-cern. "But his death would raise questions. Better to wait until after the sale to do that. In the meantime I'd place a tail on him and see if he runs his mouth. It's always better to know who to watch out for than it is to kill the competition."

He rose slowly to his feet, a smile once again tugging at his lips. "I'll be sure to bring the matter to Warbucks's atten-tion. Until then, enjoy the party tonight. I'm sure I'll be in touch again soon."

"I look forward to it." She nodded briskly before turning and moving for the door.

Unlocking the door, she left the room without looking back, the sense of watchful eyes raising the hairs on the nape of her neck.

She was being watched, and not just by Raymond. Some-one had been listening in, looking in on that meeting. She had been dissected, every word, every expression, every shift of her body analyzed.

Warbucks had made his move and she had stated her conditions. Now, she hoped he accepted them, rather than having her killed as he did others who had had the temerity to make demands he didn't like.

Entering the hallway, she watched as John straightened from the wall, his arms falling from their crossed position against his chest. Eyes narrowed, his taut body filled with tension, he watched as she made her way to him.

"Mary okay?" he asked as his arm curled around her waist and they headed back into the foyer.

"Mary's fine." She felt the subtle shift of his body, the si-lent sign that he knew she wasn't merely talking about Ray-mond's wife. "You?" she asked. "Are Ian and Kira okay for lunch tomorrow?"

"They appreciate the invitation," he told her. "Ian has a bit of business he wanted to discuss anyway."

She certainly hoped so. After tonight, both John and Ian were going to come across with information, details and plans. She was not going to be kept in the dark at this stage of the game. Warbucks wasn't just testing her, he was seriously considering a partnership, which meant the stakes had risen in this little game.

"Good." She nodded thoughtfully, glancing around and wondering once again who was watching, who was listening.

"Are we ready to leave this little get-together yet?" John lowered his head to caress the shell of her ear sensually. "There's a light snow falling, a full moon. We could have the chauffeur drive us around for a while."

In other words they could discuss whatever had happened in her meeting with Raymond.

"That sounds nice." She turned her head, lifting it, and smiled as his lips settled on hers for a light, affectionate kiss. "Shall we say goodnight to our host?"

"Definitely."

Their host, Ford Grace, was thankfully just entering the marble foyer from the ballroom. John made their apologies with a thoroughly unapologetic male grin that he wanted to enjoy Bailey on a long romantic ride in the snow.

Bidding them a goodnight, he turned back to the couple who had followed him out as John collected her cloak and settled it over her shoulders.

The doorman opened the wide double doors, and to Bailey's delight, the snowfall was just as beautiful as John had proclaimed it. Large fluffy flakes fell in a slow-motion drift that gave an airy, gentle feel to the air around her. Lifting the hood of her cloak, she held on to John's arm as they stepped from the house, lifting her face to allow the cool weight of the ice crystals to melt against her flesh.

She needed the sense of innocence, of unhurried beauty that came with the night and the snow around them.

"It's beautiful," she whispered as her head lowered and her gaze was momentarily blinded.

Blinking, a sudden knowledge shattered into her brain at the same time as a red laser dot settled on her chest. Slow motion. She could feel every heartbeat as she cried out, pushing John aside at the same time that the blast of a rifle shattered the stillness of the night.

She felt him dragging her down, pushing her to the icy, snow-covered stones of the steps. Her hands slid across the surface, a burning sensation covering the tender flesh as the world around her seemed to erupt with sound.

Another sharp retort of gunfire shattered the night as screams filled the air. Other screams, feminine cries, and male shouts as John jerked her across the steps to the relative safety at the side of the limo.

"Stay here," he yelled at her as the chauffeur slid around the vehicle and shoved a lethal, black MPA Defender at John.

"Like hell." She grabbed at his arm as he moved to jump from her side. "You're not going anywhere. They'll be after you as well. Let Ford's men take care of it."

Those men were moving around the house now. Black-clad, faces impassive and dangerous, they tore across the yard toward the woods where the blasts had come from.

"Get her back in here." Raymond was suddenly at their sides, his expression furious as he grabbed John's arm. "She's safer in the house."

With the two men flanking her, she felt John's arm curl around her waist again, lifting her as he pulled her back up the steps and into the house.

They didn't pause. Leading the way, Raymond rushed them through the foyer and back through the hall to the small office he had taken Bailey to earlier.

Once the door was closed and locked behind them, John set her on her feet, and for the first time she caught a glimpse of his furious face. His eyes were like thunderclouds, his face set into a dangerous scowl as he turned on Raymond.

"What the fuck is going on here?" he snarled in Raymond's face.

Raymond, surprisingly, seemed to have paled. Concern marked his expression as his gaze roved quickly over her.

"I'm fine," she snapped, glaring back at him as he moved back marginally. "Damn. You two act like I've never been shot at before."

"Not here, not like this." Raymond shook his head in a quick, jerky motion. "You should have never been targeted."

"Well, she was," John snapped. "And I want to know why. Now, Raymond."

"We'll know why." Raymond stepped back as his cell phone rang. Jerking it from the pocket of his jacket, he flipped it open before pressing it to his ear and turning his back on them.

"She's fine," he said quickly. "I have her secure. Have they found the shooter yet?"

Bailey glanced at John as they listened to the conversation.

"How the hell am I supposed to know who it is?" he snapped suddenly. "My best guess would be one of the competitors. I warned you they wouldn't take kindly to losing out on the deal so quickly . . . Fine. I'll take care of it . . . Just let me know."

He disconnected the call before turning back to them.

"Professional brokers don't attempt assassination because they lost out on a deal," John snapped, his gaze thunderous as he rose to his feet, glowering back at Raymond. "If anything happens to her, Greer, you can bet your ass that the loss of reputation that your employer will suffer won't be easily regained. I'll make certain of it."

"Don't threaten me, Vincent," Raymond warned him, his voice deepening in anger. "This is a risk you take when you play the game. She knows it as well as you do."

"Like hell." John was in his face as Bailey rose to her feet.

She almost rolled her eyes at the testosterone filling the room as well as the male posturing going on here. As though they thought yelling at each other would actually solve the problem here.

"John, enough." Bailey stepped between them before the

confrontation could actually turn to blows. "Raymond." She turned to the other man. "Check Ralph Stanford's whereabouts. If he's in the mansion, then have your men question if he was here during the time of the shooting. I would bet he's your shooter."

Both men turned to her now.

"What the hell makes you think it was Stanford?" Raymond snarled.

She did roll her eyes at that. "You should check the reputations of the men you're considering." She shook her head. "Stanford doesn't like games of competition. He's prone to even the playing field with a bullet whenever possible."

"He was warned," Raymond growled.

"Perhaps not strenuously enough," she pointed out as she turned back to John. "Please inform the chauffeur that we're heading out, again. I'm not standing around here and waiting for the bloody little show sure to be played out if they actually manage to catch him."

"You're as stubborn and hard-headed as ever," Raymond accused her as she and John headed to the door.

"Yeah, yeah, yeah." She waved her hand over her shoulder. "Goodnight, Raymond, and please inform your boss that I haven't left happy tonight. He owes me."

CHAPTER 10

BAILEY LAY STILL AND SILENT in the bed when John entered the bedroom. She watched him, her gaze devouring him as he stood at the foot of the bed and stared back at her. There was a darkness to his expression that didn't make sense, a heavy brooding silence that surrounded him.

As though he was holding back some part of himself, unwilling to allow her to see it, or to see the implications of it.

He had been quiet since leaving the party. His entire demeanor had shifted, turning dark and dangerous in the wake of the attempt on her life.

"Did you call your buddies and inform them of tonight's events?" she asked him, careful to keep her tone casual.

"Not yet." There was a growl in his voice, an underlying tone of warning that she was certain she was going to ignore. As she watched him, her heart clenched, emotion welling inside her as she fought to hold back years' worth of grief and loneliness.

Staring at John now, the pieces of the puzzle that had been laid into place clicked. There was no suspicion, no coincidence. She knew. With the heart of a woman who had only loved once in her life, Bailey knew who her lover was, and she knew he would never reveal himself to her.

So many years alone. She remembered those first weeks after he had "died." She had existed in a place of such dark grief that she hadn't known if she could pull herself out of it. She had only just recovered from her parents' deaths. Hell, she hadn't even recovered, but Trent had helped her to focus, he had helped her to live again. Then he was gone.

And now he was back.

She had to blink back the tears at the feeling of betrayal, even as she wondered if she wouldn't have done the same. When he had informed her that Warbucks had been behind Trent's death, he had been telling her why he had left.

He'd had no choice. Warbucks wouldn't have rested until he was dead. There would have been no safety for him, no way for him to escape the powerful reach of the criminal whom no one could identify and therefore no one could watch or catch.

And Trent alone wouldn't have been in danger. Anyone he loved, anyone who could have been used as a weakness against him would have been in danger.

"Ralph Stanford was in the ballroom at the time of the shooting," he told her as he paused at the bottom of the bed. "Greer is still searching for him, but I'd say we've lost the trail for tonight."

"Whoever it is will try again," she stated. "There's a lot of money hiding in this deal. They won't like losing out so quickly."

The house party would pull the players into place. Whoever or whatever Warbucks was trying to maneuver, this would allow him to place everyone in a controlled area where he could watch and wait.

"Last year, Raymond Greer hosted this same party at the same time. It coincided with the sell of a list of agents working a delicate operation in Europe. Two weeks later, those agents were dead," he told her.

"Operation Seascape," she murmured. "The agents were in place to watch and track a terrorist cell that was using England's coast to smuggle in people, supplies, and weapons. They were waiting for the arrival of one of the organization's leading generals when that list was sold."

John nodded. "The general made it into England, and he

was lost after that. He's still on the move rather than neutralized as he should have been."

It wasn't the subject that was truly on both their minds. Bailey could feel the tension, the emotions that swirled in the air around them, that infused them, that burned inside her chest with the force of a wildfire.

Tears threatened to fall as her heart actually ached with the knowledge of everything she had lost, everything she couldn't have. She wanted to be in his arms, she ached to feel him against her, and yet a part of her refused to bend or to ask for what she needed most.

"I'm going to shower." He moved away from the bed and turned toward the bathroom. "We can talk later."

Later. There was always later.

She watched as he disappeared into the other room, noting the stress in his voice, in his shoulders. There were still so many things that she didn't know about him, that she hadn't known about him five years before.

They'd had so little time together. Not nearly enough time to know everything they needed to know about each other.

She lay in bed and stared at the ceiling as she heard the water in the shower turn on. She imagined him stepping beneath the spray, water pouring over his body.

She didn't want to imagine.

Flipping the blankets away from her body, she moved from the bed and on silent feet entered the bathroom.

Shedding the long T-shirt she had worn to bed, she watched through the shower doors as he put his head back and let the water run over his face and head. His dark blond hair plastered to his head and neck. Water streamed over his hard, muscular body, giving it a golden sheen that tempted her hands to touch.

She watched, simply watched as he kept his back to her, poured shampoo into his palm, then replaced the bottle before working the gel through the thick strands of his hair.

Thick, heavy lather streamed down his back and buttocks, sliding down like a lover's caress before slipping to the floor of the shower.

Bailey reached out, touched the glass as though she could actually feel the warmth of his flesh, and felt the need exploding inside her. Just to touch him, to taste him, to kiss the bronzed flesh and feel the flex of muscle beneath. To feel him against her, inside her.

She licked her lips as he stepped beneath the water once again, the suds flowing down his body, disintegrating beneath the force of the water as she slid the shower doors open.

He had known she was there. She watched him tense as she entered the cubicle and glimpsed the heavy length of his erection.

Warm flesh met her palm as she reached out and touched the flexing muscles of his back. His head lowered beneath the spray, one hand reaching out to brace against the wall.

"Wrong time, Bailey." His voice was rough, guttural. "Go back to bed, baby."

She paused, hearing something in his voice that she had never heard before, something she had only sensed in him a few times in Australia. Those had been the times he had simply disappeared a day or so before returning with his familiar, ever-present smile.

"Go back to bed?" She slid the door closed behind her, enclosing them in the heated moisture of the shower.

His other arm rose, his hand bracing against the shower wall as he drew in a hard, deep breath.

"Why would I want to go back to bed?" She let her fingers trail down the tense muscles of his back. "What are you hiding from me, John?"

She knew parts of what he was hiding. He was hiding who he was, what he was. He was hiding the man he had been, not just the man he was.

"Maybe I'm trying to protect you." His voice was a rough growl.

She stared at his profile. His eyes were closed, his thick, long lashes spiked from the water as he obviously fought for control.

"It's too late to try to protect me," she whispered as she

leaned her head against his shoulder. "And protection isn't what I want from you. It's not what I need from you."

Before she could finish, he moved. One arm snaked around her waist, jerking her in front of him before he pressed her back into the shower wall.

His expression was tight with lust, his gray eyes nearly black with it. The erection that pressed against her belly was steel-hard, iron-hot.

Water flowed around them now, washing between their bodies, over their shoulders, enclosing them in a heated world of hunger and need.

She reached out to the side of the shower cubicle, her fingers closing around the bottle of shower gel that sat on the narrow shelf.

"Don't, Bailey." His arm tightened around her back as she snagged the clean cloth hanging on a ring to the opposite side.

"Don't what?" she asked as she felt his cock throb against her lower belly. "Don't be here with you, John? Don't touch you when you can feel everything you want or need slipping through your fingers? Or are you just too damned scared to reach out and touch it?"

She poured the soap onto the washrag, staring into his eyes as she worked up the lather. There was something tormented, something desperate in his gaze as he stared down at her.

"Don't you want me, John?" she asked him then. "Did you ever truly want me?"

There was an edge of pain in her voice, a shadow of it haunting her gaze, as though she were asking not just about the present, but a past she couldn't know that they shared.

John stared down at her, feeling the dark, overwhelming lust that rose inside him for this woman. It was a hunger, a need he had always had to force himself to combat. From that first meeting with her, from their first kiss, it had risen inside him like a fire he couldn't control.

It had been like this before. There had been times in Australia that he'd had to simply walk away from her, to put distance between them as he fought the unfamiliar hunger that he couldn't name and sure as hell didn't understand.

It had grown worse, he admitted. Five years ago, it had been like an ache he couldn't put a name to. It wasn't an ache now; it was a tide rising inside him, filling every part of his senses and demanding more from him, from her, than he had ever expected.

Being someone else hadn't helped. He had thought it would. He had believed that coming here as John Vincent rather than Trent Daylen—working with her on his terms, with the knowledge between them that when the mission was over, they were over—would ease the desperation inside him.

It hadn't. In ways, he believed it had only made it worse. She looked at him as though she knew who he was, what he was, and he couldn't allow her to ever know.

Tightening his arm around her he jerked her to him, felt her indrawn breath, and watched the excitement that lit her green eyes.

"You should have stayed in the bed," he growled as he felt that hunger ripping through him.

"Why, so you could stay in control?" The rasp of the lathered cloth moved over his shoulder as her nipples stroked against his chest with every breath she took. They were silken fire against his chest, burning into his flesh with sensual destruction.

"Control can be a good thing." He proved his point by pressing a thigh between hers and pressing it tight against the heated mound of her sex.

He could feel the heated slide of her slick juices, feel them searing his skin as she drew in a hard, deep breath.

Taking the cloth from her hand, he shoved it back into its ring, then caught her wrists, placing them in one hand and holding them over her head.

"What are you fighting, John?" she whispered. "Me? Or yourself?"

He stared at her, wondering himself what he had always been fighting, even though he knew. He had fought the bonding, the need, the hunger that he was trying to hide from now. The certainty that life without this woman wasn't worth living.

It was the reason he had tried to leave her in her bed, alone and escape to the shower. To hide from himself. To escape the need to give her more than he had thought he had to give to any woman.

"You don't know what you're doing to me, Bailey," he rasped. "You don't know what you're doing to both of us."

She was breathing heavily, her breasts rising and falling against his chest as he moved back from her slowly. But not to let her go. Hell no. There was no letting her go now.

"What am I doing to us, John?" Her soap-slick hands flexed within his grip as her hips arched to press his cock tighter against her belly.

"Destroying us?" he asked her softly, because he knew that was exactly what she was doing. Destroying them, one soft caress, one heated kiss at a time until he could feel his soul unraveling.

"Destroying us? How can touching you destroy us worse than this situation could?"

The question of the ages, a question he couldn't answer because no other thought could penetrate the hunger growing inside him.

His head dipped, his lips taking hers in a kiss that only fueled the flames tearing through him. Looping her arms around his neck, he gripped the back of her head to hold her in place and fought himself, fought the impulses tearing through him.

It was like fighting a demon inside his soul. It refused to allow him any peace, refused to release him.

And this was the part of himself that he hadn't wanted her to see. The dominance, the hunger, the sheer desperation for her touch that ruled his every sense.

"Damn you, I warned you not to be here," he growled, fighting back the hard rumble in his voice, a flavor of an accent that he didn't dare allow her to hear.

Throwing his head back he gripped her hair, moved her lips to his chest, and fought back the compulsion to simply take her.

Her hands caressed from his neck to his chest, then to his abdomen. The muscles of his stomach clenched almost violently at the feel of her silken fingertips tickling over them, moving lower.

Breathing in roughly, he stared down at her now, watching as he guided her head, watching her go lower, her swollen lips working over his chest, brushing his hard male nipples before angling to his abs.

As though she moved in slow motion, each caress took forever and seared into his soul as he watched her. Her lashes lifted, beaded with water that made her green eyes brighter, more brilliant than ever before.

"You know what I want," he groaned. "Give it to me, Bailey."

His fingers fisted in her hair as he pressed her lower and felt her hot breath against the swollen crest of his cock. Her fingers gripped the shaft and held it along his lower belly.

Violent sensations of pleasure racked him at the feel of her moist breath, the knowledge that her lips were so close, that pleasure was just a breath away.

She stared up at him, watching him, snaring his will with her gaze as her head moved lower, her lips parted, and the sweet, heated caress of her mouth struck a bolt of ecstasy hard and deep inside the taut sac of his balls.

"Fuck." One hand slapped against the tile shower wall as he blinked water from his eyes. "Suck me."

Her lips closed over the brutally sensitive crown as her tongue swiped over it, caressed it and stole his mind. He could barely maintain a semblance of control, so fiercely did the pleasure resound inside him.

God help him. He needed her in ways that he didn't understand himself. He needed to possess her, to own her sexuality, her sensuality. Her heart.

His hips jerked, driving the iron-hard crest deeper into

her mouth as her cheeks began to flex and the suckling motion of her mouth sent white-hot flares of sensation tearing through his senses.

There was nothing else quite like Bailey's lips at his cock, sucking him into her mouth, taking him with an intimacy, a silent promise that weakened any resolve he had to hold himself distant from her.

He could do nothing but let the lust have its way now. She stripped him of control. She had followed him when he had warned her to stay away. She had continued touching him when he had warned her she might be getting more than she was bargaining for.

Need was like a ravening beast inside him now. It was a hunger he couldn't hold back.

He watched as she took the head of his cock into her mouth, laved it with her tongue, sucked him deep within her hot little mouth.

His hand clenched tighter in her hair as he fought to hold back the impulse to spill his release in that moment. God knew he wanted to enjoy this. The feel of her sweet mouth, so hot and snug as she sucked at the crown of his cock.

The sight of her, lashes half closed, lips reddened from sucking at him; the sight of his cock thrusting shallowly between her lips. It was the most erotic vision of his life. Bailey had the ability to do that. To make each encounter with her more erotic than the one before.

Fire whipped over his nerve endings, surrounding his cock and tightening in his testicles. The muscles of his thighs were so tight they ached, his arms bulging as he fought to hold on to just enough control to enjoy this a few moments longer.

To feel her mouth suckling him, her silken palm cupping his balls as she moaned against his overly sensitive flesh.

It was destroying him. He watched the shallow thrusts he made between her lips, the way her expression shifted, the pleasure on her face.

"Sweet Bailey," he groaned as her tongue swiped over his dick. "Ah love, you're destroying my control."

She was destroying him, inside and out. He couldn't hold

on. He could feel the need boiling in his veins, his cum rising through his cock.

He couldn't hold on. His fingers clenched tighter in her hair, his teeth clenched, and before he could pull back, a shattered groan tore from his throat.

His release tore from him. He felt it shoot from the tip of his cock, filling the inside of her hot mouth as he felt her take him, swallowing the essence of him. He groaned her name, not caring how it sounded or what it gave away.

All he cared about was Bailey and the arousal that kept him brutally hard. As her tongue gave another long, delicious lick over the head of his cock, he pulled back, jerked her to her feet, and lifted her to him.

Bailey cried out in surprise and pleasure as she was lifted against John's chest. His head lowered, his mouth covering a hard, sensitive nipple before sucking it into his mouth. Wicked hot and brutally ecstatic, each hard draw of his mouth sent shards of sensation striking through her womb before it wrapped tightly around her swollen clit.

She could feel each stroke of his tongue over her nipple, first one, then the other, as he kept the firm, suckling pressure on the tip.

Her head fell back on her shoulders as she gripped his hair and fought to hold on. To keep him to her, just for a little while. To make enough memories to hold her through the rest of her life, to keep her warm at night when he was gone again.

"Fucking beautiful," he groaned as his head lifted.

Pressing her back against the shower wall, Bailey felt his lips move lower. She felt his tongue between her breasts, running down her belly. As he dropped to his knees in front of her and spread her thighs, his lips moving to the swollen, distended bud of her clit, Bailey felt her senses exploding.

Heated water showered around them as the hot warmth of his mouth surrounded her clit.

His tongue was velvet heat as it licked around the swollen bud, worked it against the underside, and laved it with hungry strokes.

He kissed it. Sucked it inside, then licked again and again, until Bailey was fighting to hold back her screams, pleas that he give her what she needed, that he sent her spinning into the star-studded void she could feel awaiting her.

"John!" His name was a shattered cry on her lips as his tongue stroked, his lips sucked. His fingers moved between her thighs, two sliding high and deep, filling her, working inside her with tight, heavy strokes.

He stretched her, burned her as he filled her. Bailey spread her thighs wider, panted his name, and fought to breathe just enough to make sense of the sensations tearing through her.

It hadn't been like this before. It had never been this hot, this vibrant before and she found herself at once frightened and exhilarated by the sensations tearing through her.

Excitement wound in her chest. Blood thundered through her veins. Pleasure tore through her senses.

She couldn't hold on to her senses like this. Was she supposed to? Was anything supposed to be this good, this hot?

Pleasure wound inside her, tightening in her womb, her pussy, swelling her clit and sending pulses of sharp electric sensation tearing through her.

Bailey felt her hands latch into his hair, her nails digging into his scalp as the tension escalated, tightened, and exploded into a starburst of rapture so sharp and intense that her knees weakened, her legs collapsed.

And he was there. John caught her, held her close to him, lifted her as he wrapped her legs around his hips and pressed the heavy tip of his cock into the violently sensitive tissue beyond.

"Ah yes." Her lips moved to his shoulder, his throat. "Oh God, John. Like this. Just like this."

Hard and deep. There was no control left for either of them. His hands cupped her rear, his fingers clenched there as he began to thrust inside her. His groans and her cries filled the shower, wrapped around them, bound them.

She could feel the bond as it began to tighten, felt it settle inside her, tighten through her as her orgasm rushed over her again.

She tightened around his thrusting flesh. Her legs gripped him harder, her fingers dug into his hair and her back arched as she felt his lips at her neck. And she felt his release. Unbidden, unsheathed, his cock throbbed, swelled, then sent his seed spurting deep and hot inside her.

Bailey's eyes flared open to stare into his eyes. Feeling the last pulses of his release, the last echoes of her orgasm, their gazes connected, held and they both stared into the face of reality.

It wasn't the release, it wasn't that she wasn't protected, because she was. Bailey didn't leave her protection in any man's hands. It was the knowledge that this intimacy had never been shared with another. Not even Trent.

She had felt this, known this. She had never given this to another man, until now.

John held something Trent hadn't.

Her soul.

CHAPTER 11

MARY GREER'S MOUNTAIN cabin was a twenty-five-room three-story mansion set in a pristine valley surrounded by aspen, oak and huge fir trees. A large lake bordered one side of the property while stables and a snowmobile shelter bordered the other. A huge evergreen garden maze stretched out behind the house, while the front and side were reserved for the driveway and a multicar garage.

Limos were lining up in the huge circular driveway as the Serborne vehicle pulled in. Chauffeurs, butlers and housemen were carting luggage into the house and following the directions of Mary's excellent staff in the placement of guests and their possessions.

There were more than two dozen couples attending. Invitations were much sought after and prized, even among the social elite who spent most of their winter in Aspen.

Dressed in winter-white cashmere pants, sweater and long coat, Bailey allowed John to help her out of the limo two days later as she stared up at the imposing structure overlooking them and wondered once again whatever possessed these people to live their lives as they did.

Bailey would be bored silly within two weeks and she knew it. A life of balls, parties, social luncheons, and shopping had never been her thing, as she'd proved when she left home just after she turned eighteen.

It had been her mother's life, though, as well as that of her mother's friends. They had lived for the next party, the endless rush of social functions and were crushed if invitations to their own weren't accepted.

Security had been doubled from previous years, Raymond had assured her on the phone that morning. Every precaution had been taken to make certain that there would be no risk to her.

Bailey was beginning to believe that Raymond was truly upset over the attempt to kill her the week before. He had placed a security team outside her cabin, while inside both John and his bodyguard Travis ensured her protection.

Living under the constraints of that "protection" was starting to get on her nerves. She wasn't a hare-brained debutante, she had assured them. She knew how to take care of herself.

"Nice place," John commented as he let his hand linger at the small of her back to lead her to the open double doors to the marble foyer of the cabin.

"Do you think so?" she muttered. "I always felt it was a bit ostentatious. Too large and much too glitzy. It's the one piece of property that Mary owns that causes me to question her taste."

No one else heard the muttered insult, though John doubted Bailey would care if it had been. It was rather a known fact that Bailey shared housing and clothing tastes with few other people.

He could hear something more in her voice, though, a sense of disappointment, a soul-deep ache as she stared at the glittering, glitzy dwelling and those who were entering it.

Chauffeurs and house staff called back and forth. Luggage by the ton was being hauled in for a two-week stay, and many of the twenty-four guests had retreated to the ballroom and the buffet and drinks provided there.

"Ms. Serborne. Mr. Vincent." Raymond and Mary's butler met them at the door. "The Greers have requested your presence in a private gathering in the library. If you'll follow me."

Nose in the air, highbrow, and definitely status-conscious, the middle-aged gentleman led the way through the foyer to a marble-floored hall that in turn led to another wing of the house.

"Mr and Mrs. Greer." The butler opened the door with a flourish before addressing his employers. "Ms. Serborne and Mr. Vincent."

John placed his hand on Bailey's back as they entered, felt the fine tension that held her muscles tight, and ached for her. She hated Raymond Greer. There hadn't been a single noted confrontation between the two when they had been in the agency that had ended with anything less than animosity. She had known her former boss was on the take. Had known it, and had been unable to do anything about it.

Until now. But the road to the final goal was paved with heartache and pain for her. He had seen it in her eyes before their arrival, and he felt it now emanating from her body.

"Bailey, John." Dressed in black silk pants and a matching black sweater, Raymond rose from where he sat with his wife in front of the fireplace and approached them with a friendly smile.

"Greer." John accepted a hearty handshake and watched as Raymond turned to Bailey, gripped her shoulders, and gave her a warm kiss to the cheek.

A smile curled Bailey's lips, even sparkled in her eyes, but it was no more than a testament to how hard she was reaching inside herself to carry on the charade.

"Call me Raymond, John." Raymond clapped him on the shoulder as he turned back to Bailey. "Let me get you a drink. What are you having?"

Bailey's voice was soft, gentle, so sweet it was almost enough to give him a toothache. Raymond's smile was pure charm on a weasel's face as he turned back to John. The illusion the man presented was almost amusing.

Requesting a straight whiskey, he kept his hand at Bailey's back as Raymond motioned them to the small gathering. Ford Grace and his ex-model mistress Rose sat on a love seat parallel to the fireplace. Mary sat on the love seat directly in front, which left another free for Bailey and John.

"Wagner." Ford nodded back at Bailey almost hesitantly.

"It will be good to see him," Bailey stated. "I haven't had much time to spend with old friends."

Ford nodded. "I'm glad to see you survived the last party well," there was a hint of concern in his gaze. "I worried your past would follow you when you left the agency."

Ford glanced at Raymond, then back to Bailey. "Your father worried constantly that one day you wouldn't return home," he stated as Raymond handed them their drinks.

Bailey stared back at Ford, hiding the hatred that welled inside her, that threatened to damage the goal she had kept in the forefront of her mind for so long.

She hated the sincerity he faked so easily. The concern that darkened his gaze and gave his expression the appearance of affection. She wanted to scream at him, to rage over the elaborate game he was playing and force him to admit to being the cold-hearted son of a bitch that she knew he was.

"If my past is returning to haunt me, then I'm certain I'll have it dealt with soon," she assured Ford before glancing at John with the confidence of a woman who knows her lover is taking care of the matter as they settled on the love seat in front of Mary.

"I've hired extra security staff for the party, dear," Mary expressed, her concern genuine. "We've had to do this several times when Ray's enemies have found him as well. It's a shame that serving your country comes with such risks right when you should be able to relax and enjoy your lives."

"It would be far easier to tolerate if the country you risked your life for gave a damn," Ford injected smoothly, critically. "I've not seen a time that Raymond's life was in danger that the agency gave a damn."

Unfortunately that was true. Bailey wished she could argue the fact that more was done to protect retired agents, but she knew her argument would sound hollow at best. Besides, arguing for her country would do very little to engender the trust she needed to draw Warbucks further into this little partnership.

"The agency barely gives a damn when you're active," she lied. She knew better. She knew the extremes that went into trying to protect agents, both active as well as retired.

"A shame," Mary sighed, her delicate face creased in sympathy.

"Raymond, I believe Rose and I will see our way to our room now." Surprisingly, Ford rose to his feet and extended his hand to his mistress as she joined him.

"And I believe I will as well." Mary lifted her hand to Raymond, allowing him to help her from her seat. "I'm certain you and Bailey would like to discuss old times and those tales simply give me nightmares." She grimaced.

Living those times still had the power to give Bailey nightmares.

Saying goodbye to Mary, Bailey restrained her own desire to escape to the privacy of her room with John. The sitting room felt stifling, the very air within it heavy with deceit.

"Bailey, would you mind if I talk to John alone for a bit now?" Raymond surprised her with the request. "I'd like to discuss a few security details with him, if you don't mind."

She narrowed her gaze at him. "John and I are partners, Raymond," she reminded him coolly.

"And I understand that clearly." He nodded. "Unfortunately, your choice of broker is going to have to prove himself to me, as well as to Warbucks, to gain approval, Bailey. John won't be accepted instantly simply because he's the one you chose."

Of course, it couldn't be that simple, could it?

Staring back at Raymond, her gaze cold, she rose slowly to her feet. "Very well. I'll leave you two to discuss whatever manly things you have to discuss without me."

Raymond appeared a little too amused by her statement. Comedy wasn't exactly her forte, so she wasn't a bit pleased by it.

"We do appreciate your patience with us, my dear," Raymond drawled. "I promise I won't keep him long."

John had to restrain a smile as Bailey shot him a worried look from beneath her lashes. To give her credit, she didn't argue further. Rather she donned the polite, femininely arrogant look that made him hotter than hell before she turned and left the room.

He knew the interrogation that would come later. She didn't like being cut from any phase of this operation. The fact that she hadn't been involved during his meetings with the team pissed her off enough. Now, he was going to have to deal with her anger toward Raymond. And she did know how to get pissed at the other man.

As the door closed behind her, Raymond followed and locked it quietly before turning back to John.

"You're taking control of things nicely," John told the other man as he stared around the sitting room. "I hope your marriage isn't too constraining."

"My marriage is the one thing in this farce that gives me any pleasure." Raymond grimaced as he moved back to his drink and tossed it back, then narrowed his eyes on John. "Does Bailey suspect my involvement with the unit?"

John shook his head. "Not at all. Does Warbucks suspect your involvement?"

Raymond gave a hard shake to his head as he rubbed his hand over his face and breathed out roughly. "It's a dangerous game we're playing here, John."

"But a necessary one," John murmured. "How close have you gotten?"

"His second in command is Myron Falks, just as we suspected," Raymond answered him. "I haven't pieced together the rest of the group yet, though."

"It's a group rather than an individual, then?" John probed.

Raymond shook his head again. "At this point, I don't know. I've managed to move in close enough in the past years that Myron trusts me implicitly with everything but Warbucks's identity. I'm wondering if he even knows himself. As you know, I've identified several of Ford Grace's security personnel, as well as at least one of Waterstone's and Claymore's. There's no way to track exactly who it is, because no one singularity ties any of the men."

"But he trusts you enough to interview the broker involved with this sale," John stated.

Raymond nodded. "I was put in charge of brokers three years ago, as you know, until Warbucks focused on Bailey. I've tried to make certain I've shown no preference for any one broker. Several times it's been noted that each transaction you've overseen has been equated with greater financial benefits as well as discretion. Jerric Abbas, as you also know, despite his lack of expertise in the area, was running a close second."

John nodded. Raymond was unaware that Micah Sloane was now Jerric Abbas, and part of the unit. John didn't always support Jordan's decisions on keeping relevant information from the players involved in missions, but in this case he agreed.

If Bailey knew Raymond was a part of the mission, then she would spend the majority of her time trying to prove he was betraying them. Raymond wasn't betraying them. He had too much to lose, and his hatred for Warbucks matched Bailey's.

"Just ensure that I get the contract on this," he told Raymond as he rose to his feet. "Let's make certain we get him this time, Raymond. We may not get another chance."

Raymond rose to his feet with a sharp nod. "You and Bailey seem fairly close. Will she end up hurt when this is over?"

Was there any way any of them could end up not hurt? John wondered.

"I'll worry about Bailey," he informed Raymond. "You worry about your end."

"Is she still determined that Grace is Warbucks?"

"What are the chances that Ford Grace is involved with this?" John asked, his eyes narrowing on the other man.

Raymond breathed out roughly. "About as high as the

chances any of the other men we're looking at are. Warbucks is well hidden, John. He's surrounded himself with men who guard his identity like junkyard dogs. Our only chance to find him out is full disclosure on this deal. Thankfully, it's something Jerric Abbas seems to be demanding as well. The sensitivity of the item, the amount of money involved in the transaction and the risk factor are all things Warbucks will have to look at as he makes his decision."

"Make certain Myron understands that neither myself, Bailey, nor Abbas will accept anyone but Warbucks," John told him as he headed to the door. "Let's not fuck this up at this stage of the game."

"Now." John leaned forward, feeling the rage he had been trying to contain for a week now bubbling to the surface. "Who tried to kill Bailey?"

"God, I don't know." Raymond grimaced as he dragged his fingers through his hair, frustration lining his expression.

John could see the concern that marked the other man's face and for just a second, fear for Bailey flashed in his eyes. She thought Raymond held her in such contempt, that his attitude toward her had been one of dislike.

It was an impression Raymond had worked to convince Bailey and others of, but the fact was, the other man held her in very high regard. Most people who truly knew Bailey did care for her.

"Warbucks went through the roof with that attack," Raymond continued. "Surprisingly, I believe I heard a note of fear in his tone during the conversations we've had. For the first time he hasn't gone through Falks, but came straight to me instead." His gaze turned thoughtful. "A few times, John, I could have sworn I recognized his voice."

They had known going in that whoever Warbucks was, he was a member of this particular society. Raymond had worked these past years to infiltrate and work himself into a position of trust to learn the identity of the traitor.

"Not enough to be sure, though?" John asked.

Raymond shook his head. "Just enough to make me crazy

trying to figure out who it could be. He has Falks running himself ragged trying to secure Bailey while still working for his employer. I think Falks is a man ready to break. Too many years of trying to please too many masters maybe."

"That will do it to you," John sighed.

"He's a scared man, John," Raymond stated thoughtfully. "Warbucks keeps Falks with Waterstone, me with Ford, and several other men with the other families in security positions to draw suspicion from him. But in doing so, over the years I've noticed that the strain is beginning to show on the men he's using. They can't quit, or he'll kill them. Mess up and they die. They're stuck between a dagger and a grenade and they know it."

"Interesting analogy," John grunted. "Makes sense though. His men are divided."

"Exactly." Raymond nodded before glancing at the clock above the fireplace. "We better cut this short. Falks will be arriving soon and I'm supposed to be available as soon as he arrives."

Of course, Myron Falks would want an update as soon as possible, John thought as he rose to his feet and headed to the door.

"Keep me updated," he ordered. "I want to know what's going on immediately.

Raymond nodded before moving to the doors and opening them with a flourish. The arrogant persona was back the second he gripped the doorknobs. Nose high, his expression pinched and self-aware, he stared down his nose at John.

"It's been a pleasure getting to know you, Mr. Vincent," he expressed in stilted tones. "And it's a pleasure to know our lovely Bailey will be so well taken care of."

Several couples were milling in the hallway as they shook hands. John moved from the room to find his lover. At least two of the men standing in the hallway were on the unit's suspect list: Stephen Menton-Squire and Samuel Waterstone. Both men had the connections, the background and the ability to acquire the weapons now coming up for auction.

He nodded to the couples as he moved past, aware that behind him guests were moving toward Raymond, greeting him in friendly tones.

Raymond had settled into this society nicely since the operation that had placed him in sight of Mary Altman six years before. The widow had been ripe for a love interest, but had made a point of steering clear of any man her brother set before her. She had expressed an interest in dangerous men. In men who walked a darker path than those she knew. Raymond had been placed in her path. They had married a year later.

Not that John didn't see genuine affection between the couple. He did. And Raymond had a flair for business that had cemented Mary's interest in him.

Raymond had been more than a CIA agent, even then. He had been part of a very select group of covert Internal Affairs agents searching for a link between Warbucks and the CIA. Bailey had been under suspicion immediately. It was a suspicion that had been quickly terminated and later used to benefit the unit. Her refusal to pull back on Orion had worked perfectly. It had led to her disenchantment with the agency as well as the renewed inner-agency suspicion that she was indeed working for or with Warbucks.

She was their ace in the hole, but in ways, she would be to Warbucks as well. Because of her close association with all the men involved, as well as her contacts, it was hard for her to suspect anyone outside Ford Grace.

Moving to the opened doors of the ballroom, he caught sight of Bailey at the other end, engrossed in conversation with Kira and Ian Richards.

"Ah, Mr. Vincent. There you are. It seems you and Bailey brought a bit of excitement into our little group."

If you call attempted murder excitement, John thought.

John turned to face Samuel Waterstone and Ronald Claymore. Claymore was watching Bailey broodingly. Turning back to John he glared at him in disapproval.

"How so, Mr. Waterstone?" he asked curiously.

Samuel winked back at him subtly. "Did you think you

could sweep one of our heiresses off her feet without an investigation? A very thorough investigation, I might add. Then the attempt to kill her last week? Be careful son, we would not appreciate losing her."

John arched his brow. "Neither would I."

"He's a smart boy," Ronald commented with a hint of ire to the other man. "It's not as though Bailey really gives a damn what we think, anyway."

John's brow arched in question. "Should she?"

"You're a bit unsavory, Vincent," Samuel stated. "Not exactly unacceptable, though you'll need a bit of polishing if you know what I mean. We can't allow one of our group to be caught up in anything illegal, you understand. *Discretion* is always the key word. And only then if you protect what you're responsible for."

"Discretion?" John asked. "You mean as discreet as you and good ol' Stephen here were in that trade scandal last year?"

Ronald Claymore glowered, though Samuel Waterstone grinned in pride. "Well, a bit more discreet, but in all fairness we did skate by that one fairly well."

The US government had nearly brought the two men to trial for their involvement in trading delicate national secrets with China. The charges had been dropped for lack of evidence, and the two men had retained their government contracts with their companies simply because they'd been too powerful to warrant pulling them. The pressure that had been brought to bear on several senators, as well as the president himself, had been extreme.

"I'll be certain to be just as discreet," John murmured. "Though I'm not certain how my business dealings could come under the same scrutiny."

His cover had always remained cohesive: He was an international negotiator between American and foreign interests in various business dealings. The less savory side he was always careful to deny, even to those who knew the truth.

Samuel grinned at his response. "Sticking to your story, huh? My contacts say you're a bit more extreme than you let on. That perhaps you negotiate more than international contracts. I could use a man like you. We should talk business sometime."

"Really?" John murmured. "Business in what fashion?"

Samuel glanced around in concern.

"The kind of business that isn't discussed in company," Ronald grunted with a fierce frown. "Let's say Samuel and I have a few business dealings that could require a bit of a rogue. The sort of rogue we understand you can be."

John stared back at them as though assessing his chances of a true business deal. This weekend was designed for Warbucks to size up the buyers he was considering. John and Abbas were there, obviously the two major players in the running. He'd expected to be contacted, though he doubted these two men were going to hand over information on the *CROSSFIRE* contract.

"I'm more than happy to discuss business at your convenience," he stated. "You can contact my assistant for scheduling."

Samuel's brows lowered at the information. "There's no sense in dragging anyone else in on this," he argued. "We can deal with this among just us men. No sense in dragging in that female. She demands too much information."

Which meant they had already been in contact with Tehya at one time or another.

"That's an assistant's job," he reminded them.

"Could be dangerous considering your line of business," Samuel suggested quietly. "For you and her. Possibly for Bailey."

The thinly veiled warning had John smiling back at them coldly.

"Your influence and power don't extend to my world, Samuel," he stated calmly, his tone dangerously quiet. "Remember that before you make the mistake of threatening me, my assistant, or my lover. It could be a fatal mistake on your part."

He turned his back on both of them, found Bailey again and headed across the ballroom to join her. He didn't move angrily; he showed no visible signs that he was within seconds of turning this little house party into a brawl.

He had his reputation, just as Warbucks did. His reputation involved taking no bullshit, no threats, no matter the client. He'd stared down men more dangerous than Warbucks had proven himself to be, many times over. Men who would rather shoot him in the back than look at him. And he'd survived it.

Warbucks didn't trust or deal with men who catered to his ego. He liked a challenge. He enjoyed forcing those he felt beneath him to recognize that he was the superior being.

It was a readily known fact that John considered no one but God as his superior. He wasn't a humble man and he didn't pretend to be.

"John, we were getting ready to send a search party out for you," Kira laughed as he moved in behind Bailey. "Raymond's known for holding interesting guests for hours at a time in that library of his."

He moved against Bailey, let his arm circle her waist, pulled her to him, and tucked her against him.

"Raymond enjoys retelling his former adventures." John grinned easily. "And I enjoy listening."

"Raymond led such an exciting life." Mary Greer sighed in delight. "And he gave it up to spend his days with me." It was obvious she was extremely proud of her husband.

"At least he talks about something other than stock interests and the falling dollar," Janice drawled with an air of boredom. "Which are the only tall tales I get to hear."

As the group laughed, John lowered his head to Bailey's ear.

"Are you ready to retire to our room with me?" he asked her, though he was pretty damned certain she was more than ready.

"Surely you aren't stealing our girl away from us so soon, Mr. Vincent?" Mary smiled with no small amount of affection as she stared back at Bailey. "It's so rare I get to spend much time with her."

"I'm sorry, Mrs. Greer," he apologized with what he

hoped was the greatest sincerity. "She's not been sleeping well this last week and I thought she'd enjoy a nap."

"Oh dear, yes." A frown instantly marred Mary's expression as she leaned closer, her arms going around Bailey. "Go rest, dear. We'll see you at tonight's party."

Bailey accepted Mary's hug and returned it with one of her own as she shot John a reproving look. It really wasn't nice to lie to such a gentle creature, she thought with a flare of amusement. Trust John to be the one to do it. He was smooth, sincere, and completely unrepentant.

Accepting his hand, she allowed him to lead her from the ballroom and the buffet that had been set up there. It wasn't as though she had been able to eat while he had been locked in the sitting room with Raymond.

She was just about fed up with being locked out of meetings. John slipped off while she was asleep to meet with his team, Raymond so very politely ordered her to leave the room. As though she were the little woman without a brain in her head to protect herself.

"I'm not happy with you," she stated with a soft whisper as they moved up the stairs.

"Should I be upset?" She didn't like the vein of amusement in his tone either.

"You should be scared," she informed him. "Very scared."

Rubbing his fingertips against the small of her back, his head lowered closer to her ear as they reach the landing. "I'm trembling in my briefs."

Damn him, he didn't wear briefs and they both knew it. He was blissfully naked beneath those jeans he was wearing.

"You should be," she muttered as they reached their bedroom door.

Handing him the key, she waited until he unlocked the door, then with a smile, stepped back so he could precede her inside.

The laughing glance he shot her was wicked, sexy, and filled with sexual intent.

She'd learned in the past week that he could be incredibly sexual, even more so than she had imagined. It never failed to amaze her just how inventive he could get, how hot he could make her while he was doing it.

Suddenly, the need to be alone with him was like a fever in her blood. The minute they were inside and the room was swept, she had half a mind to demand what she wanted. All of him. Inside her, around her, burying himself deep between her thighs while the world around them simply faded away.

Just a few more seconds, she thought. Just a little longer, and then she could escape the games, the lies and the reality she knew she was going to have to face soon.

CHAPTER 12

AS THEY STEPPED THROUGH the bedroom door, Bailey came to a stop and stared at their visitor as John locked the door behind them.

Tehya was now in disguise as Catalina Lamont, Jerric Abbas's ex-lover and partner. Her red-gold hair was now a dark, stunning brown, thicker and longer, falling nearly to the middle of her back. Her eyes were a dark chocolate brown, her eyebrows more defined, her cheekbones higher and sharper, her lips a shade plumper.

Dressed in a snug bronze silk dress that barely passed her thighs, with matching heels, she looked like the seductive, dangerous woman she was, both as Catalina and as Tehya.

"Room's clear." Tehya held up the small electronic bug sweeper and waggled it in her hand as she propped the other hand on her hip and stared at them with raised brows. "I would have expected them to at least leave one bug. I mean, hell, how else are they supposed to know what the two of you are up to?"

"Give them time," Bailey snorted as she stepped out of her high heels and moved to the small seating area where a white-noise box was activated. The small black box emitted a low-level static that would interfere with most listening devices.

"Give you time to get lazy?" Tehya harrumphed as she

took the chair across from the love seat that Bailey was sitting in. "John doesn't get lazy."

"No. John does get irritated, though," he stated.

Bailey glanced up at him, seeing the irritation that did fill his gaze now.

"Samuel and Ronald?" she asked.

He gave a brief, hard nod before relating their conversation to her and Tehya.

Bailey watched as he spoke and wondered if Warbucks would have approached him so blatantly.

"They approached Jerric in a similar manner," Tehya revealed when he finished. "They could be fishing to see who snaps up the job faster."

Bailey shook her head. "It would be a test, no more because I still have to submit my choice. It follows Warbucks's methods, though. He's been known to approach potential brokers with other jobs, especially new ones to test them on reliability as well as their ability to avoid any traps he sets for them."

"We're not playing that game here," John stated as she watched him shed the jacket he had worn and lay it across the back of the love seat. "Jerric can play the games if he feels the need to. In the end Warbucks will go with Bailey's choice."

Bailey stared at him, seeing the confidence and lack of concern in his expression.

"How can we be certain?" she asked. "Warbucks always tests the brokers he has lined up. If they don't play the games, then they're out of the running for the job."

John shook his head. "I have you. As you stated, you have yet to submit your choice, but all the players here know you'll choose your lover."

"I expect Raymond or Myron to make their move on me soon," she mused. "They'll need to test my loyalty in some way, whatever choice I make."

"We have another problem as well." Tehya leaned forward and stared back at Bailey. "Do you remember Alberto Rodriquez?"

Bailey stared at her in surprise. "Alberto is a major Colombian drug runner. Very fanatical, a psychopath. He was captured about three years ago by the Colombian police and imprisoned."

"Well, he's out of prison," Tehya said. "He's in Aspen and looking for you. Somehow he discovered your identity and decided you're going to pay for the death of his brother."

Bailey was aware of John leaning forward almost protectively as she stared back at Tehya.

"Alberto should have never been able to discover who I was," she said quietly. "No one there knew, not even the authorities. His brother, Carlos, was a bloodthirsty son of a bitch who deserved to die. He killed two young mistresses in two months and he was working on a third when we moved into the hut he'd taken her to in the jungle. He was killed when he turned his weapon on us."

"He's blaming you for the hit." Tehya shrugged.

"Where was he sighted?" John's tone was clipped now.

"In town last night, flashing Bailey's picture and asking her whereabouts at a little diner there called Casamara's."

Bailey nodded. "It's one of my favorite restaurants. It won't be hard to find me."

"We sent out two of our backup teams to locate him, but he disappeared around daylight," Tehya reported. "As soon as we know more, I'll get that information to you. Keep your sat phones on you and keep them turned on just in case."

"Alberto could throw a kink in the plan here." She turned to John as she sat back in the couch and breathed out warily. "He's a true killer. Unlike his brother, he doesn't let himself be ruled by anger, only cold hard determination. We were on his trail for more than a year before we captured him in Colombia. He won't be easy to track, especially in these mountains. The good thing about him, though, is that when he decides to kill, he doesn't do it from a distance. It's face-to-face."

"Well, bully for him," John muttered darkly before turning back to Tehya. "I want him found, now. We don't have time for this."

"We believe he was given a bit of help in breaking out of his Colombian stronghold," Tehya told him. "And he obviously has help here."

"Warbucks?" Bailey asked. "What would be the point?"

"Unless it's another test," Tehya said, shrugging, "we're not certain at this point, though we're pulling in new intel at the present. We also have a buyer named Jaeko in Aspen. He's rumored to have been sent to be in place for the auction when it begins and to verify the product for sale before bidding begins."

Jaeko. Bailey narrowed her eyes and thought for long moments. "Jaeko doesn't have the connections or the money for this. He's a low-level buyer with little or no backing. He mostly buys guns, grenades, and ammunition for rebels."

"He began branching out about three years ago," Tehya stated as she glanced at John. "Rumor has it that Jaeko made some high-level friends while he was incarcerated in a Russian prison for a few months before he escaped."

"There was also a rumor that he was killed by his American wife four years ago," John said slowly.

"Rumor." Tehya waved it away. "We have definite sightings of Jaeko after that, and none of them was in a body bag."

Just as there were sightings of Jerric Abbas and Travis Caine—Caine being the bodyguard and chauffeur who worked for John Vincent.

Travis Caine was once an international two-bit assassin whom no one had ever been able to gather enough evidence against. About seven years before, rumor had circulated that he had attempted and failed to kill the wrong victim. A drug lord, Diego Fuentes. Diego had sent his own assassin after him and that assassin had supposedly returned with proof of the kill. Caine's head.

Weeks later Fuentes's assassin was dead and Caine had popped back up, alive and well.

Suspicion began to pound at Bailey's head and suddenly, she was very interested in meeting Jaeko again. There was no way John or Tehya, or their little group of agents, could know that at one time, Jaeko had been one of Bailey's Russian informants.

What the hell kind of team was John involved in? She glanced over at him as he and Tehya discussed the various players involved in the upcoming bids. Rumors of terrorist cells, terrorist leaders, and terrorist countries that were getting their money together to bid on the product of a lifetime.

"Do we have everyone in place?" John was asking as Tehya rose to her feet long minutes later.

"Everything's ready." Tehya nodded. "Jerric is pacing the floors waiting on a phone call . . ."

"Jerric doesn't pace," Bailey murmured as she looked up at Tehya.

She watched as John stilled, suddenly becoming dangerously wary.

"Really?" Tehya looked down at her, her brown eyes narrowing. "Are you certain?"

"Jerric Abbas doesn't pace and Catalina Lamont has a jealous streak a mile wide. Don't forget that when the two of you are playing your little game here. Because trust me, everyone else of interest will be watching as well."

"Catalina and Jerric are no longer an item," she stated with a smile.

"Catalina and Jerric haven't been an item several times," Bailey said with a shrug. "Catalina still cut off a woman's earlobe for allowing him to whisper in it. She's sworn she'd never let him go short of death and he has yet to kill her. That means they're still an item." She rose to her feet and stared at John, then Tehya. "I wonder how *Jerric's* new wife feels about his new lover?"

She turned to head for the shower when John caught her arm, pulling her to a stop. "Meaning?" he growled, his voice dark, warning.

Bailey widened her eyes innocently. "Oh, do I have my information wrong?" "Jerric isn't married? How bad of me." She shook his hold loose. "Excuse me while I go shower. This game makes me feel dirty all of a sudden."

John watched as she stalked through the bedroom and into the shower before he turned and stared back at Tehya.

Tehya sighed. "It's a good thing Risa trusts Micah and likes me, huh? Otherwise, we'd be having problems with this mission."

John pushed his fingers through his hair wearily. "She knows who Jerric is. I don't have a doubt in my mind that she's also piecing together other bits of information we don't want her to know."

Teyha shrugged. "She *thinks* she knows, John. Without proof or someone to verify it, then she's still in the dark." She gave him a warning look. "Just make certain you aren't the one providing the proof."

John shook his head as a mocking smile crossed his lips. "Jordan thinks he can control this, doesn't he?"

Tehya rolled her eyes. "Jordan thinks he can control many things. Whether or not he can is another thing." She glanced around the room, her expression sobering as a hint of wariness crossed her face. "I'd better go. I have to at least pretend to be Jerric's mistress. Do you have any idea what a bitch he can be when it comes to working with a woman? You'd think he's possessed by his wife rather than married to her."

"He's possessed by his love for her," John said quietly. "There's a difference."

"He's still a bitch to work with." She shrugged. "I'll keep you up to date on Alberto, and you keep an eye on her."

"I have her back," he stated as he moved to the bedroom door. "Do you have a viable cover for being in our room?"

A faint grin touched her lips. "Several people heard Jerric more or less order me to come here and attempt to negotiate with you to drop out of the running. Simple business transaction."

He nodded at that and opened the door, aware that the cameras aimed at the hallway would monitor her exit from the room.

Bailey was getting fed up with the lies, he could see it in her expression, sense it in the tension that was tightening within her day by day. Bailey didn't suspect anything. Hell, no. She knew . . .

Running his fingers through his hair, John moved to the door, turned the knob easily and stepped into the steamy confines of the bathroom before closing the door behind him.

He could see her through the glass shower doors, her head braced against the tile wall, her shoulders hunched against the anger. The knowledge. And the pain.

This was destroying her, it was destroying him to watch her hurt like this. Like a beast digging in sharpened claws, the knowledge that the end was coming soon tore at both of them.

Shedding his clothes, he moved to the shower, slid open the doors, and watched as her head jerked up.

John saw the betrayal in her eyes, the fear, the need to know that something, just one thing in her life was a constant. That it was real.

"Come here." He pulled her into his arms despite her attempt to turn away from him. "Come here, baby. I have you."

He felt the sob that racked her body as he closed his arms around her, and felt the feminine need for comfort, for security, that she so rarely showed.

Bailey was used to dealing with everything on her own. She wasn't used to sharing her pain or leaning on anyone. Right now he needed her to lean on him. He needed to protect her against something, he needed a dragon to slay for her, because God knew he couldn't find a way to slay the situation they were in, or the lies he was forced to live.

He cupped the back of her head and stared across her head, feeling the anger rise inside him that she had to hurt this way.

He kissed her forehead, beside her eye.

She shook her head. "I hate the lies, John."

She stared up at him, anger vibrating in every line of her body. "I know you're lying to me. I know Jerric is a lie, just as I know Travis Caine is one. I know it. And I still have to allow it to continue. I hate it."

Bailey knew how to lie. She knew how to deceive in her job. If there was one thing he knew about her though, it was that outside that job, Bailey was as honest as the day could be long.

This was tearing them both apart.

"There are lies we have to live, for one reason or another," he said. "That still doesn't mean the reality is what we want it to be."

He couldn't tell her the truth. God knew he wanted to. He needed to. But right now the truth would be more dangerous to her than the lie was painful.

"I'll end up hating you," she whispered fiercely.

"And I'll always dream of you," he sighed as he lowered his lips to hers.

His hard shaft pressed against her belly, though it was a need he could control now. He needed to comfort her just as much as he needed to love her.

"Did I ever stop dreaming of you?" She cried softly as she melted against him.

He ran his hands down her back, holding her close to him as he felt her hands stroking around his back, her sharp little nails probing at his flesh with slow, sensual rasps.

He could feel the heated hunger rising inside her now. It was there in the prick of her nails, in the feel of her hot tongue licking against his chest.

Oh yeah, he liked that. His hand cupped the back of her head as he lifted his face and blinked against the water flowing around them.

"I need you." The sound of her whisper against his flesh tore through his senses. "I need all of you, John. Everything. Just this once."

Just this once, and she wanted things he was sworn not to give her. Things he knew better than to give her—and yet he knew he would.

Simply because she asked for it, because she needed it. Because she was immersed in a world that he could see was destroying her.

"You have me, love." He kept his voice low, let the Australian flavor of his natural accent free, and gave her all of him.

He stared down at her as her head lifted, her eyes filling with tears, her lips shaking as she parted them to speak.

He couldn't let her speak. He couldn't let his soul break apart any more than it already was for her. His head lowered and he stole the words in a kiss that immediately sparked a conflagration of heat.

Her hands buried in his hair, fisted in it, and tried to pull him closer as he cupped the rounded globes of her rear and lifted her closer.

Her legs twined around his hips, her ankles crossing at the back as he braced her against the wall and stared into her exquisite, hungry expression.

"I remember, love," he whispered as a soft sob tore from her lips. "I remember every touch, every kiss. I remember you like a dream that saves my soul."

Her head rolled against the shower wall as her hips lifted against him, rubbing the slick folds against the head of his cock.

The sensation was sharp, fiery. Like a thousand pinpoints of pleasure racing over the hardened crest. He felt the silken folds of her pussy part for him, felt the heat of her as he nudged inside.

Snug, clenching tissue surrounded the tip of his cock as he fought to breathe through the pleasure. Being with her like this, holding her, feeling her acceptance of him tore through his senses like wildfire.

"Hold on to me, babe." His voice was thick with passion, with an accent he'd sworn he'd never use again.

She needed all of him, he would give her all of him.

Pressing inside her, he worked the hard flesh of his cock deep as he held her gaze. Heavy-lidded and intense, her emerald eyes glittered as water condensed on her lashes.

"We'll never speak of this again," he insisted roughly, his own heart breaking as her eyes filled with tears again. "Tonight, Bailey. Just tonight, we forget where we are, who we have to be. Just for tonight."

"Just for tonight," she agreed, her voice filled with tears. "Just for tonight."

Gripping her rear tighter he lifted her to him, braced his feet against the shower floor, and began to lower her again. Each blistering inch of velvety female flesh that gripped him sent a lance of sensation tearing into his chest.

As though she were firing barbs into his heart, tying her to him forever in ways that she hadn't already.

How could one woman have such a disastrous effect on a man?

How could one woman fill so much of a man's soul, even as he knew that the day could come when he would lose her?

He was risking everything for her. To give her this one night. To give her a few moments of comfort that would eventually do more harm than it could ever do good.

But he couldn't resist her. He couldn't resist the need, the hunger, or the plea she had whispered.

She had known, in her heart, in her woman's soul, she had always known who he was, what he was, and what he was to her. There was no denying it any longer, just as there was no denying the need clawing at his balls.

Hips straining, he thrust deeper inside her, feeling her clench and tighten around him as a muted cry fell from her lips.

"I dreamed of this," she whispered on a sob as she buried her lips against his neck. "I dreamed of you touching me, holding me again. Loving me. Love me, Trent. One more time."

Trent. The forbidden name, a man who was dead, the man who had claimed his woman so many years before and had never been able to let her go.

"Shhh." He breathed the shushing little sound against her ear as he pressed deeper and deeper inside her. Taking her by increments until he was lodged to the hilt, stretching her, feeling the erotic bite of muscles that were stretched to their limit.

The feel of her was like heat and lightning surrounding his dick. It was the most erotic, most sensual sensation of his life. The feel of Bailey taking him, loving him, each feminine clench of her sheath rippling over the too-sensitive flesh.

"I can't wait," he groaned as he tried to hold still inside her, tried to hold on to the sensation of her clenching and stroking his cock with delicate internal muscles.

It was a sensation unlike any he had ever known, even with other women. Women he had cared for, had at times perhaps even loved. Still, none could compare to taking Bailey naked, without a condom, with nothing separating their flesh, nothing standing between them physically, or emotionally.

In that moment, with the water pouring around them, he could touch her heart, her soul. Just as she touched his.

"God help me, I love fucking you," he groaned, watching as a flush worked over her face and her eyes darkened in arousal.

Around his cock he felt her pussy convulse, felt her heated juices pressing around his engorged flesh.

"Fuck me some more," she whimpered.

His hips jerked involuntary, thrusting against her, lodging his shaft deeper inside her as they both groaned with the gathering firestorm of sensations.

It was going to blow his mind, taking her like this. When they were finished he would drown beneath the spray of water because he'd be too damned weak to push himself from it.

Bracing her more firmly against the wall, his hips moved. He pulled back, swallowing tightly at the feel of her pussy gripping him, trying to suck him back in as he forced himself to withdraw all but the engorged crest. Breathing in deep, he fought for control. Staring into her heavy-lidded eyes, he lost it as her grip tightened, rippled and she moved, driving him inside her once again.

He couldn't hold back. There was no way to recapture his control after it splintered, no way to halt the tide that rose inside him, spurred him, demanded that he take all she had to give. That he give everything that she demanded of him.

Moaning her name, he braced one hand against the shower wall and held her to him with the other wall. His hips thrust and churned, shafting inside her with hard, brutally exquisite thrusts that had them both panting, fighting to hold back, to hold off a release that he knew would drain him not just physically, but emotionally.

He wanted it to last forever. He wanted to hold himself inside her until the world itself disappeared and there was nothing but the man and the woman, hearts pounding, souls merging. Until nothing mattered but the pleasure, and the pain washed away with the water pouring around them.

"I love you. Oh God, Trent. Trent. I love you so much."

His name on her lips sent a shaft of ecstasy tearing through his testicles as he groaned in near rapture.

"I love you, babe." Thick and heavy, the rough drawl of Australia in his voice whispered around them, bringing back a past neither of them had been able to forget.

As the words whispered past his lips, he felt her lose control. A low, fierce tremor began in her hips where his arm braced her to him. That tremor built, grew in intensity as it raced through her pussy, worked over his cock, and tore through her senses.

He felt her orgasm ripping through her, felt the clench of her body, heard the cry of pleasure that mixed with the sound of the water, and he lost his mind in the rush of her juices around the thrusting length of his cock.

He lost his mind and his control.

Throwing back his head, he gave himself to his own release. He felt it tear through his balls, drawing them tight to the base of his cock as his seed began to spurt from him, filling her, mixing with her release and searing his flesh as he groaned her name and poured himself into her.

It was like dying inside her, becoming a part of her, melting so deep inside her soul that he knew neither of them would ever be free.

It was like finally finding the home he hadn't believed truly existed for him. And in that moment he knew why his fellow agents were so damned possessive and particular about assignments such as the one Micah was working. He belonged to Bailey. He belonged to her, body and soul. And he knew from that moment on, never again could he allow another woman to touch, to take what was Bailey's alone.

Clenching her rear in one hand to hold her to him, he fought to press his hand tight enough against the shower wall to keep himself upright.

Bailey's legs were tight around his hips, shudders still working through her body as he fought to catch his own breath.

"I will always love you." He couldn't hold the words back. "Until my last breath, sweet Bailey. I'll love only you."

She sobbed against the pleasure, against the pain. Her eyes locked with his now, her body melded to him. She whispered, "I'll love you forever."

John only prayed that somehow, some way, they could have forever. Together.

Chapter 13

RAYMOND AND MARY GREER knew how to throw a house party, Bailey had to give them credit for that. The next afternoon as she eased away from the ballroom where a full buffet lunch and champagne bar had been set up, she marveled at the massive amount of money that had to have gone into the catering of the affair.

Chefs had been flown in from France, Greece and California. Fresh produce and seafood was brought in, as well as superior wines and champagnes. No expense was spared for this once-a-year party that Mary so enjoyed throwing. The fact that her husband used the event for his criminal activities was evil, in her eyes.

Mary was one of the gentlest ladies Bailey had ever known. During her childhood Mary Altman had been a strong guiding force for Bailey and Anna. She had taken the two girls under her wing, guided them in their coming-out balls and taught them how to laugh at themselves when their parents had exhibited disappointment or disapproval in them.

Slipping out of the ballroom, Bailey made her way through the foyer and away from the clash of voices. She couldn't handle the crowd of overgrown teenage females any longer. That was what they reminded her of. They were mothers and grandmothers, yet they seemed to think they were still eighteen. The petty backstabbing and social climbing sickened her. Being a part of it was something to avoid at all costs.

As Bailey escaped the ballroom and moved quietly through the house, she was aware of the security cameras that followed her progress. Raymond had spared no expense in the security of his home, or his secrets. It seemed that every room she had been in so far, except bedrooms and bathrooms, were equipped with the electronic devices. Some of the larger rooms contained several of them.

Movement through the house was tracked diligently, the images displayed into a secure room in the basement level that was manned by several security guards.

Outside was no less secure. The evergreen maze was filled with them, the only privacy to be found there was in the sheltered, private grottos that Mary had insisted on and had spared no expense in creating.

The place was a virtual fortress, leaving her very little opportunity to slip into Raymond's office and rifle through his papers. The good ol' days of the spy game that her cousin Garren Abijah had once talked about were well and truly gone.

Everything was electronic now. Gadgets and sensors, virtual access and computer viruses. One damned near had to be a rocket scientist to figure out how to slip into secured areas undetected. That or have a team with varying skills covering every move.

She wasn't a rocket scientist and she didn't have a team. That left her at loose ends as she roamed the house and eventually made her way outside.

John was with the men, most likely pursuing much more interesting activities this afternoon. Shooting pool, playing poker, possibly out hunting. She would have given her eye-teeth to be socializing with the men rather than the women. Buying jewels and clothes wasn't exactly her idea of a fun time. She wasn't there to have fun. She was there to catch a murderous traitor and she had to admit, at least to herself, that she was beginning to grow impatient.

Her world, unfortunately, was still a man's world. They conducted business, made financial decisions and ran the vast array of companies beneath their personal umbrellas.

The women spent their days with their charities, their shopping, lunches and social calenders. God, could that life get any more boring?

Moving through the house, she found herself drawn to the library. The intimate, cozy room was filled with books, reading nooks, and a fire that crackled cheerily in the hearth.

The warmth of the fire sent a soft glow of heat to the seating arrangement in front of it. As Bailey entered, her only thought was to curl up on the comfortable couch she and Anna used to share when they had slept over at Mary's and reminisce on a childhood friend who should never have died.

Her hopes were doomed to disappointment. Moving toward the fireplace, a slight movement to her right had her swinging around, her hand going to the small of her back, beneath the cream-colored cashmere sweater she wore for the weapon hidden there in its butter-soft leather holster.

"Ease up, Agent Serborne." From the shadows, one of the brokers invited to the house party stepped forward.

"Landon Roth." She kept her hand on her weapon. "No one told me you had been invited."

A wide toothy smile in a less-than-charming face was her answer.

Landon was one of those plain little men that one met sometimes. If you didn't know him, didn't know the pure genius and pure evil inside him, then he was so easily overlooked and underestimated.

"I rather had a feeling you would be drawn here." Plain hazel eyes glanced around the room as he straightened the edges of his charcoal-gray jacket over his white shirt. Finely pleated pants and black leather shoes completed his appearance. He wasn't short, he wasn't tall. At five feet eight inches, he was just the right height to blend in. Neatly trimmed hair a shade of dark blond or light brown, she had never really determined which and thin wire-rimmed glasses.

"And what made you think I'd be drawn here?" she asked, careful to keep an eye on him.

He looked around again, a smile playing at his lips. "I

think a library rather becomes you, Agent Serborne," he stated. "Classy, refined, quiet. An oasis of peace." He clasped his hands in front of him. "I always rather saw you as a woman of class and refinement, though I must admit I never made the connection to the Serborne fortune until I arrived here. The CIA omitted that from your file, I do believe."

She arched her brows. "I'll have to remind them to correct that oversight."

He chuckled at her response as he wagged a finger at her. "Very deceptive, my dear. Very deceptive. The past they created for you was quite inventive, I must say. Kansas farm parents, dead. No living brothers or sisters. An orphan with no family. Very, very good."

"Thank you." Bailey watched him carefully as he moved to the seating arrangement and took a seat in one of the comfortable wing-backed chairs.

"Do have a seat, Agent Serborne," he invited as he waved his hand toward the couch. "We need to discuss a few details if you don't mind."

"And if I do mind?" she asked archly.

He smiled, a rather chilling curve to his lips that she knew was designed to inspire fear. She wasn't afraid of him. Fear of Roth wasn't something she had ever known. She was wary, though.

"I do believe as Warbucks's emissary you are required to consider all brokers invited to this little get-together in the hopes of convincing you that they are the best man for the upcoming auction," he pointed out. "I'd have to have to complain that I wasn't given a fair and impartial chance at the job."

"Last I heard, Warbucks didn't exactly follow traditional employment guidelines." She almost rolled her eyes at his statement. "Really, Roth, do you believe there's an argument you can give that would convince me that you should have this job over John Vincent?"

"Your lover isn't exactly the best man for the job." His lips twisted into a curve of distaste. "If you were looking for a business partner, my dear, I'm certain you could have found a much better match. One who at least understands the world you were born within."

And of course, Roth would understand it. He was a distant runner in line to England's throne, and raised amidst the pomp and arrogance of European royalty. His parents were aristocrats, cold and brittle, but even they were wary of the child who hadn't seemed to have an ounce of mercy, compassion, or warmth.

He'd poisoned his nanny when he'd been no more than five. At ten he had nearly killed a playmate, a boy several years his senior. At sixteen he'd been under suspicion for the murder of his lover, who had been pregnant at the time. At the same time he had been suspected of cheating on finals at the prestigious school he'd been enrolled in.

At eighteen his parents had died in a suspicious vehicle accident. Roth had believed he would inherit the vast fortune his parents were thought to have had, only to learn that they had been little more than paupers living on the charity of friends and family.

"I'm quite satisfied with the lover I've chosen," she assured him as she took a seat in the corner of the couch, watching him closely.

His lips twitched as he propped his elbow on the arm of the chair and ran an index finger over his upper lip.

"He's a bit common, don't you think, my dear? He doesn't exactly have upper-class connections or a background that could complement yours. There are surely men much closer to your stature."

"Men such as you?" she queried lightly.

"Precisely." His smile was knowing, condescending. "I would be a much better choice. We could move mountains with the power we could attain."

"I can already move mountains." Bailey could also feel her skin crawling at the thought of this man touching her.

His lips pursed as dark hazel eyes narrowed on her.

"Even out the playing field, Agent Serborne," he ordered her, his voice lowering, becoming rasping, a serpent's hiss of fury. "I don't relish the idea of losing the particular contract."

"The contract hasn't been given yet," she pointed out. "Warbucks makes the final decision, I only suggest the best man for the job."

"The best man being that upstart Vincent?" he sneered. "He's a worthless piece of white trash, and you know it as well as I do."

"He's worth quite a bit to me." She eased to her feet, straightening as she watched him carefully. "The best man for the job is the one who can get the job done and done correctly. Unfortunately, your record doesn't speak nearly so well for you as John's does for him. You leave a trail of blood and a wake of suspicion in your path. We don't need that."

He pushed to his feet, a wave of red anger rushing over his cheekbones as he glared back at her.

"I get the job done."

"John gets it done efficiently, without suspicion and without a mess. Sorry for your luck, but you're falling way behind in the quality department here."

She turned to leave the room. She'd had enough of his attitude and superiority. Landon Roth was known for his ability to get a job done, there was no doubt about it. He had the contacts and the reputation to make the sale. But he clearly wasn't the best choice.

Turning her back on Landon Roth wasn't the wisest move she could have made either. She knew his reputation, but she hadn't truly believed he was stupid. Until she felt his knife at her throat.

"You're a nasty little bitch," he hissed at her ear as the cold steel caressed her neck. "I never did care much for you. Despite your vast fortune, you have no breeding whatsoever do you, you little whore?"

"*Bitch* and *whore*, your vocabulary is improving." She drew in a hard breath as the razor-sharp blade bit closer to her flesh.

"I could leave you on this floor bleeding and go straight to dinner," he snarled. "I'd relish the feel of it flowing over my fingers simply because you're trash. Just as your whore-mongering little boyfriend is trash."

Bailey lifted her eyes to where the all-seeing eye of the carefully hidden camera looked down on the library from above the door.

If security was watching, how long did she have? she wondered. If they weren't watching, then she was simply just screwed.

"You won't get away with it," she warned him.

"Of course I will," he laughed. "Warbucks can't afford to have me arrested because then it would bring his own activities to light. And he would have to catch me to kill me, wouldn't he, darling?"

"You'll never make it out of here."

Would she make it out of here? She felt the cold steel pressing into her skin and knew that if she even breathed the wrong way, then she was going to die.

"This is no way to convince me to use your services, Landon." She kept her voice calm, cool. "Actually, it's a damned good way to become a casualty to this game. Because I promise you, even if Warbucks allows you to live, John won't."

She felt him pause behind her.

"No woman is that important to John Vincent," he snickered. "It's a proven fact, Agent Serborne."

"Until this woman."

Bailey's eyes flew to the door where John stood. At his sides were Raymond Greer and John's rarely seen bodyguard, Travis Caine. Behind them were three of Greer's security personnel.

"I kindly ask you to release Ms. Serborne," Greer gave a grade-A impression of arrogant superiority with a commanding sneer. "You'll receive a six-hour head start before Warbucks sends a man after you."

Roth stilled behind her. The knife seemed to tighten against her throat and she could almost feel Roth's intent behind the blade. If he was going to die anyway, he might as well take her with him.

Her gaze connected with John's then. His gray eyes swirled with fury, his body was taut, controlled, his fists clenched at his side.

"Don't do it, Roth," John stated quietly.

"Warbucks would kill over this?" Anger vibrated in Roth's tone. "His rules are fairly simple, Greer. There are no rules in business. Isn't that the message he sends out when he begins his competitions?"

"No message was sent other than an invitation to appear and to be considered for the contract," Raymond informed him coldly. "You have stepped over the line. Release Ms. Serborne, or I promise you, you'll die hard."

The knife wavered at her throat. Bailey didn't dare swallow, she could barely breathe. She had assumed Roth wouldn't attack her here, she had been wrong. Perhaps fatally wrong.

"Release me, Roth, and I'll discuss this with Warbucks," she stated. "Perhaps a small fee for my trouble can be arranged rather than your blood."

"I'd listen to her if I were you," Greer informed him. "Because only she could convince him to rescind this order."

"Whore, your time will come," he hissed in her ear before jerking the knife from her throat and pushing her roughly in Greer's direction.

Turning, Bailey's foot flew out and up, the heavy pad of her boot striking him in the jaw, sending him careening across the room before he tipped over the back of the couch and landed on the coffee table with a resounding crash. The legs buckled, toppling him to the floor as a heavy groan spilled from his lips.

"Stay back," she ordered Greer and his men before moving to Roth, jerking the knife from the floor and gripping his hair, pulling his head back and letting him feel the blade on his throat for a change.

"You're fucking messy," she snapped as she stared into

his suddenly horrified gaze. "A brainless little viper without the means or the ability to perform reliably on any job. I wouldn't let you walk behind my dog and clean up its shit, let alone handle a contract that I direct."

She let the knife bite into his neck enough to draw blood, to have his eyes widening in fear.

"Let me see you again, and I'll make certain you're skinned before you die. Do you understand me?"

"Yes." The word was barely a breath.

Sneering back at him, she pulled back, still holding the knife, and tossed him a contemptuous glance. "You're not worth killing. Get the hell out of here now and make damned certain I don't ever have to look at your plain little face again."

She turned her back on him, this time confident, knowing he wouldn't dare move on her.

As she neared John, she tossed her head to dislodge her hair as it threatened to spill over her face, then nearly gasped as his fingers gripped her arm.

"Raymond, take care of this," he snarled back at Greer. "I expected better security and I sure as hell expected better taste in the candidates chosen for this game your boss enjoys playing."

"It will be taken care of . . ."

"And don't kill him." She glared back at Raymond. "Don't make me break my word. That son of a bitch will give me his prized Monet he stole last year if he wants to live." She turned back to Roth and smiled in triumph. "You have two weeks to arrange delivery or you won't have to worry about it any longer."

She didn't have a chance to say much more. With great subtlety and no small amount of fury, John directed her out of the library and through the foyer to the stairs that led to their room.

"Ease up," she muttered, jerking at her arm as they started up the stairs. "What the hell is your problem?"

"Not another word." His voice cracked like a whip despite the quiet tone. "Not one more, Bailey. Don't argue with me, don't struggle against me. Just keep your damned mouth shut."

She glanced at him in disbelief before being forced to watch where he was dragging her as they went up the stairs.

"I don't know what your problem is," she snapped. "He was bluffing."

"Roth doesn't bluff," he snarled.

"Of course he bluffs," she hissed. "If he wanted to kill me, he would have gone ahead and sliced my throat rather than waiting. He was fishing and he caught a prize fish with your and Raymond's reaction. Now the entire criminal element is going to know that both John Vincent and Warbucks place value on my life."

That could be a hazard. They had enemies. Warbucks's identity wasn't known, but neither were his perceived weaknesses. Until now.

"Your logic completely pisses me off." He paused long enough to unlock their bedroom door before pulling her through it and slamming it behind them.

"My logic is perfectly sound." She rounded on him furiously as he released her, anger surging through her veins at his pure, high-handed, male-superior arrogance. "And what the hell makes you think you can drag me around like this?"

"This."

He moved faster than she could evade him. Between one breath and the next, she was in his arms, her head pulled back by the simple expediency of his fingers tangling in her hair.

His lips covered hers, his tongue pushing fiercely between her lips as he kissed her with a hunger and heat that shocked her, scorched her to the tips of her toes.

If there had been any doubt in her mind that John hadn't placed some emotional claim on her, then it was gone in that second. Pure male possession marked his kiss. As his tongue pumped between her lips, stroked along hers, and his hands jerked her closer, she knew in that moment, that with his hunger, his need, he was branding her. Her senses, her flesh, her very femininity were being marked by this man's kiss, by his touch.

"Damn you." He jerked back long enough to grip the hem of her sweater and push her arms up.

It came over her head before she could even consider fighting him for possession of it. Tossed to the floor, forgotten, his lips moved down her neck, nipped at the flesh and sent her senses reeling with pleasure.

Anger and lust, need and hunger burned through her now, burned between them. She could feel the desperation in his touch, in the stroke of his lips and his harsh breaths.

Danger was a spike of adrenaline, but only emotion could spike a lust and a hunger that raged this hot, this intense. Perhaps, she thought, only love could spike the white-hot desperation that began to whip around them.

Only love.

John felt Bailey's breath hitch, heard the excited little whimper that left her lips, and had to fight to keep from jerking their jeans down, turning her, and taking her immediately.

Something savage, something burning and primal had torn through him the second he had seen that blade at Bailey's throat. The second he had realized he could lose her.

For a second, one heart-stopping second, he'd seen a glimpse of what she must have felt when he had "died." Pure, unadulterated fear had surged through him. For the first time in his life, he had known what true fear felt like. What it tasted and smelled like.

It was wrapped around his senses now and nothing could pull him free of it but this. Her kiss and her touch. Marking her body as his. Branding her senses with his touch, with a pleasure they could only find with each other.

He released her long enough to allow her to tear the shirt from his shoulders. Picking her up in his arms, he moved to the bed, tossed her to it, and moved his hands to the snap of her jeans.

She hadn't worn a bra. The smooth, unblemished mounds

of her breasts were topped with tight, delicate pink nipples that stood tight and hard. They tempted his lips, his tongue to taste them.

Pulling her jeans down her long, exquisite legs, he stopped long enough to jerk her boots from her feet before removing the denim quickly.

Silk covered the wet folds of her pussy. Damp silk, proof that she was as aroused as he was, as ready for his possession as he was to possess her.

The panties tore free of her easily.

Watching her face as he ripped the fragile silk from her, he saw the widening of her eyes, the flare of excitement that flushed her face.

"You turned your back on him," he snarled suddenly as he tore at the belt cinching his hips. "You knew not to turn your back on him."

"So punish me." She stretched her arms over her head and arched, thrusting her breasts out to him. "I was a very bad girl, John."

Damn her. Damn her for being the only woman in the world who could make him crazy, make him insane to have her.

"He could have killed you." He rid himself of his boots and jeans, his hand gripping the base of his cock as he fought to hold back the need to thrust inside her.

Her gaze fell to where he held himself, her tongue swiping over her lips sensually. Lips swollen from his kisses, reddened from them.

"If I thought it would make you think twice, then I damned sure would," he bit out roughly as he pulled her legs apart, gripped her hips, and pulled her to the edge of the bed.

Pushing her legs back, John bent his head to the dew-glistening folds of her pussy and swiped his tongue through the narrow, syrup-laden slit.

God, she was as sweet as an early morning rainfall. Her pussy was heated, her clit standing out hard and glistening, need tightening every muscle in her body.

The taste of her was pure nectar. Stiffening his tongue, he pushed it into the velvety grip of her vagina, feeling it clench around him, shuddering with pleasure.

Her juices spilled to his tongue, filling his senses with the addictively sweet taste of her. He could take her like this for hours. Fucking her with his tongue, tasting her pleasure and her hunger, searing her taste into his senses.

"Oh God. John," she called out his name, her voice husky, vibrating with sweet sensual intensity. He could hear the surrender in her voice, feel it in her body.

Fucking his tongue deeper, harder inside the snug grip of her pussy, he couldn't help but moan at the liquid passion that flowed from it. Licking at the soft fall of juices, caressing her, tasting her, he grew drunk on the very essence of her.

Lifting his lips he bestowed a swift, hard kiss to the plump, swollen folds before his tongue found the distended little button of her clit. His fingers moved to the soft folds his lips had left, parting them, finding the soft entrance to her body that his tongue had raided moments before.

He sent two fingers working inside her as his lips covered her clit. Sucking it inside his mouth he let his tongue play with it as his fingers stroked past the tight grip of tender muscles that clenched around them.

Her pussy was hot, gripping, tightening on the digits as he sucked at her clit, licked at it, felt it swell and throb beneath his tongue.

She was close. So very close. Fear and danger had spiked sensation. Need and hunger had intensified it until John felt as though he were burning in the center of a white-hot flame.

She was his. His woman. His life.

Flicking his tongue faster over the distended bud, he claimed with his mouth, he felt her arching in his grip. Her hips writhed, impaling her snug pussy on his stroking fingers, working her clit against his tongue until he felt her exploding around him.

Groaning, forcing himself to bite back his own cries he jerked back, positioned his cock and as her pussy vibrated with the force of her orgasm he began penetrating her.

His eyes focused on the center of her body, watched as the soft, sweet folds of her flesh parted for the flared head of his cock, watched her body take him. With quick, desperate thrusts he worked his way inside the shuddering entrance, groaning now as she took him, inch by inch, her cries echoing in his head until he was seated to the hilt inside her.

And then he just let himself feel. The way her pussy rippled around his cock, milked it, clenching on it with a fiery suckling sensation that had him shaking his head as he fought to hold on to his control.

"Never again." He lifted his gaze, staring into her eyes as he fought to hold on to the need to spill inside her. "Never again, Bailey. Never do that again. Never risk yourself like that again. Do you hear me?"

She stared back at him and for a second he saw the flash of pain in her eyes.

"Like you did?"

His jaw clenched. His hips moved. He couldn't hold back the need to thrust inside her, to force her to acknowledge, if only to herself, that she could never risk her life like this again. Never again.

"Never, Bailey." Pushing her legs back again, he worked his cock inside her, hard, filling strokes that had her lifting to him, had her crying out his name, begging him, pleading.

"Never again," he snapped as he began to lose control.

He couldn't lose her. As long as she lived, he breathed. She was the light in a world of darkness. He couldn't survive if she wasn't in it.

She shook her head. Her pussy clenched tighter, rippled around his cock, stroked him with fingers of flaming sensation that nearly destroyed his mind.

Control was shot.

Groaning her name, he moved over her, his lips burning against hers as he began to fuck her with deep, fierce strokes, thrusting inside her as she cried out beneath the kiss and exploded in his arms.

Her orgasm rained liquid fire over the violently sensitive

head of his cock. It clenched and tightened, sucked at his shaft, and tore the final threat of control from his grasp.

When he came, he felt as though a part of himself, his soul, shot inside her with his release. He couldn't hold back the throttled groan, her name, a prayer. Ecstasy blistered his senses, tore through his soul, and left him gasping in the wake of sensations he couldn't describe. All he knew was that this was why he lived. For Bailey. For her touch, her kiss.

He lived for Bailey.

CHAPTER 14

"EXCUSE ME, MR. VINCENT, but Mr. Greer has asked for a moment of your time."

John turned from his perusal of the poker game playing out in the billiards room the next afternoon. He hadn't joined the game yet himself, mostly because he'd already caught two of the other players cheating. Not that he couldn't cheat, or wasn't better at it; he was simply watching how they cheated to give himself an edge when he did take a seat at the table.

"Of course." He turned from the poker table and followed the houseman through the room and out to the long hall that led from the recreational wing of the first floor toward Raymond Greer's office in the far wing.

The cabin was huge. It was a monstrosity, just as ostentatious as Bailey had accused it of being.

"Here we go, sir," the houseman announced as they stopped at the door of the office. He gave a brief, firm knock.

"Enter," Raymond called out, his voice muffled by the door.

The houseman opened it with a flourish before nodding back to John.

Entering the room John was aware of the door closing behind him, but he was more aware of the two men watching him from across the room.

Raymond sat in a high-backed chair, close to a bank of windows that looked out on the snowcapped forest beyond them. Myron Falks sat in a matching chair to his side, which left the third chair to face the two men. A low marble-topped table sat in the center of the arrangement with a coffee tray service waiting in the center.

"Have a seat, John," Raymond invited, his expression stern as he extended his hand to the empty chair.

"Thank you." John arched his brow as he moved to the empty chair and took his seat.

The pair facing him were dressed in dark business suits. Jeans and a loose sweater weren't exactly business attire, but neither did John feel in the least beneath two men outfitted for an office.

"You have a quite a background, Mr. Vincent," Myron began with a dour expression.

John's brows arched. "As do you, Mr. Falks. Or should I say, Mark Fulton?"

The alias wasn't well known. It was a name that John Vincent shouldn't know, unless he had gone beyond the normal channels to find the other man's identity. Channels that only a CIA contact could have had. A contact that the most powerful in underground circles trusted.

Falk's eyes dilated in surprise before he glanced quickly to Raymond Greer.

"Very impressive," Raymond drawled, and John had to give him credit for his acting abilities. The fact that he was still alive and working for Warbucks attested to those skills.

John tilted his head and glanced back at Falks. "You're not the only one who insists on knowing who he's working with," John informed him. "Only a stupid man doesn't ensure his own survival."

"And as we already know, you're not a stupid man," Falks stated coolly. "I have to admit, though, I didn't expect that Bailey would have taken you that far into her confidence."

"Bailey and I are more than lovers, Falks, we're partners. Evidently you missed that part somewhere."

Falks shrugged at that. "As I said, she surprised me. It's a rare occurrence, and I'll ensure it doesn't happen again."

"Myron has often wondered over the past years, when

Bailey has covered up for various little gaffes Myron's made, if she was sincere in protecting her friends or merely baiting them. She does have an odd sense of humor."

"I haven't heard her laughing about it," John shot back with a sharp look toward Falks.

Falks's brows lifted. "With Bailey, you can never be certain." He waved John's ire away. "She can be a bit of an enigma."

"I have to agree with him, John," Raymond inserted. "We've all had our doubts about Bailey at one time or another. And I must say, I myself was a bit surprised when she began a relationship with you. Bailey normally avoids the criminal element."

"Bailey's been up to her neck in the criminal element for years," John said. "CIA agents don't exactly socialize with the upper crust. Even agents with Bailey's background."

"He does have a point," Falks drawled with a snicker. "We expected her back in the familiar embrace of family and friends within the first year. She stuck it out longer than I imagined she would."

"I warned you that Bailey wasn't easy to predict." Raymond smirked back at Falks.

"So you did." Falks smiled at the comment before turning to John. "I imagine you know why you're here at this moment?"

John sat back in his chair and stared at the other man quietly for long moments. "The same reason Abbas will be here later?" he asked. "Warbucks likes to interview his potential brokers before he chooses which one to assign the job to. Been here, done this, though I have to admit I've never warranted executive-level attention before."

Falks's chest seemed to expand in pride at the comment. "The item up for auction is rather expensive, and demands a certain amount of discretion if we're going to keep various law enforcement officials from turning their attention to us. You've come highly recommended and several past engagements that you've conducted with lesser liaisons have proven your reliability."

"It doesn't hurt that you've partnered with a favorite daughter of our inner circle," Raymond pointed out. "We owe you a debt of gratitude for reinforcing the beginnings of trust that we were extending toward her."

"Think nothing of it." John smiled. "As long as I get the job."

Falks chuckled at that. "There will be several conditions to the assignment. One is that Bailey will be present during the auction you're conducting. We would hate for her to later decide that she wasn't a part of the event."

Trust came in many forms, John thought.

"She would actually demand to be a part of it," he informed them both.

"Verification of the product will be arranged once Warbucks has made his final decision on the broker," Raymond informed him then. "You'll be taken to the storage point, but you won't be given its location. You'll be permitted to verify the product and ascertain its legitimacy, with Bailey at your side. You'll be given the same opportunity just before the auction."

"The product will be in my possession once the auction begins," John stated. "It won't leave my sight. If it does at any time, or if the buyer doesn't receive final confirmation from me after the sale before the transfer of funds, then the buy will be invalidated."

Falks's smile was slow, confident. "We'll abide by that. The buyer will immediately transfer half of the funds; the other half we'll accept on delivery of the product."

"I'll be with the product at every stage from the time the auction begins until delivery." John nodded. "Bailey will be handling the exchange of money between the two accounts as well as communication. I'll provide all protection and transportation."

"Your men are highly rated," Falks replied. "You have an exemplary record, Mr. Vincent."

John inclined his head in acceptance of the compliment as Raymond poured coffee and set John's cup before him. The rich, black liquid steamed invitingly.

"My men know what they're doing," John continued. "Just as I do."

"I have to admit, I've been in favor of your particular talents since the beginning," Falks informed him. "You're one of the more reliable brokers. Abbas doesn't have the experience I feel this product deserves. But I'm only the employee, not the employer. Warbucks will make the final decision."

John shrugged. "There will be other jobs. Should your employer decide to accept my services, my fee is fifteen percent of the agreed price of the item. A third at the time your employer makes the decision in my favor, a third at sale, and a third at delivery."

Falks's brows lifted. "Abbas has agreed to drop his terms to ten percent."

"Abbas can afford to drop his terms to ten percent." John grimaced. "He hired mercenaries rather than keeping a team he can trust and men he knows. That's how rumor begins and how transactions get fucked up. He has very little overhead and he doesn't rate his time as valuable as I rate mine."

A glimmer of respect began to gleam in Falks's gaze. It was hard to impress men of his ilk, men who followed someone who'd been as mysterious as Warbucks over the years. John had worked the past five years on a reputation that had begun close to ten years before he took John Vincent's identity. The broker had been killed in a freak accident on a mountain road while under surveillance by the first two members of the unit, Micah Sloane and Nik Steele. His body had been buried, and his identity stolen.

John didn't mind taking a dead man's name or building his career in the interest of breaking the bastard who had taken his own life.

"Your time is very valuable, I agree," Falks stated as he lifted his coffee cup to his lips. Setting it back down, he turned to Raymond. "Please ensure that Mr. Vincent is compensated if Warbucks does decide on Abbas. Future goodwill is immeasurable."

It was an attempt to put him back in his place.

John rose to his feet without invitation, causing both men to glance at him in surprise.

"I don't need your future goodwill," he stated. "Or your charitable contribution toward my financial stability." He let a grin touch his lips. "Financial stability is now the least of my worries. My reputation, though, is very expensive. My terms are as stated, gentlemen. I await word on your decision."

He didn't give them time to argue as he moved for the door and left the office.

He knew how to handle deals and he knew the man he had fashioned John Vincent into. The once-struggling broker hadn't had the charisma or the daring that John used after his transformation.

As he left the office and moved through the hallway to the main portion of the cabin, he pulled his cell phone from his jeans and tapped in a text to Bailey.

Your friends are a bit arrogant, he texted with a grin.

Seconds later she came back with the prearranged response. *You don't need them. Just me. Wanna mess around?*

He didn't answer the question. Instead he headed to the back entrance of the house and the evergreen maze that made up the gardens behind the house.

The maze held a variety of small sheltered grottoes with gas fireplaces, each creating an enchanted private atmosphere that guests were invited to partake of.

He and Bailey set up an arrangement of meeting places there. If one was being used, the next on the list they'd created would be checked.

He moved to the first on the list. It was midway into the maze, difficult to find, and highly private. It was the perfect setting for a tryst, or a covert meeting.

He slid into the grotto, his gaze raking over her slender figure as she shed the jacket she had worn. Beneath it she wore a light loosely woven sweater, jeans, and boots. Her hair brushed past her shoulders, framed her quiet expression, and picked up the rich color in her emerald-green eyes.

God, she's beautiful, he thought as an image of her the

night before, taking his dick, crying his name, shot through his mind. He'd had problems with that all day. The memory of it distracted him and never failed to tighten his cock as his balls throbbed in hunger.

Damn her, he couldn't get her out of his system and he couldn't get enough of her. He didn't want her out of his system. He wanted her in his arms until they both took their last breath. Hopefully years and years from now.

"It's about time you showed up," she murmured with a smile as he moved to her and took her in his arms. "I didn't think you'd ever make it."

Her body snuggled against his, accepting a part of him that he never wanted to lose. It was almost impossible to pull his head out of his cock enough to concentrate on the mission.

"Are we clear?" he asked, his voice barely a breath of sound as he kissed the shell of her ear.

She caught his wrist and moved his hand to her rear, to the back pocket where she had tucked the slim electronic detector she had been given to sweep their room.

Lowering his hand, he clenched it over the rounded globe and pulled her closer to him, letting her feel the erection that throbbed beneath his jeans.

"I could eat you up right here," he whispered. "Lay you out on that bench and show you just how inventive I can get with my tongue."

Her breath caught. He heard the sound, felt the little jerk of her body as her hands moved beneath his jacket to tighten on his shoulders.

"You're distracting me," she breathed out roughly.

"I'm distracting me." His hand petted and stroked over her rear as the image of her spread out on the padded bench nearly had him spilling himself in his jeans.

God, the things she did to him.

"Our friends are definitely a part of the problem." He kept his voice so low that she had to press her ear to his lips to hear him.

"You met?" The feel of her lips rubbing against his ear in turn had his balls drawing tight.

"With both of them," he affirmed. "The job is on the table between myself and our other party of interest. Your attempts to investigate as you covered for them over the years were successful. They believe they can trust you, as well as me. We should know within a few days."

Her hand stroked over his shoulders, her nails scraping against his sweater as her hips moved against his, teasing him, torturing him in the most pleasurable way.

"You'll be chosen," she stated. "One of them will come to me soon enough. Myron has yet to meet with me, but I'm expecting him to do so very soon. When he does I'll let him know I've chosen you for the job." He could hear the distaste in her voice.

Have you received any information on Roth? He couldn't stop himself from caressing her ear as the hand that rested at her waist dipped beneath the hem of her sweater. The memory of that knife at her throat still had the power to terrify him.

"No." She shook her head. "He hasn't been seen since leaving Aspen last night, but I don't expect to hear anything for several days."

"He'll be careful for a while until he's certain he's not being tracked," John agreed. "Do you think Warbucks will pull back and allow him to live?"

"It's according to how bad he wants to please me," she said. They were hoping Warbucks's intent to draw her in went deep enough for a favor. It could give them an edge they could use later.

John nodded. "We should know something soon then."

The waiting game was the hardest. They had everything in place, their intent had been made clear. Now they just had to wait to see what Warbucks did with it.

"I've demanded full disclosure, either way," he told her. "The price, the item and the buyers involved will demand it simply because of the risk factor. I need to know who to come after if I get screwed."

And John Vincent was known to come after his enemies.

"How do we know we'll meet the true Warbucks?" Her

hands were as busy as his. They stroked beneath his sweater, her fingers combing through the fine mat of hair on his chest before rasping against a hard male nipple.

He damned near shuddered at the pleasure. Fuck him, she was like a fire herself, burning him from the inside out.

"We'll know." They'd worked too long, too hard and this sale was too important to Warbucks's reputation.

She finally nodded as her tongue slipped between her teeth to lick over the lobe of his ear. His palm cupped her breast, his thumb stroking over her nipple.

The hard tip was warm silk, tempting his mouth even as he fought to hold back.

"What about our other party of interest?" She breathed against his ear as her hands rasped down his chest to his taut abdomen.

"Either way, full disclosure will be demanded," he assured her.

She nipped at his ear. "Tell me who he is."

He almost grinned. "Abbas? A true bastard."

"Uh-huh." Her lips moved to his neck as the mission began to take second place now that she had the information she needed in case Falks or Greer approached her.

"Fifteen percent fee." He finally remembered as her tongue stroked beneath his ear.

"Hmm," she murmured as her fingers moved to his belt and slowly loosened it.

Hell, they would end up melting the snow from the shelter faster than the warmth of the fire would.

Moving back slowly, he sat down on the bench, staring up at her as he gripped her thighs and pulled her to him. He needed a taste of her, just a little bit. He couldn't get enough of her, no matter how much he tried.

Jerking the hem of her sweater over her silken stomach he laid his lips against her flesh and listened to her breath catch, felt her hips arch.

He touched her and she caught flame along with him. It was like spontaneous combustion, and it was destructive.

"Straddle me." He pulled her closer as his head lifted.

A flush mounted her face as she moved to straddle his hips. Leaning back, he arched his hips as she came over him, driving his denim-covered cock between her thighs.

"Damn, you're hot, even dressed," he growled as he gripped her hips, ground against her and moved her over him.

"Dangerous game here," she panted. "I could end up tearing your clothes from that sexy body of yours and having my way with you."

"You'd have to beat me to it," he promised her. "Because I'm less than a second from doing the same to you."

He gripped her hair and pulled her to him, demanding a kiss that he knew would sear his senses. And it did. It burned into his brain, sent flames shooting over his nerve endings and exploding in his balls.

He could lay her back and strip her, have her, taste every inch of her body, and pray to God no one caught them. The chances of being caught were slim to none, he assured himself. Only a few people would know where they were. The guests at the party wouldn't be slipping out here until after dark. They were a bit more circumspect in their liaisons.

John felt her hands thread through his hair, her fingers clenching as she tried to pull him closer. Her lips moved beneath his, her tongue accepted his, rubbed against it, tasted him as he tasted her. They both groaned, the sounds of pleasure washing around them as they strained closer.

His head tilted as he moved to taste more of her. His hands were beneath her sweater, cupping and caressing her unbound breasts, stroking her nipples and dying for a taste of them.

There was a mission here that he was supposed to be concentrating on. A job to do. Hell, Jordan would kill him if he found out how distracted he was becoming and just how important Bailey was becoming to him.

The unit was all that mattered to Jordan Malone. Bailey was all that mattered to John. This wasn't going to work out for the other man where missions were concerned. And nothing else was going to work out for John if he lost Bailey.

Holding her to him, his lips sipping at hers, his hands stroking her breasts, her nipples, he knew he couldn't live without the taste of her, the touch of her. He needed this simply to survive.

"Well, it looks like we're definitely interrupting something here." The low, irritated foreign drawl had John's head jerking back as he pulled Bailey from his lap to the relative protection of his side.

"You're so bad, Jerric." Catalina's cool, feminine tones were filled with amusement. "You could have given them a few minutes before interrupting."

Bailey stared back at the couple, her senses alive like never before, and felt a flush work over her face as she faced Jerric Abbas.

He was glowering at her as though in disappointment or disapproval before his expression cleared and his black eyes were once again cool and all too familiar.

This wasn't the Jerric Abbas she had known, but that look was definitely the cousin she had known as David Abijah, and the agent she had met in Atlanta, Micah Sloane.

The pieces were falling in place for her. Trent had become an international penny-ante broker, John Vincent, and built his reputation into that of one of the most trusted, reputable black-market brokers in the world.

Micah Sloane was fairly unknown, but Jerric Abbas wasn't. This Jerric was making a name for himself, though. Travis Caine. She knew the man she had recently met as Travis Caine wasn't the same one she'd met in England several years before.

They were all dead men reborn.

"Should I leave?" She rose slowly to her feet and jerked her jacket from the edge of the bench where she had laid it. Pulling it on, she suddenly felt less like a schoolgirl caught making out and more like a woman with a mind of her own.

Of course, David had always had way of making her feel like a child whenever he caught her in something she shouldn't have been a part of. He had been a steadying influence in her life. He and his father Garren, before their deaths, had represented stability in a world that often hadn't made sense to her.

"Miss Serborne." He nodded his head to her before turning to John. "I hear we're still in a bit of friendly competition."

John rose slowly to his feet as Jerric and Catalina both remained still, too careful, too wary.

They had been followed or somehow suspected they were being spied upon. She could feel it. Had someone been watching them before Jerric and his rumored lover had come upon them?

"I trust we'll both handle it like the professionals we are," John drawled as Bailey watched Catalina closely.

"Always," Micah stated, his expression hooded as he gave John another long, intent look. "Sorry to have interrupted you, but I do so enjoy getting my little pokes in where I can."

Catalina's laughter was silky and smooth. It was natural, though the look on her face was warning.

They were definitely being watched.

"Then Bailey and I will retire to our room, where your little pokes don't matter," John said mockingly as his hand settled at the back of her waist and he led her toward the doorway. "If you'll excuse us."

"Of course," Jerric murmured, then his voice became a breath of sound as they moved past. "Be careful, my friends, you've picked up some attention."

John and Bailey moved past them as though they hadn't heard the brief warning. John's arm wrapped around her waist, pulling her to him as though they had every intention of finishing what they had started as soon as they returned to their room.

Bailey would have loved to finish it. The need for it was burning through her system like a flame she couldn't extinguish.

He had always done that to her. If he touched her, her response tormented her for days on end. When she had lost him, she had never forgotten that touch, never forgotten the man who had claimed her heart.

Glancing around, Bailey caught sight of movement in the edge of the shrubbery that led into another path of the maze. There, sheltered by the shadows, Ralph Stanford shifted back, almost hidden completely by the evergreens he was hiding within.

Bailey could feel the malevolence reaching out to her, the rage that filled the other man.

Bailey felt John's hand at her back, a subtle warning to ignore the man as he watched them. She could ignore him for now, but she knew the time would come that ignoring him wouldn't be an option. Ralph hated to lose and he hated Bailey. It was a combination Bailey knew would soon strike out at her, and perhaps John as well.

Chapter 15

ON THE SURFACE, JOHN was the perfect businessman. He conversed with the elders of the society Bailey had been born into with a charisma and intelligence that over the next few days they would learn to respect.

Ford Grace, Samuel Waterstone, Stephen Menton-Squire, and Ronald Claymore were all on the board of directors of Serborne Enterprises, a vast umbrella of businesses and major shares in businesses that made up the Serborne fortune. It was these men who would lose a large source of income if Bailey died without an heir or changed her will to leave her fortune to a nonrelative rather than charity, as had been set up.

They were also the four men who had made the short list of suspects in the investigation she had been conducting herself for years, as well as the investigation John's unit was involved in.

The four of them were her godfathers as well. Her father hadn't picked one man, just as her mother hadn't picked one woman. No, she had four sets of godparents, thank you very much.

They were also the men whom John had convinced that he was smart enough, savvy enough, and deceitful enough to help Bailey control her shares once she took them over. Not that any of them was happy that he would no longer be voting those shares. But at least they weren't opposed to the man it seemed she was choosing to vote them.

"You're making quite an impression," she murmured to John as he returned to her several nights later in the ball-room after meeting the four men for drinks.

"There's no way those four men work together," he growled. "Do you realize that in the past six years they have argued over the simplest vote, and almost come to blows over each idea that has been broached to making your companies more efficient and employee-friendly?" He looked outraged. "Do you know one of those bastards nearly hit *me*?"

"Really?" She hadn't known that. She had been too busy trying to pin the name Warbucks to one of them.

"Bailey, those four are psychopaths posing as business-men." He was in her face, his expression bordering furiously amazed. "They need to be locked away for the safety of every-one they know."

Bailey stared back at him in surprise. "I'm sure it's not that bad."

She turned back to the shrimp bowl on the buffet table and debated a few more when he caught her arm and pulled her around to face him once again.

"Bailey, it is that bad," he growled, horror obviously re-flecting in his gaze. "If you ever, and I mean ever, decide to actually take responsibility for the inheritance your parents left you, then you have a fucking mess on your hands."

"That boy likes to overexaggerate!" Bailey turned around, reeling from the obvious criticism that she neglected her in-heritance, to meet Ronald Claymore's furious, brows-lowered, forehead-drawn expression. He looked just as pissed as John. "If you end up marrying this brazen little upstart, then we're going to have words."

"Ronald, you never could tolerate anyone who could out-yell you," Samuel Waterstone expressed in precise, cold tones from behind him. "Don't punish her because he's louder than you are." He then glowered at John. "He's louder than all of us."

When exactly had the Twilight Zone decided to visit As-pen, Colorado?

"Ignore them, Bailey." Ford was the only one who

showed a reasonable amount of goodwill. A smile quirked at his lips and his gray eyes reflected something she hadn't seen since she was a child. A sense of fun. "They've gotten too old to enjoy a good fight."

Stephen Menton-Squire was glaring at all of them. "The boy is a damned bastard," he muttered, drawing disapproving glances from the other three men.

"Excuse me, gentlemen." John gripped Bailey's arm at the elbow, his expression filled with irritation. "I don't think you need to be a part of this conversation."

"Wait, this conversation involves us." Stephen turned on John with a fierce frown as he jerked his evening jacket into place and straightened his thick shoulders. "We should obviously be present."

"In a padded room," John bit out with a frown just as dangerously dark as the other man's. "And only if you show some respect when a lady is present."

He drew her quickly away. Looking over her shoulder, she caught Ford's obvious chuckle as the other three men began to argue among themselves, again.

It was normal. For the first time since returning home, Bailey remembered something good about the times she and her parents had spent with the four men and their families. When Ben Serborne engaged in a war of words with these men, it made an all-out brawl look gentle.

"They're like children," she murmured with a sense of nostalgia.

"I'd rather deal with terrorists armed with nuclear capabilities," John muttered as he drew her to the dance floor and took her in his arms before glaring back at them. "You need to do something about them where your companies are concerned."

She looked back at him in surprise. "Not my area. The business was Father's love affair, not mine."

"It's your children's inheritance," he informed her, anger still vibrating in his voice as his hand pressed her closer to him and she felt the warmth of his larger body surrounding her.

"I don't have children," she pointed out. "And I don't intend to have any."

He almost stopped in the middle of the floor, surprise drawing his expression tight once again. "You will eventually," he finally stated carefully.

Bailey met his gaze with one of determination. "No, John, I won't. The father of my children died. Remember?" She kept her voice carefully low, kept her lips hidden so they couldn't be read. But she didn't hide the truth from him.

She'd rather be alone than to be with a man simply because she wanted a family or children. It wouldn't be fair to the man, but it especially wouldn't be fair to the children.

He didn't say anything. Hell, what could he say? It was the truth. He was going to disappear from her life just as he had the first time, except this time she would know he was out there, without her.

"The business is your legacy," he finally stated as he tucked her closer to him. "It will go to someone, Bailey. Leaving it to charity is unconscionable."

"And taking care of it myself is outside my range of abilities," she told him. "I'm not a businesswoman, John. I don't want to be one."

Once this was over, she would take enough of her inheritance to retire. A nice little house someplace quiet, a peaceful little neighborhood where she could retreat from the battles she had faced over the years.

She deserved it, she told herself. She was looking at losing the man she loved twice in one lifetime. There would be no children, no family, and the white picket fence would be for looks only.

How was he supposed to answer that one? John wondered then. She had been an agent from the age of eighteen until she had been fired the year before. She had lived to destroy the person or persons responsible for killing those she had loved. The only time that love had overwhelmed that desire, it had been taken from her.

Jordan was going to be pissed, he thought as he felt determination well inside him. He wasn't letting her go a second time. And she wouldn't sit back and let him fight those battles on his own, she would be at his side. She would be a part of the unit, one way or the other, or John would have to break a promise that could very well put both their lives in danger.

"And if you could have the man you loved?" he asked her then. "Would you want children?"

He felt her smile against his shoulder and had a feeling it wasn't a gentle smile. He could almost sense what lay behind it.

"That option isn't open to me," she said softly. "Until it is, that's not a question I can answer."

He tucked his head against hers and reined in the sigh that would have slipped from him. This mission was getting to him, the entire situation was fucking getting to him. He needed to give her reassurance, he needed to promise her that he was never going to leave her life again, but until he made the necessary arrangements, he couldn't promise her anything. He didn't have the promises to give her.

"Excuse me. I'd like to claim this dance." They drew to a stop as John stared back at Wagner Grace.

Bailey turned and stared at the other man. John could feel the tension building in her body, working through her system.

"Just for a moment," he requested as he stared at Bailey. "I promise I won't keep you long."

The man looked haunted, but he also looked spoiled and put out, John thought. He admitted, though, that the offspring of the four icons who were here this weekend hadn't impressed him much. They were spoiled little children parading as adults. They were smart as hell, but their intelligence was invariably put to use in less-than-intelligent areas. Wagner for instance, according to the unit's report, had spent most of his life trying to get out of work rather than showing any interest in the various business interests his father had accumulated.

"Of course." Polite society would have frowned on him for refusing, he guessed. Besides, this was one for Bailey to handle.

Moving from the dance floor, he bit back a grimace and joined the four men he was certain should be committed for the safety of the public at large. Not to mention their own safety.

"That boy has some growing up to do," Samuel commented as John turned and directed his attention back to the ballroom.

"They all do." Stephen sighed. "We didn't raise our kids right, Sam. That's our problem."

"Ben raised his right," Ford interjected. John turned to stare back at the other man. Ford's eyes met John's and in them, John glimpsed a bit of calculation mixed with the respect. "Ben raised his girl right," he stated again. "He was smarter than the rest of us."

With that he turned and moved from the gathering. Watching, John saw him join Raymond, speak for a moment, then leave the ballroom.

John turned around again to watch Bailey, his gaze narrowed on her cool expression and the stiffness of her body. Wagner looked sincere, intent, convincing as he talked quickly.

BAILEY PLACED ONE HAND in Wagner's, her other hand on his shoulder, and stared up at him curiously as he led her around the ballroom floor.

She could feel the tension radiating from Wagner. A watchful cold tightness to his body that she had never associated with him before. She hadn't seen him much during the house party. He and several of his friends, such as Grant Waterstone, had found other pursuits to entertain them.

"I'm worried about you, Bailey," he finally stated as he stared down at her in concern. "One of Raymond's security personnel mentioned that you were attacked the other day by another guest. One of the more unsavory individuals that Raymond likes to invite."

Bailey stared back at him in surprise. She had assumed Raymond would cover up the event.

"It was nothing to worry about," she waved the event off. "A minor inconvenience."

"I see." He frowned back at her. "As I understand it, you were seconds from having your throat slit."

"And as you can see, I'm doing fine," she assured him. "Really, Wagner, don't worry."

"I do worry," he stated. "As does Grant. Vincent isn't a safe bet for you, dear. He'll only add to the danger of your own past."

Grant Waterstone was a bastard and everyone knew it. Even worse, he was a stupid bastard. He ran with the wrong crowd, did too many drugs, and paid too high a price for them.

She ignored his jab at John, instead keeping her expression carefully composed and simply letting him rail.

"Father doesn't even care what I uncovered investigating that bastard Vincent." He glared down at her suddenly. "Do you know he's suspected of brokering deals with terrorists? For God's sake, Bailey. You're with the CIA."

"I was fired," she pointed out with a lack of heat. "I'm a free agent now, Wagner."

"You were with the CIA," he amended. "Where's your patriotism?"

"With my 401(k), my pension, and my service record," she replied with obvious boredom. "Shot to hell when I was fired."

He stared back at her curiously. "I never believed you'd back Father over anything." He shook his head. "He's not the man he's obviously convinced you of, Bailey. We both know that."

She remained silent. She could understand why he was questioning her. To him, the change he saw in her would be confusing.

"You know he isn't," he said,

"None of us are." She shrugged. "As you said, I was an agent. I've been one since I was eighteen, Wagner. In all those years I was never able to put a crime to your father's name, and trust me, I've tried. Perhaps I'm the one who has been wrong all these years. And even if I wasn't, then it doesn't matter. I won't turn on the only family I have left."

"Maybe there is proof," he suggested carefully. "Proof that would prove he's not what he seems to be."

She narrowed her gaze and watched him carefully. "Be careful, Wagner," she began.

"Listen, meet me later." His voice lowered as his hand tightened at her hip. "Give me just a few minutes, Bailey. Let me show you that he doesn't deserve your loyalty."

Her lips pressed together as she appeared to consider the request.

"For Anna, Bailey. Do this for Anna," he whispered.

She breathed out heavily. "Tonight, after the ball," she told him. "Whatever you have, bring it to the room."

"Come to mine," he urged her. "Alone. Vincent can't be there. He's too tight with the fathers to suit me. And what one is doing, you can bet the others are involved in."

And what the hell did that mean? Could Wagner actually have proof that any of them were Warbucks? Or were involved with that traitor?

"I'll be there." She nodded. "I can't promise when."

"That's good enough," he nodded. "I'll be waiting for you."

The music drew to an end. Wagner took her hand and led her back to John.

"Thank you for the dance." He nodded graciously. "Good night."

Bailey watched him leave as she felt John's hand move to the center of her back, where his fingertips massaged her spine subtly.

"I have to meet with him later," she said quietly. "He says he has some kind of evidence against Ford. Something that proves he doesn't deserve my loyalty."

"Did he mention what?" John nuzzled her ear slowly, sending a wave of pleasure rushing down her back. She felt like arching like a cat beneath his touch.

"He didn't say." She shrugged. "He'll be waiting on me tonight after the festivities down here are over."

"We're getting closer." His lips were still close to her ear, caressing the shell with sensual strokes.

"Perhaps." She couldn't get over the feeling that something wasn't right, though. Ford was too damned nice, and too determined to keep Wagner and Jules apart. Just as he was too determined to draw John into any and all business discussions.

This was a side of Ford Grace that frankly terrified her. He wasn't a nice man and she got nervous when he pretended to be.

"We have company arriving," he told her quietly before straightening and moving his hand to her hip, where he cupped it warmly.

"Bailey." Grant Waterstone stepped up to them, his haughty features almost effeminate as he stared down his eagle-straight nose at her.

His hair was perfectly styled, his face smooth and classically handsome, and she knew for a fact his hands were baby soft.

"Hello, Grant." She turned her head for his brief kiss, accepting it on her cheek despite the vague feeling of distaste that chased down her spine.

There was just something about Grant that she had never truly been able to like—something that just never rang true about him. It wasn't just his drug habits, or his low-class friends. She had always felt he would sell her out in a minute if he ever had the chance.

"You should be careful of Wagner," he warned her quietly. "We all know how he enjoys his schemes."

She arched her brow. "Wagner has never been unkind, Grant."

"You were just never in reach," he stated arrogantly. Simply be careful, my dear. I'd hate to see you hurt."

"Insurance is good for something." Her lips twitched in amusement.

Grant shrugged. "Just a word of warning." He turned and moved away from her, his shoulders straight, his head held high.

"Grant's been buying his drugs from a man associated with a homeland terrorist cell," John murmured at her side.

Bailey nodded slowly. She knew that, she just wished she didn't.

"I've had enough." She shook her head. "Get me the hell out of here."

Immediately he began leading her to the wide double doors that led to the foyer and the staircase. To say she'd had enough was putting it mildly.

They made it back to their room with few interruptions. The flow of champagne in the ballroom was heavy enough that most of the groups that had congregated together were more inclined to stay in one place than seek out other amusements.

Entering the bedroom, she kicked off her heels as John swept the room for listening devices. He found one, stared at it for long moments, then shook his head before crushing it beneath his heel and leaving it lying for housekeeping to clean up.

"That is beginning to get old," Bailey stated as she unzipped the back of her dress and shimmied out of it.

Laying it across the back of a chair, she moved to the walk-in closet, where she pulled free a pair of loose sweats and a T-shirt.

Re-dressing in the relative privacy of the closet, she tried to push back the weariness that tugged at her. A weariness that seemed to have followed her most of the day. It wasn't just physical, it was mental. Her adult life had been spent running away from these people, and each day with them now reminded her why.

She felt out of place, out of sync with the men and women she had been raised to consider her family. Couples who considered themselves above her, more intelligent, superior to her simply because she hadn't spent her life trying to fit in with them.

"When are you meeting with Wagner?" John stepped to the doorway, his gaze brooding, dark. "I don't like you seeing him alone."

"Wagner's harmless." She sighed. "The information he has could be important."

"He's the least dangerous of the entire crowd," he agreed. "But I'm still not comfortable with it."

She turned fully to meet him as she pulled a pair of sneakers from a shelf and slipped her feet into them. Bending to tie them, she glanced up at him again, seeing the concern on his face.

"He won't talk to me if I bring anyone with me," she told him. "If Wagner has proof against Ford, then it's something we need to deal with now."

She made certain to keep their conversation in Ford's favor, to never speak of the mission unless they were certain of security, and to keep any reference to Warbucks silent.

They had eight days left on this assignment. Eight days to figure out who Warbucks was and prepare for the meeting with him. Eight days to put the past to rest, she thought. Eight days before she lost John, again.

That thought had her pausing as she straightened, staring back at him with the knowledge of how little time they had left together.

How was she supposed to survive this time? she wondered. How was she supposed to sleep at night knowing he was on a mission without her, knowing that another woman could touch, could hold what belonged to her? Knowing that without him, she was alone; that it wouldn't matter where she lived, because that place would still be unbearable without John.

And she couldn't cry over it. She couldn't rage over it. There was nothing she could do to ease the pain burning in her chest.

"It's going to be okay." He mouthed the words at her. "Trust me."

She did trust him, but still, she couldn't see a way out of this one. Whatever agency had reformed him wouldn't want her within it. She had been fired from the CIA; she was considered a security risk to any other agency.

"Sure it will," she mouthed back. An empty platitude.

"I'm going to go talk to Wagner." She moved to the doorway as he stood in front of her. He didn't move. He stared at her, his expression brooding as he obviously searched for something in her expression.

"Are you armed?" he finally asked quietly.

She shook her head. "There's no place to hide it effectively, and I wouldn't want Wagner to suspect. If I'm not back in an hour, then come looking for me. But I can guarantee you, I'll be back before that."

He still wasn't moving.

"I'll need to get past you, John." A tired smile pulled at her lips as she watched him.

God she loved him. There was something about him now, just as there had been before, that drew her irrevocably to him. She wanted to curl into his arms again and for a little while forget that the world around them existed.

"Not yet." He stepped forward, his hands moving to her hips before he pulled her against his body.

She felt his erection instantly. There was a hunger, a need in his touch as his hands stroked down her back to cup the curves of her rear before moving back to her hips.

She was waiting on him when his head lowered, when his lips brushed against hers. Her hands slid to his neck, her fingers dipping into the cool strands of his hair as her lips parted for him.

His kiss was like a fire in winter. A sweet benediction of pure hunger, of need. Beneath his kiss she felt both cherished and ravished. Flames leapt through her system and seared her nerve endings as she fought to hold on to her senses just enough to remember what the hell she was supposed to be doing here.

Because in John's arms it wasn't as though she could actually think or plan for anything past the brush of his lips or the touch of his tongue.

Long sipping kisses revived that part of her that had grown weary and too tired to face another day of the deceit and manipulations. His hands stroking along her back, beneath her shirt, touching her flesh, caressing it, brought the warmth back to her body and left her sighing in need against him.

"Hurry back," he whispered against her lips as her eyes

opened languorously to stare into the dark recesses of his gaze. "I need you tonight, Bailey."

"And tomorrow night?" she whispered. Though it wasn't tomorrow she worried about. It was eight days from now, when this investigation wrapped up, one way or the other; when Warbucks was either revealed or triumphant over them. It was then that her heart would need answers.

"I need you every night."

He needed her, but they were both aware that they couldn't always have what they wanted. That sometimes, you were just left holding an empty heart and an even emptier life.

"I'll hurry," she promised as she drew back from him. "Be waiting for me."

"Always," he promised.

She just wished that were true.

Chapter 16

BAILEY SHOVED HER HANDS in her pockets as she made her way from the second-story wing—where her and John's suite was located—to the other side of the house, where Wagner had been assigned a suite.

The structure was huge, more mansion than cabin. It was ostentatious and glittery and a waste of money in the extreme, she thought.

But it was also a work of art in places. She couldn't take that from it. It just wasn't her, any more than her parents' cabin was her.

Moving past the nearly soundproof doors of the other suites, she took several long minutes to make her way to Wagner's. She ignored the sound of a door opening behind her and the quiet click of it closing. She wasn't afraid of being attacked, yet. That would come later, if it came at all.

Someone had paid Orion to leave her alone, to let her live despite how close she had come to him several times. Whoever that person was, they wouldn't allow her to be killed here, within familiar territory. Especially not after the attack by Landon Roth.

Stopping at Wagner's room, she knocked softly and waited until he opened the door.

He had been drinking. He held a glass in his hand, and the scent of whiskey that surrounded him, though faint, was a testament to the fact that it wasn't his first of the night.

"Come in." His tone was cold, icy.

She had rarely seen Wagner like this.

"I only have a few minutes before John will notice me missing," she told him as she stepped inside the suite and looked around slowly.

The room was immaculate. The bed was made without the first indication to suggest that anyone slept in it.

"I seem to be pouting tonight, according to Father." He lifted the whiskey glass with a sardonic smile. "It rather sucks when your father falls from the pedestal you've placed him upon."

Bailey watched thoughtfully as he finished the whiskey before thumping the glass on a nearby table.

"Most of us have to face this when we're in our teens." She finally shrugged. "Our parents aren't perfect, Wagner, no matter how much we wish they were."

"No kidding," he grunted as he wiped his hand over his face before shaking his head wearily. "But not all our parents are monsters, Bailey."

"Is your father a monster?"

Wagner sighed wearily at the question.

"You know father's personal assistant was killed in a skiing accident several months ago?"

Bailey shook her head. "I hadn't heard." She had, actually. She had even managed to search the man's apartment days after his death, but had found nothing that would incriminate Ford Grace.

"Charlie was a good man." He sighed heavily. "He was only about ten years older than we were, but he was damned smart. He ran Father's life like a well-oiled machine."

"That's a personal assistant's job," she stated as she maintained a carefully calm attitude, almost cold. It wouldn't do to show emotion or curiosity too soon.

"Yeah, ol' Charlie was smart." He gave a hard grunt of mocking laughter. "Father had no idea how smart, I don't believe."

"What are you getting at, Wagner?" she finally asked tiredly. She didn't want to deal with this tonight. She wanted to return to her room and curl against John's body. She wanted to feel his touch, his possession, and save up another memory for the time she wouldn't have him any longer.

Wagner shook his head, his eyes narrowing on her. "You've surprised me, Bailey," he stated sadly. "I had thought your sense of justice was much stronger than it appears it was."

"Wagner, my sense of justice got a clue when I realized how little others really gave a damn," she bit out impatiently. "Now I really don't give a damn myself. And what the hell does my patriotism have to do with your father or your relationship with him?"

"There is no relationship with him," he stated as he turned and moved to the television set to retrieve the remote sitting on top of it. "I realized that the other day when I received a very interesting package."

Holding the remote, he crossed the room to her.

"What sort of package?" she asked him.

His smile was mocking, disdainful. "What makes the world go around, Bailey?"

She watched him for long moments before a brittle smile crossed her lips. "Power."

"Not money?" He arched a brow with a mocking curiosity.

"You can have money and still retain no power." She shrugged. "Power can bring you unlimited funds, though. So power makes the world go around, Wagner. Not money."

He chuckled at that. "Father says the same thing."

She lifted her shoulders in a negligent shrug. "So did mine. It was his favorite philosophy."

"Did you know your father and mine fought the night he died?"

Bailey felt that swift, brutal stroke of pain inside her soul and fought to hide it.

"Our fathers were always arguing." She pushed her hands back into the pockets of her loose sweats and regarded him with a hint of amusement. "They enjoyed it."

He shook his head. "No, they really fought. A fistfight in

the middle of Father's office. Ben stormed out, swearing he'd see Father in prison. That was an hour before your parents were killed."

She shook her head as rage threatened the careful calm she had pulled around herself. "I had no idea. But what does this have to do with now?"

"As I said, Charlie was smart." He lifted the remote and turned on the television. "He believed in insurance, and he had a bit of his own." His composure seemed to crack then, along with his voice. "God, Bailey." He turned back to her. "Charlie had a package that he left with a friend to give to me if something happened to him. There was a DVD in that package."

Bailey could feel her palms sweating now. She stared into Wagner's face and saw the brittle rage that reflected in his eyes.

"What do you have, Wagner?" she whispered almost in dread, sensing, somehow knowing that life as she knew it was going to be changed.

Wagner shook his head. "Sit down." He indicated the chair across from the television. "Trust me, you don't want to be standing for this."

Bailey sat down warily as Wagner hit PLAY and the DVD started up.

It was in Ford's office. He was standing behind his desk as her father stalked into the room.

"What the fuck do you think you're doing?" Her father growled, his deep voice resonating inside Bailey as she watched his beloved features.

"Searching for some papers." Ford looked up from the desk. "What's your problem? Getting cold feet?"

"Cold feet, your ass!" Ben cursed. "You little bastard. Who the fuck is Warbucks and what the hell is he doing with the test designs Serborne Research has been working on for the military? What the bloody hell are you up to?"

Bailey's heart nearly stopped. Ford sat down behind the desk slowly. "What are you talking about, Ben?"

"I'm talking about the fucking rumor that the Mossad

caught wind of. The rumor that an American traitor has military designs entrusted to my company. Designs that only you could have gotten access to. Designs you gave him." Ben's voice rose in volume as fury creased and flushed his face.

Ford regarded him silently over the desk for long moments.

"Forget you heard that rumor," Ford advised him. "And advise your cousin Garren that he has his facts wrong. If you want to live, Ben, if you want your family to live, you'll drop it."

The fight progressed from there. Her father was out of his chair, fists flying. The fight turned bloody before Ben stormed out of the office, threatening to call Homeland Security.

As the door slammed shut, another door opened. Bailey wanted to scream in rage as Orion stepped from another room into the office.

"Take care of him," Ford ordered him coldly. "Tonight. Before he has a chance to call anyone."

"It's going to cost you." Orion's smile was a monster's grin of anticipation. "This won't be as cheap as Mathilda and Anna's was."

She was going to pass out. Bailey stared at the scene with a sense of horror, praying the emotionless mask she had plastered on her face was still in place.

So many years she had fought to prove that Ford had hired Orion to kill his wife and daughter, and then her parents. So many sleepless nights spent trying to find proof, fighting to make Ford Grace pay for the deaths of those she had loved.

And here was the proof. Right here, in living color, taped by a man who had been smart enough to think about insurance.

"Price is no object," Ford stated arrogantly. "Just make certain it happens tonight."

Orion shook his bald head and gaze a mocking little laugh. "It's always a pleasure doing business with you, Grace. Always a pleasure."

Ford sniffed at the comment as Orion turned on his heel and left the room the way he'd come. That night, her parents had died.

She could feel the tears she needed to shed, ached to shed burning in her chest as she watched Ford return to his desk, straighten his papers, replace the phone on the desk, then pour himself a drink.

He was calm, humming to himself, as though he hadn't just ordered the deaths of two people who'd loved him like a brother. As though he hadn't just admitted to killing his wife and child.

And she couldn't do a damned thing about it. Not yet.

Rising to her feet, she moved slowly to the television, found the controls, and ejected the disk. Holding it in her hand, she stared down at it, felt something shatter inside her soul, and prayed to God that she knew what the hell she was doing.

If Wagner tried to use this, then he was dead. Ford would have no compunctions about killing his heir if he turned against him like this.

"Tell me how to handle this, Bailey," Wagner whispered roughly behind her. "Tell me how to make him pay."

"Have you copied this?" she asked softly.

"Not yet," he answered. "I can't believe I even have it."

She held the disk between her hands, took a deep breath, and snapped it in half.

"What the fuck!" Wagner was suddenly in front of her, incredulity marking his face as he jerked the pieces from her hand. "What have you done?" He stared at her as though she had gone insane. "Bailey, what have you done?"

She faced him, forcing ice over her expression, watching as he looked at the broken halves, then back to her.

"It doesn't matter what you know," she told him calmly. "Remember where your loyalty lies, Wagner. Remember who your father is. Before you end up as dead as your mother and sister."

It broke her heart. She was going to strangle on the tears that fought to be free. She wanted to curl onto the floor and die, the agony was so intense. Nothing, except losing Trent, had ever hurt like this. Nothing else but the loss of the man she loved had ever ripped into her with the needle-sharp talons that raked over her now.

Agony pierced every bone and muscle, every joint and cell. She felt as though she were moving in slow motion, as though the air itself had thickened around her, forcing her to plow through it, making her body feel as though it weighed a ton.

She didn't want to return to her room. She didn't want to face John, she didn't want to face herself. She wanted to find a hole, a very deep, very small hole, and crawl into it for a very long time.

"Is your sense of loyalty to the bastards really this strong, Bailey?" Wagner's voice was a hard rasp as she reached the door and gripped the doorknob.

"It is." She didn't turn to face him; she couldn't. "It always has been, Wagner. No one just ever cared to realize it."

Her loyalty to her friends. Her loyalty to her parents. It had always been strong, it had always driven her to find their killer. As it should have driven Wagner.

"Good night, Wagner."

Walking from the room was incredibly easy. As she moved down the hallway she watched as another door opened. Myron Falks stepped from his suite next to his employer's and watched her, his gaze narrowed.

"Bailey." He nodded to her as she neared. "Could we talk?"

She glanced at the watch on her wrist. Fifteen minutes before John came looking for her. Could she make it that long before she allowed herself to curl into the comfort of his arms? Could she bear talking to this monster for fifteen seconds, let alone a few minutes or more?

"Sure." Did she really have a choice?

He moved back from the doorway, allowing her to enter. As she walked into the room, she glanced at the sitting area. Raymond stared back at her.

Rising to his feet, he moved to the bar, fixed a straight whiskey, and brought it to her.

"Sorry, whiskey is the only choice tonight." He handed her the glass.

"Thank you." It was exactly what she needed. She sipped at it rather than throwing it back as she needed to, to burn the shock and horror from her system.

"You met with Wagner," Myron began with an air of curiosity. "We've been worried about him lately."

"Really?" She sipped at the whiskey again and stared back at him with false interest. "Why would you be?"

His brows lifted as though in surprise. "The last few days he's been rather upset with his father."

She tilted her head and gazed back at him silently for long moments.

"Wagner will be fine." She finished her drink and set it on the side bar before shoving her hands in her pockets again with an air of impatience.

"Perhaps if we knew what was wrong with him," Raymond suggested, "we could help him."

Her smile was tight as the fury brewing inside her threatened to spill over. Bullshit—they knew what was wrong with Wagner, or at the very least strongly suspected.

"Wagner will be fine now," she repeated her earlier reassurance. "He had a few issues, but they've been resolved."

"You took care of it then?" Myron asked.

"I took care of it." She tightened her lips as though irritated with the fact that she had been forced to do it. "Of course, if others were more aware of their responsibilities, I wouldn't have to take care of nearly so much."

Myron's lips twitched at the comment as she moved back to the doorway.

"If you'll excuse me, it's late, and John is waiting on me."

"Are you going to marry him?" Myron didn't beat around the bush. "I think you should know he's gained approval of the families here during Raymond's little house party. We'd hate to see that relationship come to an end."

"As would I," she agreed. "Trust me, Myron, I would hate to see that happen myself."

Without giving them any more information, she turned the doorknob and left the room, praying she made it back to her own suite before she was waylaid again.

She forced herself to remain calm, to walk slowly and steadily, to keep her expression controlled. She forced herself to remember the prize, the punishment she could mete out if she just held on to her control a little while longer. Just until she was back in John's arms.

Opening the door to the suite, she stepped inside, her gaze meeting John's as tears filled her eyes. She closed the door behind her slowly, locked it, and stared back at him miserably.

"Bailey?" He moved toward her slowly. "Are you okay?"

She was crumbling inside. She could feel her emotions imploding inside her soul as she fought to hold on to her control, to keep from wailing in agony.

Pushing shaking fingers through her hair, she moved across the room to the sitting area before curling into the corner of the couch and pulling one of the small pillows over the ache in her stomach, fighting to hold back her sobs. They couldn't be entirely certain the room was secure, and she didn't have the control to be quiet. To rein in the agony if she actually let the sobs free.

She watched as he moved to the dresser and flipped on the white-noise generator he had there.

Tears filled her eyes. As though the machine had given her a measure of freedom, her emotions began to overwhelm her.

John moved to the sitting area and crouched in front of Bailey. She had curled her legs beneath her, fitting herself into the corner as if attempting to draw in on herself.

He stared into her swimming eyes, her pale face, and realized that he had never seen Bailey like this. Shell-shocked, so filled with pain and grief that it seemed to radiate around her.

"Baby?" He reached out to her, touched her cheek, and felt the first tear fall.

Some primal, primitive part of his being tightened in anger at the look on her face.

"So many years," she whispered as she bent over the pillow, as though the pain inside her couldn't be borne anymore.

God, what had happened? He should have never let her go alone. He should have stayed with her. It was his job to protect her, to shelter her.

"So many years for what, baby?" He cupped her face and wiped the tears away, only to have more replace them. "What happened, Bailey?"

She swallowed tightly as her breath hitched and her expression convulsed in agony. But she held it together. Even when he was sure she was going to break, she held it together.

"So many years I searched for proof," she said, her voice jerky. "Proof that Ford Grace had killed Anna and her mother, and then my parents. And then there it was." She held her hands out and stared down at them as though in disbelief. "It was right there in my hands. All the proof I could have ever asked for." She shook her head, her gaze coming back to his as the tears fell faster. "And I destroyed it." A sob tore from her chest as she bent over. "Oh God, John. I destroyed it."

He caught her in his arms, jerking her against his chest as she seemed to fall apart from the inside out. She was shaking, shudders racking through her body as he fought to hold on to his own grief. A grief spurred by hers, because he knew, to the depths of his soul he knew, what it would have done to her to walk away from the proof she so desperately needed.

"I broke the disk," she cried hoarsely, her arms tightening around his neck. He lifted her against him, pulling her into his arms and across his lap as he sat down in the chair behind him.

There was nothing he could do but hold her. There was no way to comfort her, no way to promise her that the decision, whatever it had been, was the right one.

"What happened, Bailey?" He smoothed her hair back, whispered the words in her ear, and prayed to God that she was finding at least a small amount of comfort from him.

He couldn't bear to see her hurt like this. His Bailey was so strong, so proud. The wound it would have taken to produce this kind of pain would have to be devastating.

She shook her head again, another sob ripping from her chest and tearing through his heart.

"It was right there," she cried, her voice low. "Ford admitting to killing Anna and her mother, ordering my father's death. It was taped by his assistant and sent to Wagner after the assistant was killed last month. 'Insurance' was what the man had called it in a letter that accompanied it. His insurance. And it was in Ford's office, with Orion. My father showed up, furious, questioning him about military design secrets that had been stolen and sold to the highest bidder. Father was enraged. They fought. He stalked out." Her voice was broken, rasping with agony. "And Orion walked into the room. He walked in and Ford ordered him to kill my father." Her nails dug into his shoulders as a low, broken wail tore from her throat and through his soul.

He could imagine what it had taken for her to maintain her control. To hide her pain.

"Oh God, I told Wagner to remember where his loyalty was." Self-disgust colored her voice and mixed with the tears and the sobs. "I told him to remember it before he ended up as dead as his mother and sister. I broke the disk. And I warned him to remember where his loyalty should lie."

Her fist clenched against his shoulder as a low scream vibrated against his chest. Her body tightened in her fight to hold back the rage tearing through her, nearly destroying her.

"I want to kill him." She fought to breathe, and John felt his own eyes fill with tears as he tried to comfort her. Without words, because there were no words that could ever ease the pain he knew she was feeling.

"It was right there in my hands," she sobbed against his chest again. "Right there, John, and I walked away. I walked away."

Because she had no other choice. She knew it, and he knew it. Warbucks was too important, the recovery of the missiles too imperative to jeopardize it at this point. The needs of the many versus the needs of the few, and the agony tearing through one small woman.

"I have you, Bailey," he whispered against her hair as he tightened his hold around her, kissed her tear-drenched cheek and wished he could find a way to ease that pain. "It's okay, baby. I promise it's okay. We'll get him. We'll make him pay for all of it."

Because John knew what Bailey didn't. The unit had been called in not to bring Warbucks to justice, but to gain the proof against him and execute him.

There was too much power contained here, in one place. If Ford Grace was Warbucks, then he had the connections to have any charges against him tampered with. Evidence would come up missing. Witnesses would die. It was that simple. There was no way in hell to preserve the facts of the case and ensure that justice was served.

No, Warbucks would die. It was that simple. At the hands of a member of the unit, whoever was holding the sniper rifle when the meet was arranged. The order had been signed before the unit had ever taken the job. It had come to them because the law enforcement agencies that had tried to capture him were too hampered by rules, regulations, and laws.

"He's going to pay for this," John swore again as he rocked her in his arms and felt a slice to his soul each time a sob tore from her chest.

"I hate him," she cried out, a strangled low sound that the white-noise generator could cover, a grief-ridden, agonized sound that he knew he would never forget. A sound he would ensure Ford paid for.

"He took everything from me," she charged. "Anna, my parents. You. He took everything, John. All of it, and never flinched. He didn't care. God help me, he didn't care."

Death was too good for Warbucks, but there was no other way to make him pay. No other way to ensure that he didn't destroy another life.

Brushing her hair back, he kissed her cheek again and simply let her cry. There was no way to fix this, no way to make it better, and if she was going to mend her shattered control, then she would need a chance to hurt first. To grieve.

The game could continue tomorrow. For now, Bailey needed this chance to rail at fate and at the job she had signed up for.

An agent who had truly turned would have to remain loyal to Ford, no matter what he had done. Thus, for now she would have to keep the end goal in mind and ensure that Ford Grace—Warbucks—had the chance to to continue his treasonous activities.

That would come to an end. John made the vow to himself. If he had to pull the trigger himself, Warbucks's treachery would end. And it would end soon.

CHAPTER 17

BAILEY OPENED HER EYES as John lifted her into his arms
and carried her to the bed. He laid her against the cool comfort of the silk sheets and began to draw the blanket over her
body, his expression tortured.

She couldn't sleep. There was no way she could sleep,
no way that she could ever drift off fast enough or deep
enough to still the agony, the betrayal she had dealt, or her
own guilt.

"No." She pushed the blankets away as he braced one
knee on the bed and moved to him instead. "I don't want to
sleep."

"You need to rest, baby." His voice was deep, dark. It was
as tortured as she felt, but she felt something more as well.
The need for a comfort that could only come from his touch.
An affirmation that there was indeed something Ford Grace
hadn't been able to kill. He hadn't killed the man she loved.

No matter the name he took, no matter the shape of his
face. This was still Trent. He was still her soul.

Moving to her knees, she gripped the hem of her shirt
and pulled it from her body, the cool air of the room striking
her nipples, sensitizing them.

So many nights she had lain alone, crying, aching because there had been no justice for those she loved. Because
there had been no comfort in the darkness of the night for
her own soul.

Her comfort was here now.

She tossed the shirt to the floor, stared into his eyes, and cupped her own breasts, her fingers finding the hard tips of her nipples and pinching them slowly, pulling at them as he suddenly swallowed tightly.

She had never teased him like this. She should have, she realized, because his gray eyes turned almost black as a hard flush mantled his cheekbones.

"Baby," he breathed out roughly. "This won't help you rest."

"I don't want to rest." One hand continued to cup a breast as she moved the other down, between her breasts, over her stomach until she pushed her fingers past the elastic band of the loose cotton pants she wore.

She found herself with her fingers. As he watched, his gaze narrowing on the movements beneath the material, she found the dampening folds of her pussy and caressed the sensitive pearl of her clit softly.

"I want you," she whispered. "All night, John. Take me. Take me until I know nothing but your touch, know nothing but the pleasure you can give me. Don't leave me alone."

She slid her fingers from the pants, the tips wet, glistening with her juices, and moved them to touch her lips, to taste herself.

He caught her hand before the tips touched the curves, his breathing suddenly hard as he pulled them to his mouth instead and tasted her, sucked her fingers between his lips and raked the sensitive tips with his tongue.

Bailey moaned. She couldn't stop the sound, still rough from her tears, rasping with the pain that burned inside her and the hunger rising to scorch her.

"What the hell do you do to me?" he asked as her hands moved to the buttons of his shirt and fought to undo them quickly. When the tiny disks slipped through her fingers, she gripped the edges of his shirt and jerked them apart, sending the buttons flying.

"The same thing you do to me, perhaps?" she panted.

She could forget the world in his arms. She did it every

time he touched her. She needed to do it now. She needed the world and the guilt to recede, to evaporate for just a little while.

She watched his jaw clench as his hands moved to the waist of her pants and with a smooth shift of muscle in his shoulders, jerked the material over her hips and to her knees.

His hands weren't rough, but they were insistent, dominant. This was what she needed. That blazing hunger that burned inside him. She needed all of it, every desire that had filled his imagination as well as hers.

"I used to dream," she whispered as she stared into his hungry eyes, her hands going to the belt that cinched the waist of his pants. "When I was alone." When she had thought he was gone. "When it was dark. I would touch myself, and imagine you. You would forget yourself with me. You would touch me like you were never going to touch me again. You took me as though it were the last time you would ever have the chance."

The belt came loose and she sucked in a hard breath as his hand suddenly cupped between her thighs, covering the swollen, sensitive flesh of her pussy while his upper palm rasped against the engorged bud of her clit.

"What did I do to you?" His voice was dark, dangerously sexy. It whispered of rain-swept nights and fierce passionate storms.

She pulled the clasp of his pants loose, lowered the zipper.

"Your lips went to my nipples," she breathed out roughly. "You sucked me, hard. Your teeth and tongue rasped them."

Her head fell back as a cry tore from her throat. His lips moved to a nipple, covered it. He tugged at it with his teeth, lashed it with his tongue, then sucked her in deep as she pushed his pants over his hips, freeing the thick, fierce length of his cock.

She loved him, loved his touch, his kiss, loved the heavy shaft that she knew brought the edge of pleasure and pain so destructive to her senses.

Her fingers tried to wrap around the heavy flesh, but they wouldn't reach. She contented herself with stroking it, feeling the dampness that coated the wide crest and the fierce throb that pounded through the heavy veins.

Her other hand gripped the hair at the nape of his neck, held him to her breast. She gloried in the heated feast he was making of her flesh.

He wasn't holding back. So many times she had felt him holding back, taking her gently when he needed to take her harder. Suppressing his own needs for what he thought were hers.

His teeth tugged at her nipple again before releasing it and moving to the other. Bailey whimpered at the incredible sensations that tore through her. It was like strokes of lightning tearing from her nipple to her clit, clenching her womb. The burning sensations overwhelmed her and tore another cry from her lips as her head dipped, her teeth moving to his shoulder to clench at the tight flesh there.

A hard male groan echoed from his chest and he pulled back, one hand clenching at the back of her head, as her lips moved lower, her teeth rasping against his flesh, nipping, taking heated, stinging tastes of his skin while he used his fingers to lead her down his body.

"D'you think you're the only one who dreamed?" His voice was almost a snarl above her, the lightest flavor of an accent coming through as he shed his pants and knelt fully on the bed before her. "Come on, love, give me what I need. Let me watch you take me, Bailey. Suck my cock, baby."

She moaned as her lips reached the wide, glistening crest. Her tongue licked over it as she teased him, evading the caress she could feel he sought.

He wanted in her mouth. She wanted him there. But she wasn't about to give in to him so easily. Bent before him, she braced one hand on the mattress and raked down his thigh with the nails of the other.

She felt him shudder and felt the juices flowing from her sex at the knowledge that she could affect him like this. That he needed her as much as she needed him.

She had never felt him like this, never felt that hunger

clawing so close to the surface of his lust before. It was there in the tight tension of his body, the steady pressure of his hand at her hair, holding her in place as his cock nudged insistently at her lips.

She licked over the demanding crest again, blew a rough breath of air over it, and tempted him to take more, to demand more from her.

"Little tease," he growled.

Holding her head still, he pressed his cock more firmly against her lips, parting them, pressing inside as she felt flames lance over her nerve endings.

She could feel his fingers tight in her hair, tugging at the tender roots just enough to send fresh flares of ecstatic sensation tearing through her.

"Suck me," he demanded roughly. "Suck my cock, baby. Hot and deep." The last was a harsh, heavy groan as her lips parted and sucked him inside, hot and deep.

Her mouth closed around the thick flesh as she felt it throb against her lips. The thick shaft clenched beneath the caress of her fingers, and his body tightened until she wondered how he could bear the strain.

Hot, electric lust flared between them, burning Bailey with its intensity as John began to move in short, shallow strokes, fucking her lips with an almost desperate hunger.

This was what she had dreamed of as she'd touched herself through the years. Her lover, the man she loved, giving her those parts of himself that he had always held back.

John wasn't holding back now. Both hands were in her hair, pinning her in place as he took her mouth with slow, shallow thrusts that had moans rising in her throat.

Her tongue worked over the head of his cock with each thrust, rasping against the sensitive underside and drawing a hard, deep growl from the depths of his chest.

The taste of him was heated male, rich with lust and a burgeoning hunger that throbbed through the heavy shaft. His fingers pulled at her hair, his short nails flexing against her scalp as she filled her mouth with him.

She wanted more. So much more. She wanted the hunger

burning like a conflagration between them, destroying them before they were both reborn.

"Damn you." His voice was rougher now, his strokes inside her mouth gaining in speed as his flesh seemed to swell and tighten, the hard throb of blood increasing in pressure.

It was already like a heated iron beneath her lips, so hard and hot she felt bruised even as her arousal grew.

She worked her mouth over the throbbing crest, sucked at it, deep and firm, loving the feel of his cock pulsing in her mouth, the knowledge that he was fighting release, that his body was straining to hold back.

He was close. So very close. She could almost feel the deep, heavy pulse of his semen working up the shaft when he suddenly drew back, drawing the prize from her just seconds before it was in her grasp.

Within seconds she found herself on her back, the pants torn from her legs, and John's lips between her thighs. Her legs fell open, spreading wide as he pushed them apart with his hands, his head lowering.

His tongue swiped through the wet folds, pausing at the entrance to ream it hungrily before licking up, circling her clit, then drawing it into his mouth.

Hard, brutally hot strikes of sensation tore through her, arching her hips to him as she felt the first one, then two fingers slip inside the clenched entrance of her pussy.

She drove herself onto the penetration, gasping, crying out as she felt the stretching pressure fill the sensitive portal. The feel of his fingers inside her, the suckling pressure of his mouth, and the sound of his heavy moans were too much to bear.

Bailey could feel the waves of sensation centering in her womb, radiating outward through the rest of her body. Flames were licking over her body, sizzling across her flesh, and slickening her skin with a heavy layer of perspiration.

She could feel her juices building, gathering, easing between his fingers and saturating her flesh as he thrust them into her, sending her senses reeling.

She was lost in a kaleidoscope of pleasure, of sensations

that struck hard and fast, never ending, racing through her body and her bloodstream with a force and speed that left her breathless.

His suckling mouth was a demon as it held her clit captive, his tongue a fiery force of rapture as it stroked, caressed, and lashed against the sensitive bud.

Bailey swore she couldn't survive another second of it, but her hands were locked in his hair, holding him to her as she begged for more.

She had never known pleasure like this except in John's arms. And never had he let himself go like this. Never had he ravaged her senses as he was tonight, drawing her into a world in which only pleasure and the two of them existed.

"So good," she moaned, arching closer to his suckling mouth. "Oh God, John. It's so good. So hot."

She writhed beneath his mouth, so close to orgasm that she could feel it aching to explode through her system. So close, and yet he held her on the edge, refusing to allow her to slip over just yet.

His fingers worked deeper inside her, thrusting into the snug entrance as she arched her hips, rotated them, a strangled scream escaping her throat as the sensation evaded her once again.

"Please," she panted, unable to stand the intensity of pleasure, dying for a release that stayed just out of reach. "Please, John."

His answer was a dark, low growl as he released the pressure on her clit to kiss it instead. Deep, sharp little kisses that had her moaning in need as she arched closer, fighting to find that peak.

"Not yet, baby." His fingers slid from the aching depths of her pussy as he gripped her thighs before pulling himself up along her body.

"Now." Her hands fell to his shoulders, gripping them as she tried to push him back down her body.

"Not yet. Together. We'll come together, Bailey, or we'll not come at all."

He hooked his hands beneath her knees, lifted them, brac-

ing them against his biceps as his hips moved into place, his
cock pressing against the snug entrance that wept for him.

Bailey froze, her gaze locking with John's as his head
lowered farther, his lips grazing hers, stroking against them
as he began to work his cock inside her.

It was exquisite. It was a pleasure unlike anything else
she could have imagined. It was a pleasure unlike any other
he had ever given her.

Holding her gaze, his lips taking sipping kisses, sharp
little tastes of hers, he worked the heavy, engorged head of his
cock inside her. He stretched her, filled her until the sharp bite
of pleasure was like a fiery central ache. It radiated through
her body, struck at her clit, her nipples, tightened them until
they felt too sensitive, too swollen to bear.

"God, you're sweet, love," he groaned as the head of his
erection lodged inside her. "So sweet and tight. You burn me
alive."

But the flames were tearing through her.

Her arms tightened around his neck as she tried to breathe,
tried to control at least a small measure of the heated, desperate pulses of need that racked her body.

"Stop teasing me," she cried out as he pulled back before
working his cock deeper inside her. "Please, John. Now. I
need you now."

"Sweet Bailey." The sigh of his voice rippled across her
lips as he lifted his hands and pulled her arms from him.
Clasping her wrists in one hand, he pulled them over her
head, holding them there as his hips bunched.

She could feel the need striking through her with violent
intensity now. It was throbbing deep inside her, her clit was
a swollen mass of nerve endings, her womb convulsing with
the need for release.

Bailey was shaking, shuddering with the need that she
couldn't control. Her legs tightened around his hips as a strangled scream tore from her throat. Then her cry echoed around
her as he tightened and thrust inside her, deep and hard.

Her back arched. Pleasure streaked up her spine, wrapped
around her skull, and sizzled through her nerve endings.

Brilliant pinpoints of light dazzled her senses and left her burning in the middle of a maelstrom that she had no hope of controlling.

"Fuck me, you're tight." John's strangled groan sent another rush of sensation tearing through her. Pleasure upon pleasure. She wasn't going to survive this, even though she had begged him to give it to her.

She arched to him, moaning as he slid back again until only the engorged head remained lodged inside her. A second later another fierce, deep throat lodged him to the hilt again, stretching her open and revealing nerve endings that flamed with the heated stroke.

"I can't stand it." Her head tossed against the bed, her legs tightening around his hips as the fiery whirls of sensation centered in her pussy and at her clit.

"Just a bit longer, baby," he groaned. "Hold on to me just a bit longer. God, there's nothing like fucking you. Like being so deep inside you I can feel your heartbeat."

She could feel his heartbeat. It throbbed against the sensitive tissue of her pussy, vibrated into her clit, and had her senses spinning.

Perspiration gleamed on his face, a rivulet of moisture easing down his forehead and dampening his thick lashes. He looked like a sex god rising over her, impaling her with paradise.

Looking down between their bodies, she watched as he drew back, his heavy flesh glistening with her juices, parting her, then surging inside her again until not even a breath could pass between them.

It was the most erotic sight of her life. He moved slow and easy, thrusting inside her with deep, slow strokes, letting her watch him take her. Watch her flesh part and hug the silky wet column of his cock as he took her.

"I want to hold you here forever," she sobbed, unable to tear her eyes from the sight. "I don't want to lose this, John. I never want to lose this."

She wanted to stay right here, stuck in a time warp,

watching his flesh merge with hers, his heavy erection impaling her, releasing her, stretching her again.

Releasing his hips from the vise of her legs, she planted her feet in the bed, tilted her hips, and took him deeper, dragging a hard, heated moan from his lips.

"Sweet baby," he rasped. "God help me, Bailey, I'd die without you now."

The Australian accent, faint but there, had her convulsing around him, nearly orgasming from the sound alone, from the sense of the past rising up to swamp her, to merge with her present.

This was how she had dreamed. Just like this. Of the pleasure, each stroke slow and easy, the need spiraling inside the both of them until they could contain it no more.

Until they had to act. Until they couldn't bear it another second.

His thrusts became heavier, harder. He gripped her thighs, pushing them back as he braced himself with his knees and began to thrust inside her. To shaft into her with hot, long strokes over his cock.

His hips surged against her, over and over, impaling her with a pleasure that burned hotter and bright with each stroke.

She cried out his name. Her neck arched, her legs tightening as she felt the breath rush from her lungs and sensation imploding inside her.

His pelvis stroked her clit, sending a surge of electric intensity swarming through it until it erupted in ecstasy at the same moment that her pussy began to convulse in orgasm.

Above her, his heavy groans signaled his own release. A second later, deep, blistering pulses of warmth attacked her vagina and threw her higher, deeper.

She was flying through time and space, jerked out of reality and thrown into rapture. Stars exploded behind her closed lashes, violent pleasure streaked across her nerve endings, and his name was a wail of such utter completion that she wondered if she would ever survive without it again.

Collapsing against her, John released her legs, his body coming over hers as he caught his weight on his knees and elbows, his head burying at her neck.

She could hear him whispering something, his voice a hard thick growl filled with that forbidden accent. The man who had been dead lived in her arms for that moment. He held her, his cock pulsed inside her, his lips pressed to her neck as his fingers buried themselves in her hair.

Exhaustion swamped her as she felt the last fragile waves of pleasure ebbing through her. The shudders that racked her body eased, the blinding hunger was sated for the moment, and the world around her had disappeared.

Locked close to his body she felt a sense of peace slowly easing through her, the guilt easing away.

What she had been forced to do hadn't been easy. She had lost friends, she had lost her last ties to the past. But in doing it, she was ensuring the future for more than just the friends she loved. She was ensuring her own future, the future of perhaps thousands.

John had done that for her. With just his touch, his possession. He had taken her past the world where nothing had made sense, given her a pleasure so overwhelming that it had made her realize exactly why it was so important.

It was just there. As the peace slid around her, sleep overtook her and that knowledge became cemented inside her. Wagner and Jules would survive, because she was doing what she had to do. She hadn't been able to save Anna and Mathilda. She hadn't been able to save her parents. But she could save Wagner. She could ensure that Warbucks never forced John to "die" again. The past she remembered might be cracked a little, but those she had so loved as a child would survive.

That survival was what mattered.

Sleep slid through her. Weariness sucked her under until her breathing eased and blessed numbness overcame her. There were no dreams. There were no monsters chasing her.

There was just this. Comfort. Warmth.

John.

* * *

JOHN SLID SLOWLY FROM the heated grip of his lover's body and stared down at her, loving her so damned much he felt as though it were ripping his soul from his body.

Shaking his head at the surge of emotion, he dragged his weary body from the bed and moved to the bathroom. Wetting a soft washrag in warm water, he grabbed a towel and returned to the bed. There he washed her gently, drying the dampness from her flesh before she could become cold.

Easing the rag between her legs, he wiped his seed from her thighs, from the swollen folds of her pussy, and then dried them gently before lifting her against the pillows and pulling the blankets over her.

Other than a moaning little protest as he moved her, he didn't disturb her. She slept deeply, heavily, exhaustion finally sucking her into a dreamless void where she could hopefully find a bit of peace.

Back in the bathroom, he washed himself before drying, turning out the lights, and returning to the bed.

Lying on his back, he stared up at the darkened ceiling and considered what she had been forced to do. No one, especially a woman with Bailey's capacity for love, should have to face what she had faced tonight.

To turn her back on the proof she had waited for over so many years—proof against the man who'd had her friends and parents killed—had nearly destroyed her. He had seen it in her eyes, in her face. He had felt it as she had shuddered in his arms and fought to hold back the hysteria that had torn through her.

Then she had to maintain that act in the face of Myron Falks and Raymond Greer's quiet interrogation. It was more than most women could have borne, even one as well trained as Bailey had been as an agent.

She had done it. She had held back that rage to do what had to be done.

Her strength amazed him.

He felt her move, her body shifting, seeking his warmth as she rolled against him. Opening his arms to her, he pulled her into his embrace, wrapped her in his hold, and let his own eyes drift closed.

Yes, Jordan was going to be pissed, because there wasn't a chance in hell John was letting this woman go. Only death, a true death, could tear them apart now, because he would be damned if he would ever walk away from her.

She was his mate. His soul. A man didn't walk away from his soul and survive.

"I love you, Bailey," he whispered, allowing his true self to slip free.

A little hum of pleasure vibrated against his chest. Even in sleep she heard him. Felt him. Knew he was there to watch over her. He would make damned certain he was always there to watch over her from now on.

The unit be damned. He wasn't losing her again.

CHAPTER 18

NOTHING HAD EVER BEEN harder for Bailey than putting on a good face and accepting the horrific decision she'd been forced to make with Wagner.

To hear that he had packed up and returned to his own home was a welcome bit of information for her. She didn't know if she could have borne facing him each day with the knowledge between them that she had betrayed not just Anna, but also her own parents.

Two days after Wagner had left the Greer cabin, Bailey stepped from the bathroom, dressed for another boring day of socializing. She couldn't believe there was actually another virtual fashion show planned for that afternoon. Of course, today it was evening dresses, she assured herself mockingly.

"How one woman can make a pair of sweatpants and a T-shirt look fashionable, I haven't decided yet." John was leaning against the heavy post at the end of the bed, buttoning his shirt while regarding her with an amused smile.

"It's a talent." She adjusted the hem of her olive-green FORGET THE DOG, IT'S THE WOMAN YOU NEED TO WATCH T-shirt over the band of her matching sweatpants.

Pulling a pair of socks from the dresser, she sat in the chair next to it and pulled on the dark green socks that matched her sweats and T-shirt. She pulled white sneakers from beneath the chair and laced them up before standing and pulling her hair into a low ponytail.

"I saw several of the other women downstairs earlier," he mentioned. "It seems silk slacks and blouses are the 'in' thing today."

She paused and stared back at him through the mirror. "Are you counseling me on my clothing choices, John?" She arched a brow and stared back at him haughtily. "Do I really come across as a silk-on-silk girl to you?"

"If the situation warrants it," he murmured.

"And you think the situation warrants it?" she queried a bit sarcastically.

He paused, his lips pursing as he stared back at her. A grin tilted the luscious curves of his lips. "Perhaps not."

"Good man." She nodded decisively as she gave her appearance one last check to ensure it conveyed the proper amount of disrespect toward the day's events.

He shook his head, finished tucking his shirt into his silk pants and adjusting his belt. He wore his cell phone in a case at his hip, a backup weapon in a holster at his ankle.

Moving to the walk-in closet, Bailey pulled a sheathed knife from under a stack of sweaters, pulled up the loose leg of her sweats, and secured it to her leg.

That was the best she could do. There was no way she could get away with carrying a gun herself. She and John had agreed on that. To create the impression they were looking for, they had to show that she relied on John for the muscle, and the guns. Ladies didn't carry a gun in polite society, she mocked to herself.

As she stepped back into the room, a firm knock sounded at the door.

John stiffened as the door to the connecting room opened and Travis Caine suddenly entered. When the hell had he arrived?

John waved him back. Travis stepped back into the other room, almost closing the door as John moved to the exit to answer the knock.

"Raymond." He stepped back as Bailey steeled herself to face the other man.

"John, I hope you're doing well this morning." Raymond's smile was quick as he held out his hand.

"Excellent, Raymond." John nodded as they shook hands.

Bailey felt like rolling her eyes. Just what she needed, pleasantries from a killer.

"Bailey, you're looking refreshingly casual today." Raymond of course looked down his nose at her.

Bailey smiled brightly. "I thought so."

Raymond shook his head at her, his lips appearing to almost twitch. "You don't conform well, do you, my dear?"

"Is conformity required?" she asked as she moved beside John. His arm instantly wrapped around her waist as he pulled her to him. "I was unaware of that."

He shook his head. "Not at all. There are times it's actually a bit refreshing, as I stated." He turned back to John. "If I could have a moment of your time after you've had breakfast, I'd like to discuss some business with you."

"Of course," John agreed with no haste or apparent excitement. "It might be an hour or two after breakfast, though. As you know, my bodyguard returned last night and I need to discuss a few issues with him before the day begins."

Raymond nodded. "You have my cell phone number. Call me whenever you're ready." He turned and moved back into the hallway as John closed the door behind him.

Locking it, he moved back to the dresser and flipped the white-noise generator back on. The connecting door opened more fully and the tall, well-dressed form of Travis Caine moved into the room.

Who was he? Bailey stared at him intently. There was something about the tilt of his head, the shape of his eyes, and the way he held his shoulders that was disturbingly familiar.

"You heard?" John asked him.

Travis nodded, his face expressionless. "The other security personnel are on call as well. I was in the kitchen this morning and several of them were there. Myron Falks has pulled in two men, supposedly for Waterstone. Greer's bodyguard is in attendance, as are at least one bodyguard for Menton-Squire, Claymore, and Grace."

"Any reason why they were called in?" John asked. "I have to admit I was surprised when Greer suggested I might want to call my own in."

John moved to the coffee service that had been delivered by a housemaid earlier and poured himself a cup.

"There was something said about a hunting trip in a few days' time," Travis revealed. "Evidently, these men don't all trust one another as much as they let on. There's nothing in the report we were given that mentions this hunt."

"It's a yearly thing," Bailey told them. "Father and his bodyguard used to go every year. But it was usually the last day of the house party. This is the first time I can remember that it's been scheduled so soon."

"Then we wait for the surprise." John shrugged as he turned to Bailey. "Wear your backup weapon rather than the knife."

Bailey shook her head. "Not here. If Raymond or Myron glimpses a backup on me, he's going to slip back into a mode of distrust. I'm letting you handle the 'man' business," she sneered. "I'm keeping to the role they want me in for the time being. It's the only way we're going to get what we want here."

John grimaced. She could tell he didn't like it. She didn't think much of the unwritten rules herself. This was how it was, though. Several of the women in the group downstairs were very astute businesswomen, but they pushed back their intelligence while attending this party and pretended they were nothing more than clothes-buying, charity-organizing little socialites.

It was almost like the Middle Ages. The antiquated rules were enough to piss off any independent-minded woman. Not that it had ever done her any good here.

"The two of you do what you have to do." She waved her hand back at them. "My turn will come soon enough." She narrowed her eyes back at John. "You're in charge of negotiations, that they're aware. But they're aware we're partners. Correct?"

His lips twitched, though she glimpsed the approval and respect in his gaze. "They're well aware of that, sweetheart."

She nodded before another thought crossed her mind. "Have our friends managed to track down our Colombian visitor?" she asked him.

She knew Alberto Rodriquez a little too well. He wouldn't be in Aspen if he wasn't there for her. He detested cold weather. But even worse, he was hiding, which meant he had a plan in place.

"Nothing yet." John's jaw clenched with what she knew was an edge of frustration. "I have several friends on it, but he's buried deep."

"That's not a good thing," she told him, voicing her earlier concern.

"Stay close to the house," John ordered her. "If you need to go out, contact Travis. He'll go with you."

She restrained a smile at the arrogant command. Sometimes John forgot that she did indeed know how to take care of herself. It was that male–female thing, she thought. He couldn't help the need to protect her, the feeling that protecting her was his responsibility.

"Yes, boss." She saluted him with a flippant smile to ease the tension in the room.

He frowned at her as Travis sipped at his coffee and watched them closely. Too closely.

"We should go to breakfast," she decided rather than continuing the conversation. "Raymond gets testy when he has to wait."

She noticed the look that passed between John and Travis and made a mental note to pursue the subject with John later. He had been acting a bit distant whenever Raymond's name had come up, as though he knew something he wasn't yet telling her.

Not that she didn't doubt he would tell her. The past days

had been busy, filled with not just the emotional trauma she was still dealing with in regard to the information against Ford that she had destroyed, but also the meetings Raymond and Myron had been having with both John and Jerric.

As they moved downstairs and went into the dining room for the buffet breakfast that had been set up, Bailey was struck by the fact that two main players up for the brokerage contract happened to both be agents of the mysterious unit.

Both men had "died" and taken other identities, not just once but likely several times. They were both searching for Warbucks, working together, and they had both managed to fool both Myron Falks as well as Raymond Greer?

She glanced at John as he ate, his attention supposedly on his food and on her, when in fact he was keeping close tabs on everyone in the room.

It didn't make sense that Jerric Abbas and John had made the final cut with Warbucks, did it?

Both identities were very well established, she had to admit. Both men had the right build, the right information, the right impersonation. But still, there was something that suddenly struck her as off. It was something she was going to have to get to the bottom of before too much longer.

She hated going into anything blind, and suddenly she had the idea that there was a part of this mission that she was definitely blinded in.

After breakfast was cleared away by the servants and the groups of men and women began to form and drift away from the dining room, Bailey watched as John met with Travis and moved to the back of the house. No doubt to the library, where it seemed women were not allowed when the door was closed.

She noticed John casting her several long, concerned looks before he moved off for his meeting. Was she too quiet to suit him? She narrowed her eyes on his disappearing back as a sudden suspicion began to form in her mind.

He had an asset within Warbucks's ranks, she could feel it.

But who was it? It couldn't be anyone low-level. Did Warbucks even have low-level associates? He was paranoid where his identity was concerned. Bailey suspected that even Raymond might not know his true identity.

She did suspect that Myron did. From Warbucks's first appearance fifteen years before, Myron had been there. At first he was a cautious presence overseeing several sales under an alias, acting as broker himself until the deals became too hot for him to risk exposure himself.

It was about eight years before that Warbucks had begun using brokers. The first few hadn't worked out so well. Money had been lost; the deals hadn't been the best he could have gotten for the items up for auction.

The emergence of Warbucks as an international procurer of classified information had been a slow one. His reputation had grown in degrees, but always Warbucks had been very careful to keep his identity, or any suspicion of his identity, a secret.

He placed others in the path, disposables. People he had a grudge against, or lives he simply wanted to play with.

Shaking her head at the certainty now that John was hiding something from her, Bailey moved through the house, careful to avoid any of the groups and headed to the evergreen maze and gardens in the back.

It was the most peaceful part of the property. It was the one area where she actually had good memories from her childhood. She had never liked the house, but she had always loved the garden grottoes hidden within the huge maze of evergreen abundance. The heated fountains, hidden shelters, and vine-covered, heated hideaways had always tempted her to linger and lounge. To hide.

Today the spot tempted her to think. Her emotions had been in such turmoil; the decisions she'd had to make, the delicate balance she'd had to achieve had kept her mind fractured. Her ability to assimilate a mission had been affected in noticeable ways.

In dangerous ways.

Making her way through the maze, she found the small hidden areas she had loved as a child, and marveled at the fact that they seemed so much smaller now. So much colder.

The gas fires still burned, the shelters were still shadowed and tempting, but the place didn't hold the appeal it once had. Or perhaps she had grown past it. The lessons she had learned at the hands of the men and women who now attended this party hadn't always been pleasant ones. But she had realized as she'd grown older that they were lessons she had needed to know and understand if she was going to stay and survive within it.

Staying wasn't something she had ever intended on doing, though.

Making her way deeper through the maze, she smiled at the memory of the paths she had taken as a child. She remembered her way through it, her way out of it.

And getting out of it was suddenly imperative.

She came to a slow stop and watched as the shadow materialized from the last, hidden shelter in the maze. He wasn't tall, perhaps an inch taller than she was. He was burlier, darker. Thick black hair fell in slick waves to his neck as dark, cold eyes stared back at her in satisfaction.

"Alberto Rodriquez," she said quietly. "Now, how did you get on the estate?"

Raymond Greer had excellent security. Alberto couldn't have slipped onto the property; he had to have had help.

White teeth flashed in an icy, cruel smile as thin lips curved upward.

"You have made enemies, my dear," he said quietly. "Let us see now, what name did you use in Colombia? Maria Estova, yes? Ahh, who could have known that our dear faithless Maria was in truth one of America's richest heiresses. I must say, I was rather shocked."

She just bet he was.

"So how much would it cost me to convince you to turn around and make your way back to Colombia?" she asked, though she was rather certain no amount of money was going to accomplish that.

"I do not know," he mused. "What price do you place on a brother's life?"

His brother, Carlos. Carlos wasn't nearly as intelligent as Alberto, but he had been more bloodthirsty, less cold, just as merciless. If possible. And she had a feeling Alberto wasn't willing to accept any price for the part she had played in his brother's death.

"Carlos made his choice, Alberto," she stated as she stepped back. "You know that as well as I do."

Carlos had made the decision to fight the night she and her team had swarmed through the drug-processing warehouse Carlos had set up. It had been his decision to fight rather than be arrested. It wasn't as though he wouldn't have been released just as quickly as he was arrested. He just would have lost millions of dollars in cocaine and heroin.

"Carlos trusted you." Alberta smiled at that. It wasn't a smile of amusement. "You were his good friend, were you not, Maria?" He gave a mocking grimace. "Ah, Bailey. Not Maria."

"Bailey," she agreed, wondering how quickly she could get to the knife beneath the leg of her sweats and if she could reach hers before he reached his.

"You know you're not going to get away with killing me," she informed him calmly. "This isn't Colombia, Alberto, and I'm not one of the innocent young women you and your men kidnap off the streets. Others know you're in the area. You'll be hunted down."

He laughed at that. "Ah you have the same naive belief in your people here as you had in your men in Colombia," he accused snidely. "Would you be surprised to know that one of your good friends here sold you, my dear? That I was searched out, paid to come here and eliminate you. They had no idea I would so gladly do it for free."

Warbucks. Now what had she done to piss him off? Or was this one of the infamous tests that his employees were forced to endure? He liked games. He enjoyed playing with both employees and enemies. There was no difference in his eyes, it seemed.

"Really?" She didn't have to pretend curiosity, but she was having to fake the calm. "And who would that be?"

He chuckled at the question. "You would like to know badly, yes?"

"*Badly* would describe it." She stepped back farther. If she could get ahead of him, take the right turn, then she might have a chance of losing him in the maze.

"You know, I have been studying this maze for several days," he stated with a smile. "I know it well by now. As well, I would say, as do you."

Okay, nix that idea. Evidently someone hadn't just hired him, but had also gone out of their way to prepare him.

"Well, since you intend to kill me anyway, you could be nice enough to just let me know who hired you," she suggested reasonably. "Consider it a last request."

"But I was never one to provide last requests." He sighed. "It tends to allow the soul to rest in peace. Do you imagine I would wish your soul to rest in peace, Ms. Serborne?"

She arched a brow. "Well, I could haunt you rather than drifting around miserably," she promised chillingly. "How would that feel, Alberto? To have my ghost fucking with your daily life?"

He laughed at that. Okay, so he wasn't spiritual. Surprise there.

Reaching behind his back, he withdrew what he was well known for. A long, wicked-looking knife that gleamed in the cold sunlight as she bent and removed the small knife she had strapped to her leg.

Damn, she should have listened to John and carried the gun.

His smile was bright, a bit amused, and filled with triumph as he twirled the knife beneath the thin, weak rays of the sun.

"You were not as proficient with the knife as you were with other weapons," he reminded her. "Poor Ms. Serborne. Looks like today is the last day you breathe. I hope you have enjoyed the time you have spent upon this earth."

"Well, I was starting to," she sighed. "I hope you enjoy what John Vincent is going to do to you when he catches up with you."

He did pause at that. He was a criminal, of course he knew who John Vincent was. Even more, he was an international drug-dealing, arms-buying and -selling bastard. There was no way he couldn't know who John Vincent was.

"I had heard perhaps you were sharing his bed," he said with a nod. "It is too bad. But Vincent, he is a businessman, yes? He will not risk his business to come after one lowly Colombian drug dealer. You will be forgotten, just as I'm certain his past lovers have been forgotten."

"Wouldn't bet on that." She stepped back again.

She was going to try to run for it. He knew it, and she knew it. She wasn't going to make this easy for him. She wasn't nearly as experienced with a knife as he was, and he had a lot more muscle on his frame when it came to a fight.

Bailey dug her feet into the thick snow beneath her, turned, and took off. If she could get far enough ahead of him, she might have a chance.

She heard his laughter behind her and knew she had given him exactly what he wanted. Alberto loved the hunt as well as the fight.

She tore around the first turn, raced down the connecting corridor, and felt perspiration begin to run down her back as she looked back to see how close he was.

He was too damned close. So close that it was apparent he was only playing with her. Pushing her legs harder as she gripped the knife with her other hand, she raced around the next turn, then dug her feet harder, shot past the next turn, and struggled to maintain her speed as she went through a short corridor before turning again.

She gained a little distance. He was having to work to catch her now, but she couldn't keep this up for long. There was no way she could actually race through the maze and make it back to the house with him this close on her ass.

If he caught her, there was no way she could hold out for

long in a knife fight. She was, quite simply fucked. And praying.

"BAILEY SEEMS RATHER CALM about allowing you to handle the negotiation phase of our little endeavor," Myron commented as he handed John a drink and took a seat next to the warmth of the fireplace in the library.

Sipping at his drink, John lifted his brows as though in surprise.

"Negotiations are my strong suit," he informed the other man. "Bailey's coordinating possible transport and drop areas as well as monitoring underground chatter concerning new sales up for bid. Talk in this business can be deadly," John reminded him.

Myron nodded slowly. "As I understand it, she was quite adept at coordinating the missions she was placed on. She was a good agent."

John waited silently, sipped his drink, and wondered where the other man was going with this. Raymond was silent, watching the exchange in interest rather than participating in it.

"Bailey proves to be exceptional in any endeavor she undertakes," John assured the other man.

"She's been quite helpful as well," Myron stated. "She's covered for us in several operations that could have been endangered. Without knowing who Warbucks truly was."

John simply stared back at him now.

Myron's lips twitched in amusement. "I'm quite certain she knows that my alias is Mark Fulton. I wasn't as careful as I should have been in the early days of this venture, as Warbucks has pointed out quite strongly several times. I've been aware that she knew who I was for several years now."

"Where is this leading?" John asked him calmly. "Bailey really doesn't give a damn who you are. Her concern was in protecting this little society she loves so dearly, not any one man."

"And that is commendable. Very commendable." Myron

nodded as he glanced at Raymond. Raymond gave a small nod.

As Myron's lips parted to say more, there was a heavy, imperious pounding on the door. Turning to the panel with a glare, Myron stalked to the door and swung it open as John and Raymond came to their feet.

Jerric pushed past Myron, his icy gaze finding John.

"Bailey's in the garden under attack. West end of the maze in corridor seven-twelve," he stated. "Catalina saw everything from our window."

John didn't wait for permission. Fear pumped hard and fast through his system as he moved quickly from the room and motioned Travis to follow him. They were running down the stairs and tearing through the empty ballroom to the French doors within seconds.

Bailey was being attacked. Only one person would dare to attack her here, only one man was insane enough to believe that he could get away with it.

Alberto Rodriquez.

"JERRIC." MYRON'S VOICE was a smooth, silky drawl as Jerric—aka Micah Sloane—turned to head back out of the room. "You interrupted a very important meeting."

Jerric kept his expression cool, composed. His gaze didn't even flicker at the carefully voiced warning.

"Why would you do such a thing? I would think you would consider Bailey's death advantageous to your gaining the contract that is about to come up."

Yeah, having the last member of his family exterminated would be as advantageous as taking a hole in his head.

"I owe him." Jerric stuck to the cover they had developed over the years. Friendly enemies. There were a lot of those in this business. "This repays the debt."

"And that debt would be?" Myron asked carefully.

"The explosion in Afghanistan designed to kill myself and Catalina," he stated. "John warned me of the hit." His lips quirked mockingly. "I'm standing here today because of him."

Myron's brows lifted in apparent surprise. "Interesting. The man is said to have unusual morals where this business is concerned."

Jerric nodded abruptly but remained silent. To say more would only raise suspicion in Myron and do more harm than good in the acquisition of the contract John was after. His silence implied an unwillingness to make John appear the stronger broker of the two of them, though. That knowledge should be clear-cut. John had been set up as the stronger of the two brokers, just as the real John Vincent had worked strenuously to cement his own reputation.

"You trust him then?" he asked Jerric.

"With a deal." Jerric nodded abruptly. "I wouldn't cross him, though. It could be deadly. And letting his woman die would definitely be considered crossing him." He paused as though waiting on them to speak. As though he were curious about the meeting that had been in progress until his interruption.

"Thank you for that clarification." Myron nodded, glancing at the door in a silent signal that the other man could leave.

Jerric nodded abruptly before turning on his heel. The door closed quietly behind him.

MYRON TURNED TO RAYMOND, watching as the other man retook his seat and stared back at Myron coolly.

"Are we going to check out this attack?" Myron asked him.

"Of course we are." Raymond lifted the remote on the side table, pressing a programming button as he pointed it toward the quiet noise of the television in the corner.

Instantly surveillance cameras flipped into view. Another button and the large screen was suddenly filled with a battle of knives between Bailey and a heavyset Colombian.

"Rodriquez," Myron murmured as he watched the struggle. He frowned then. "How did he get on the property?"

"I was rather curious about this myself," Raymond stated. "Did you sell out her identity?"

That was a strict no-no. Myron glanced at him in surprise. "Warbucks would kill me," he murmured. "He's been very particular about keeping her alive."

"Considering he killed her parents, that's rather a surprise." Raymond glanced at the screen in boredom.

Yes, it was a surprise, Myron agreed silently. But Warbucks still had a bit of conditioning to acquire, as well as a bit of self-preservation. Bailey Serborne should have been killed years ago despite the financial toll that her death would have exacted. So her fortune went to charities rather than the four men who oversaw her business concerns? It wasn't as though Warbucks needed the damned money.

Was it guilt? Myron wondered. No, Warbucks didn't know guilt. It could be no more than greed, pure and simple.

But that greed was one of the reasons Myron enjoyed his job so much. Because he was greedy, too, and he received his cut in a timely, safe manner.

He took his chair to watch the fight as it played out. It would be interesting to see if John could reach her in time. Even more interesting would be learning exactly who betrayed her. Unfortunately, he might have a pretty good idea there—and it would be so simple to use it.

CHAPTER 19

SHE WASN'T GOING TO MAKE it.

Bailey felt the slice of Alberto's knife across her upper arm, the fire-and-ice pain lancing through her body as she felt the blood gush from the wound.

Jumping back, she stumbled, slid on the slick layer of snow underneath as she felt Alberto's foot land heavily on her rear, throwing her face-first on the ground.

Rolling, she tightened her grip on the knife and barely evaded a foot to her abdomen. Another quick succession of rolls gave her just enough room, just enough time to jump quickly to her feet and sprint out of the way of the knife heading for her stomach.

She was running out of energy. Even the adrenaline pumping through her veins wasn't pouring enough strength into her smaller body to fight off the much bulkier, more muscular Alberto.

Panting for air as she held her knife ready, her body braced as he faced her across only a few feet of distance.

"Playing with you is fun." He grinned. "Arousing." His free hand dropped to his crotch, and he gripped it firmly. "Maybe I make you bleed some more, then fuck you as you bleed out."

The idea was clearly an exciting one for him.

"Don't make me puke on top of everything else, Al," she

sneered. "We both know you can't handle the sight of it. You have a weak stomach."

He shrugged, smiling again as he waved his knife in her direction.

"You, gringa, have been a worthy adversary," he praised as he circled her like a hungry coyote. "The hunt has been a good one. Yes?"

"You cheated," she told him, breathing hard, trying to find the energy that she knew she was going to need for the next attack he made.

"Cheated?" He glowered back at her in outrage. "How did I cheat? I found you. I gave you the chance to fight. You have failed."

"You were hired to come after me, remember?" she mocked him. "You didn't find me on your own, Alberto."

"Eh, a minor thing." He rotated his wrist, twirling the knife in her direction again. "Very minor. I will count it a victory anyway."

That was just her luck.

She watched him closely, knowing he would rush her any second and when he did, he would likely kill her.

Where the hell was security? She knew there were monitors placed throughout the maze to allow Raymond's security team to keep an eye on it during the house parties. The richest men in the world congregated here for two weeks of the year. They couldn't afford a crack like this in their surveillance.

"When I kill you, I will send a prayer up to Carlos," he told her. "He will smile down at me."

"Smile up at you, you mean." She smiled herself, a tight curve of her lips that mocked his statement. "I rather doubt Carlos made it into heaven, Alberto. He's burning in hell and waiting on you."

Could have been the wrong thing to say.

She managed to jump from the first thrust of the knife, the blade barely missing her abdomen before he came back with another parry.

Bailey managed to grip his wrist and moved to break it. Unfortunately the fingers that wrapped in the long strands of her hair clenched and jerked, hauling her back as she maintained her hold on his wrist.

"You bastard!" she screamed furiously, kicking back, her foot connecting with his knee and nearly throwing him off balance.

His hand loosened in her hair for just a second. Just long enough for her to jerk her head back and away from him as she fought his wrist, struggling to keep the knife out of harm's way. As well as her throat. She made a mental note to ensure that if he actually managed to kill her, she would haunt him until he took that knife to his own throat. The bastard.

"Little bitch," he snarled as she managed to ram her fist into his nose. "Cunt. Whore."

Filthy-mouthed prick.

She didn't have the energy to hold back that knife and curse him at the same time.

A second later she was flying through the air, landing on her back heavily and staring up at the sky as the wind left her body in a rush.

Oh God, that hurt.

She wheezed through the pain as she tried to roll to her side to get back to her feet.

She didn't have the time. Within a breath that she didn't have, Alberto was straddling her, one hand locked in her hair to pull her head back, exposing her neck as she flailed about with her hands in an attempt to latch on to his wrist again.

She couldn't do anything with him. He was too big. Too strong. He was smothering the breath from her chest as he sat on her, strangling her air even as he prepared for the killing stroke of his knife.

She was going to die. And unlike Trent's "death," hers would be forever.

Dots danced before her eyes as she struggled to breathe. Darkness edged at her mind and her eyes grew dazed as she watched his arm pull back. Watched the blade glint, sunlight striking off it, nearly blinding her.

As she accepted the fact that she couldn't throw him, couldn't evade that night, a curious roar filled the air. It was enraged, animalistic, and made the hairs on the back of her neck stand up in primal response.

As the swift arc of the knife closed on her throat, she was suddenly free.

The unexpected rush of air had her strangling, oxygen wheezing through her lungs as she was jerked roughly from the ground and shoved into the dubious protection of the tall hedges that made the corridor.

She slumped in the snow, shaking her head as she fought to understand exactly what had happened. When she managed to clear her vision and focus, it was over.

John's fist rammed into Alberto's bloody face, the force of it driving the other man's head back and slumping him to the ground.

"Take care of this." John jumped back from the body, scooping the knife up as he moved as he turned to Travis, his gray eyes snapping with storm-cloud intensity. "I want to know who hired him and why before you return. Understood?"

Travis nodded sharply before using the ripped sleeve of Alberto's long-sleeved shirt to secure his hands. He ripped the material away casually, tied it tight around the other man's wrists, then hauled him up until he could toss him over his shoulder.

"Bailey." John was beside her in a second, his hands going to her arm where a long, narrow slice oozed blood.

She blinked up at him.

"Took you long enough," she managed to wheeze. "Where the hell was Greer's security? He has cameras every other fucking foot and no one saw this?"

She could feel the anger beginning to burn in her fast and hot. If he wanted her dead that bad, why not just use a bullet?

"The security force was called to check an intrusion on the other side of the property." Raymond and Myron stepped into the corridor. "We had a break in the fence. A young boy who had been hired to distract us. Supposedly so your good friend Alberto could sneak in to see his girlfriend."

She glared at the two men. "Someone hired him, told him where I was." She moved to her feet as John wrapped his arm around her and lifted her against him. "It had to have been someone here."

They looked at each other, frowned, then turned back to her.

"No one involved in our special negotiations would have done this," Myron informed her. "They would have known better. Warbucks doesn't want you dead, Bailey. As you yourself know, there's no desire to see your vast holdings left to charity. Why else would an order have been given to Orion to keep you alive?"

Myron made the statement so casually. As though the death of her parents meant nothing, whereas her own would mean a loss of financial holdings.

"I'll find out who it was," John stated. "Travis will question Alberto before dumping his body where it will serve as the best message to anyone else stupid enough to threaten me or mine."

Could a man's tone, or his words, more clearly declare ownership? Bailey shot him a glare beneath her lashes. She didn't belong to anyone, least of all an arrogant "dead" man who had no intentions of sticking around once his mission was complete.

"You trust your man in this, then?" Myron asked. "We could have taken care of it here."

"You didn't take care of your security, gentlemen," he snarled. "I'm beginning to doubt the safekeeping of any item my clients may purchase as well. You can't ensure the safety of your guests."

With that, he lifted Bailey into his arms, carrying her as though her leg had been sliced off rather than her arm scratched deeply.

She'd actually come out of this little fight much better than she had expected to, she told herself. She was still alive.

She might not need stitches. She was still breathing and John was rabid with anger and concern.

What more could a woman want?

Pain shot through her, perhaps mockingly, as the slice in her arm throbbed. She let herself relax in John's embrace, though, and allowed him to slip her through the back of the house and up the stairs to their room.

Guests were none the wiser, and hopefully there would be no gossip to take care of later. If she could just get through this, get the wound cleaned and bandaged, then she should be good to go. At least until the next attack. Damn, she could use a vacation.

"From now on, you don't enter that garden," John ordered roughly as he laid her on the bed. "Understood?"

"Yes, boss," she murmured mockingly as the door opened again.

Looking up again she watched, her expression closed, as Jerric Abbas and his rumored lover, Catalina Lamont, entered the bedroom and closed the door behind them.

"Is she all right?" Jerric asked quietly, his voice, his manner calm and unfeeling.

Bailey felt tears come to her eyes. How like David he still was, despite his attempts to appear otherwise. The same look in his eyes, the same tight controlled line of his lips when concerned.

She remembered that same look on his face when she had trained with the Mossad during her first year with the CIA. Each time she'd been hurt he'd carried the weight of it, as though he blamed himself.

"I'm fine, just a little scratched," she told him, wincing as John moved back to her and tore off the one sleeve of her T-shirt.

"Stitches?" Catalina moved closer. "Is Greer or his henchman sending a surgeon?"

"A surgeon?" Bailey muttered. "It's a scratch."

"It requires stitches," John informed her tightly as he jerked his cell phone from his pants.

Hitting speed dial, he waited a second before saying, "She needs stitches." He listened to whatever the response was on the other line before flipping the phone closed and shoved it back into the clip.

"Greer already has someone on the way," he stated, his voice low.

"Probably a butcher." Bailey groaned as she turned and stared at the wound, frowning. "It's not that bad. Some salve and a bandage and I'll be good to go."

"Stop being so stubborn." It was Jerric who voiced the order, his tone as commanding as any general's. "The wound needs proper care no matter your . . . feelings."

He started to say something else. Bailey turned her head and narrowed her eyes.

"No matter my aversion to needles," she finished quietly for him. "Why didn't you just say it?"

"Enough." John was suddenly in her face, his expression furious. "You need stitches whether you want them or not. Just as you'll need an antibiotic shot. What about tetanus?"

"Updated." She glared back at him. "Don't order me, John. You're not the boss of me no matter what you believe."

"Stop arguing with me or I'll have you sedated on top of it," he threatened. "And stop baiting Jerric. He has enough problems dealing with that one." He jerked his head to Catalina, who smiled innocently.

Catalina. Tehya. God, these people had more names and identities than she had socks. Jerric was married as Micah Sloane, to one of the nicest young women he could have found. Risa Clay had been terrorized by her father before his death, and after. When Micah had been sent in to protect her from Orion, there had been no doubt he had fallen in love with her.

"Some men enjoy being difficult." Catalina crossed her arms over her breasts as she gave the men another falsely sweet grin. "Jerric is one of the most difficult."

Jerric grunted at that before turning back to John as he straightened from the bed.

"If everything is well here, then Catalina and I will leave

for the time being," he told John. "If you require any help, please let us know."

Bailey nearly rolled her eyes.

As they left she turned back to John, watching as he moved to the bathroom and seconds later returned with a damp rag. Wiping the blood away, he surveyed the cut again.

"It doesn't need stitches." She sighed again. "Come on, John. I know my own body. It's not hurting nearly bad enough to have to do that."

"And I said stop arguing."

He obviously wasn't going to pay attention, and honestly, she was so bruised and sore at the moment that she really didn't give a damn.

"Make sure he has painkillers," she muttered. "And that he numbs it. I'm not in the mood for more pain if you don't mind."

Like Jerric, he grunted at the comment, obviously put out.

It wasn't long before Raymond Greer's surgeon arrived. A plastic surgeon even. What the rich and famous could accomplish in a small amount of time.

John ushered in the two men, standing back with Raymond as the surgeon checked out the wound.

Bailey closed her eyes at the first shot and winced.

"That better be a painkiller," she told him.

The white-haired doctor chuckled. "Of course. I know my job, my dear," he assured her before he laid out what he needed to work.

Bailey turned her head, refusing to look as he sterilized the items he pulled free. Minutes later she felt a sharp prick, her head jerking back to the surgeon furiously.

"It will numb the area, young lady," he said, frowning back at her. "Or would you prefer to feel each stitch going in?"

She would have thrown up. Her stomach roiled at just the suggestion. She turned her head again, watching John and Raymond from her peripheral vision curiously. The painkiller was making her head a bit woozy, but even she could detect that there was more going on here than there should have been.

They were talking in low whispers, their voices too soft for her to make out the conversation.

Her lashes were drifting closed as, once again, she made a mental note to ask John exactly what was going on. Right now, she was tired. The crash from the adrenaline, the shock of the wound, the certainty she'd felt that she was going to die, only to take that next breath, all combined and piled down on her.

She was drifting in a nice, warm sea, surrounded by darkness, a feeling of security wrapping around her as long as she could hear John, sense him in the room.

He was there. She could rest. There was no reason to struggle to remain awake to protect herself. John would protect her.

"I'M FINISHED." DR. DREYDEN rose from the side of the bed and meticulously packed away the bloody gauze and items he had used to stitch the wound shut.

A bandage covered her upper arm, stark white against bruised flesh. The doctor tucked the blankets around her and stared down at her with a crooked smile before shaking his head. She seemed to have that effect on everyone.

"Thank you for coming in, Dr. Dreyden, and as always for your discretion." Raymond shook the doctor's hand before leading him to the door. "Send me the bill, please. I'll make certain everything is taken care of."

"It's going to be quite a bill, my friend," the doctor informed him. "This was my vacation, you know. My wife will pout for days."

"I'll call the resort myself," Raymond said. "I understand you've been trying to get reservations into one of the exclusive restaurants in town. Casamara's?"

The doctor paused. "We've yet to obtain a time."

"I'll make certain you have an open reservation," Raymond promised. "On me. I'll take care of everything and have the owner of the restaurant contact you soon."

The doctor's brows arched as he thanked Raymond before leaving the room and closing the door behind him.

"Who was it?" Raymond murmured at his side. "Has Travis contacted you yet?"

John shook his head. "Not yet. He will soon."

"It wasn't Warbucks," Raymond promised him. "The moment Myron informed him of the attack, he went crazy. I could hear him screaming in rage over the phone myself." He paused for a moment. "I've never heard Ford scream like that. I've never known of him to be that furious."

"I'll find out who it was," John promised before glancing at Bailey again. She was sleeping. Finally. "I'm going to have to tell her," he stated quietly as he turned back to Raymond.

He was going to have to warn her soon that Raymond was actually working for the good guys. Not that he expected her to believe it. Not at first.

Raymond grinned at that. "She enjoys hating me, John. And I have to admit, it's been fun having carte blanche to irritate her. Mary knows me too well now. I can't irritate her near as easily."

Raymond and Mary's marriage was truly a love match. Raymond loved his new wife despite her money and the power it had given him. It hadn't gone to his head. He'd used it as he could, though, to further the investigations that his position placed him in the path of.

He was a damned good agent himself. Sometimes, too good. He enjoyed pretending to be the bad guy far too much.

"Find out what's going on," John ordered as Bailey shifted against the bed restlessly. "Tell Warbucks I'm pissed over this. I suspect he's behind it. Suggest finishing this deal up to appease me. If word gets out that he attacked my partner, then it could damage his standing among those willing to bid for the product. They may not trust the product enough for an optimum bid if they don't trust him any longer."

"Good thinking." Raymond nodded. "I know Myron has already suggested that fear to me, so it should be simple enough."

John nodded as Raymond turned and walked from the room, leaving him alone with Bailey and the knowledge that he should have kept her closer to him. He should have refused Warbucks's demands that she not be a part of the negotiation process, that he preferred to work with John alone for that. The good-ol'-boy system had placed Bailey in danger, and he didn't like that. It wouldn't happen again.

Checking his watch, he picked up his cell phone and dialed.

"Richards," Ian answered on the first ring.

Moving closer to the white-noise generator, John checked on Bailey again quickly.

"She's fine," he stated into the connection.

"Kira was concerned," Ian said carefully. "We were coming to check on her later, before we leave. Kira's uncle has had a small emergency and requires her presence."

It was code. Kira's uncle was actually in perfect health; the phrase was a signal to pull the group together and prepare for the final phase of the mission.

It was coming together. John could feel it moving closer, that surge of adrenaline, that sense of danger coming closer.

"Give her uncle my regards. I hope everything is well with him," John said.

"I'll do that," Ian murmured. "We should be there in an hour or so to tell Bailey good-bye. Will she be awake?"

John didn't see how, but knowing Bailey, it wouldn't surprise him.

"Perhaps," he answered. "In any event, we'll see you when you get here."

He disconnected the call and paced back to the bed before pushing his fingers through his hair and exhaling a hard breath.

He couldn't believe he had very nearly let her down. That he had almost allowed her to be taken out of his life. One thing was for certain. It wouldn't happen again. And when he found out who had given Alberto Rodriquez her identity and hired him to kill her, then John promised to exact a very painful revenge.

He checked his watch again, paced the room, and waited

for Travis to call. Waited to know the name of the man who would soon die.

RAYMOND ENTERED HIS PRIVATE office rather than the library and glanced at Myron, who sat with his hands in front of his head before the blazing fireplace.

The man looked haggard, but he invariably did whenever he was forced to deal with Warbucks. There had been a time when Raymond had wondered if Myron's employer, Samuel Waterstone, was the traitor, but he had dropped that idea rather fast. Waterstone more amused Myron than anything else. Warbucks kept Myron's nerves on edge, though.

"He's still upset?" Raymond asked as he moved back to his desk.

"The man is a psychopath." Myron sighed.

Over the past years Myron had taken to confiding in him, as though he needed someone with whom to discuss the issues that concerned him over Warbucks. In the past years, the traitor had been concerning Myron more and more. The rages were becoming more violent, the orders often more dangerous.

"Perhaps after this deal, we'll have a bit of a break," Raymond stated. "He usually takes a small vacation before planning his next venture."

Myron shook his head. "Do you realize how many men died stealing those missiles, Raymond? Good men."

The men who stole those missiles hadn't been good men. They had been mercenaries who worked for an exorbitant price. All the same, many had been killed during the theft Warbucks had set up. It didn't matter how many generals you blackmailed for certain information; you'd still have loyal soldiers. A lot of good soldiers had died. American boys whose lives should have mattered more than they had. That was the waste there. Those were the good men who had lost their lives.

"It's going to be hard for him to top the sale of these missiles." Raymond shrugged as though it didn't matter either way to him. "Hasn't he stated that each sale will be bigger than the one before it?"

Perhaps that was what worried Myron. It sure as hell worried Raymond, because the only thing bigger would be biological weapons.

"He's going to get us all killed." Myron rose to his feet, paced to the mantel, and stared down at the fire before lifting his gaze to Raymond once more. "I've worked with him for sixteen years now. I've watched him, year by year, getting more and more dangerous. He's convinced he can't be caught. That luck so favors him, he can't lose."

That didn't sound like Ford. Still, Raymond knew there was much he didn't know about his brother-in-law. Ford kept his own council except for the three men he had grown up with. Waterstone, Claymore and Menton-Squire were his only friends. His only confidants. Raymond couldn't see him confiding this in the other three men, though. He sure as hell knew they weren't working together on it. They couldn't agree on the time of day, let alone something as important as the theft and sale of American military weapons.

"His concern with Ms. Serborne's safety eludes me." Raymond moved to the bar and fixed himself and Myron a drink. "It's not as though shares in her companies could make or break him, is it?"

Myron shook his head. "Fucking pocket change."

"Then why go to such lengths? Orion was on a monthly retainer to keep her alive. Why would he care? Let the bastard kill her if she's causing him that much trouble."

Myron gave a hard, mocking laugh. "You'd think so, wouldn't you?" He accepted the drink Raymond handed him. "It's not the money."

"Really? What else could motivate him?"

Myron looked thoughtful a moment before giving a heavy sigh. "I asked him that once." He shook his head. "Right after he placed Orion on retainer to keep her alive." Myron looked confused for a moment. "He said she was all he had left to remind him of something. He never said what?"

His child perhaps, Raymond thought. If Ford Grace was

indeed Warbucks, then the murder of his child could be playing on his conscience. But then, if he was Warbucks, he likely didn't have a conscience.

"Ah well, it likely won't matter for long," Raymond stated as he took his chair in front of the fire.

"Why is that?" Raymond sat down slowly in the chair across from him.

Raymond shook his head. "Vincent is a bit irritated. He believes Warbucks may have hired Rodriquez."

"No way." Myron shook his head quickly. "He's enraged. He's ordered me to bring whoever it was straight to him the moment I found out. He wants to kill him himself."

Raymond shrugged. "So I suspected and informed Mr. Vincent. He wasn't convinced. I would suggest making some gesture of goodwill or encouraging our employer to hurry this process, perhaps in Vincent's favor. I fear when Ms. Serborne is ready to travel, he may be disappearing for a while. He seems rather fond of her."

Myron sighed. "Vincent is known to have had few relationships, but in those he did have, he was rather protective of the ladies. He's known for his valiant attitude toward them. Almost chivalrous, despite his sexual relationships with them."

"Strange," Raymond murmured as though he didn't quite understand it.

"Just so," Myron stated as he sipped at his drink. "I'll meet with Warbucks and see what I can do. I agree with you, a gesture of goodwill is definitely called for. And I believe he's merely been stringing Vincent along in some asinine little game of his. He would accept no one but Bailey's, choice, I believe."

Warbucks's affection for Bailey confused Myron, as it did Raymond. Warbucks didn't seem to be the type to feel affection for anyone, let alone a woman.

"I would suggest accomplishing this before Bailey's ready to travel," Raymond said with a sigh. "Vincent's not in a pleasant mood and time will only enrage him further, I believe."

Myron rose to his feet. "I'll call him again tonight." He set his empty drink glass on the table between them before moving to the door. "Wish me luck. He's not easy to deal with these days."

"Good luck, my friend," Raymond stated softly.

After Myron left, he stared into the flames of the fire, but it was the past he was seeing. He saw bright green eyes, long red hair, and a smile that had lifted his heart.

He saw the sister he had loved with all his heart. Bright, shining, innocent. He saw her laughing one minute, he saw her in a casket days later, that beauty and laughter wiped away because of one man. Lucy had been a courier for the CIA. Posing as a college student in Milan, she had been transporting classified information between two sources when she had been waylaid.

Rather than taking the information and leaving Lucy laughing, they had killed her instead. The information he had uncovered was that the men had taken her to Warbucks. The bastard had raped her before giving her to his men. He had fired the bullet into her brain himself, stealing her life.

That had been fifteen years ago. Lucy had died and he'd been unable to attend her funeral, unable to grieve for the connection he had shared with the young woman, because no one had known of their family relationship.

Raymond had been the bastard. His father had never acknowledged him, and Raymond had never asked for the acknowledgment. But Lucy had found him. And she had loved him. She had taught him what innocence was, what loyalty was.

This is for you, Lucy. He lifted his drink to the fire in a toast to the flames that so resembled her hair. *This is for you.*

CHAPTER 20

IT WAS THE NEXT AFTERNOON before Bailey felt more like herself. She was stiff and bruised, but bouncing back despite the stitches in her arm and the bandage wrapped around it.

She felt good enough that her hormones did a major backflip when John moved from the bathroom with nothing but a towel wrapped around his hips and approached the bed.

She'd showered earlier. Insisting on it despite the wound. She felt refreshed, her aches easing, and definitely ready for something that would affirm she had lived rather than died.

Something that would give her one more memory to hold in reserve against the loneliness she knew was coming. The shot the doctor had given her the night before for pain had knocked her out. Painkillers tended to do that for her. It had given her a full night's rest, and a morning's appreciation of waking up.

"Feeling better?" he asked as he sat on the bed beside her.

"Better," she agreed, staring up at him before she reached out and slowly pulled the edges of the towel apart to reveal the arousal he hadn't even been trying to hide.

The darkened crest was thick and throbbing, a pearly drop of liquid glistening at the tip.

Bailey felt her nipples harden painfully as her clit became unbearably swollen. Heated liquid warmth spilled from her sex, dampening the folds of her pussy and leaving her feeling tender, weak with hunger.

She had faced death. She had faced the fear of never touching him again, never knowing his kiss, or his laughter. Never knowing his warmth. She had faced oblivion, escaped it, and now she just wanted to revel in his touch.

"Fuck, you look like a goddess lying there," he growled as he stepped nearer, staring down at her with naked demand. "Wearing nothing but panties and a T-shirt. Do you know how hard it's been not touch you the last day? Not to kiss you or taste that luscious little body?"

Her lips parted as she drew in a hard, sharp breath. Dark and erotic, the words sent visions of lust dancing through her brain. She needed that touch, that warmth. She needed him.

"Look at you, love," he whispered, that dark, earthy hint of Australia sliding into his tone. "So flushed and heated. Does it turn you on to know that you make me half insane with lust for you? That no other woman has ever done to me what you do?"

Bailey smiled back at him as he reached out to her, his hand lifting, the backs of his fingers caressing over the slope of her breast, causing her nipple to tighten almost painfully.

Moving farther onto the bed, he pulled her into his arms, letting her feel the hard length of his cock against the bared flesh of her tummy where the T-shirt rode up. The heated crest flexed and throbbed against her flesh as it sent a pulse of blistering sensation to attack her womb at the memory of him pushing inside her.

"You make me crazy for you." He nipped at her lips before taking a deep, drugging kiss from them. His tongue licked and stroked against hers. Her senses were rioting, spinning out of control with the need racing through her.

"Damn you, I can't think of anything but this some days. You're my weakness, Bailey. And my strength."

There was a dominance that brewed inside him again, despite his tenderness. A dark, brewing lust that had her breath catching.

It was pure lust. Power. It was a desperate hunger she had never felt before, never known before.

"I could have lost you," he whispered as he brushed his lips over hers and pushed her panties down her legs to her knees, where she lifted her legs and managed to kick free of them.

Her hands moved over his naked body, feeling that warmth, that need as he pressed her thighs apart and moved over her.

"Wrap your legs around me." The wicked flavor of his voice was deeper now, darker, as though he couldn't hold back who and what he was when he was with her like this.

His hands gripped the outside of her thighs as her arms went around his neck. The heavy width of his cock nudged against her sex, slid against the slick folds, then found the clenched, tight entrance it sought.

The lack of foreplay was only more erotic. The desperate hunger that suddenly raged between them had her heart racing, her body trembling as pleasure raced through her.

Bailey's head fell back as a whimper of hunger, of pleasure fell from her lips. She felt him working the hardened flesh inside her. Her legs tightened around his hips, her breathing was gasps of pleasure, her cries were of desperate need.

His fingers kneaded her rear, gripped it, moved her as his hips bucked against her. She was flying in the face of a torrent of sensations and fought just to catch a breath that eluded her.

Ecstasy slammed through her, over her. Heat surrounded her. The feel of his arms flexing beneath hers, his hands holding her, his hips shifting, moving, thrusting harder against her as her hips arched, her head grinding into the pillow.

Bailey needed, ached, and hungered. She had never felt this desperate, this hot. She had never before felt as though the world were focused on this one point in time, this one moment when nothing mattered but the pleasure tearing through her.

"Hell yeah," John groaned at her ear as she pressed closer to him, her hips moving, shifting, dragging ragged groans from both of them.

Tender, ultra-sensitive tissue rippled and clenched around his shuttling cock as she fought to hold him inside her.

"You'll kill me like this." His lips were at her jaw, her neck, stroking and caressing. "Sweet baby." Pressing her closer against him, he moved one hand from her rear to her breast. His thumb and finger gripped her nipple, plumped it, stroked fire through it.

"You'll survive," she gasped as sensations began to burn and tighten inside her, merging into a conflagration of intensity.

Bracing his elbows into the bed, John thrust inside her again, hard and deep, and she felt her breath gasp from her lips.

This was how he wanted her. Wicked and wanting to be in his arms, John thought. Her nails bit into his shoulders, sending pinpoints of fire racing through his system. The sweet grip of her pussy tightened like a fist around him, slick and hot.

He would never forget this, never forget her like this. Her head thrown back against the pillow, eyes closed, her lips parted as she fought, and sometimes failed, to breathe.

She held on to him as though he were the center of her world, as she was the center of his.

"My Bailey," he groaned, unable to hold back the claim, the demand.

God, he wanted to possess her, heart and soul. Holding her, loving her completed his life.

He had nearly lost her. He had turned along that maze, slid into the corridor where Alberto had trapped her, and seen him holding her down, his knife coming around to stroke her neck. Terror had jackknifed inside him.

He could not imagine life without this. Without the sweet heat of her pussy gripping his cock. Without her nails digging into his shoulders, her voice, husky and demanding, calling out his name, begging for more.

He might not be able to claim her before the world, but he

could claim her in the dark, away from prying eyes. He could have her. As he was having her now. He could love her, hold her. He could belong to her.

"John." Her hands moved from his shoulders to his hair. They tangled in the long, sweat-dampened strands, tightened and pulled, and he felt her unraveling.

Her pussy gripped, tightened, and rippled around his dick until his balls became tortured with the need for release.

Not yet. Bailey first. He wanted to feel her coming, he wanted to feel that wet heat racing over his flesh, convulsing around his cock.

"John, please," she gasped in naked need. "Give me now." Her head shook, her body trembled. "Oh God. John . . ."

He watched her eyes flare open, watched as they widened and her body tightened while her orgasm rushed through her, over her.

She was like a flame in his arms, burning him, tearing through his soul and leaving the very essence of his need for her laid bare.

"There, sweetheart." He nipped at her neck as she began to shudder in his arms. "Come for me, Bailey. Come for me, sweetheart. All over me . . ." He thrust harder, deeper, prolonging her pleasure, wanting to live inside her forever.

But that last cry that escaped her lips did him in. He buried himself inside her and lost control, lost that edge that he had always prided himself in. Against his will, against the desperation that burned inside him to wait, to hold on, to relish her just awhile longer, his release tore through him.

And it was like dying inside her. He felt his release tearing from him, shuddering through his body, tightening in his balls, and laying his soul bare.

Over and over it ripped through him until he gasped her name, buried his head at her neck, and gave himself to it.

"Baby. Baby." He couldn't bear letting her go. Shudders, tremors raced through him. His knees were weak. It seemed the strength he had always depended on was failing him, and it was going fast.

He'd buried one hand in her hair, holding her head to his shoulder as he poured himself inside the tight grip of her pussy.

"I want to hold on to you forever," she sobbed against his shoulder. "Don't let go of me, John. Not yet."

"I have you, baby," he whispered, holding her closer, trying to bring her body fully into his. "I have you. Right here."

She stared up at him, her beautiful green eyes dark with satisfaction and the edges of pain.

"It's going to be over soon," she said softly against his shoulder. "Warbucks will be neutralized, the missiles will be safe, and it will all be over."

And he could hear the hollow pain in her voice that they would be over as well. He wouldn't let it happen. He couldn't let it happen, and Jordan would have to understand that. There came a time when a man had to accept where his priorities lay. His were with Bailey. They should have been with Bailey all along. Vengeance was nothing compared with the hell he had faced without her.

Everything wasn't going to be over, though. He would make sure of it. *They* weren't going to be over. He wasn't letting her go. But first, he had to face Jordan. There was always the chance that Jordan could just have him canceled. It was in his contract, after all. The warning that ignoring or disobeying orders could result in a silent order to terminate.

Not that he thought Jordan would do it. But he owed it to Bailey to know exactly what they were going to be facing before he broached the subject with her.

It would mean a lot of trust from her; it would require a lot of trust from the other team members to bring her in.

She would love it, though. Bailey was a damned good agent. Too good to just quit.

"I think I'm hungry," she said softly into the silence as she sat up and pushed her hair back from her face before looking down at him. "What about you?"

"We missed dinner." He turned and glanced at the clock on the bedside table. "And your friends are getting worried about you. The story is that you fell in the gardens and cut your arm. You've been recuperating."

"I'm surprised you've kept them out of our bedroom." She laughed, a low sweet sound that wrapped around his heart.

He grinned back at her, then grimaced as his cell phone rang. Picking up the device, he flipped it open. "Vincent."

"I'm coming back in," Travis told him quietly. "I'm about five minutes from the cabin."

"We'll be ready." He jumped from the bed as he disconnected and turned back to Bailey. "Get dressed, Travis is on his way in."

She breathed in roughly. "Does he know who hired Alberto?"

He shook his head. "He won't report until he can do it securely."

He moved to help her from the bed, then stepped back at her playful glare. "I can still walk, John." She rolled her eyes. "I'm not exactly an invalid from that little scratch."

"Give me a few years to get over the sight of that bastard ready to slice your head from your shoulders," he bit out, his voice rough as the image of it rose in front of his mind again. "That wasn't one of my better days, Bailey."

"Yeah, well, I don't rate it very high either, John. But see, I'm just fine." She spread her arms away from her luscious body as he felt his balls tighten in an impending erection.

"You look fine as rain, baby." He sighed with the knowledge that he couldn't have her again, not yet. "But if you don't get dressed, Travis is going to end up seeing just how fine you really are, because I'm going to have you flat on your back again."

That brought a smile to her face, but the quiet, somber intensity in her eyes was still present.

BAILEY PULLED ON JEANS, a sweater, and thick socks. She was leaving the bathroom when Travis's quiet knock heralded his return to the mansion.

Opening the door, John let him in as Bailey turned on the white-noise generator and poured them all a cup of coffee.

"Thank you." Travis accepted the cup as he sat at the small table on the other side of the room, farthest from the door.

Taking the other two cups, John moved to the table to join him as Bailey trailed behind him.

"We interrogated Rodriquez," Travis said softly. "He didn't have a lot of information, though. He was contacted anonymously. The money was deposited electronically into his account and he was given your identity. All he knows is that whoever hired him informed him that they would be at the party and they would know if he actually succeeded in earning the money."

"I guess it was too much to hope that whoever hired him would get stupid, just once," Bailey stated in disgust.

"The men here aren't stupid, and neither are the women," Travis mused. "They can get careless, though, as can their security personnel. I'll see what I can find out from there in the next few days." He looked at John. "The boss is getting concerned. It seems the CIA is making noise about investigating Warbucks again. They caught a hint of this sale. So far he's managed to keep them off track, but that won't last long."

"It's likely not working at all," Bailey told them. "The men here aren't the only smart ones. The agency wants Warbucks, and they want him alive."

"Too bad," John murmured as he turned back to Travis.

"Rodriquez didn't survive interrogation," Travis said, keeping his voice quiet. "His body will be left where local law enforcement can find it in a few days. He didn't suffer greatly. He just didn't survive."

Bailey knew what Travis wasn't saying. Rodriquez had been executed. When his body was found that would be apparent, and it would fit with his history. There would be no investigation outside the team Travis and John worked with.

"I've suggested Warbucks may have been behind it," John warned Travis. "As I expressed to Raymond Greer, a goodwill gesture, if he wasn't involved, may be appropriate."

There was that look again. As though they were keeping something from her that they knew they shouldn't be.

"What's going on with Raymond?" She lowered her voice to a breath of sound as that mental note kicked in. "And don't bother telling me nothing."

Travis and John shared "the look" again. It was beginning to get on her nerves.

"If the two of you didn't want to tell me, then you'd better watch your expressions," she stated irritably. "Spit it out now and get it over with, if you don't mind."

Travis glanced at her with a brooding look as John breathed out heavily.

"Not yet." His voice was a breath of sound. "We're not safe enough. Not yet."

She wanted to kick both of them. "Whatever." She rose from her chair, finished with the conversation now. She had her own suspicions, suspicions she wanted to reject simply because she detested Raymond Greer so thoroughly. But she had to admit that she detested a lot of the men she'd worked with.

If Raymond had been setting himself up to move into Warbucks's sphere, then his attitude would make perfect sense. It would also explain his sincere affection for his wife, which she would have never believed if she hadn't seen for herself.

She grimaced at the thought. She didn't want to suspect what she was starting to suspect. It meant she was going to have to change her perceptions, and she really didn't like doing that.

Turning back to both of them, she considered them with a narrow frown before mouthing, "Raymond's covert."

John glanced at Travis, then to her, and nodded sharply.

Fuck. Dammit.

She stomped her foot against the rug before kicking out a pillow that had lain forgotten in the floor. With her good arm she swept the blankets off the bed, kicked them, and cursed silently again before turning on the two men again.

She didn't want to believe it, she really didn't. She detested Raymond. Arrogant. Superior. Conceited. The man was an asshole. He couldn't be a good guy. She wouldn't allow it. She didn't want to accept it even as she knew she was going to be forced to.

She'd spent years investigating Raymond, so she knew his cover was damned deep. That took careful planning. It took an agent setting himself up, effectively going rogue, and aligning himself with a backup team no one would suspect.

John's team.

She glared at him. Her teeth clenched until she was afraid she was going to crack her own molars.

"I hate him," she mouthed.

John's lips tightened as he fought back the grin that she knew wanted to shape his lips. Travis's head ducked as he hid his amusement. He was a hell of a lot smarter than John.

And they were keeping her blind. They had held this information back, giving those damned silent signals and making her figure this out on her own. They could have just told her.

Raymond's cover was sensitive, though, she knew that. If he was covert here, they couldn't take the chance that even a breath of it reached Warbucks. They could cover their own conversations, they could hide their true purpose beneath a million excuses. But an explanation of Raymond's position couldn't have been covered or excused.

She pushed her hair back from her face, almost wincing at the pain that sliced through her upper arm.

She hated this, she really did. She had actually plotted and planned Greer's death with great precision and pleasure. Backpedaling from that mind-set was not going to be fun.

"Assholes," she muttered before picking up the blankets and pillows and tossing them back on the bed.

Both men were so obviously holding back their amusement that she could have shot them both.

Now she had to do some serious rethinking about a man she completely hated.

She blamed John for that. It was going to be all his fault until hell froze over.

As she stomped over to the coffeepot, a firm knock sounded on the door. She wanted to groan at the thought of yet more surprises coming her way.

Rising quickly to his feet, Travis took his coffee cup and retreated to the connecting room as John moved to the door and opened it carefully.

"Mr. Vincent." Myron stood on the other side of the panel. "A moment of your time, if I may?"

John stepped back as Myron moved past him, his gaze raking over the room before taking in the state of the blankets. Bailey glanced at them, let her lips twitch, then turned back to Myron. It looked as though they had been playing in the bed. Well, actually, they had been.

"How can I help you, Myron?" John closed the door behind him and moved to the wet bar at the side. "A drink?"

"No thank you," Myron said politely as he stepped over to the seating area. "Could we sit, please?"

Moving to Bailey, John settled a hand at her back as he led her to the love seat across from the chair Myron had taken.

"You're doing well?" Myron asked her as she and John sat down.

"I'm better." She nodded, keeping her expression calm.

"Good. Good." He rubbed his hands together as he leaned forward and braced his elbows on his knees. "I'd first like to extend Warbucks's apology for the attack. We're not exactly certain who ordered it, but we're tracking the money sent to Rodriquez's account. We should have answers soon."

"I'm tracking the information as well," John informed him. "I have my own sources."

Myron nodded. "I expected as much. Warbucks has asked that you allow him the pleasure of taking care of this for you, though. He has, over the years, taken extreme measures to protect Bailey from any danger. It disturbs him greatly to believe that one of our own, more or less, would strike out at her for any reason. This society polices itself when possible. Warbucks will police this issue."

Bailey was aware of John staring back at Myron for long, tense moments before replying. "If he can produce results," John finally said, shrugging. "If he doesn't, then I'll take care of it myself."

"Good enough." Myron sat back in his chair and stared at them for long, silent moments before continuing. "I always knew I liked you for a reason, Bailey," he finally stated. "Over the years you've surprised me more than once with the operations you've covered for Warbucks. You knew he was part of your extended family. How?"

Her brow arched. "Really, Myron, it wasn't that hard. The thefts were connected too many times and in too many ways back home. There was no mistaking it, if you grew up surrounded by certain men and their idiosyncrasies."

"Yet you haven't identified him," Myron stated.

"I tried not to get too involved," she answered. "I knew who I suspected, just as I knew how dangerous he could be. If he wanted me to know who he was, he would have told me."

Myron nodded slowly. "Yes, you were always very cautious as a child as well. Curious, inquisitive. But cautious. That very much suits your personality."

He seemed subdued, Bailey thought. She had never seen him this quiet or hesitant in anything.

"Warbucks has built his persona carefully," Myron went on. "He built it by ensuring that only one person knew who he was. It was the only way to be certain. That person is myself. Even Raymond has no idea of his identity."

John shifted beside her. "That can't continue, Myron." He voiced the warning softly. "Warbucks's deals are growing. He's not going to get the price he's demanding for his acquisitions without a level of trust. The only way to succeed in that would be in using you as a broker rather than hiring it out."

Myron nodded. "I'm not as young as I once was," he

breathed out regretfully. "That job is for a younger man. As I expressed to Warbucks, what we need is our own personal broker. A man we can trust to hold our secrets, and one whom our clients will trust to verify the products and ensure their legitimacy." He looked between Bailey and John. "If this is a position you'd be interested in, then Warbucks will approve your contract for the job and meet with you to verify the acquisitions and discuss the terms."

Bailey barely managed to hold back the rush of adrenaline that surged through her. This was the break they had been waiting for. This was what they had worked toward. So many years, and so many deaths, and the end was now within reach.

"Terms can be discussed." John finally nodded thoughtfully, cautiously. "That would require a great amount of trust from both parties, Myron. As well as a much larger cut. By associating as a retainer of sorts, I'd have to be extremely careful to ensure other interests weren't affected, and if they were, I'd be forced to drop those clients. That could cost me."

Myron grinned at the information. "You're a superior businessman," he commended him. "That's pretty much what Warbucks expected from you. He's preparing his offer. The two of you can discuss terms and percentages after you've had a chance to inspect the acquisitions for auction."

John nodded again, his expression, his entire demeanor thoughtful. "I'll look forward to that meeting then."

Myron rose slowly to his feet. "You and Bailey will come alone," he informed John. "No security. You'll have to trust that Warbucks considers you important enough to provide for that. The meeting will take place tomorrow night."

John rose slowly to his feet. "He's expecting a lot of trust for very little in return," he stated.

Myron inclined his head in agreement before turning to Bailey. She could see something in his eyes, a tiredness, a wariness that warned her everything wasn't as calm as Myron wanted them to believe between himself and his employer.

"Bailey has extended her trust and has been rewarded countless times in return. Haven't you, my dear?" he asked her.

"Many times," Bailey agreed, even as she hated acknowledging it.

"Very well," John finally said, though it was apparent he wasn't comfortable with it. "I'll accept Bailey's trust in this." His arm went around her back once again as he pulled her close. "We look forward to the meeting."

"Very good." Myron smiled again before rising and moving to Bailey.

Gripping her hands, he stared down at her fondly. "I watched you grow," he said softly. "I didn't always agree with you, but I must say, you've turned out to be a fine young woman. One I have the highest respect for."

He bent, kissed her cheek, then moved away from them.

"I'll see my own way out," he stated. "Good night."

The door closed behind him seconds later.

Emerging from the connecting room, Travis stared at John and Bailey curiously. John moved to the dresser, pulled the electronic listening device detector from the drawer, and went over the area Myron had been in.

He found two devices he'd left in place. Drawing Bailey over to the door, he indicated that they keep their voices low.

"Call the boss?" Travis asked softly.

John nodded. "We don't have much time. Get it together."

Bailey moved away from him as Travis retreated to his room, her gaze returning to the door before moving to the position of the listening devices. Myron had been smooth, very smooth. She hadn't even noticed him placing the bugs on the chair and beneath the little table that separated it from the love seat.

Turning back to John, she watched him with a strange sense of regret. It was almost over. Almost. Twenty-four more hours and they would achieve both their goals. Warbucks would die.

Would John Vincent then "die" as had Trent had, leaving her forever?

She told herself she was prepared for this, but as she stared back at him she realized that no preparation could have steeled her for it.

They had one more night together. It would have to last forever.

CHAPTER 21

BAILEY HAD PROMISED HERSELF over the past two weeks that she wouldn't regret the end of the mission. She wouldn't beg John not to leave her, she wouldn't hurt either of them with anger or recriminations. She had built her memories. She had loved him with everything she had inside her. She had given him every part of her heart, her soul. She hadn't held back. She hadn't saved enough of herself to go on, and she knew it.

The next evening she dressed in jeans, a heavy sweater, and hiking boots. A long leather jacket was laid out on the bed. A search of the garment would reveal nothing, but she knew where the weapons were. A small knife here and there, but no gun.

They were to go unarmed, and there was no way hide a weapon other than the smallest and most inconspicuous.

Such as the derringer in the heel of her hiking boots. That was the best she could do. The other heel held ammunition. She could possibly get by with it. She was damned sure going to try.

John was dressed similarly. Jeans, a heavy sweater, boots, and a long black leather jacket.

At least they could be tracked. Several skin tags dotted her bare skin, just as they did John's. The small trackers had only a few seconds of activation, just enough to pinpoint their location for the backup team that would move in once Warbucks was identified and the missiles verified. How they would know that, she wasn't certain. She knew it had something to do with the watch Travis had given John earlier. Hopefully, it would work as it was supposed to.

They were to take no cell phones, Raymond had told them earlier that day. No communication devices at all. This was a meet, greet, and verify. They would see the missiles again when the auction took place in seven more days.

This was a gesture of trust and goodwill, plain and simple, as far as Warbucks was concerned. As far as Bailey was concerned this was the end of Warbucks's little game. Once the night ended she and John would be dead, or Warbucks would be.

"Ready?" John glanced at her before looking at his watch. "We have ten minutes to meet Myron and Raymond in the garage."

She pulled her coat from the bed and shrugged it on, wishing she had a dependable weapon for that last bit of added security.

"Ready." She glanced out the window to see the heavy snow falling outside. She wondered if the weather would make tracking more difficult.

John hadn't been able to describe the safeguards he and Travis had in place. Travis had left an hour before, his cover being orders from John to begin work on the transportation lines they had already prepared for the sale. It was a reliable story, and one that neither Myron nor Raymond had questioned.

Moving from the bedroom, she felt John's hand against her lower back as they descended the back stairs to the hall outside the kitchen, then walked the short distance to the heavy metal door that led to the garage.

The four-by-four Hummer limo was waiting for them, warmed and running, a driver and guard standing by the doors.

"Mr. Vincent. Miss Serborne." The driver nodded as John helped Bailey into the back where both Myron and Raymond awaited them.

The two men were silent as the limo pulled out into the falling snow, following the driveway that curved around the cabin, cut through the small valley, and merged into the main road.

"I think you'll be very pleased with our acquisition, John," Myron stated as the limo began to gather speed. "It's the culmination of a lifetime of connections and contacts. Warbucks has found that most men and women, even the most patriotic, will do anything to cover their human weaknesses. Everything is for sale, if you simply know that weakness." Myron seemed almost paternally proud of Warbucks's ability to procure America's ultra-secret weapons.

"What makes a man weak can also make him undependable," John reminded the other. "Warbucks has been incredibly lucky as well."

"Yes, Lady Luck does often smile down on him." Myron grinned fondly. "As though he's blessed."

Or cursed, Bailey thought.

"Warbucks will meet you at the warehouse," Raymond stated then. "You'll verify the product before your meeting with him in case you have any questions."

It was all very business-like, very civil. Bailey was once again amazed at how normal criminals could sometimes seem. As though it never once entered their mind that they were breaking the law, or that they were responsible for lives lost. All that mattered at the end of the day was that almighty dollar and how many of them could be accumulated in the shortest amount of time.

"Transportation routes have been laid out for you," Myron said. "The routes we have in place are exceptionally secure. You're more than welcome to use those, or you can use your own. But once the missiles are in your possession, Warbucks is no longer responsible for them."

John inclined his head slowly. "I'm well aware of that, Myron. Travis is gathering our team together now and preparing for transportation. If your lines are better than ours, though, I'd be more than happy to accept your generosity."

Myron gave a quick, brief nod of acceptance, his expression approving, as though he were staring back at two well-behaved children.

The bastard.

"The missiles were definitely a coup," John stated. "How did he pull it off?"

Myron's smile was filled with pride now. "As I said, some men will do anything to ensure that their weaknesses are hidden. Warbucks came across a rumor that a particular general enjoyed a rather perverted sexual taste. He managed to acquire pictures of the man partaking of the act, showed them to him, and then requested the information he needed to acquire the missiles."

Bailey felt John's bicep as it tightened behind her head. A dozen soldiers had been severely wounded and several had died when Warbucks had acquired the weapon. Myron spoke of it as though it were something to be proud of, rather than the heinous act it was.

As the Hummer moved through the heavy snowfall, conversation waned into an almost comfortable silence. Bailey was plotting, planning the acquisition of a weapon. She knew John would be doing the same. Weapons would be the first priority.

If John's plan succeeded, then the team backing him would be in place within minutes of their arrival at the warehouse. Once the weapons were verified and Warbucks identified, the eight-man team backing John would move in.

It was John and Bailey's job to acquire weapons and restrain Warbucks.

As John's fingers played with her hair along the neck of her jacket, she felt the skin tag on her arm activate and begin to heat.

The sensation lasted for two minutes, the heat building to a pinprick burn before easing away.

"Warbucks has been hoping to bring you back into the fold for many years," Myron mentioned as he pulled a flask from his jacket, opened it, and drank from it. The scent of aged whiskey drifted through the back of the limo.

"I was never out of it," Bailey stated. "I was merely rebelling for a while."

"As all children do." Myron nodded as he returned the flask to his pocket.

Bailey caught the concerned look Raymond shot John. There was something not quite right here. Not dangerous, but not right. The hairs on the back of her neck weren't standing up in warning; rather, they were tingling in distrust.

As the Hummer approached the city, it turned off onto another paved road and headed around the back of Aspen. Bailey had a pretty good idea where they were going now.

The warehouses had been abandoned ten or fifteen years before. They were still standing, still sturdy, but heavily guarded.

The tracking tag on her collarbone heated as they passed through the guard post. Military-erect, weapons held ready, the guards were impassive and cold.

They were mercenaries, she thought; she knew the sort. Icy-eyed, merciless, bloody. She might even have recognized that one.

The limo pulled through the warehouse yards, moving to the very end of the row of half a dozen huge buildings.

"He doesn't have a regular security force?" Bailey asked. She could see several other mercenaries milling around.

"He doesn't need one," Myron told them as the Hummer pulled into the open door of the last warehouse.

They pulled in a few feet from another Hummer limo. Four guards stood around the vehicle, watching them coldly, intently.

"We'll check the items up for auction first," Myron stated, his voice strangely hollow as he turned back to Bailey.

Bailey nodded, watching him carefully as she felt John's arm tighten around her.

The door opened and Myron got out. As Raymond followed he turned back and glanced at her before nodding slightly.

They were checked for weapons immediately. The guards

were chillingly polite, well trained, and thorough. Finally, they nodded at Myron.

"Move back." He waved the guards away as he held out his arm to Bailey and John. "Come along, children, let's check out the newest toys up for sale."

Bailey moved closer to him despite the concern in John's gaze. She felt Myron's arm go around her shoulder, and with a sense of shock felt the weapon that slid into the pocket of her coat.

The handgun was heavy, clip-loaded. When her gaze met Myron's, she saw something more there. Wariness, fatality. He knew tonight was going to see Warbucks's reign coming to an end. Somehow, he knew it was all an act.

"I've known you since you were a child," he said quietly as they moved along the warehouse. "You were almost my favorite, did you know that?"

She swallowed tightly and shook her head.

"Warbucks was always temperamental. He didn't care for others as you did."

Her heart was racing now as she realized he was talking too low for John or Raymond to hear him.

"What's going on?" she asked him.

"I disabled the jammers this morning," he said quietly. "Whatever devices you've managed to use have been working. I know what you are, I know why you're here. I always have."

She almost paused. She would have if he hadn't kept her moving.

"I'm old and tired," he said quietly. "And I voted for our current president. I believe in him."

"God, what are you doing?" she whispered.

"Saving you, I pray," he stated. "Don't take anything at face value. Don't believe in friendships of the past, don't trust in them. Remember, psychopaths have no friends, no family."

They moved to the end of the warehouse and a small enclosed office.

"In here." He moved away from her, unlocked the office,

and stepped inside. "I'll remain with Raymond and leave you to inspect the product at your leisure."

Bailey and John stepped inside.

There was no chance to warn him of the conversation. The cameras in the corner of each wall were wired with audio and—she was guessing—pretty damned sensitive.

In the middle of the room sat a long table, and on that table was a portable launcher and four missiles.

Bailey stood back so John could have the room he needed to check them out. As he brushed against her, she maneuvered her body until his hand brushed against the heavy weight of the gun she was carrying.

His head jerked back to her in shock, his gaze narrowing as he felt the weapon before he turned back to the table and began to check the weapons.

This was it. It was almost over.

She leaned back against the wall and shoved her hands into her pockets. Her fingers curled around the butt of the gun, and in it she found a measure of comfort, as well as concern.

Myron had betrayed Warbucks? It didn't make sense. Nearly two decades of following the traitor and suddenly he was turning on him. Why would he do that?

"This is it," John murmured as he checked first one missile, then the other. "The product is viable and authentic."

She watched as he covered the watch with his other hand, his fingers activating whatever it had been designed for. Shit was going to hit the fan, she could feel it.

"We have an auction then?" she asked.

At the same moment the skin tag at her lower back begin to burn. That one was for one purpose. They had ten seconds to take cover.

One. Two. Three. She stared at John, seeing his face as he carefully laid a wooden cover over the box that protected the missiles.

Four. Five. Six. She moved to the entrance of the office, checked the empty building beyond them.

Seven. Eight. Nine. She gripped Myron's and Raymond's

jackets and gave a hard jerk, pulling them into the office as all hell outside began to let loose.

"Here." She pulled the gun from her pocket and passed it to John as gunfire began to erupt and voices began to scream in warning.

How many damned mercenaries were there?

Turning to Raymond and Myron, she shot them a hard look as John moved to the door and looked out carefully.

"Stay here, you'll be safe," she yelled at them.

Raymond looked dangerous, furious. His weasely expression was pulled into hard, cold lines as he glared at both her and John and then the weapon.

"Ask him." She nodded to Myron. "He's the one who gave it to me."

Myron slunk to the corner of the room, then slowly let his body slide down until he was hunched into a protective ball, his face pale, frightened at the sounds of gunfight outside.

"We have to get to Warbucks before he gets out of here," Bailey yelled to John.

"We protect the missiles," he bit out, his voice commanding. "We'll get Warbucks. If these missiles get away, then we're fucked."

If Warbucks got away, then they were all fucked anyway. She couldn't promise that Myron would turn on the man he was obviously so close to.

"Fine, you protect the missiles." Before he could stop her she was out the door.

She heard him yelling before her, his voice brutally enraged, as she tore off her coat to give her freedom of movement, then jumped behind several wooden boxes for cover.

Mercenaries were trying to clear the path for the limo. A heavy army truck blocked the exit, but several men were fighting to get to it.

Heading for the limo, she worked her way around the boxes, moving behind one of the soldiers silently, her gaze trained on his body, her mind on the automatic weapon he was carrying.

She was within feet of him when a shot sounded behind her and the soldier slumped to the floor, gun and all.

Whirling around she stared in shock at John.

"Not alone you're not," he growled. "And if those missiles come up missing then we're both dead, and there will be no return."

They rushed to the body, stripped it of weapons.

"Get to the limo, I'll cover you. Wait for me before you go in," John ordered.

Bailey nodded quickly before surprising him with a hard, quick kiss. Then she turned, took the automatic rifle from him, and headed out again.

Thankfully the soldiers were more concerned with the black-garbed figures trying to kill them than they were with the broker and his lover trying to escape.

If she was lucky, very damned lucky, then Warbucks had made it plain that she wasn't to be killed now, either. She wasn't betting her life on it, but she was sure as hell hoping.

"Keep moving," John yelled as more mercenaries poured into the warehouse. "Get to that limo."

He was firing off rounds as she raced across the last distance to the vehicle. Throwing the door open, she flung herself into the interior and received the surprise of her life.

"Grant?" She stared into Grant Waterstone's clearly drugged eyes as he smiled back at her goofily.

"Hell, could've swore I got you killed," he chuckled. "That Colombian wasn't near as good as Grace told me he'd be."

Grace. Ford Grace. He was Warbucks, and he had been the one to betray her to Alberto.

"What the hell do you mean by that?"

Grant laughed at the question. "I warned you, Bailey. He's a crazed mother-fucker." He wagged his finger at her. "Loyalty, my girl. Loyalty. Too bad. Grace is packing. He's flying away." He flapped his wrists in a gesture of a bird flying. "Fly away, birdie."

Drug paraphernalia littered the back of the limo. Evidently he'd consumed quite a good part of the product.

"Where is Ford going?" she yelled at him.

"Ford?" Grant shook his head. "Not Ford. That old man is crazy. Wagner. He has the money. He's gonna fly away home."

Jules.

Her head jerked around. She watched as one of the mercenaries finally jumped into the truck blocking the entrance and began to move it away. At the same time, John jumped into the driver's seat of the car.

"The Grace mansion," Bailey yelled out to him. "Get there now. He's getting ready to run."

She heard John curse violently. But the car slid into gear and in the next second the tires were screaming as he laid the gas to it, turned, and shot out of the narrow opening that had been created for the Hummer.

They ignored the mercenaries' yells, demands, and gunfire. Grant was yee-hawing, laughing uproariously as John shot through the warehouse yards to the gate.

"We're crashing through it," John yelled back at her.

"Go for it." She braced her body for the impact and watched Grant go tumbling as the heavy vehicle sliced through the chain gate.

Snow fell around them, cold seeping into her bones. Myron's words came back to her: *Psychopaths have no friends.*

Grant's words. *Not Ford. That old man is crazy.*

It wasn't Ford Grace.

A part of her soul ached, cried out in pain. It wasn't Ford, it was Wagner, and he had Jules.

Insurance, she thought. Like Myron, he'd had his suspicions, and now he was hedging his bets. With Jules.

CHAPTER 22

"WE HAVE THREE MEN JOINING US," John yelled as he inserted an earbud communications device in his ear and drove the treacherous roads with easy skill. "Myron confirmed Warbucks is Wagner Grace and that he has Ford and Mary with him. He had two mercenaries pick her up this evening."

He passed her a communicator that she inserted quickly.

"He's going to be expecting us," she warned him. "He's suspected us all along."

"He wanted to believe you would be loyal to him. When you threw that disk away, you convinced him you could be. But he doesn't fully trust. No one in his position would have."

No one who really knew her would have believed she could have turned against her country, she thought. Myron had known, but he hadn't told Warbucks. He had taken his chances, knowing that Wagner was pushing into fields that were going to get too many killed.

The other man had grown a conscience of sorts. How and why, she wasn't certain.

"A helicopter is on its way to the Grace mansion," a female voice reported calmly over the link. "ETA is in twenty minutes."

"He's getting ready to run." She gripped the automatic

rifle she still carried in her hands. "If he flies out of here, then we've lost him."

"Well, let's just make damned sure he doesn't fly out," he cursed. "Hold on."

He hit the gas harder, causing the limo to jerk into gear as it began to power through the snow falling heavily around them. The drive to the Grace mansion wasn't a long one. Ford had always liked having his material possessions close at hand.

As they accelerated up the drive that led to the mansion, Bailey quickly checked the weapon she carried for ammo before shoving another clip in her pocket, as well as the ankle backup John had stolen off the soldier he had killed.

"You have to give me the appearance of going in alone," she told him imperatively. "Come in after me and cover me. Let's see if I can get Ford and Mary, then we'll do what we have to do once we've rescued them."

She could tell he didn't like this, but he nodded sharply. "I'll be right on your ass," he warned her as they neared the house.

"I wouldn't expect anything less," she promised him.

"All cameras in the house have been jammed," the voice at their ear assured them. "You have a four-minute window to reach the office."

Plenty of time.

"Location of all heat signatures?" John requested.

"Heat signatures show three people only in the house, Heat Seeker," the female voice on the other side of the link announced. "One in the office, two in an anteroom."

"That has to be them," Bailey murmured as John slammed to a stop in front of the house.

The limo was still rocking when Bailey jumped out, shoved her weapon into the back of her jeans, and strode to the front door.

It was unlocked. Opening it carefully, she stepped warily into the warmth of the house.

It had been years since she'd been here. The last time

she had stayed all night with Anna when they had both been no more than children. Before she had been killed. Betrayed.

But had Anna's life ended at her father's hands—or at her brother's?

Moving into the marble foyer, Bailey turned through the receiving room, then to the short hallway that led to the back of the house.

Ford's office was at the back of the house, just as Raymond's was at the cabin. There were two anterooms: a sitting room and a second, smaller office. The house was wired with cameras into the office, but only one person was in there. If he was watching the cameras, he would know something was wrong. She could get lucky, she thought. It could be Ford harmlessly working away, with Wagner waiting to pounce. They could be ignoring the monitors, but she highly doubted it.

She didn't expect to get that lucky, but she could hope.

Holding the rifle ready she moved to the office, noticing that the door was cracked open. Glancing back silently at John, she peeked into the room and saw Ford working silently at his desk. The monitors to the house were turned off, but if she wasn't mistaken there were actually more in the smaller office.

She eased the door open until it was flush against the back wall and stood in the doorway as John remained hidden at the side of the wall.

Ford glanced up in surprise.

"Bailey?" He came slowly to his feet, a frown on his face as he glared at the rifle. "What the hell is the meaning of this?"

He was genuinely surprised. She was still shocked.

"Where's Wagner, Ford?" She glanced at the door to the other office.

"Wagner left earlier." He shook his head in bemusement. "I haven't seen him all evening."

"Wagner's here." She walked farther into the room, lowering her weapon on the far door as it slowly opened.

If she lived a hundred years she would never forget the sight that met her eyes.

Mary's delicate face was bruised. Her eyes were nearly swollen shut, her lips swollen, her cheek black and blue. Dear God, Wagner had hit her.

He had her braced in front of his body, a smile on his face, a gun at her temple.

"Wagner." Ford's voice was strangled as his son stepped into the room using Jules as a shield. "My God . . ."

"Bailey." Mary's voice was thin, betrayed. Tears leaked from her swollen eyes and dripped down her face. "Bailey, what's going on?"

Bailey stared at Wagner in shock. This wasn't the man she had been raised with. The man she had thought of as a brother at one time.

"Why?" she whispered.

"She didn't want to help me." Wagner shrugged as though it were all perfectly acceptable. "I had to teach her better. Just as I always had to teach Anna better." He glared at his father's pale, shocked face.

Bailey shook her head slowly. "It was Ford," she whispered again. "He was the one beating Anna and your mother."

Ford's head swung around to her, his face almost dazed with shock now as Wagner laughed.

"Father is a wuss. He wouldn't have dared to raise his hand to either of them. The few times Mother tried to tell him, he wouldn't accept it. Would you, Pop?"

Ford turned back to his son. He was visibly shaking now. There was so much pain in his eyes, his face.

"What have you done, Wagner?" he whispered. "My God, what have you turned into?"

"A better man than you?" Wagner sneered. "My fortune is twice yours by now, old man. I was smarter and better and you were never smart enough to see it, were you?"

Ford shook his head as he stared at Jules, then back to Wagner. "You call this smarter, better? Abusing those who love you? Who trust you? Betraying them?"

"They're like lambs, they need guidance," Wagner snapped.

"Just like Mother and Anna. I told you those two bitches were trouble but you wouldn't listen, would you? You just had to let them go that night, didn't you? You couldn't see sense. They would have destroyed us. Destroyed me."

"They would have convinced Ford that you were the monster you were," Bailey said painfully, imagining the hell she must have lived with. "To know your child was a monster, that there was something this twisted inside him must have been a horrible weight on her shoulders."

"She thought she could actually get away from me," he screamed back at her. "That I'd ever let either of them go. I owned them. They belonged to me and refused to see it."

"God, are you insane?" Ford suddenly yelled back at him. "You don't possess people, Wagner."

"I possessed them," he sneered. "I owned them. Just as I own the rest of you."

"And the disk of your father ordering Orion to kill Anna and her mother? My parents?" She felt as though she couldn't breathe, couldn't assimilate what was happening around her.

He laughed at that, too. "Computers are such amazing inventions, as is the software now available. His insane assistant thought he could blackmail me with that disk. I let him believe he could for a while, then got rid of him when the time was right." He shrugged again as though it didn't matter. "I've been smarter than you, Bailey. Admit it."

She nodded slowly as she stared back at Jules's dazed face. "You were smarter than me," she said, barely believing what was happening around her now.

"I own you too, Bailey," he informed her cruelly. "I've maneuvered you for years, tested you, drawn you in."

"And I fooled you, didn't I?" she mocked him suddenly. "You never suspected, did you, Wagner? Not at first, not until tonight."

His head lifted, his nostrils flaring. "You didn't fool me, bitch. I just hoped you were smarter. Now you can die right along with the bastard that thinks he can tell me how to live my life and the little whore that thinks she can walk away from me." He tightened his grip on Jules again, causing her to cry out in pain.

Psychotic, Myron had told her. He had no friends. He was worse than psychotic.

"Do you think you're going to get away with this?" she finally asked him. "That you'll actually manage to escape?"

"Of course I will. The mercenaries have orders to kill Raymond and Myron. I'll lose the missiles, but oh well." He sighed. "And you and Father will kill each other. Just after Father kills Jules." He stroked the weapon down Jules's swollen face.

He had fooled them all so effectively. He truly had. Ford had been the one the investigation had focused on, just as Bailey had focused on him for the past twelve years. She had been so certain it was Ford because of her suspicion that he had been beating Anna and Mathilda, that she had refused to look any further. And now, they were all paying for it.

Bailey shook her head. "It won't work, Wagner. You won't get away with this."

His smile was gloating.

"I will get away with this . . ."

"Myron isn't dead, and neither is Raymond," she told him, feeling the pain that tore through her. "Myron and Grant are alive as well as Raymond. I knew before I arrived here who to look for because they told me."

Silence filled the room. Wagner's expression cleared for a long second as his grip tightened on Jules to the point that she whimpered. Bailey could see the flash of fear in his eyes, of disbelief.

Shock creased his face. "You're lying. Myron wouldn't betray me!" he suddenly screamed as Mary flinched and cried out.

He cuffed her head roughly. The next few seconds moved like slow motion.

Mary stumbled to her knees, clearly close to unconsciousness, as Ford jumped for his son. A curious animal-like howl echoed through the room as Wagner let go of Mary, straightened his arm, and fired at his father.

Ford's body jerked, then fell into Wagner, catching him off balance, as Bailey jumped for both of them. She could hear John behind her, yelling out at her as she fought to get to the gun Wagner had dropped.

His hand curled around it. His arm came up. A smile spread across his face and in the same breath a bloody red hole appeared in his forehead.

"No. No," Ford moaned in disbelief as he crawled to his son, lifting his head against his bloody shoulder and hunching over him as grief racked his body. "No. No, Wagner."

There were no tears. His voice was broken, though. Agonized. His expression was glazed as he lifted his eyes to Bailey.

"I don't believe this," he whispered. "I don't believe this. Why?"

Men were swarming into the room now. Black-garbed, masked, weapons lifted, and hard voices shouting out orders as sirens railed in the distance.

Bailey crouched next to Ford, John beside her. He'd fired the shot that had killed Wagner. He'd backed her. He'd let her have her moment, he'd let her avenge the past until he'd had no choice but to step in.

"You didn't know, did you?" she asked Ford then.

He shook his head slowly. "I wouldn't hurt Anna and Matty, Bailey," he said, shaken, weak now from the wound in his shoulder. "Your dad asked me about that. I thought you were crazy." Tears fell from his eyes to his cheeks. "I thought you were crazy."

Now wasn't the time. It wasn't the time to tell him what his son had been, what his son had done. Later, she thought. After he healed, after he had time to accept what had happened.

"He just had a temper," Ford whispered as he clasped his son, rocked him. "That was all. He had a temper."

He had a lack of conscience.

Turning from him, she moved to where Mary was being checked over by Catalina and Kira Richards. They had jerked the masks from their faces and were running their hands over the other girl's body, checking for broken bones.

"She's unconscious," Kira stated as two men moved to Ford. "We have paramedics on their way."

"Move out. Law enforcement coming," a harsh, brooding voice called out. Hard drives were being jerked from computers and files torn from cases. "Black Jack and Wildcard have the upstairs," another voice called out. "Move out. Move out."

Catalina and Kira remained in place as several suited agents rushed into the room.

"You have it, Director," the commanding voice said, turning matters over to Milburn Rushmore—Bailey's former boss and director of the CIA headquarters in Langley.

John was still behind her. She could feel him.

"Heat Seeker, move out," he was ordered again.

John stared back at Bailey as she turned to him.

"You have to go?" she whispered, trying to smile back at him. Trying to let him know she understood. She had known he would leave her again, but that didn't stop the ache of betrayal from searing her soul.

His lips tilted into a rueful grin. "Not a chance in hell."

Bailey felt the rush of light-headedness that exploded through her system. Hell, she was going to fall to her knees herself.

His arm wrapped around her as he turned to his commander.

"I'll be in for debriefing when it's over."

Dark blue eyes narrowed and reflected irritation. Bailey could see the fight brewing between these two men now. Tension suddenly filled the room as the other men stopped, stared.

Those brilliant blue eyes moved slowly to her, raked over her, narrowed further in calculation.

"You'll regret it," he warned John, but nodded anyway

before leading the way for the others and heading out of the house.

"You're staying?" She had to lean against him. She had to feel his arms around her.

"I'm staying," he promised. "Forever, Bailey. I'm staying with you forever."

She turned back to the scene before her and once again felt the overwhelming disbelief that coiled inside her chest. She couldn't believe Wagner had pulled it off for so long. That he had remained hidden, worked so hard to place the guilt on his father.

Had he sensed that Warbucks had gone as long as he could?

Unfortunately, loyalty just wasn't what it used to be. Myron had helped raise the children of the men he'd always associated with. He had held them as babies, hell, he'd baby-sat groups of them at a time. And she believed he'd cared about them.

He'd known Wagner for what he was, known the joy Wagner obviously found in destroying the security his father and his father's friends worked to build for them.

Wagner had hated them all.

She moved to where Ford was being loaded onto a gurney. An oxygen mask covered his face; he was pale, weak. Tears leaked from his eyes.

"I loved him," he whispered again.

She knelt by the gurney and touched his cheek. "We all loved him."

And she had. Like a brother.

The tears were trapped inside her for now. They would fall later, when she could sit down and assimilate what had happened, and how.

"Your director is taking care of the police," John whispered at her ear. "You have FBI and DEA here. The warehouse is secured and the missiles are being packed for transportation. It's over, Bailey."

She stood to her feet and stared around. Yes, it was over. But maybe, just maybe, something else was beginning.

She turned back to John and let his arms wrap around her once again.

"Hanging around, huh?" she sniffed against his chest as she felt his heartbeat beneath her cheek.

"Always," he whispered, that beloved flavor of Australia stroking over her senses. "Always, love."

Two Days Later

Langley. It had been a long time since she had been here. Bailey moved into Director Milburn Rushmore's office as his assistant showed her in.

The last time she had been here, she had been enraged, chafing at the restrictions placed on her, furious at the orders that had held her back for so long. And betrayed. Betrayed that her director, a friend of her father's, had actually approved her interrogation by agents that had no agency and no name.

Now, she was mildly curious, distrustful. But the anger was gone.

"Bailey." Milburn rose to his feet from behind the monstrous cherrywood desk that was the focal point of the room.

In front of the desk another man rose. Jordan Malone, former Navy SEAL, retired after the death of his nephew Nathan Malone. Short black hair revealed sharp, darkly tanned features. Brilliant blue eyes stared back at her coolly as his lips seemed to thin further at the sight of her.

She knew those eyes. She had seen them two nights before in the Grace mansion ordering John from the scene and back to his "death." John had refused to go. He still hadn't left for that debriefing, and she knew he was ignoring his cellphone. Demands that he return. Threats perhaps.

"Director Rushmore." She moved to the desk and stood before him.

This time, she wasn't an angry agent. She was a free agent. And she intended to stay free, at least from the CIA.

"Meet Jordan Malone. Jordan, Bailey Serborne." Milburn introduced them.

"Mr. Malone." She took the proffered handshake, watching him warily. She had a feeling this meeting had nothing to do with her and everything to do with the agent that he wanted back.

"Ms. Serborne." His tone was icy. "Thank you for coming in."

She arched a brow mockingly as she glanced back at Milburn.

"You're welcome, Mr. Malone." Her tone was just sarcastic enough to assure him that she knew what his game was.

"Sit, Bailey, please," Milburn invited as he waved his hand to the vacant seat beside Malone. "I wanted to thank you personally for your help with the Grace situation. None of us could have known what was going on there. Without you, we could never have neutralized Wagner." His voice seemed to crack as Bailey breathed in deeply.

Milburn had been her father's friend. He was Ford's friend. He was a friend to sheiks, kings, and to four of the richest men in the world. And he had been Wagner's godfather.

"He had journals," she said. "You found them?"

She needed answers, not just for herself but for Jules as well. There was still an edge of disbelief that it had happened like this. That Wagner had been the villain. No, more than a villain. He had been a monster. A monster that had gone to extraordinary lengths to frame his father for his own crimes.

"We found the journals. Thank you for letting us know they existed." His face creased for the barest second with grief.

Wagner had kept journals since he was a boy. Anna had told her about them once, when they were younger. Strange that she hadn't told Bailey that it was Wagner who was abusing her. She had never said Ford had done it, that had been an assumption that Bailey had made. An erroneous one.

"What happened, Milburn?" she asked. "I never suspected Wagner. I would never have believed it if I hadn't been there."

Milburn shook his head sadly. "He was twisted, Bailey. He was a missing a soul, and he was very good at hiding it."

"Wagner began early in his teen years learning how to steal information and how to use it," Jordan broke in at that point. "As Milburn said, he had no soul. As with most psychopaths, he was incredibly intuitive and intelligent. He lived for the power, directing lives, taking lives. Men like that live for a single reason, to attain a god-like status while holding everyone in thrall with fear. He thought he was invincible. He learned better."

She shook her head. She would never make sense of it. It was impossible to understand.

"He was going to kill his father. Make it look like Ford killed me, then killed himself because he knew he was caught."

"And he would have succeeded had the men working with John not been prepared for Warbucks to pull a surprise. He's been rather good at that over the years."

Yes, he had been. That should have been their first warning. Warbucks had always kept an ace up his sleeve. He'd always managed to lay evidence at others' doors and keep suspicions from himself. They hadn't learned his identity for a reason: because he knew how to keep the attention focused on his father rather than himself.

"So why am I here?" She turned to Jordan rather than focusing the question on Milburn.

Jordan leaned back in his chair as he turned to her, his hand lifting to allow his finger to stroke over his upper lip thoughtfully, a considering expression moving over his face.

"You haven't guessed?" he asked silkily, dangerously.

"You want John back." She wasn't beating around the bush.

His lips quirked in amusement. "I haven't lost John," he stated thoughtfully. "Are you under the impression I have?"

Bailey could feel an edge of panic moving inside her now.

"Then what do you want?"

"I want you to walk away," he stated carefully. "Go back

to your life, however you intend to live it, and walk out of his life. Then, he'll once again be effective. I'm afraid until you do so . . ."

"You're wasting your breath." She came to her feet, fighting the anger that had begun to build inside her. "I don't order John. I don't tell him what to do, I don't tell him how to live his life. That's his decision."

He shook his head. "He relinquished that decision when I saved his life in Australia. When I saved yours," he added. "You owe me, Ms. Serborne."

"I don't owe you my soul," she argued. "And neither does John."

"Sit down, Ms. Serborne," he commanded, his tone hardening.

"Go to hell."

"Learn how to take orders or you can learn just how powerful an enemy I can be." He came out of his chair, dominating, commanding. Forceful. "We can do this one of two ways. You can join John in the life he signed up for, of which he now has seven years that he owes to the agency. Or you can learn to do without him for very long periods at a time. And I can do that." He was in her face then, his gaze icy, steel-hard. "I can send him on missions that will hold him for a year at a time. I am not required to pander to his ego, his sex life, or his emotional promises to a woman. You want him, you can join him."

She stared back at him in shock. John had finally explained the agency to her. The Elite Ops, what they were, how he had joined, why he had joined. What they did. The idea of it had intrigued her, but she had never imagined this. Never thought this choice could come her way.

"Join the team?" she asked carefully. "I could work with him? Not separate from him?"

His nostrils flared as he straightened once again. "The two of you make a damned good team, and you've already fucked my life up by making yourselves a team. John Vincent is more than just a cover. He's a connection, a pipeline into an underground force that we can't afford to lose. You've already proven yourself as his partner. If you want to keep that position, then you damned well better learn to consider me not just your boss, your director, or your commander. Ms. Serborne, I'm your worst fucking nightmare."

She was about to believe it.

She licked her lips and glanced back at Milburn. He was watching the show with a hint of amusement and satisfaction.

"Does John know?" she asked.

He frowned back at her. "John would have to answer his phone first, wouldn't he?" he snarled back at her.

"You called me here because John wouldn't answer your summons?"

"My calls," he snapped.

"Your summons," she informed him. "I heard the messages. You, Mr. Malone, have a god complex."

"And you, Ms. Serborne, had better learn how to deal with it," he snapped back in reply. "Do you want in? Or do I see how far away, and for how long, I can commandeer your lover?"

"My husband."

His eyes narrowed. "Excuse me?"

"My husband, Mr. Malone. John and I were married in a private ceremony last night. I believe that marriage trumps your contract in several ways." She lifted her hand. "Clause seven, paragraph three: 'Married, and having formed a legally binding tenet with one whose classified rank matches or exceeds his own, requires that said agency, unnamed but existing, to ensure that said agent, namely one John Vincent, the choice of working with his spouse, or barring the ability to do such, the choice of ensuring proper marital time as befitting his rank and mission status. That time shall be not less than one month to every three, or one week to every three. Said agency is required to enact and ensure such marital time without restrictions.'"

His eyes narrowed. "He showed you the contract?"

"After the ceremony, of course." She smiled coolly.

"Clause eight, paragraph four: 'If unable to work with or aligned with said agent, spouse must accept that said agent must complete one mission before each marital benefit can be demanded.' I determine the length of time a mission lasts."

"It's a good thing I enjoy working with him then." She smiled cheerily. "You are required to allow him three months' leave for a honeymoon, I believe."

His lips parted.

"And," she continued, "I believe Milburn will be hearing from my lawyers soon. The charities that the majority of the profits of my companies go to are being redirected, Mr. Malone, under certain conditions to a charity near and dear to our president's heart. Have I mentioned the president and vice president are close family friends? The charities being redirected to are fronts, I believe, for the Elite Ops."

His teeth snapped closed.

"I'm a businesswoman," she stated. "I'm an agent and I'm John's wife. I don't need you in my face over the fact that you lost control for a few seconds of your agent's life. Console yourself that you gained an agent instead."

"It's a damned good thing I can respect a strong woman," he snapped back. "That doesn't mean you won't follow orders. You can shove that money right back where it came from if you think it's going to change how you'll be trained, or how you'll be treated."

She grinned at that. "It won't change John either. I believe he's on his way to debriefing this afternoon. You've likely missed him."

John had never had any intentions of breaking faith with the contract he had signed. But neither of them was willing to do without the other.

"You're going to make his life hell," he growled. "And mine."

"And it's something she's damned good at," Milburn laughed, causing both of them to turn to him.

He pulled his rotund body from his chair, adjusted his glasses, and smoothed back his thick graying hair.

"Congratulations, Jordan." He moved around the desk and clapped the other man on the back. "You just acquired one of my best agents."

"You said she was one of your biggest headaches when she was in Atlanta," Jordan growled.

"One goes with the other," Milburn laughed. "Trust me, son, one goes with the other."

As they stepped outside the office, the door to his assistant's office opened, and John walked through, escorted by several guards.

"I invited him," Milburn laughed at Jordan's scowl as John moved to her, curved his arm around her waist, and pulled her against his body.

"Causing trouble again, love?" He smiled down at her before giving her a quick, warm kiss.

"Always," she agreed. "How did you know?"

"Your director called just after you left." He nodded to Milburn, he glared at Jordan.

"Hell." Jordan glowered at both of them. "You do know everyone involved in the Ops is now calling me head matchmaker rather the brilliant commander I started out as." Irony filled his tone.

"You'll live?" Bailey suggested.

"Or he'll be next," John chuckled. "How's Tehya doing by the way?"

"Three months, no more," he snapped. "Don't make me send a team after you or I'll assign you both to opposite ends of the damned planet."

He stalked from the office as Bailey stared at him in surprise and John obviously fought to hold back his laughter.

"You're the troublemaker," she accused him.

"Actually, I'm the matchmaker," he assured her. "Wanna help me work on him?"

Bailey's laughter mixed with Milburn's. "I'd love to. I'd absolutely love to."

She was going to. She could just imagine how crazy both of them together could make Jordan Malone. And they'd have help. After all, she was certain they weren't the only ones he'd attempted to keep apart. He wanted his agency nice and cool and uncomplicated.

It was time to complicate Jordan Malone's life.

> **"Leigh's** *pages explode with a hot mixture of erotic pleasures."*
>
> —RT Book Reviews

Wild Card

Navy SEAL Nathan Malone's wife, Bella, was told he was never coming home. But if he can get back to his wife, can he keep the secret of who he really is . . . even as desire threatens to consume them? And as danger threatens to tear Bella from Nathan's arms once more?

Black Jack

The Secret Service can't control him. The British government can't silence him. But renegade agent Travis Caine is one loose cannon you don't want to mess with, and his new assignment is to die for.

Maverick

The only way for the Elite Ops agent to uncover an assassin—and banish the ghosts of his own dark past—is to use Risa as bait. But nothing has prepared him for her disarming blend of innocence and sensuality, or for his overwhelming need to protect her.

Renegade

Elite Ops agent Nikolai Steele, code name Renegade, is asked to pay an old comrade a favor. This friend swears he's no killer even though he's been mistaken as one by Mikayla. Nik goes to set her straight, but the moment he lays eyes her, he knows he's in too deep.

Heat Seeker

John Vincent has every reason to want to remain as dead as the obituary had proclaimed him to be. He'd left nothing behind except for one woman, and one night of unforgettable passion. Now, both will return to haunt him.

Live Wire

Captain Jordan Malone has been a silent warrior and guardian for years, leading his loyal team of Elite Ops agents to fight terror at all costs. But Tehya Talamosi, a woman with killer secrets and body to die for, will bring Jordan to his knees as they both take on the most deadly mission

ST. MARTIN'S PRESS

"LORA LEIGH *is a talented author with the ability to create magnificent characters and captivating plots."*

—*Romance Junkies*

Midnight Sins

Cami lost her sister in the brutal murders that rocked her hometown so many years ago. Some still believe that Rafe Callahan, along with his friends Logan and Crowe, were involved. But how could Rafe—who haunted her girlish dreams, then her adult fantasies—be a killer?

Deadly Sins

A newcomer in town, Sky O'Brien is a mystery to Logan Callahan. Like him, she is a night owl. Like him, she is fighting her own demons. Like him, she hides a secret in her eyes—a fire that consumes him with every glance. Could she be the one to heal him?

Secret Sins

Sheriff Archer Tobias has watched the Callahan family struggle to find peace and acceptance in the community—despite the murders that continue to haunt them. But he is torn between duty and desire when Anna Corbin becomes the next target.

Ultimate Sins

Mia, left an orphan after her father's death, was raised amid the lies and suspicions against Crowe Callahan. But nothing could halt the fascination she feels for him, or the hunger that has risen inside her.

St. Martin's Paperbacks   St. Martin's Griffin

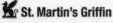